Single Ladies

Single Ladies

Blake Karrington

www.urbanbooks.net

Urban Books, LLC
300 Farmingdale Road, NY-Route 109
Farmingdale, NY 11735

ISBN 13: 978-1-62286-787-5
ISBN 10: 1-62286-787-4

First Mass Market Printing January 2017
First Trade Paperback Printing July 2016
Printed in the United States of America

10 9 8 7 6 5 4 3 2 1

Distributed by Kensington Publishing Corp.
Submit orders to:
Customer Service
400 Hahn Road
Westminster, MD 21157-4627
Phone: 1-800-733-3000
Fax: 1-800-659-2436

Chapter 1

Ducking the landlord had become a skill for Tammy around this time of the month. She watched as Mr. Louis pulled up; but he didn't get out of his car right away. That gave her just enough time to creep away from the living room window, grab her five-month-old baby girl, Sinniyyah, and head upstairs to her bedroom.

"Come on, NaNa. Don't start ya stuff," she whispered to her daughter, seeing that she was becoming a little fussy. It was a good thing that her son, Anthony, was in daycare, because he always played loudly in the house.

It was the first of the month and rent was due, and Mr. Louis didn't play any games about his money. He wanted it on the first, or no later than the fifth, and if you didn't have it by then, a late fee of one hundred dollars would be added to the rent. He didn't care what the situation was.

Knock! Knock! Knock! Knock! Mr. Louis banged on the door.

Tammy kept Sinniyyah as quiet as she could while hoping he would leave, but he didn't. Instead, he whipped out his cell phone and dialed Tammy's number.

The loud ringing sound of her phone going off downstairs startled her and Sinniyyah. *Damn!* She knew she had forgotten something. She had meant to turn her ringer off. She knew now that there was no way Mr. Louis would leave because if her cell phone was inside, there was a 100 percent chance that she was also.

Realizing that her cover had been blown, Tammy decided to go downstairs and face him. Hopefully he would understand her situation and give her more time to come up with the rent money.

As she began to turn the knob with Sinniyyah in her arms, she put on her game face before fully opening the door. "Hey, Mr. Louis. I thought I heard somebody at the door, but I was upstairs about to put my baby down for a nap," she quickly lied.

The expression on Mr. Louis's face said that he wasn't buying it, or didn't care. "Look, Tammy. I'm tired of having to come by here and hassle you for my money every month. Now either you can pay your rent on time, or you need to find another place to stay. I'm not running no charity house for women here."

Tammy knew that Mr. Louis was somewhat right, and you could tell this by the shame she had on her face. She hated not being able to pay her rent or other bills on time. It seemed lately that this was the same struggle every month.

The math just didn't add up. With only currently having a part-time job, she pretty much lived off of welfare, which only gave her $650 cash assistance every month for two kids, including daycare, and $300 in food stamps. The rent for the three-bed-room house was $500 a month by itself, and that included only water. All the other bills were her responsibility alone, and by the time she did get paid from her part-time job at Walmart, the bills had soaked up every dime that she made.

"And where is that nigga of yours? He can't give you the money?" Mr. Louis asked.

Breaking Tammy from her thoughts, the image of Chris momentarily shot through her mind. But as of right now he couldn't help her, so she quickly brushed that thought away. "He's not around right now, Mr. Louis, which is why it's been so difficult for me. I'm trying to do all this on my own and it's tough," she said with a sad face, hoping that it would draw some sympathy from her landlord.

But Mr. Louis's eyes were feasting on Tammy's breasts, more specifically her nipples that were protruding through the thin T-shirt she had on. She didn't have on a bra, so he could clearly see the darkness of her nipples. "Well, you're a pretty enough girl, and I think I could help you out and give you some more time to come up with the rent."

"Thank you so much, Mr. Louis! If you could just give me until next week I'm sure—"

"Wait a minute, young lady! Mr. Louis just offered to help you and you don't offer anything in return? Now don't tell me you're a taker and not a giver. You know it don't work like that," Mr. Louis spoke, cutting Tammy off midsentence.

Tammy knew that it sounded too good to be true, and now she understood what Mr. Louis was getting at. "Mr. Louis, I know you don't think I'm having sex with you just to get some more time on my rent!" she said, already knowing the answer.

"What kind of man do you think I am? It wouldn't just be for your rent. I would throw in a couple dollars so you could have some money in your pockets. Besides, I would hate to see you and them babies sitting out front with all your furniture. So, you just give my offer some thought, or get my money to me by the end of this week." He turned and walked out.

Tammy was about to cuss him out, when she heard her phone ringing again. It was around 2:00 p.m., so she was hoping it was the call she had been waiting for all day. She looked at the screen and the number was blocked, so that meant only two things to her. One: it was a bill collector; or two: it was Chris, her kids' father calling from jail. Praying that it was the latter, she answered it, but didn't say hello right away just in case she had to hang up.

"You have a prepaid call . . ." the operator announced into the phone.

Tammy quickly pushed 5 to accept it. This phone call was right on time, because she really needed to talk to him.

Chris was like everything to Tammy. They had been together since they were teenagers, and the love that they had for one another was unbreakable. They'd been together for a little more than seven years, and day for day, Chris took care of her in every way imaginable, all the way up until he got locked up five months ago.

"What's up, babe?" Chris asked, putting his back up against the wall.

"Ducking and dodging Mr. Louis," she responded with a little humor while looking out the window to make sure he was gone. She knew she could never tell Chris what Mr. Louis had proposed to her. If she did, he would be going right back to jail, for murder this time. Tammy knew how much he loved her, and he would never tolerate that type of disrespect to her from anybody.

Chris sighed loudly into the phone. "It won't be much longer. I'll be home soon," he said, trying to make Tammy feel a little better. "How're my babies?"

Tammy gave him a rundown, but it probably wasn't what he wanted to hear. They needed stuff too, things that she couldn't provide at the moment. The everyday struggle was hard, and the only thing that she could do about it was roll with the punches until something better came along.

"Look, I'll holla at my folks when I get off of the phone with you. You'll have some money by the end of the week," Chris told her. Beyond all the jokes and all the seriousness behind Tammy's voice, he could hear the pain inside of her. It kind of made him feel less of a man, hearing his woman and his children in distress and not being able to do anything about it. Yeah, his family had mad love for Tammy and the kids. And they were doing as much as they could for her, but it was nothing like having Chris around. With him, she didn't have any stress or worries, at least financially.

Falisha jumped into Kim's car with an excited look on her face. Kim looked back at her best friend with a curious gaze, knowing she was up to something. "What are you thinking?" she asked, hesitating before pulling off.

"You know how Lamar is always talking about how he has a job? I think we should follow his ass today to see if he really does," Falisha joked, but Kim knew she was dead serious.

Lamar, Kim, Falisha, Tammy, Lisa, and Ralphy were the best of friends. They'd all known one another since preschool, and they all had lived on Parker Street for most of their lives. Lamar was like Tommy from the TV show *Martin*. He always said he had a job, but nobody ever believed him because he never revealed where the job was or who he worked for. That and he was always available to do lunch or dinner at the drop of a dime.

Falisha, who never could control her desires to mind other people's business, was so curious to know where Lamar worked that she would stop at nothing to find out the truth.

"Girl, you're crazy as hell! I'm not following that nigga around all day." Kim chuckled.

"Come on, please!" Falisha begged. "If you do this for me, I promise I'll do the double date thing with you and that guy you met on Instagram," she bargained.

Kim had to think about that offer. She did need somebody to go with her to meet up with Ron. He was cute, and his Instagram was popular, and out of the hundreds of people who followed him, he claimed that he only wanted to go out with her. She was going to go out with him just as long as she could bring a friend to help whoop his ass if he turned out to be crazy. Kim thought about it for a minute before responding. "All right, it's a deal. But ya ass better be ready to go with me tomorrow night!" she jokingly threatened.

Deep down inside Kim had to admit that she too was curious as to where Lamar worked. She had pictured him in all kinds of uniforms: UPS, a security guard, a fast food joint. Because of his muscular build, she even thought that he could be a bouncer at a club. The thing was, she or Falisha wouldn't know for sure until they followed him, and that was now the mission they were on.

Tammy didn't even open the bills that fell through the mail slot of her front door. She didn't have any way to pay them right now anyway. Her welfare check didn't come until the third of the month, which was two long days away, and her Walmart check didn't come until Friday.

The mail she did open up was the mail from the welfare office. She wished she hadn't, though. It was her case manager writing to tell her that her cash assistance had been discontinued, and that she needed to come down to the office and file child support papers in order to keep getting any assistance. "It's always some shit!" she said, tossing the letter onto the table and grabbing her cell phone.

Now definitely wasn't the time to be playing around with that money, especially with Mr. Louis being on her mind with the rent due. It was times like this when she wished that Chris was home. Financially, he stayed on top of his game. He wasn't rich, but he was doing well for himself to the point where every bill in the house, including the rent, was like pocket money to him. It was easy for him, and Tammy was too used to being spoiled. That's why stepping up to this type of responsibility was hard.

Chapter 2

Lisa slid her hand under the pillow so she wouldn't have to look at her wedding ring while Dre slammed his dick in and out of her from the back. She knew she was wrong, but it felt so good to have her ex doing things to her that her current husband, Ralph, who went by Ralphy, couldn't do. She looked back at her phat ass slamming against Dre's stomach as he continued to pound away. She threw her pussy back at him, holding on to the headboard for support while he continued to go deeper and deeper inside of her.

Her box was so wet and tight that Dre had to pull out for a second to get himself together, before he busted off too early. "You miss daddy's dick, don't you?" he asked, slapping his dick against her ass cheek before pushing it back inside of her.

"Sssss! Boy, stop playin!" Lisa moaned, slowly pushing her ass back up against him. She could feel another orgasm coming on.

Dre could tell that she was about to cum, too, so he pushed his manhood as deep as he could inside of her, and gripped both of her ass cheeks like a set of handlebars. Her pussy tightened up around the whole of his thick member, and then came a burst of warm, slippery fluid that made his dick feel like it was drowning.

"Dre! Dre!" Lisa yelled out in pleasure. "I miss dis dick!" she admitted.

Dre began to cum as well, but instead of cummin' inside of her vagina, he took his dick out and slammed it in her asshole.

Lisa bit down on the pillow in pain. It hurt like hell, but at the same time it felt kind of good. "Come from back there!" she moaned and flopped onto her stomach from exhaustion. She was done, out for the count, and the only reason why she didn't consider falling asleep was the fact that Ralphy would be waiting to pick her up from her job.

Dre wasn't making things any easier by rolling her over on her back and stuffing his warm, wet tongue into her tunnel. She just looked down at him, and then over at the clock on the nightstand. *Choices, choices,* she thought as she began to get aroused again.

Since Kim and Lamar were roommates, it wasn't that hard for her and Falisha to find him. They sat in Kim's car two streets over waiting for him to leave the house, and that was after Kim had called him to see if he was going to work today, and at what time. This was a full-fledged stakeout, equipped with sunflower seeds and soda, and a blunt that Falisha had from earlier.

"Girl, roll that window down. Gas ain't free," Kim said, and turning the car off altogether. "And pluck those ashes outside."

"I bet you dis nigga is a stripper or some shit," Falisha said, taking a pull of the weed.

"Naw, I don't think so. I saw his dick before. He don't have a stripper's dick." Kim chuckled.

Falisha looked at Kim with a curious look. That was a piece of information Kim never shared before. She was so strict on her "not dating a roommate or friend" policy that it was a surprise to hear her say that. "You gave dat nigga some pussy?" Falisha asked, sitting up in her seat to focus on some juicy details.

"Hell no, I didn't give him no pussy! But I did see him naked in the shower one morning when I was rushing to get to work," Kim responded. "I only saw—"

"Oh shit, girl! There he goes!" Falisha yelled, cutting Kim off.

Kim fumbled around trying to get the car started. She watched as Lamar put his duffel bag into the trunk of his car and then got in and pulled off. Kim pulled off right behind him, tailing him at a good distance. He rode down North Tryon Street, then up Harris Boulevard until he jumped on the highway. Kim looked at Falisha with somewhat of a confused look. "I'm not gonna be following this nigga out to the boondocks," she said, looking at the signs on the highway.

Lamar made it a little too difficult for Kim to keep up anyway. He dipped in and out of traffic as though he knew somebody was following him.

Kim almost sideswiped a car trying to stay with him. "He's drivin' like a maniac," she said.

"I know, girl. Stay with him, though," Falisha playfully encouraged.

It didn't take but a few more minutes for Lamar to disappear into traffic, leaving Kim and Falisha scratching their heads trying to figure out where he was. The covert mission was over before it had yielded any fruit.

Kim found herself getting off on the next exit, but there was something about Lamar eluding her that made her even more curious to know where he worked. It was like a silent pact had been made when she looked over and saw the look on Falisha's face. It was a look of determination and disappointment rolled up in one.

"We're gonna find out where dat nigga works!" Kim said with a devious look on her face. She stuck her fist out for a little fist bump with Falisha, letting her know that it was game on.

***

Dre had put his dick so far in Lisa's back that she had a whole different walk. She hadn't been fucked like that in weeks. It wasn't an everyday thing for her to cheat on Ralphy, and there were times when she hated herself for doing it.

Ralphy was a good man. He was sensitive, giving, and caring, and probably one of the most honest men in Charlotte. He worked a good nine-to-five job at Ford Motor, complete with medical benefits and a 401(k) plan. The only things he lived for were Lisa and their four-year-old daughter, Naomi.

"What happened to you?" Ralphy asked, getting out of the car to meet Lisa, who was coming down the walkway.

She looked somewhat injured, but the only things that were hurting were her ass and her conscience. She could still feel Dre's dick back there. Visions of him pounding away at it made it hurt just a little bit more. "I fell coming down the steps," she lied, while getting into the car.

Ralphy didn't think anything of it. In fact, it made him want to cater to her even more. "Other than you busting ya ass, how was work?" he asked before leaning in to give her a kiss.

"Busy. It seemed like everybody and their mother wanted to get their teeth cleaned or pulled," Lisa complained. Being a dental secretary wasn't a bad job, especially when Dr. Crosby allowed Lisa to do just about whatever she wanted to do. Today wasn't that busy at all. That's why he had allowed her to take off for the day, and that's how she found her way over to Dre's house.

"Well, look, my mom said that she was gonna watch Naomi this weekend, so I planned a nice little getaway for us," Ralphy said, placing his hand on her lap.

She didn't know if it was guilt that made her jump from his touch, or the fact that her whole lower body was aching. But, whatever it was, it caught Ralphy's attention. He was so green to the fact that his wife had just gotten finished getting her back blown out by a nigga with a dick five inches longer than his.

"Are you sure you're good?" he asked again, rubbing his hand up and down Lisa's thigh while still keeping his eyes on the road.

Lisa sat there thinking about how horrible a person she must be to be an adulterer. "Naw, babe, I'm good. I just need a nice, warm bath, some rest, and I'll be fine," she told him before looking out of the window.

The welfare office was loud, stinky, jam-packed, and it was like that from the moment Tammy got there at nine o'clock that morning. Four hours later, the atmosphere was still the same, minus the old lady with a bad odor. Tammy couldn't understand why her appointment was for nine, when she ended up having to sit there all day before she was seen. By the time the case manager did call out her name, she was hungry, irritated, and tired.

"Hello, Ms. Green. Sorry you had to wait so long. As you can see it's busy as hell around here," Ms. Betty, the case manager, said, taking a seat behind her desk. "I needed you to come down here so that you can fill out these child support papers—"

"But my kids' father is locked up right now," Tammy tried to explain.

Tammy wasn't aware that welfare couldn't care less about whether Chris was locked up. In order for her to continue to receive cash assistance, she had to file for child support even if Chris wasn't able to pay it. The government was definitely going to make sure that he didn't have any money saved up in a bank, or maybe a lawsuit pending or any money anywhere. Welfare was going to get their fair cut, if not all of it.

After about twenty minutes and a couple more papers to sign, Ms. Betty looked up. "All right, Ms. Green. Your new cash assistance will start next month—"

"Next month?" Tammy snapped back. "What do you mean, next month?"

"Ms. Green, as of two weeks ago you were taken off of welfare altogether. That's why I wrote you

and told you that you had to fill out this paperwork," Ms. Betty said, pointing to the child support
papers on her desk.

"But I got bills!" she pled, damn near ready to
cry. Tammy was somewhat new to the system;
she didn't understand that welfare worked like
that. They were so unpredictable at times, and it
was always something with them, especially when
you had a case manager who didn't care two shits
about you or ya problems.

Ms. Betty wasn't one of those case managers,
though. She knew the everyday struggle of young,
single women with children. "Look, this is what
I can do for you, Ms. Green," she said, taking off
her glasses and wiping the sweat from her eyes.
"According to the possible outcome of this paperwork, you should be getting around six hundred
fifty dollars a month in cash assistance, and a
little more than three hundred dollars in stamps.
On or about the sixteenth of this month, I will get
you the six hundred fifty dollars in cash assistance
you were normally getting, and I will get you the
three hundred dollars in stamps. That's about two
weeks from today. I'll have all of your paperwork
processed by then. That's the best that I can do."

It was a relief, but it was still two weeks away.
That meant that Tammy was going to have to hear
Mr. Louis's mouth, along with paying the late fee
on her rent, or she was going to have to really

consider his offer. Just the thought of that made her stomach hurt. There was nothing about Mr. Louis that she found attractive. That, and the fact she had never cheated on Chris ever. Tammy's mind went back to her problems.

Anthony, her four-year-old, was going to be pulled out of daycare for this month, and the electric and gas bills were going to get paid late as well. All that, and she was still going to have to be broke for the next two weeks, not to mention the fact that the baby needed Pampers and the house needed a good cleaning.

Tammy left the welfare office with more stress than she did when she walked through the door. But like all bad news that she received in her life, she had to just suck it up and try to keep it moving. She really didn't have the time to cry over spilled milk, because in reality she knew nobody cared.

Chapter 3

"Hey, Ralphy!" Falisha yelled out from her porch in a sexy, sinister kind of way.

Everybody on the street knew that Falisha was a stone-cold whore. She wasn't just any kind of whore, though. She was somewhat sophisticated with her whorism, and had every right to be with an ass as phat as hers and a gorgeous face to match. She had light brown skin, thick, naturally curly hair that reached her shoulders, 36DD breasts, a flat stomach minus the baby fat around the edges, and she had the cutest dimples that sank into her cheeks every time she smiled.

"I'ma give dat nigga some pussy one day," she joked then chuckled, looking over at her girlfriend, Annet.

"Ain't he married?" Annet asked, knowing that it really didn't matter.

"Yeah, he's married right now. But I don't know how long that shit's gonna last," Falisha responded, watching Ralphy walk up his steps and then disappear into the house.

She knew that Lisa was either cheating on Ralphy, or was about to. Falisha and one of her baller boyfriends were out one night and had run into Lisa and her ex, Dre, at Dave & Buster's. When she saw Falisha she tried to clean it up and put some distance between her and Dre, but Falisha knew that they were together. The only reason why she didn't blow up the situation was because Lisa was her friend also.

Ralphy was a good friend of Falisha's too, but she opted to take the side of the female first. That was natural for a woman. If Ralphy had gotten caught with another woman by Falisha, she would have told on him in a heartbeat, especially if the woman he got caught cheating with wasn't Falisha herself. She was crazy that way.

"Girl, it's hot as shit out here. Let's go in Ms. Dana's house for a minute," Annet suggested, wanting to soak up the air conditioning.

Ms. Dana's house was the house that everybody went to just to chill out. Her husband had passed away a couple of years ago, so she was lonely, and because he had a good job with the city, Ms. Dana had received a big settlement and still had his paycheck coming in monthly. So she kept a refrigerator full of food and a mouthful of gossip for whoever wanted to hear her. She had an open-door policy with everyone on the block.

"Ms. D!" Falisha yelled out as she walked through the house.

It wasn't any surprise that Lamar was sitting on the couch finishing up a big-ass plate of tilapia fish and fried potatoes. That's all he did when he was there.

"You're always eating!" Falisha joked, and walked over and took a few potatoes off of his plate.

"When are you gonna let me eat you!" he shot back in a sexy tone, winking his eye at her.

"Boy, you can't afford to bite dis," Falisha said, tapping her kittykat through her tight, coochie-cutter shorts.

Lamar just chuckled at her remark. He always had a thing for Falisha, but she was all about a dollar. Even when they were young he always wanted her to be his girlfriend, but he was too dark for her. She liked light-skinned boys ever since she was young. They did have a couple of flirtatious moments as they got older, but it never went anywhere.

As Falisha got older, her taste in men changed. And if a nigga wasn't pushing a Benz or something close to it, he didn't stand a chance. One thing she knew beyond a shadow of a doubt was her worth, and because of it she became a little arrogant and conceited.

"Let me get to work," Lamar said, taking his plate to the kitchen.

"Work? Nigga, where you work at?" Falisha asked, following him.

"Wouldn't you like to know?" He laughed, putting his dishes into the sink.

"Boy, you don't have no job. You probably trappin'," she said, playing around.

"Naw. You'll never catch a nigga like me trappin' again. I leave dat shit to dem nut-ass niggas you're fucking wit' out there," Lamar said, walking up to her. "And for the record, I can afford to do anything I want. Put a price tag on it, and I'll show you what it do," he said, tapping the side of Falisha's ass.

"Yeah, right!" she mocked. "Boy, don't get beside ya'self." She chuckled, tapping him on the chest.

Falisha started to walk away, but Lamar grabbed her by her waist and pulled her back. Shit got serious real quick, and Lamar was pretty much at the end of his rope with her and the playing around. "Look, we're both grown," he said while looking directly into her eyes. "What will it take for you to spend one night with me? No games, no bullshit. I'm tryin' to fuck," he said flat out.

It took Falisha by surprise for a second hearing that come out the way it did from Lamar. It was kind of crazy, but she actually respected his honesty. "Are you serious?" she asked with a curious look on her face.

"Dead serious," Lamar shot back.

Falisha thought that he was still playing around, but he wasn't. She said the first number that came to her mind, knowing that it was going to put an end to Lamar's fantasy. "Shit. I need like a stack," she said with a smile on her face. "You know I ain't trickin' if you got it," she said with a smile.

Lamar shook his head and walked off into the other room.

Falisha kind of felt bad playing him like that. She knew that he couldn't afford to spend $1,000 on some pussy. No one she ever dealt with, baller or not, ever gave her a grand cash up front to hit it one time, and she didn't expect for it to happen now.

Before she could walk into the other room and say that she was just kidding around, Lamar was walking back into the room with a wad of money in his hand, counting it. He counted out $1,000, and tossed it onto the table. He counted out another $500 for a total of $1,500, and threw them bills onto the table also.

"Go find us a hotel. Get ya hair, feet, and nails done, and get a new outfit to wear tonight," he said, tucking the remainder of the money he had into his back pocket. "Let's make a date out of it," he said before turning around and heading out the front door.

Falisha couldn't believe her eyes or what she just heard while looking down at the money. She didn't think that Lamar would call her bluff, but he did, and he wasn't playing any games, either. She really didn't know how to take it. Up until now, she only halfway considered herself to be a whore. She didn't want to fully admit it, but now Lamar had really made her feel like one: a high-priced whore, but nonetheless a real live whore in every sense of the word.

"Shit, I'll give dat nigga some pussy for that type of money!" Annet joked, coming into the dining room.

Falisha was still a little stuck for a second, but she eventually scooped up the money. She counted it all before folding it up and stuffing it into her pocket.

"So, what are you gonna do?" Annet asked.

Falisha thought about it. "Shit. You feel like doing a bitch hair?" she asked Annet with a smile on her face.

"Damn! You shouldn't be working here!" a voice said, catching Tammy's attention. She looked up from the computer screen.

Her job in the customer service section of Walmart required her to be able to deal with the people, but today just wasn't her day to be friendly. She looked up with an attitude, not really in the mood for the smooth talk. She had heavier business on her plate, like how in the world she was going to pay her bills this month, especially the rent that Mr. Louis kept asking for.

"Can I help you?" she asked with frustration visible all over her face.

"Naw, I was just talking—"

"If it doesn't have anything to do with you returning items for a refund, I really don't feel like talking," Tammy snapped, cutting him off. She didn't have time for any bullshit right now. The whole single mother thing was starting to take a toll on her, and things didn't look like they were going to get better anytime soon. The last thing she wanted to do was entertain somebody tryin' to crack on her.

"Look, I am sorry if I made you upset. Here, take this," he said, reaching into his pocket and pulling out a VIP card. "Find a babysitter for Friday, grab a couple of your friends, and come down to my club. You'll sit in the VIP, and all drinks will be on the house," he said, trying to pass her the card.

"What makes you think I need a babysitter?" she asked while looking at the VIP card he held out to her.

"You're too pretty not to have kids. Besides, I know the signs of a mother when I see them," he said with a smile.

Tammy sat there, but didn't take the card. As bad as she needed to take a break and have some fun, she didn't feel like her rude manners toward him should have been rewarded.

He did, though, so he placed the card on her desk after she refused to take it. On that, the man simply turned and left.

Tammy couldn't believe how generous the man was after getting nothing but attitude. She grabbed the VIP card off of the desk and looked at it. It had been so long since she had been in a club atmosphere, and she didn't even recognize the name. "Club Live," she mumbled to herself, looking at the card.

A slight moment of excitement came over her; that was, until she realized that she didn't have any money to go to the club, nor did she have any money to pay Ms. D to watch the kids. The little money she did have from her part-time job had to go toward the bills. It was a decision to either hit the club and possibly live in the dark, or pay the electric bill and sit home with the kids. For Tammy, it was a no-brainer, and with that she tossed the VIP card into the trashcan.

Lisa stood in the shower, letting the water run over her head. Thoughts of Dre hitting her from behind ran through her mind, causing a tingling sensation between her legs. After two months she still couldn't believe that he was home. His body was so tight and so right, and his dick game was still the best she ever had, hands down.

Dre wasn't just Lisa's ex; he was the love of her life, and had been up until the day that the judge gave him a life sentence for murder. Lisa could do time, but the one thing that she couldn't do was a life sentence with Dre, and he understood. But before they separated they both made an oath that, no matter what their situations were, if he was to ever come home again they were going to be together. That was seven years ago.

Three months back, Dre won his appeal and got a new trial due to a witness changing her testimony about the night she thought she saw Dre shoot and kill somebody. After she decided not to testify this time at his new trial, the DA didn't have anything else but circumstantial evidence. It wasn't enough to hold him for the new trial so they let him go, and the first person he came looking for was Lisa, the only woman he'd ever loved in his life.

Lisa was startled by Ralphy pulling the shower curtains back. "Can I get in with you?" He smiled, taking his shirt off.

She playfully sprinkled water in his face as he got in and stood behind her. He wrapped his arms around her and kissed the top of her shoulder. It wasn't anything sexual. He just wanted to spend some QT with his wife.

"So, are you ready for this weekend?" Ralphy asked, taking the soapy washcloth and washing her back.

Before he reminded her, Lisa had forgotten all about the little outing they were supposed to have.

It was conflicting, too, because she had promised Dre that they were going to get together and figure out what they were going to do concerning their relationship. That conversation was something that couldn't be put off any longer, because she couldn't go on living a double life the way that she was. *Love triangles are such hard work.* "Of course I am ready," she said, turning to face him.

"Now, for the past few days I could tell that something has been bothering you. Is it something you wanna talk about?" Ralphy asked, pulling her closer.

"I'm good, babe. Work, work, work!" she lied, resting her head up against his chest. She just stood there letting the water hit her back. She hated the fact that she was lying to Ralphy and cheating on him. It was really starting to mess with her mentality.

The love that she had for him was strong. He came at a time in Lisa's life when she was just about ready to give up on love. None of the men who came after Dre were worthy of falling in love with, but then Ralphy came along and reminded her so much of the only man she ever loved. That was the reason why she fell for Ralphy so hard, and eventually ended up marrying him. Now that the real thing was back, she really didn't know what to do.

Chapter 4

Falisha pulled into the Bally's Hotel and Casino where Lamar had made reservations. She stepped out of her dark blue Charger looking like a celebrity. Her thick thighs and phat ass barely fit into the Dolce & Gabbana dress she wore, and her large breasts were cupped just right, showing a lot but hiding the best part.

"Damn, Falisha!" Lamar said, coming out and meeting her at the door. "I guess you're gonna be my eye candy for the night, too." He smiled.

"Why not? You paid for it!" She snickered, throwing her arm up under his while they walked into the building.

Valet parking attendants took a minute to get her car out of the way. Everybody stopped to watch Falisha walk away, and it was worth all of the horns being blown by people who were trying to get their cars parked.

Lamar had the entire night planned for them, starting with dinner at an upscale restaurant inside the hotel, then a comedy show, and then on to the grand finale. "Check dis out," he said, stopping her before they got all the way into the restaurant. "Tonight, all the friendship shit is out the door. Even if it's only for this one night, you're considered to be my wife for the night. You got me?" he asked, grabbing a hold of her waist.

Falisha looked up at him, threw her arms around his neck, and then leaned in to kiss him.

Her lips were so soft and tasted so sweet that Lamar's dick started to get hard. He pulled back and just looked into her brown eyes for a moment.

"Yes, I understand, honey." She smiled before leading him though the double doors.

Dinner was good, and the comedy show was even better. Lamar and Falisha talked about everything, and found out they had more in common than what they knew. Falisha had to be honest and admit that she was having a ball. She had been out on a lot of dates recently, but never really had this much fun. That was the difference between ballers and the average nigga on the streets. Ballers let their money do all of the talking. As long as they got the baddest bitch in the hood riding shotgun and could fuck whenever they wanted, it was cool. But with an average nigga, he couldn't afford to let his money do the talking. He actually had to do all of the talking himself.

"These shoes is killing my feet," Falisha said, walking up behind Lamar while he was at the craps table. "Can we go upstairs now?" she asked, wrapping her arms around his waist.

"Yeah, we can go," he said in a soft voice, then turned around to face her.

After cashing in his chips, Lamar and Falisha made their way up to the room. This was the part of the night they both were waiting for and hoping that it ended even better than how the night had started off.

"Wait right here for a second," Lamar said, stopping Falisha at the suite's door.

She stood off to the side while Lamar went inside. It took him a few minutes, but eventually he opened the door. He grabbed her by the hand and led her into the Presidential suite.

Falisha looked around in awe at the many candles that lit up the room, and the rose petals covering the bed and floor. She laughed, not at Lamar but at how beautiful the room looked. She saw stuff like this happen on TV, but never did she experience it for herself. "What are you doin', Lamar?" she asked while shaking her head.

"Nothing. I am just tryin' to show you something different," he said, leading her to the bathroom.

The bathroom was candlelit as well. Warm water was pouring into the Jacuzzi, and a bottle of Moscato sat in a bucket of ice next to the tub. It was breathtaking. This was definitely something new for Falisha. The hustlers she was used to messing with never took the time out to do anything like this.

"Go ahead and get you some 'me time' for about a half hour. I'ma hit the shower and wait for you out here," Lamar said, walking over to the shower.

He was done with his shower in fifteen minutes, and had been waiting for Falisha to come out of the bathroom. When she finally did, she walked into the room with a towel wrapped around her body.

Lamar was standing by the entertainment system in nothing but a pair of boxers. His body was ripped to the core, and it looked sexy, especially with the many tattoos he had on his chest and stomach. Keith Sweat's "Right and a Wrong Way" came through the speakers, setting the mood just right.

Falisha couldn't stop blushing as she walked over to him. "Oh, wait!" she said, remembering that she had forgotten something. She walked over to her bag, reached in, and grabbed a wad of money. It was what she had left of the money he had given her, less her hair, nails, and clothing expenses. She walked back over to him and tried to put it in his hand, but he pulled away.

"That's you," Lamar said.

"No, no, no," Falisha responded, walking up closer to him. "I don't want it to be like that. I'ma keep it real with you, Lamar. You earned this pussy tonight, and I'm not gonna have it any other way," she said, and tossed the money onto the entertainment cabinet.

She grabbed him by the hand and led him over to the bed. She pushed him onto the bed and then unraveled the towel from around her body.

Lamar's dick got rock hard at the sight of it. Her titties sat up like she had implants, her stomach was flat with a little baby fat around the edges, and her kitty was shaved bald with a light strip of hair running to her belly. He grabbed her waist and pulled her closer so that he could kiss her stomach while she stood in front of him. Even her skin tasted sweet.

She pushed him back onto the bed and climbed on top of him, leaned in, and kissed him softly on his lips. She tried to take over the show, but Lamar wasn't going to let her.

He pulled her body up against his and then rolled her over onto her back. She chuckled because she saw that he had caught on. "It's all about you tonight," he said, leaning in to kiss her. He kissed and bit all over her neck, breasts, and stomach like he was eating a ripe peach. Her skin was so soft. He let his tongue slide down her thigh then bit down on the inner part of it. A trail of warm, wet kisses traveled to the lips of her kitty. He began French kissing it while guiding his tongue in and out of her tunnel.

"Damn, boy!" Falisha moaned, grabbing the back of his head with one hand and a handful of her titty with the other.

Lamar cocked her legs back so that he could dig his tongue deeper inside of her. He flicked his tongue at a slow pace while the rest of his mouth pressed up against her vaginal lips.

"Oooooohhhh, shit!" she moaned, feeling her first orgasm coming on. She looked down at Lamar's head swaying side to side. She grabbed the back of it and pushed his mouth, face, and tongue deeper into her nectar box. Her legs locked up around his cranium, damn near suffocating him with her thighs. Her eyes rolled to the back of her head, just as Lamar curled his tongue up to hit her G-spot. "Ooohhhhhhhhhh!" she moaned, reaching her peak.

It was like somebody cut open a water balloon the way that her fluids splashed into Lamar's mouth. His whole face was soaked, but he continued licking and sucking her juices up like it was slop. *Dis bitch's cum even tastes sweet,* he thought while looking up at the pleasure written all over her face.

"Ooohhhhhh, myyyy God!" she yelled out again, feeling another orgasm erupting as Lamar continued to French kiss her clit. This time you could actually hear the bones in her legs cracking as they locked up.

By the time Lamar picked his head up from below, it looked like his face took a milk bath. With no time to waste, he used the comforter on the bed to wipe his face off.

Falisha tried to roll over into the fetal position, but Lamar was on point, rolling her over onto her back. "Don't run from me," he said, grabbing her thighs and pulling her to him. He slid his seven-inch member inside of her, going as deep as he could. What he lacked in length, he made up for in width. She moaned as he began to stroke slowly, pushing himself inside of her to the rhythm of R. Kelly's "It Seems Like You're Ready" coming through the speakers. His music selection was on point as well.

Falisha didn't know what Lamar was doing to her. All she knew was that whatever he was doing felt good. He pressed his lips against hers as he continued to feel his way around inside of her. He looked into her eyes with every stroke and every kiss. "I have loved you since middle school," he whispered in her ear. "I want you to be mine," he admitted, pushing himself into her deeper.

Falisha bit down on his shoulder and dug her nails into his back in pleasure. Her body began to tingle all over, and the more it tingled the more she bit down, sucked, and kissed all over his neck.

"I want you to be mine!" he whispered again.

Falisha's body couldn't hold back any longer. The orgasm took control, sending her body into convulsions.

Lamar could feel her walls tightening up, and a river of cum gushed out all over his dick and his stomach. He thought she was pissing on him the way that it squirted out.

"I'm yours!" Falisha moaned, and stuffed her tongue into his mouth. She was on cloud nine and didn't want to come down. It was intoxicating, mesmerizing, and beyond her deepest fantasy.

Lamar didn't fuck Falisha like a porn star, nor did he treat her like a whore and dog her out. He did something that had her stuck on stupid and unable to identify what he made her body go through. He made love to her as though it was his first and last time.

Chapter 5

Lisa looked down at her watch, waiting for the time to get somewhat close to five o'clock so she could take off. She didn't know how this weekend was going to turn out, or even if she was going to be married at the end of it. She had a feeling that her bullshit was going to catch up to her eventually, and the outcome wasn't going to be good.

"Lisa, you can take off if you like," Dr. Crosby said, coming out of the exam room. "I only got this gentleman here left, and I'll be leaving myself."

It was like Dr. Crosby read her mind, because she was about two minutes away from asking him if she could leave. Ralphy had made reservations for them somewhere, and Lisa had to find out where and make her move.

Both Ralphy and Dre were on her mind pretty much every moment, from the time that she woke up until the time she closed her eyes at night. She couldn't believe that she was in love with two men. Each of them she loved for different reasons, but at the end of the day somebody had to go, and that had to happen immediately.

She bolted out of the building and jumped into her car. She took her car today so that Ralphy wouldn't have to pick her up. She needed a little space and distance from him in order to do what she planned on doing.

Before she pulled out of the parking lot, she had to call Ralphy to find out about the plans for tonight. If he was trying to make it a surprise where they were going, it was going to be a little hard getting it out of him. But she had a trick for that, too.

"What's up, beautiful?" Ralphy answered the phone while looking out on the highway on his way home from work.

"Hey, babe. I know we're supposed to be going out tonight, but I'm kind of stuck at work right now," Lisa lied.

"Come on, babe," Ralphy said in a disappointed manner.

"I'm not tryin' to cancel, babe. I'm just gonna be a little late.

"You know how hard it is to book at the Forrest Tree," he said with an attitude.

The Forrest Tree Cabins was like a snow lodge couple's retreat for relaxation time. It was very romantic but hard to book, not to mention the very steep reservation fees. "Babe, babe, babe," she said, trying to calm him down. "How about I meet you there? Just grab my things and head on out there. I swear, I'll be right behind you," she pled.

Ralphy really wasn't trying to hear any of that right now. He was irritated at the fact that they wouldn't be driving out together. Nevertheless, he was going to enjoy his weekend with or without Lisa being on time. He had too much money invested in this getaway. "Yo, don't have me waiting out there by myself, Lisa. As soon as you're done at the office, you make ya way up the highway."

The Forrest Tree Cabins was only about an hour and a half away, which gave Lisa plenty of time to work with. She had a little bit of running around to do before she hit the highway, and going to see Dre was her first stop. She really didn't want to go all weekend without seeing him, and as long as she didn't get caught, she wouldn't have to.

"You make sure you pick these kids up first thing in the morning!" Ms. D yelled out from the kitchen to Tammy, who was sitting in the living room with Kim.

It had been a long, stressful week for Tammy, and a little time out with the girls was something that she could really use right about now. No ducking Mr. Louis, no doing house chores, no dealing with the kids, just loud music, dancing, and as many drinks as her pretty face could get her.

"And make sure that you go to the store and get some cereal and milk for this boy!" Ms. D yelled as she fed Sinniyyah.

Not only was Ms. D cool as hell, she was also the go-to babysitter for the block. She was good with kids and probably babysat every child on that street at one time or another.

Tammy actually used her as a childcare provider for both Sinniyyah and Anthony. That's how she was getting the childcare check from welfare. Ms. D only wanted fifty dollars in cash and twenty-five dollars in food stamps per week to watch her kids. She was cheaper and provided a better service than the daycare center.

"Hey, bitches!" Falisha yelled, coming through the front door. "Hey, Ms. D!" she yelled toward the kitchen.

"You're late!" Tammy joked, rising up off of the couch.

"Shut up, girl!" Falisha said, and ran to the kitchen to mess with the kids.

Falisha was Sinniyyah's godmother, and she loved that little girl like she was her own. She wanted to be Anthony's godmother too, but Kim beat her to the punch.

"Falisha!" Kim yelled in a loud whisper as she looked out the window at Lamar coming out of the house with his duffel bag over his shoulder like he was going to work.

Falisha walked over to the window just in time to see him throwing his bag into his trunk. Kim whipped out her phone and started pushing buttons. The phone rang twice before Lamar answered it.

"Yooo!" he answered, leaning up against his car.

"What's up, brother? What do you got planned for tonight?" Kim asked, looking out the window at him, undetected.

"I'm about to go to work in a few minutes," Lamar answered. "Why, what's up?"

"Nothing. I just wanted you to be on point because I'm going out with the girls. I'll fuck around and need a designated driver by the time I leave the club," Kim lied, only to see if he would stick with the work lie. Messing around with nosy-ass Falisha, Kim had become somewhat obsessed about finding out where he worked also. In fact, everybody was curious to know, even Ms. D.

"All right, just call me if you need me. I get off around midnight anyway," Lamar said, and then hung up.

Kim, Falisha, and Tammy all watched as he got into his car. "He's going to work. Y'all wanna follow him?" Kim asked in a juvenile way. "Ain't nobody at the club this early anyway."

Surprisingly, her comrade Falisha didn't seem too interested in the covert mission tonight. She was still kind of confused about what had happened between her and Lamar a couple of nights ago. At this point, she couldn't care less about where he worked. She really just wanted to get clarity on where they stood because, since that night, they hadn't said a single word to each other.

"Fuck it!" Tammy smiled. "Let's hurry up before it gets too late," she said, grabbing her bag.

"Come on, bitch. Stop acting like you don't wanna come," Kim joked, pulling Falisha by the arm and leading her to the front door.

They all sat around and waited for Lamar to pull off before they exited the house. They didn't want to give him any indication that they were going to follow him. After a few minutes of letting his car warm up, Lamar pulled out of the parking space. Kim knew from before the route that he would probably take, so she could afford a separation of a block or two between them. "Let's go, y'all!" she said, leading the pack.

She was about two hours late, but Lisa eventually made it to the lodge. She could see that Ralphy still had a little attitude the minute she walked through the door, but he quickly tried to hide it behind a weak smile.

"You're not going to be mad at me all night, are you?" she asked, walking over and giving him a kiss. "I brought treats." She smiled, reaching into her bag and pulling out a bottle of Cîroc.

There was no way possible that Ralphy could stay mad at her. They had all weekend to be together and chill out. "You hungry?" he asked, wrapping his arms around her waist. He had already whipped something up before she got there, since he had the time to waste.

"We can eat a little something. I'm not gonna be able to do what I wanna do to you on a full stomach," Lisa said in a seductive way and grabbed a handful of his dick.

"Shit, we can eat later!" Ralphy responded and palmed both of her ass cheeks and lifted her off of her feet.

"That's an option too," Lisa said, wrapping her legs around his waist.

Ralphy was good and roused up by now. He started to walk her toward the bedroom door, but Lisa jumped out of his arms and stopped him. "How about you go sit on the couch and wait for me to change into something better?" she spoke in a sexy tone.

He smiled and looked at her while he backed slowly away from her. He knew he was in for a treat, so her instructions were important to follow. He went over to the flat screen hanging over the fireplace and turned on the screen saver. There was a fireplace burning, covering the whole screen. He then turned off all of the lights and took a seat on the couch.

"Close your eyes!" Lisa yelled from the bedroom.

When she walked into the room she went to the radio and put on a lovemaking CD. It was a special

CD that she made with all of her favorite slow songs on it. Janet Jackson's "Any Time, Any Place" was the first song to come on. She then walked over and stood right in front of Ralphy. "Open ya eyes," she said.

When Ralphy did open his eyes, his jaw hit the ground. Lisa stood there with a pink see-through panty and bra set from Victoria's Secret, and she had on a pair of white Jimmy Choo open-toe heels. Her body was flawless from head to toe. Her 34-26-39 frame looked like she was supposed to be modeling for *Black Lingerie* magazine. "Damn, mommy!" he said, mesmerized by her beauty. If he had it his way, he would have sat there for hours just looking, and admiring how good his wife looked.

That wasn't going to happen, though, with Lisa taking it upon herself to straddle him while he sat there. She leaned in and kissed him softly on his lips and neck while he grabbed two handfuls of her ass.

"You know you're in trouble, right?" Ralphy said, thinking about all of the things that he was going to do to her.

"Don't lose him, girl," Tammy told Kim, who was trying her best to keep up with Lamar.

Kim did well while he was on the highway, but once he got off the highway things started getting difficult. Red lights here, stops signs there, and a bunch of drivers who didn't have a clue how to drive were getting in her way.

Lamar had a certain route that he took to work every day, and it involved a lot of turns and going through city blocks. It wasn't that he wanted to shake any unwanted cars that may have been following him, but it honestly was the easiest way to get to his job. Otherwise, it would take him an hour and a half to get there, instead of forty-five minutes.

"It's dark as hell around here, girl," Falisha said, looking out the window.

"Yeah. Where the fuck are we?" Tammy chimed in, not noticing the names of the streets that they were passing.

They made so many turns and followed Lamar for so long that they got lost. Not only did they get lost, but they also managed to lose Lamar in the process. It was like one minute he was there, and then the next minute he was gone.

"Does anybody recognize any of these streets?" Kim asked, looking at the street signs.

Nobody noticed anything familiar.

Falisha quickly pulled out her iPhone 5 and went straight to her Google Maps. It told her exactly where they were, and from an aerial view she couldn't believe how far away from home they were. "Yo, it's gonna take us at least an hour and a half to get back home, y'all," she said, tapping on her screen. "We're all the way da fuck out in Greensboro," she added.

Nobody could believe it. It didn't even seem like it took them that long to get to where they were.

"Why don't you check to see if they have any clubs around here?" Kim suggested. "Since we're out here, we might as well make the best out of it." She pulled over so she wouldn't waste another drop of gas while they decided on what they were going to do.

Falisha was already at work, tapping away on her phone. "Ooh! There's a couple spots jumpin' around here," she said, looking at the screen. "There's a club called Impulse like fifteen minutes from here, and there's another one called Mandingo's Den. I think this shit might be a strip club.'"

"I wanna go to the strip club," Kim whined.

"Hold up. I don't have any money for a strip club," Tammy spoke out, not even wanting to jeopardize the forty dollars she had in her pocket.

"You're right," Falisha said, agreeing with Tammy. "Let's just see what Impulse is doing, and then go back home if it's not jumpin'," she suggested.

Everybody agreed to that, and without further questions, Kim put the car in drive and they were on their way to Impulse.

***

Lisa got out of the shower and dried off as quickly as possible. By the time she was through with Ralphy, he was curled up in the bed with his thumb in his mouth like a baby.

There wasn't an area in the cabin that Ralphy didn't sex her in, and there was nothing sexual that she didn't allow him to try. She just so happened to have a little more energy than he did tonight, so round two was now in full effect.

She periodically looked into the bedroom from the bathroom as she was getting dressed, slipping on a different type of lingerie for the next escapade. For some reason she was still horny as hell and could feel her pussy getting wetter by the minute. She had to move fast before she messed up her brand new panties and bra set she just put on.

She walked over to the bed and stood over Ralphy. She leaned over and kissed him lightly on the cheek before grabbing her jeans, sneakers, and tank top off of the floor, and then putting them on.

Kim could see all over Tammy's face that something was wrong with her. She threw back drink after drink at the bar, and at no point did she ever get up and dance to a song.

After awhile, Falisha noticed it too and became a little concerned. As she came off the dance floor she yelled out to Tammy, "Come on, girl! Get ya ass up and dance with us!" She tried to pull Tammy by the hand, but Tammy refused, feeling the effects of the three shots of Cîroc she threw back.

Kim danced her way over to the bar as well and tried her best to encourage Tammy to take a load off and dance. Again, Tammy refused, this time with a sadder look on her face.

"Walk me to the bathroom," Falisha told Tammy and Kim so that they could get away from the loud music.

When they got to the bathroom, Falisha waited for a female who was in there to finish using the toilet before she started talking. She didn't want anybody in their business.

"What's going on, Tam?" Falisha asked while watching the young lady leave the bathroom.

Tammy shook her head, not really up for talking about her problems. Life was pretty much kicking her ass right now, and the only thing she could do was roll with the punches. Chris not being around made life so much harder, and every time she tried to do the right thing, something always knocked her down. "I really don't feel like talking about it," she responded in a low voice.

"Come on, Tammy. Don't do that to us. We're family," Kim butted in. "If something's wrong with you, give us a chance to help you."

Tammy just stood there in a daze, thinking about her situation. The Cîroc was doing its part, too, because the more she thought about it, the more she started to cry.

When Falisha saw the tears coming down her face, she knew it had to be serious.

"My life . . . is so fucked up right now," Tammy began, letting out a sob. "I can't even pay my damn rent. I can't find a job for shit no matter how hard I try. I'm tired, y'all. I'm tired of everything!" she cried.

Tammy had Mr. Louis threatening to have her evicted. When she finally did open up the utility bills, there was a shut off notice for the electric if she couldn't come up with $342 by the end of the month. The other day when she was at work, she watched two employees walking into the manager's officer with a smile, and then exit without a job, and they were full-time workers. The rumor got around quickly that the firings were actually layoffs. Chris's people didn't bring the money they were supposed to, and the kids were in desperate need of some new clothes.

Tammy just sat there and let it all out. She had so much weighing her down, so much that, at times, she wished she didn't have any children.

"Tam, we're gonna get you right, girl," Falisha said, comforting her with a hug.

"Yeah, we got you, sis," Kim added, joining the hugging session.

These were true friends, the kind of friends Tammy needed right now.

Lisa crept out of the cabin in the middle of the night, only having the moon as her light to guide her down the trail about a quarter of a mile east. The sounds of the wildlife screamed through the air, and the only thing that she had for protection was an ice bucket she brought from the cabin.

As she approached another cabin she could see that the lights were on. She walked up, tapped the door twice, and waited.

A huge smile came over her face when Dre opened the door wearing nothing but a pair of sweatpants. His stomach was so inviting, and the bulge in his pants let her know that he was thinking about her.

After she entered, Dre closed the door tightly, and then grabbed her by the throat and slammed her back up against the door. "Where da fuck you been?" he snapped, and leaned in to kiss her. His lips locked on to hers, not giving her a chance to answer the question as he passionately stuck his tongue into her mouth.

Lisa was submissive to his will, watching as he took one hand and yanked her pants down to her ankles. The sight of her blue satin panties made his dick even harder. Lisa was frozen. She couldn't fight her way off of that door if she wanted to, not that she did, because this was the kind of shit she liked.

Her body trembled when Dre ripped her tank top straight down the middle, exposing her breasts. He grabbed a handful of one of them and then bit down on the other, sending her into a trance. "Dre!" she whispered, feeling her moist cookie getting softer.

He stepped on the middle of her pants so that she could climb out of them, grabbed both of her thighs, and lifted her up against the door. He wanted to fuck her with her panties on, so he just moved them to the side and stuffed his large, thick, rock-hard member inside of her.

"Aaaaaaaawwwwwwwwww!" Lisa yelled out, feeling every bit of his long dick inside of her. He dug into her pussy with every stroke, bending his knees and pushing his dick up into it as far as he could. She came within minutes of him being inside of her. She bit down on his shoulder in pleasure, only wanting him to keep going.

He did, too, all the way to the point where Lisa could no longer feel her legs that were now too weak to wrap around his waist.

Chapter 6

Lamar was in front of his door with a hose and a bucket, washing his car early in the morning. Lately, he had been thinking about what he wanted to say to Falisha the next time that he saw her. It was bothering him that ever since they had sex together that night, neither one of them had much to say to the other. When they saw each other they spoke, but it was obvious that they had some unresolved business.

In the midst of him detailing the inside of his car, a cream Escalade turned onto the street, catching his attention. The large SUV stopped right in front of his car, and paused for a minute before the passenger side door swung open.

"I'ma call you later," Falisha told the driver before slamming the door shut. She didn't notice Lamar sitting in his car until the truck pulled off. She didn't know why, but she felt like she had just gotten caught cheating on him, and that was pretty much the look that he gave her. "What's up, Lamar?" she asked, crossing the street.

Lamar didn't say anything, but rather nodded his head and then leaned back into his car to clean under his seat. For a moment, he was mad as hell that he had to live directly across the street from her.

"Oh, you can't speak?" Falisha asked, walking up and standing over him. She was feeling some type of way that all she got was a nod from him.

Lifting his head to see her, he said nonchalantly, "What up, Falisha?"

"What, you mad at me or something?' she asked while taking her keys out of her bag.

"Why would I be mad at you? We're friends, right?" he asked with an eyebrow up, trying to be smart.

Falisha could tell that he had an attitude. If it weren't for the fact that she'd been out all night long she would have stayed there and unleashed a verbal attack on him. She did have a few things she wanted to get off of her chest, too, but now wasn't the time for all that, especially since it looked like he was ready to go a few verbal rounds with her. She didn't say anything. She just turned and disappeared into the house.

Lisa's heart damn near jumped out of her chest when she cracked open her eyes and Dre was lying in the bed next to her. The sun was shining through the window curtains, letting her know that she had fucked up and fallen asleep last night after

Dre ravishingly had his way with her. She sat up in the bed and put her head in her hands. She had told herself that she was only going to lie there for a couple of minutes before she headed back to the cabin with Ralphy, but exhaustion had gotten the best of her. "Shit!" she mumbled to herself before jumping out of the bed to look for her clothes.

She ran into the living room only to find her jeans and the ripped-up tank top on the floor, balled up by the door. She covered her face with both of her hands, damn near ready to cry. She didn't know how she was going to explain this to Ralphy. The thought of her entire marriage ending because of something like this brought tears to her eyes. She knew Ralphy, and there was no way in hell he would ever forgive her if he found out that she was cheating on him. That was a guarantee beyond a shadow of a doubt.

"Think, Lisa. Think!" she said to herself, wiping the tears away from her eyes.

She had to try to find a way out of this situation, and the way things looked, it wasn't going to happen. It was already eight-thirty in the morning, her clothes were ripped, the sun was up, her hair was sweated out something crazy; and who knew how long Ralphy had been awake and waiting for her to come back in?

"Think, Lisa! Think!" Lisa mumbled to herself as she looked around the cabin.

She jumped at the first idea that popped into her head, and stormed back into the bedroom where Dre was snoring away. She walked over, grabbed his pants, and dug into the pockets, finding a wad of money, which was needed. There had to have been a couple grand there, but she only needed a hundred dollars, which she peeled off quietly before putting the money back in his pocket.

On her way into the Forrest Tree campsite, she remembered passing by a surplus mini market that sold just about everything. It's sad, but the only idea she could come up with was to bring Ralphy some breakfast, hoping that he wasn't awake by the time she got back to the cabin; or, if he was awake, he hadn't been for that long.

Lisa ran to the store in record time, covering the half-mile walk within a couple of minutes. By the time she got there she had begun to sweat both from the walk and out of fear she was about to get caught.

The store was actually bigger on the inside when she entered. She looked around and went straight to the food section, grabbing a small basket to put her items in.

It wasn't until she grabbed one of the hot breakfast sandwiches from the food counter that she realized the entire breakfast excuse wasn't going to work. Ralphy wasn't the least bit slow. Plus, he already had the whole weekend planned out, including breakfast, lunch, and dinner.

"Ma'am, can I help you?" a store worker asked as he walked over to Lisa and saw the obvious stress written all over her face.

Lisa didn't hear him at first. She just stood there in a daze, thinking about Ralphy and Dre killing one another once they found out what was going on.

"You know, we have a beautiful trail that runs about four miles alongside a creek," the man said, trying to be polite. "Sometimes I run that trail when I'm feeling down," he said, finally getting her attention.

In situations like this, a woman's brain thinks faster and more deviously than a man's does. Before the clerk could even finish telling her about the trail, she had a plan B brewing in her head. She looked around the store, but she didn't know if they carried what she was looking for. "Do y'all sell running shoes and jogging pants?" she asked the young clerk, who was more than happy to direct her to the small clothing section of the store.

Lisa only had a hundred dollars, so she had to make it work. She grabbed the cheapest running shoes she could find, along with a pair of sweatpants. They didn't have sports bras so she bought two tank tops and a SAVE THE WILDLIFE T-shirt.

"How long does it take you to run that trail?" she asked the clerk as she placed her items on the counter.

"Well, I'm not a fast runner so it takes me about an hour. If I'm walking, it'll take me about two hours, only because I like to take in nature's beauty," the man answered in a chipper tone.

Lisa dug into her pocket and pulled out the money she took from Dre, and paid for her items. She looked up at the clock hanging on the wall behind the counter. It was 8:55 a.m., and at this point she knew for sure that Ralphy was awake and probably wondering where in the hell his wife was.

She was on her way, and she only prayed that her plan would work. It was either that, or prepare for the worst.

Chapter 7

Tammy sat in her bed with her laptop, searching for jobs on the Internet. The kids were asleep, so she used this time wisely, knowing how difficult it could be to do anything while the kids were awake. A full-time job was needed, and not just any full-time job, but a good job with benefits.

She quickly learned that she needed to have a trade or even some college education, which she didn't have. It was only a year ago that she had gotten her GED, and she got it by the skin of her teeth.

"Who da hell is it this early in the morning?" she mumbled while looking over at her phone blaring on the nightstand next to her bed. "Hello!" she answered.

"Damn, bitch! What you doin'?" Falisha replied as she looked through her bedroom window blinds at Lamar carrying all of his car washing supplies back into his house.

"What do you want, Falisha?" Tammy shot back playfully as she continued to look at her computer screen.

"I need you to ride wit' me to go see my brother. The feds sent his ass all the way out to Pennsylvania to a jail called Canaan or some shit like that," Falisha said, frustrated about the recent move.

Falisha's brother had been down for almost eight years now and was wrapping up his bid. But a recent fight got him kicked out of Butner, the jail he was in, which was closer to home. Falisha used to go see him at least twice a week when he was in Butner, but now with a six- to eight-hour drive to the new jail, she'd be lucky to make it up there once a month.

"Girl, I can't go out to no damn Pennsylvania. Besides, I have to go see Chris tomorrow. You know I'm there every week to see my boo," Tammy shot back. "And how in da hell did Mac get sent all the way out there?" she asked.

"You know the feds will send you anywhere. I had to go online to find out how da hell to get there," Falisha said as she walked over to her bed. "Shit, you better get a head start and find out where they're gonna send Chris's ass. They got this Web site where they let you know everything, from where he's at to when his earliest release date will be," Falisha explained.

"Well, what's the Web site? 'Cause I'm on my laptop right now," Tammy asked out of curiosity.

"It's FBOP.com. All you have to do is type in his name and register number, and that's it," Falisha said.

Tammy wasted no time typing in his register number. It took a few seconds, but in an instant, Chris's information popped up on the screen clear as day.

"You see it?" Falisha asked, breaking the silence on the phone.

"Yeah. Hold on, girl. I'm reading," Tammy replied, looking at the screen.

When she got down to Chris's earliest release date her jaw dropped. She had to go back and check to see if it was her Chris, and not somebody else by mistake. There he was: Christopher Douglas, born March 3, 1990. He was the only one in the federal system with that name and date of birth.

"Yo, let me call you back," Tammy said into the phone, and hung up before Falisha could even respond.

The earliest projected release date for Chris was June 22, 2020, which was seven years from now. Tammy honestly didn't have any idea that he was looking at all that time. He had told her that he only had another year and a few months to go. He was lying the whole time, and she couldn't figure out for the love of God why he would do something like that.

The tears began pouring out of her eyes at the thought of his release date. It was hard enough on her as it was, but to have to go through another seven years without Chris was like torture.

The tears poured out even more as she began to think about the kids. Sinniyyah would be seven years old by the time he came home, and Anthony would be eleven.

So many thoughts ran through Tammy's mind. Tomorrow, on the visit, Chris was going to have some explaining to do, and Tammy wasn't in the mood for any bullshit.

Lisa ran all the way from the store back to the cabin at top speed. That, along with dousing her head with a bottle of spring water, gave her the effect like she had been running for a while. A little water under her armpits and some in the front of her sweatpants really made it look convincing.

When she got to the cabin, the front door flung open before she could even get up the steps. Ralphy stood at the entrance with fury in his eyes. Lisa leaned over and put her hands on her knees like she was tired from the jog. She played it cool, not looking suspicious or nervous.

"Where da fuck was you at? I been up since seven-thirty waiting on you to come back!" Ralphy snapped.

Again Lisa just kept her cool. She sat down on the steps for a moment, faking like she had to catch her breath and acting like she didn't notice his attitude. She looked at the cheap watch she had bought and saw that it was 9:05. "Baby, you gotta run this trail with me tomorrow. It's so beautiful out there. It runs along the side of a creek for about four miles, and the scenery is so amazing!" she said, remembering the details that the clerk at the store described them to her. She began walking up the steps, still huffing and puffing like she was tired.

Ralphy was so mad at first that he didn't realize how wet her shirt was until she said something about running. At this point he was convinced that she was telling the truth about the whole running thing, but he was still mad, mainly because he was more worried about her safety and well-being than anything. "Why didn't you say something? Why didn't you wake me up?" he barked.

"I didn't want to wake you because you looked so peaceful lying there," she said, walking up to him and wrapping her arms around his waist. "Oh! Plus, I had to go see my *other husband* down the road!" she dangerously joked, seeing that he was buying everything else.

He reached up and placed his hand on the back of her head, grabbed a fistful of hair, and pulled her head back so that she looked up at him.

"Hmmmm! Just how I like it, daddy!" Lisa moaned while looking up at him with lust in her eyes.

"Don't get fucked up!" Ralphy shot back, looking down the road toward the other log cabins in the distance.

Lisa didn't want him looking too hard, so she leaned in and softly kissed his neck, knowing that he would turn his attention back to her. She pushed him back into the cabin and closed the door behind them as she continued kissing him.

His attitude and anger slowly started to dissipate, and before he knew it, Lisa was peeling off her sweaty clothes. "Come get in the shower with me," she said in a seductive manner, leading Ralphy to the bathroom.

Lisa was slicker than a can of oil, but what she did was typical among women who cheated on their spouses. Never in a million years could men cheat as well as women. It would never happen. A woman's thought process was on a whole other level of play. Most of the time if they ever did get caught, it was because they wanted to get caught, whereas when men got caught, it's because they were sloppy.

The most dangerous tool a woman could possess in this world was the power of the pussy. It literally short-circuited the brains of men daily. That's the reason why Ralphy was joining Lisa in the shower, and thrusting his dick inside of her without the slightest clue that another nigga just got finished having his way with her less than eight hours ago.

At that moment, all he was worried about was getting his dick wet, and that was all fine and dandy as long as it kept the attention off the reason why Lisa had been missing for half the night.

Falisha came sashaying out of the house and right across the street to where Lamar was cleaning out the trunk of his car. He didn't even have to look her way to know that she was approaching. The house shoes skipping across the street gave her up; that and the cracking sound of the gum she had in her mouth. She walked right over and leaned up against the back end of the car.

"What do you want, Falisha?" Lamar asked, not really in the mood to be playing the flirting game.

"Don't be talking to me like that!" she responded, throwing a playful punch at his arm.

He flinched and smiled at her, then threw a T-shirt at her that he took out of the trunk. He tried his best not to pay any attention to her body, but it was hard considering the fact that all she had on was a tank top and a pair of spandex shorts. Too much skin was showing for him to ignore.

"I need a favor from you," Falisha said, throwing his T-shirt back in the trunk.

"What? The almighty Falisha needs a nobody like me to do something for her?" he joked.

"Boy, shut up! I need you to ride out to the prison with me to go see my brother."

"Who, Mac?" Lamar asked. "He still out in . . . um . . ."

"No, he's not out in Butner. They moved his ass to Pennsylvania. Some jail called Canaan," she replied.

"Pennsylvania? Got damn, shawty! That's like an eight-hour drive," Lamar shot back. "Who's supposed to be doing all that driving?"

Falisha began whining like a child. "I was gonna drive down there, but I was hoping you could drive back," she said, walking around to the back of the car and standing right in front of him.

Lamar thought about it. This was going to turn into a mini trip. He did want to spend some time with her in order to get a few things established concerning the possibility of them being together. And the more he thought about it, the more perfect the idea sounded. On this trip, he would get a clear understanding of where they stood. It was going to be a make or break it for him. They were going to be either together or not, and if they weren't going to be together, then this would be the last time he would try.

"You gonna owe me for this one," he said, agreeing to take the ride with her. "And I'm not paying for the hotel this time!" He smiled, closing the trunk of his car.

"Thank you, boo!" Falisha cried out, throwing her arms around his neck.

She then got up on her tiptoes and reached up and kissed Lamar. Her soft lips pressed up against his, making his dick get hard. She didn't even realize what she had done until her feet landed flat on the ground.

They both stood there for a moment looking into each other's eyes. Falisha couldn't believe that she just publicly showed affection to a man. That rarely ever happened. She even cut her eyes in a shy manner to see if anybody had seen her. Luckily, nobody was out there, and as she walked back across the street to her house, Lamar grabbed a handful of his dick as he watched her thick ass switch from side to side. The trip to Pennsylvania was gonna be worth it!

Chapter 8

"I don't wanna go home!" Lisa whined, cuddling up closer to Ralphy as they lay naked in the bed.

It was the end of the weekend, and checkout was in a few hours. For the most part, Lisa enjoyed herself, except for the juggling show she had to put on all weekend in order to please two men. It was hard, but she pulled it off, even though her pussy was swollen from all the fucking she had done.

"We gotta do this again," Ralphy suggested, gliding his hand down the center of her back.

Yeah, but next time just with you! Lisa thought. "Yeah, babe. I think we should come back in the wintertime to see how it looks with snow on the ground," she said.

"I agree," he replied, and lifted her chin to kiss her. "You know I love you, right?" he said, looking her in the eyes.

"Of course I know you love me, babe. And you know I love you, right?"

Ralphy chuckled then kissed her again. The passionate kissing eventually ended up in Ralphy rolling over on top of her. "Let's get one more for the road." He smiled, and leaned over to take in a mouthful of Lisa's breast.

No matter how swollen her box was, it still got wet at the touch of Ralphy's mouth anywhere on her body. He began kissing her down the center of her stomach until he reached her pussy. Lisa's hand rested on the top of his head, and once he was down there she pushed his face into it, spreading her legs apart so that he could taste it all.

Ralphy did just that, starting by stuffing his warm, wet tongue deep within her tunnel. His lips caressed her outer walls while he did his best to curl his tongue up into her G-spot.

Lisa was going crazy. She grabbed his head with both of her hands and began rotating her hips to the rhythm of his head swaying from side to side. She could feel herself about to cum. It felt so good that she started fucking his face unconsciously. "Oh yes, daddy!" she screamed while reaching down and rubbing her clit while his tongue remained inside of her. She wanted nothing more than to cum all over his tongue and into his mouth, which she ended up doing. Her legs locked around his head, her back arched up, and her eyes rolled to the back of her head.

Ralphy could feel himself swallowing her juices as she went through her act.

As she was cumming, Lisa did the unthinkable. She didn't know how she allowed herself to do it, but she did, and just like a drunk driver who fell asleep at the wheel, she crashed. "Oh, Dre!" she whispered in pleasure.

Ralphy's head stopped moving for a split second, long enough for her to realize what she had said. He didn't stop though, and kept eating her pussy like nothing ever happened. That confused the hell out of Lisa. She really didn't know if he heard her, seeing as how it was only a whisper.

But Ralphy did hear her, loud and clear. He just didn't feel like making a scene about it right then and there. His dick was still hard so he wanted to finish what he started. Instead of making love to her like he had planned, he picked his head up from the pussy, put Lisa in the doggie-style position, and began fucking her like she was a two dollar whore. He pulled out from the pussy, and then slammed his dick into her asshole with force, something he never did before. It hurt like hell, but Lisa felt like she deserved every bit of it.

"Dumb bitch!" he mumbled under his breath as he continued to pound away in Lisa's ass.

She heard him, and it was at that point she knew that Ralphy had heard her whisper Dre's name. She wanted to cry and almost did, but instead, she just planted her face into the pillow and let Ralphy finish crushing her insides.

After changing into a visiting uniform, Chris headed out to the floor to see his family. This was the best time of the week for him. After dealing with the jailhouse politics each and every day, it was refreshing to hug and kiss his woman, even for the short period of time that he had in between playing with his kids.

The visiting room wasn't as packed as it usually was on the weekends, but that wasn't what caught Chris's attention at first. It was the fact that Tammy was sitting there with her face balled up like she was mad at the world. That, along with the fact that she didn't bring the kids with her, had him thinking that something bad had happened.

"Damn! Wassup, babe?" he asked as he walked over to her with his arms outstretched for a hug.

Tammy didn't even get up out of her seat. Instead, she just rolled her eyes. "I don't feel like all that right now," she replied with an attitude.

Chris cocked his head back and twisted up his face. He didn't expect to be greeted in this fashion.

A female visitor sitting next to them while waiting for her man peeked over to see what was going on, but she quickly straightened up and looked away after seeing the look in Tammy's eyes that said it was going down.

Chris was embarrassed, but he sat down in a calm manner so that he wouldn't draw any more attention to the situation. "Fuck is yo' problem?" he asked.

"Yo' ass, nigga! I was on the computer yesterday, and I searched for your name on the FBOP Web site, and it said that your earliest release date was June 22, 2020!"

Chris just sat there with a dumb look on his face. He thought about lying to her, but there was no need to. He always knew that Tammy was going to figure it out. "Tam, I'm sorry," he said, reaching out to grab her hand.

Tammy snatched her hand away before he could reach it. She didn't want to be touched at that moment. Her blood pressure was through the roof. "What da hell am I supposed to do for seven years while you're stuck in jail? I got two of ya kids I'm tryin' to raise, and every gotdamn day it's a struggle! You got me thinking you're coming home soon, and I'm putting my life on hold for you!"

"Tam, you're trippin' right now," Chris tried to cut in.

"I'm not fuckin' trippin'! You're trippin' if you think that I'ma sit out here by myself for the next seven years!"

"So what da fuck are you sayin', Tam?" Chris asked, becoming angry at what she was insinuating. He sat up in his chair and scooted closer, waiting for her to say the wrong thing. He never put his hands on her before, but she had him so hot that he wanted to smack fire out of her ass.

Tammy, on the other hand, felt the same way. She was about ready to set it off in the visiting room. That's the reason why she didn't bring the kids, just in case she felt froggy. "Look, I'm not gonna hurt ya feelings and say what I'm going to do, so I think it's best that I just tell you that it's over. Don't—"

Before she got another word out of her mouth, Chris smacked the shit out of her. It happened so fast that the guards watching over the visiting room didn't even see it.

Tammy sat there stunned for a second, and licked the blood coming from the inside of her bottom lip. She couldn't believe he just did that. Anger quickly covered her face.

Chris could see it, too, and knew that it was about to go down. "Act like a fool if you want to!" he threatened.

Tammy wasn't trying to hear any of that. She jumped up out of her seat, but so did Chris. Before she could even start swinging he wrapped his arms around her tightly, and pinned her arms down at her sides. The guard still wasn't paying them too much mind because he thought that they were only hugging.

"Listen to me, Tammy, and listen to me good! If you cause a scene in this visiting room, I swear on our kids that I'ma break ya fuckin' jaw before the guards make it over here!" Chris whispered in her ear as he held on to her tightly. "You want it to be over, then it's over! Let's not make this uglier than what it has to be."

Even though Tammy was mad as hell and wanted to get off a couple punches, she really didn't want to have her jaw broken. Chris never swore on their kids before, and never set out to do what he said he was going to do. Even if he didn't manage to break her jaw before the guards came over, he sure as hell was going to try. Either way, Tammy was going to be the one getting the short end of the stick. "Just let me go, Chris!" she said in a low, nonthreatening tone. "You're right; it is over," she said, and pushed away from him. She reached down, grabbed the locker key from the little table, and then walked off.

Chris just stood there and watched as the guard escorted her out of the visiting room. He didn't want to show it right then and there, but he was sick.

Lamar lay in the bed flicking through the channels, trying to find something else to watch. Visiting hours were over at three o'clock, so Falisha should have been back at the motel by now. And, just like clockwork, as he was thinking about her she was pulling up in front of the room.

"Whoooo, shit, it's hot out there!" she said, coming through the door. "I thought it only gets hot like this down South."

Lamar sat up on the edge of the bed and motioned for Falisha. "Come 'ere," he said while holding his hand out.

Falisha walked over to him, took his hand, and then straddled him as she sat on the bed. The air conditioner behind him blew cold air right in her face. It felt refreshing.

"Wassup wit' Mac?" he asked, resting his hands on her waist.

"He's good. He told me to tell you that his workout game is crazy. He said he'll be ready by the time he gets out, whatever that means," Falisha said. "What's he talking about?"

Lamar chuckled at the message. "You know Mac, young'un. While he was on da block, I was at the gym getting right," Lamar said, and pulled his T-shirt over his head. "He's still tryin' to get to where I'm at." He smiled and flexed his muscles. "I told him I would get him a job working with me whenever he gets right."

"Boy, you ain't got no damn job!" Falisha joked. She hopped up and walked over to her overnight bag.

Lamar jumped up and walked up behind her. "You're just mad 'cause you and Kim can't ever seem to keep up when y'all follow me to work," he said, and smacked her on her ass, then wrapped his arms around her.

She turned around and playfully punched him in his chest. She was shocked that he knew that they had been following him. "Why you can't just tell us where you work at?" She giggled, and draped her arms over his shoulders.

"If I tell you, then it won't be fun anymore. Y'all are just gonna have to wait until I get caught slippin'," he responded.

Falisha just smiled and shook her head at the thought of knowing that he was aware of them tailing him. She also knew that she had to come up with another way to crack the mystery. She leaned in and pressed her lips up against his, pulled back, and then kissed him again.

Her full, soft lips tasted like she just got finished drinking strawberry juice, even though she hadn't. Lamar's dick woke up and rose to attention.

"I think we can work something out," Falisha said in a seductive manner.

"Oh, yeah? What do you have in mind?" he shot back, pulling her body up against his.

Falisha pushed him back onto the bed and climbed on top of him. Lamar looked up at her while grabbing a hold of her waist. She looked into his eyes while removing her tank top and then her bra, exposing her large, firm breasts. He reached up, grabbed her by the back of her neck, and pulled her face down to his. He began kissing her passionately, accepting her tongue into his mouth.

Falisha reached back and began pulling her shorts off. Lamar did the same while neither one of them broke the kiss.

They both looked into each other's eyes the whole time, and before she knew it, Lamar grabbed the top of her ass and pulled her juice box down onto his rock-hard member. She gasped at how much of it she took in. Her walls caved in around his dick, and once she completely devoured it inside of her, she sat up, looked down at him, and began rocking back and forth, taking his dick like a champion bull rider.

From the way they were so into each other, anybody in their right mind could tell that what they had was more than just occasional sex.

Neither Ralphy nor Lisa said one word to each other after they checked out of the cabin.

Lisa drove home in her car in total silence, thinking about her rookie mistake. She still couldn't believe that she called out Dre's name. He didn't even eat pussy as good as Ralphy did for her to be thinking about him.

She reached over and grabbed her phone. Being that they weren't too far from home, she wanted to call Ralphy just to check the temperature in the atmosphere. She wanted to see how much damage she had done, and the only way that could happen was by hearing his voice.

"Yo!" Ralphy answered his phone in his normal tone.

"Hey, babe. I was wondering which one of us was going to pick up Naomi," Lisa said while looking in her rearview at his car behind hers.

"You can go get her. I gotta take care of something once we get back into the city," he responded while watching her car in front of him.

"So, are you going to make it home for dinner tonight?" she asked, still not able to get the read she was looking for.

"I don't know. I'll call you and let you know," he answered, and then hung up the phone.

Lisa didn't have time to think about it because the exit to their neighborhood was coming up. She pulled over to the exit, but Ralphy didn't. He kept going down the highway. She turned to see his car speed past her and was tempted to call him back to see where he was going, but decided against it. She figured that more than likely he was going to need his space.

Lamar sat in the bed with his back up against the headboard. Falisha sat in between his legs with her head resting up against his chest. They were both completely naked and exhausted from the sex session.

The silence in the room was broken by Lamar wanting to put his cards on the table. "So, what are we gonna do?" he asked, nudging her arm with his leg. "You hear me?" he asked, looking down at her to see if she had fallen asleep.

"I hear you, Lamar. I just don't know what to say right now," Falisha responded. "I know what you want, and sometimes I think I want the same thing, but you already know that I'm with somebody else right now. I feel bad cheating on him as it is."

"But you know that's not a real relationship you're in. All you are to him is a piece of ass, just like the rest of the bitches he messes around with," Lamar stated.

Falisha knew that what he was saying had truth to it, but she had one thing on her mind, and that was her financial security. Big Fox was one of the biggest dope boys in North Carolina, and his money was as long as the West Nile River. He was an old head, too, in his mid-forties, but he ran around the city like he was twenty-one. "I wanna be honest with you, but I don't want you to look at me different," she said, looking up at him.

"Come on, shawty. That's the best part of our relationship. We always keep it one hundred with each other no matter what," Lamar shot back.

"I'm not a whore like everybody thinks I am, Lamar."

"You think if I thought you were a whore I would want to be wit' you? Tell me something that I don't know!"

"I'm only with dat nigga Fox because he takes care of me. I can pretty much get whatever I want from him, and for me that's important when I'm with somebody. Shit, he's supposed to be buying me a house next month. Not too many of his bitches get houses." She smiled.

"So it's all about the money with you?" Lamar asked.

"See, I knew you wouldn't understand!" she said with an attitude and attempted to get up.

Lamar wrapped his arms around her before she could. He could see that her feelings were hurt by what he said. "Come 'ere, yo. Cool out," he said playfully, trying to kiss her on the neck. "I understand what you're sayin'."

"No, you don't, Lamar!" Falisha said, breaking away from him and standing up on the bed. "Look at me, Lamar," she said, striking a pose in front of him. "Don't you think I deserve to be taken care of?"

Lamar looked up at her and couldn't deny that she was a dime piece. She definitely was wife material, and if given the opportunity he would be doing the same thing as Big Fox. Maybe not on the same level as Big Fox, but he would provide for her the best way he could.

"Come back down here," he said, grabbing her arm and pulling her back down to him. "Listen, Falisha. I don't have millions of dollars like ya man Fox, nor can I buy you a house next month. But let me tell you this: I'm far from broke, and for the most part I can provide for you. I make close to seven grand a week, and my money is all legal. I'm not out on da block, nor am I running around sticking guns in people's faces and robbing them. That means you will never have to worry about me going to jail or getting murdered out here in the streets. Can you say the same thing about Big Fox? What's going to happen when his old ass gets locked up or killed by one of these young thugs out here? Then what?"

Falisha never really thought about it that way. She was so caught up with all the glamour and gold that she forgot about the downside of messing with Fox. It was something that she definitely was going to take into consideration. "I just need a little bit of time, Lamar. I need to think about some stuff. Can you at least give me that? I swear you won't have to wait long for your answer," she promised, looking up at him with the most innocent look on her face.

Lamar didn't want to give up on her, and ultimately he respected the fact that she had to take some time out to get her mind right. One thing was for sure, and that was a guaranteed fact that he wasn't gonna sit around and wait forever. If she didn't make a decision in a week or two, he was going to make the choice for her.

Chapter 9

Tammy had a few hours before she had to get to work. Anthony was in his room watching TV, and Sinniyyah was asleep, so this was a good time for her to catch up on some much-needed sleep herself.

As soon as she lay down in the bed her cell phone start ringing. She reached over and grabbed it off the nightstand quickly so that it wouldn't wake up the baby. She looked at the screen and saw that the call was coming from an unavailable number, which only meant that it was Chris calling. It had been a few days since the visit, and out of his many attempts to call her, she didn't answer one of his calls. She was still hot about him lying about the time he had gotten. It was a tough pill to swallow.

Many females say that they can do time with their men when shit hits the fan and those handcuffs get slapped on, but Tammy wasn't one of them. A little bit of time—like months or maybe even a year or two—was doable, but seven years was a very long time, and she wasn't even trying to fake it like she was strong enough to do it.

After the phone stopped ringing, less than ten seconds later it began ringing again. She looked down at the screen and saw that it was him again. She was going to send it straight to voicemail, but instead she decided to answer it this time. "What!" she said after pushing 5 to accept the call.

"Yo, what da fuck is wrong wit' you not answering this phone? Anything could be goin' on wit' me, yo!"

"What do you want, Chris?" Tammy asked as if she was irritated by him already.

"Damn, can we talk?" Chris responded in a more humble tone.

"There ain't nothing to talk about, Chris. You're in there and I'm out here. You do ya time, and I'ma do me."

"So what da fuck is that supposed to mean? You out dere fuckin' around on me, Tammy? That's how you wanna play?" he said, finding himself getting mad all over again.

"Well, I don't consider it cheating since we broke up. Don't call my phone no more. Ya kids will be taken care of," Tammy said, and then hung up the phone.

This time she turned the phone off, placed it back on the nightstand, and lay down in the bed.

The law firm that Kim worked at was one of the top firms in North Carolina. They dealt mostly with criminal cases, but also took on lawsuits if the money was right. Timothy Duncannon was an animal when it came to the law, and that's why he was the boss. Every lawyer who just passed the bar wanted to work for him, but his elite team was already built, consisting of four criminal lawyers, two accident lawyers, and six paralegals: one for each attorney.

Kim was a paralegal for Tina Rosedale, a Jewish woman who specialized in murder cases. She was one of the best coming out of North Charlotte, and had high expectations for anybody who worked under her.

"Kim, I need that brief on my desk by one o'clock," Tina said, walking past Kim's cubical.

Kim didn't hear a word she said. She sat there in a trance, appearing to be looking into her computer screen.

"Kim! Kim! Did you hear me?" Tina said, seeing that she didn't get a response the first time.

"Huh! Oh, I'm sorry, Tina! What were you saying?" Kim asked, snapping out of it.

"The illegal search and seizure brief. I need that on my desk by one," Tina repeated.

Kim was on point when it came to her work. She reached over and grabbed the brown legal folder from her desk and passed it to her. "The cases I cited are all from within the past year. Judge Castle even presided over a case where he suppressed evidence in a case almost identical to ours," Kim explained. "I also cited two federal cases to close the deal. I tell you, Judge Castle doesn't have any other choice but to suppress the murder weapon and the drugs the cops found in the house."

Tina smiled, tapping Kim on the shoulder with the folder before walking off. Her work ethics were the main reason why Tina liked Kim so much; that, along with the fact that 90 percent of Kim's briefs got granted once Tina filed them. Kim was hands down the best paralegal in the firm.

When Tina walked off, Kim looked around the room to see if anybody was watching her. The coast was clear, so she reached down under her skirt and removed the bullet from inside her vagina. She gasped a little from the previous orgasm it gave her right before Tina walked up on her. "Damn! You're gonna get me in trouble!" she mumbled to the bullet as she wrapped it up and put it back in her bag.

She got up, bag in hand, and headed straight for the bathroom to change her panties. She always kept a fresh pair with her every day for exactly this reason. The bullet had become addictive, so much so that she took it with her just about everywhere she went.

The lack of dick in her life was the cause. It wasn't that she couldn't find any, but rather she just didn't have time for it. She was chasing money and trying to pass the bar so that she could move up in the ranks of Duncannon and Associates. She put her career first. A relationship was the last thing on her mind, but she had to admit that the road she was heading down was getting lonely, and eventually something was going to have to give.

Lisa couldn't focus at work to save her life. She mixed up patients' names and appointments all day and, at one point, she almost caused an accident in the operating room while Dr. Crosby was pulling out a tooth. Her mind was somewhere else.

Ever since the weekend at the Forrest Tree Cabins, things had changed between her and Ralphy. They hardly said two words to one another, and it was like their sex life had a funeral and was buried twelve feet under the ground. Ralphy wouldn't touch her no matter how many times she tried to initiate contact. It wasn't looking good at all.

Lisa went into one of the rooms that wasn't occupied and pulled out her phone. She needed to talk to somebody about what was going on and possibly get some advice on the matter. She dialed the first number that came to mind: Kim's. In a situation like this, she felt more comfortable talking with Kim instead of Falisha or Tammy.

"Hey, bitch! What do you want?" Kim playfully answered her phone as she hiked a fresh pair of panties up under her skirt.

"Kim, I fucked up big time!" Lisa said, wiping the tears from her face. "I'm about to lose my husband!" she cried.

"Whoa! Whoa! Whoa! What's goin' on, girl?" Kim asked in a concerned manner.

Lisa paused, and all Kim could hear was her friend crying. She thought something had happened to Ralphy. "It's gonna be all right, Lisa. Just tell me what happened," Kim said, trying to comfort her.

"I called out Dre's name while me and Ralphy were having sex!" Lisa spoke through her cries.

"Ooooh shit, girl!" Kim said, and leaned against the sink. "What did he say?" she asked while looking around the bathroom to make sure that she was alone.

"That's the thing. He didn't say anything about it, but I can tell he's upset. We don't say much to each other in the house. And if I ask him something, he gives me short answers."

Kim just stood there and listened to all the problems Lisa was having behind her blunder. She was very sympathetic, but even she thought that calling out another man's name was a rookie move. "Did you have sex with that boy yet?" she asked, not sure if Lisa had made the mistake of running back to her ex.

"I've been fucking Dre since the day he came home," Lisa admitted, looking at herself in the mirror across the room.

"Noooo, Lisa! You weren't supposed to sleep with him!" Now Kim was starting to feel bad, because she was the one who cited the cases in his appeal brief that got him a new trial. Her office took the case after the witness came forward with a new story, and Dre came up with the forty grand that Tina charged him. When Kim had told Lisa the good news of the appeal, she didn't do it so that they could hook up again. She just wanted Lisa to be aware that he was coming home. "Look, girl. You're gonna have to sit down and talk to Ralphy."

"I know. I tried that already, but he's not giving me the chance to say anything. He just leaves the room, and sometimes even the house," Lisa responded.

"You can't give him an option, girl. I don't care what you have to do. Y'all both need to air this shit out. But no matter what you do, don't tell Ralphy that you slept with Dre. You do that, you can kiss ya marriage good-bye!"

"Yo, every time you come to work you be looking mean as hell," Darious, one of Tammy's coworkers, said when she walked in and took a seat behind the customer service desk.

"There ain't nothing to be happy about coming in here for four hours every day and only making $8.50 an hour!" Tammy shot back.

"You gotta try and see the good in this job. It can be worse than this," Darious replied.

"Yeah, well, what good do you see? 'Cause I don't see shit that makes me happy by working here," Tammy said as she wiped down her working station with a Clorox wipe.

Darious turned around in his chair to face her and pointed at her with his ink pen. "You know there are two things I enjoy about working here. One: I finish school next month to be a pharmaceutical technician, and this job helped pay the bills while I was taking those courses. If it weren't for this job, I'd be broke as hell!" He laughed.

"Oh, yeah? And what's the other reason?" Tammy asked.

Darious smiled shyly, feeling a little embarrassed about what he was about to say. "To be honest wit' you, I look forward to you walking through that door every day at four o'clock," he told her, and then got up and walked off to go retrieve some items from the back.

For the first time in a long time, Tammy smiled at another man's compliments, outside of Chris's. Darious was handsome. He was tall, and had light brown skin and a thin frame. He always kept a positive attitude, and he always dressed nice when he came to work. Secretly, Tammy thought that he was kind of cute. She would never tell him that, though. That was going to stay her little secret . . . at least for now.

The entire drive home, Lisa thought about what she was going to say. She didn't even know how to begin this type of conversation. Ralphy was going to have a lot of questions, and she knew that. She was also expecting to be called names, and the possibility of getting smacked wasn't too far off either, even though Ralphy wasn't the abusive type. Hell, in this kind of situation, anything was liable to happen.

As Lisa was pulling up to the house her phone began to ring. Her gut instinct told her that it was Dre calling. She hadn't spoken to him since the vacation, and he had been calling every day, all day, only to be sent to voicemail.

When she grabbed her phone out of her bag, she looked at the screen and exhaled deeply at the sight of his number flashing. She looked up at the house, and then up and down the street for any sign of Ralphy. She wasn't going to answer it, but she had to. She had to tell Dre that it was over. "Hello," she answered, only to get an earful.

"Yo, why da fuck did you leave me out there wit' no way to get home?" Dre snapped into the phone. "And why ain't you answering my calls?"

"Oh, shit!" Lisa said after moving the phone away from her mouth so that he wouldn't hear her. She totally forgot that she was the one who drove him up to the cabin. She was so messed up about what had happened between her and Ralphy that the only thing she wanted to do was go home. That's the reason why Dre was calling her so crazy. "I'm so sorry, Dre. I had to leave because—"

"Man, fuck dat! Look, I need to holla at you about something. When can we meet up?"

"That's cool, 'cause I need to talk to you about something as well," Lisa said. "I can't see you right now because I got some shit I need to take care of. Just give me a couple of days and I'll call you so we can meet up." She was about to hang up when she heard Dre's voice change into a softer tone when he started singing "I Miss You" by Aaron Hall.

Lisa found herself sinking back into her seat, listening to him blow. Hearing him sing brought back so many good memories. For a hardcore thug, Dre could sing his ass off, especially when he used to sing to her. Those were the good old days, times both Lisa and Dre missed but knew that it was almost impossible for them to get back to. So much had changed since then; and, now, somebody else's heart was involved. It was a heart that Lisa didn't want to break, and it belonged to Ralphy.

Lisa sat there for a few more minutes listening to Dre before she finally hung up the phone and went into the house. When she walked in, she was shocked to see Ms. D sitting on her couch with Naomi, watching TV.

"Mommy!" Naomi yelled when she saw Lisa walk through the door.

"Now you know I don't do house calls, but yo' crazy-ass husband insisted on it," Ms. D said while rubbing the top of Naomi's head. "We was about to eat dinner. Are you hungry?"

"Wait! Hold up! Where did Ralphy go?" Lisa asked, and whipped out her cell phone to call him.

"I don't think calling him is a good idea. He left his phone here," Ms. D said, nodding toward Ralphy's phone sitting on the table in front of her.

Lisa took a deep breath, then exhaled, shaking her head as she walked over and grabbed his phone. This was the first time that he ever did something like this. "A'ight, Ms. D. Thanks for watching her. How much do I owe you?" she said, digging into her bag for her wallet.

"Little girl, didn't you just hear what I said? We're about to eat dinner. I cooked an hour ago," Ms. D told her. "Besides, yo' husband already paid me." She then got up off the couch and headed to the kitchen with Naomi in tow. "Now, I don't know what you did to that boy, but he left out of here wit' an attitude!"

Lisa kicked her shoes off and took a seat at the dinner table with Naomi, and listened to Ms. D as she began serving the food. Ms. D went on with 101 suggestions on how to fix a broken home. Most of her ideas involved kinky, sexual favors, which gave Lisa a laugh more than anything. She knew none of that stuff was going to work for this particular problem. This was going to require something more, and Lisa didn't have the slightest idea what that was. This was drama . . . real drama. And one way or another, she was going to have to deal with it.

Chapter 10

"Now look. You're gonna be the first person in the hood who knows where I work," Lamar told Falisha as he threw his duffel bag into the trunk.

Falisha stood at the passenger side door. She was excited that she was going to finally find out where Lamar worked. It was like uncovering an ancient Chinese secret, except that Lamar made her promise not to tell anybody. It took a minute for her to agree to those terms, but in the end, she did. "So, what's in the bag?" she asked, smiling from ear to ear and hoping to get an idea of where they were going.

"You'll see when we get there," he teased, slamming the trunk closed and walking over to the driver side.

Just as he was about to get into the car, a cream-colored Cadillac Escalade turned onto the block. Lamar caught an instant attitude because he knew that it was Big Fox, and he was there for none other than Falisha.

Falisha noticed the truck too, and inched away from Lamar's car so that it didn't look like she was about to go anywhere with him.

Lamar peeped her move. "Oh, yeah?" he said to Falisha as she started to walk across the street.

"Don't do this, Lamar. Just give me a minute," she replied right before the truck came to a stop in front of her.

Lamar just stood there and waited to see what she was going to do.

Fox rolled his window down and sat up in his seat. "I see you out here wit' ya li'l boyfriend," he said, looking over at Lamar, and then smiling.

"You play too much!" Falisha shot back, and playfully pushed his arm. "I thought you was taking ya daughter out today," she said, looking into the truck to see if the little girl was with him.

"I just dropped her off. I had her all afternoon. I thought me and you could catch a movie or something tonight," he said while rubbing his freshly groomed beard. "Come on," he calmly told her with a nod of his head.

Falisha didn't want to go, but at the same time she couldn't deny him either. It wouldn't look right with Lamar standing in front of his car waiting for her. Also, she didn't want to give Fox the impression that she was about to go somewhere with Lamar. Finally, she walked around to the passenger side of the truck and got in. She didn't look at Lamar, nor did she say bye.

Lamar and Fox made eye contact before he was about to pull off. No words were exchanged, but Fox did manage to crack a slick grin at him.

Lamar only replied with a simple nod of his head to let Fox know that he won this round. Among men, it was the gentlemanly thing to do. Lamar could only respect the OG's game. One or two things could happen at this point, and that was for Lamar to either bow out gracefully and let Fox take his bitch, or step his game up a notch.

The last thing a female would want was for her man to get to snooping around, if she in fact was a cheater. It's easy for women to cheat and not get caught. That's a well-known fact.

But if a man has any indication that the love of his life is sleeping around on him and there's a good chance that it's true, he can become a problem. Just like women, men have their ways of finding out whether their woman is being faithful. Men can become bloodhounds and won't stop until they find what they are looking for, and the most crucial mistake Lisa made was leaving a scent for Ralphy to follow.

Dre was a name Lisa used to throw around in the beginning of their relationship, so Ralphy knew exactly who he was. But he was a little confused, because the last word on him was that he had gotten a life sentence for murder. Thinking that Lisa might still be in contact with him, Ralphy checked into it.

First he had to get Dre's real name, which was easy seeing as how his cousin still lived on the block. Annet was more than willing to give up Dre's full name and his state ID number, thinking that Ralphy knew him and was going to put some money on his books. It was crazy, because Dre's release came so suddenly that hardly anybody knew that he had been home for almost three months. Ralphy was about to find out, though.

Ralphy had taken refuge in a local bar, away from home. He didn't feel like dealing with Lisa right now, nor did he want her to know that he was digging into her past.

You can pretty much get any information off the Internet, especially pertaining to convicted felons. When he typed in Dre's real name, Andre Tucker, his case popped up on the screen. He read that the case had been overturned, but it was pending further prosecution. It didn't state whether he was released, but Ralphy had his fair share in the criminal system to know that once you win your appeal, you either get released or get a lesser amount of time.

Reading further, he saw that the law firm that represented him on his appeal was Duncannon and Associates. The name sounded familiar and it took awhile, but he finally remembered that it was the law firm that Kim worked for. He remembered because Lisa always bragged about it, saying that if she ever had a problem with the law, Kim would get her out of trouble. It was starting to look like one big conspiracy, and everybody was in on it but him.

He looked around the bar and then down at his watch. It was a little after four o'clock, which meant that he still had a little more time to investigate further. Without wasting any more time, he packed up and left the bar with one thing on his mind. He was going to get to the bottom of things if it was the last thing he did.

Ralphy made it down to Duncannon and Associates law firm right before everyone was about to leave. As soon as he walked through the door the receptionist was packing up her things. "May I help you?" she asked when Ralphy walked up to the desk.

"Yes. Is Kim in? I need to talk to her about an appeal," Ralphy responded as he looked around.

The receptionist picked up her phone, and moments later Kim came walking down the hallway. She was kind of surprised to see Ralphy standing there when she came out into the lobby area. "Hey, Ralph. Is everything all right? Where's Lisa?" she asked, seeing that he looked stressed.

"I need to talk to you," he responded. "It's kind of important."

"Yeah? Okay, follow me," Kim told him. She had a gut feeling that she knew what this was about. She led him to the back and into an office that wasn't being occupied.

The entire time, Ralphy kept his cool, not getting mad or aggressive. He spoke in a calm manner, too. "Kim, I know your loyalty is with my wife, and I don't expect for this to be easy for you, either. But I just need to know one thing and, I'm begging you, don't lie to me," he began after closing the door and leaning his back against it.

"I don't understand, Ralphy. What are you talking about?" Kim asked, now becoming a little nervous.

"Did that nigga come home?"

"I don't know who you're talking about. What nigga?" she asked.

"Andre Tucker; or should I say Dre," Ralphy said, raising his voice a little in frustration. "Don't lie to me. I already know that your office repre- sented him on his appeal."

Ralphy was right when he said that Kim's loyalty was with Lisa. They grew up together, whereas Ralphy came into the picture just a few years ago. She wasn't trying to give her friend up to a nigga, but he wasn't going for anything. "Look, I'm not trying to get involved in this—"

"You're already involved. The only thing you can do now is minimize your part in this," he said, cutting her off. "Trust me, Kim. You don't wanna be on the opposite side when this shit hits the fan. I'm trying to give you a way out. All you gotta do is answer the question."

His threats were becoming a little more serious, which made Kim a little more afraid of what he might do to her if he didn't get an answer to his question. She thought about it long enough, and there wasn't any harm in telling him that Dre was home . . . or, at least, that's what she hoped. "Dre's been home for a little more than two months now. But, I swear, that's all I know," she said.

Ralphy shook his head, and then balled up his fist. He didn't even think about it when he turned around and punched the door. Kim jumped from the loud bang. She backed up to the desk and looked around for something to use as a weapon. She prayed that she wasn't to be punched next.

Without any further questions or comments, Ralphy flung the door open and stormed out of the office.

Kim was relieved that he had left, but she was more concerned for Lisa. She knew beyond a shadow of a doubt that Ralphy was on his way home to confront her, and the outcome didn't look good.

Kim quickly whipped out her cell phone to call and warn Lisa that she had some serious drama coming her way. Hopefully she'd be smart enough to leave before he got there.

"What time are you picking me up tomorrow?" Falisha asked Fox as he pulled up to her house.

"I don't know. I got some shit I need to take care of. I'll call you and let you know," he said while watching the small crowd of young females sitting on the porch across the street from Falisha's house.

"A'ight, boo. Call me," Falisha said, and leaned over and poked her lips out for a kiss.

Fox looked over at the young females who were looking into the truck. He turned to Falisha, raised his hand, and playfully mugged her away. "You know I ain't good wit' dat public affection shit." He chuckled.

Falisha cocked her head back and frowned at the comment. She looked over and saw Annet and her girlfriends sitting there watching. She looked back at Fox, and then rolled her eyes at him before getting out of the truck. He wasn't the perfect gentleman at all that night, and was being disrespectful when he pulled off before Falisha even got to her steps.

She was so bothered by his behavior that she didn't even feel like sitting outside with the girls tonight. A simple, "Hi!" to everyone sufficed before she disappeared into the house.

"Hey, Mom!" Falisha called out as she walked over and kissed Ms. Angie on her head. "Did I get any mail?"

"No, baby. No mail. But ya plate is in the microwave whenever you feel like eating."

Falisha could never deny her mom's cooking no matter what she had already eaten. She grabbed her plate then shot up the steps to her bedroom.

"It's almost twelve o'clock, Mom! Get off dat couch and go to bed!" she yelled back downstairs before entering her room.

When she opened her bedroom door, she was startled and almost dropped her plate when she saw Lamar sitting on the edge of her bed with his elbows on his lap and his hands crossed. "Boy, you scared da shit out of me!" she said, placing her plate on her nightstand. "How did you get up here anyway?"

"You know ya mom loves me. This is just one of the many advantages I have. I'm dat nigga!" he said, getting up and walking over to Falisha, who was standing up against the wall and smiling at what he said.

"What do you want, boy?" she asked in a low but submissive way while crossing her arms over her stomach.

Lamar reached in his pocket and pulled out the remote control to her stereo system. He pushed a couple of buttons, and then tossed the remote onto the bed. The sounds of Jagged Edge's "I Gotta Be" softly serenaded the room, changing the whole mood. "Come 'ere," he said, and gently grabbed Falisha's arm and pulled her to the middle of the room.

She went without putting up a fuss. Lamar wrapped his hands around her waist and pulled her up against his body. She reached up, placed her hands over his shoulders, and rested her head against his chest.

> *Is it real, what I feel? Could it be you and me,*
> *'Til the end of time, never part?*
> *Take my heart, hold it tight; it's true love,*
> *You know I gotta be.*

Lamar didn't have to say a word. The song was saying it all. The way he felt about Falisha was obvious, and she knew it. She could feel it, too, by the way he looked at her, the way he touched her, and by the way he spoke gently to her. Even at this very moment, she was intoxicated by the way her body fit perfectly and snugly in his grasp. "What are you doin' to me, Lamar!" she spoke as she continued to dance slowly with him.

"I'm only tryin' to be here for you. I'm not goin' anywhere, Falisha. I don't care how long I gotta wait for you, I'ma be right here at the end of the day. And if Big Fox thinks for one second that this shit's gonna be sweet, he got another think coming. He better be ready to fight for you, 'cause I am!" he said, and wrapped his arms around her tighter.

A fight was exactly the thing Lamar was putting up. But he wasn't fighting with his fists or in a yelling match. His weapon of choice was something that Fox didn't have, something Fox couldn't give Falisha, which was love and affection: a combination only Lamar introduced into her life so far. The battle for Falisha's love was on and poppin'.

By the time Tammy got home, she didn't feel like going back out to pick the kids up from her mom's house, so she called and asked her mom to bring them to her, which she didn't have a problem with. Tammy was tired, but it didn't come from work. It came from depression. The stress of being a single mother made her want to just lie in bed all day.

Sifting through the mail she picked up when she walked through the door, she came across a letter from Chris. She was hesitant about opening it, thinking all he did was curse her out in it, but she decided to read it anyway just to see what he had to say. It read:

Dear Tam,

I have a couple of issues to address, so let me just get right to it. You are absolutely right; I do have seven more years to do, as of right now. They gave me a total of ten years for the crack that I got caught with, and in the feds you only do 85 percent of your time, which brought me down to seven and a half years, including the time I already been locked up.

I know it's hard to accept. I too struggle with the numbers. I don't blame you for being mad at me for not telling you. I really didn't know how to break that kind of news to you. I knew how much it was going to hurt you, and that's the last thing I ever wanted to do. I guess a part of me was being selfish, too. I thought that once you found out, you would leave me. I didn't want to lose you.

I love you so much. I love our kids, too, and I miss y'all with every day that goes by. I really don't know how I'm going to manage the next seven years. My family is all I ever lived for when I was home, so to sit back and watch you struggle is hurtful in itself. To lose you is like losing everything, and I completely understand if you want to move on with your life. You deserve to be happy even if it's with someone other than me.

At the end of the day, I brought this all on myself. I made choices and sacrifices that ultimately got me taken away from you. I fucked up, so I can only blame me. I take full responsibility.

As far as our children are concerned, all I ask is that you allow me to continue to be a part of their lives. If you want to leave, that's fine, but don't take my kids away from me. Everything I did out there on those streets was to give them and you a better life. The sacrifices I made would be in vain if you took them away. I know I can't do much financially for them, but let me try to be the best father I can be. If you got any love left in your heart for me, then let me at least do that.

In closing, I just want to apologize for putting you through these difficult times. For now, I'ma fall back and get out of your way. I wish nothing but the best for you, and I'll continue to keep you in my prayers.

I love you, Tammy. Always have, and always will.

Chris

Tammy wiped the tears from her eyes before putting the letter back into the envelope. She really did love Chris, and only said half of the things she said because she was mad. She didn't mean any of it pertaining to her moving on, but it seemed like Chris already had it in his mind that she was going to do just that. In his letter, it sounded like he had already given up on their relationship. She really didn't want for it to go that far.

Seven years was a long time, and she honestly didn't know if she could last that long being alone. But what she did know was that she didn't want her and Chris to end like this. She was confused. They had too much time in, and two kids invested in their relationship, so before she decided to leave him for real, she at least wanted to try to ride it out for as long as she could, and hoped that the seven years would go by fast.

The only problem with that was once Chris had his mind made up on something, it was pretty much a wrap. So, when he said that he was going to fall back and get out of Tammy's way, there was a possibility that he might have finalized the separation. If that was the case, Tammy's attempt to do the time with him was pointless. It was over.

Chapter 11

"Get out da car, bitch," Gena yelled, pulling at the passenger side door of Fox's truck.

Falisha looked at the prehype young lady without a care in the world. The girl had to be a few years younger than her, so Falisha was trying to be patient. She looked over at Fox, who was sitting there smiling like this was some type of game to him.

"You better get ya little girlfriend before I beat shit down her legs," Falisha warned, trying to give Fox the opportunity to fix the situation.

This wasn't the first time Falisha had to deal with one of Fox's scallywags. He had a few young chicks he dealt with, none of whom knew how to play their part, leaving it up to Falisha to have to put them in their place. To be as cute as she was, Falisha knew how to fight and she did it well, but every now and again it seemed like somebody had to test her.

"I'll take care of it," Fox said in frustration as he got out of the truck.

When Gena saw Fox open his door she darted around to the driver side hoping she could catch the door before it closed. Before she could get to it,

Fox grabbed her by the arm and pulled her down the street away from the truck.

"Didn't I tell you to stop acting like a fuckin' kid?" Fox snapped, towering over her.

"And didn't I tell you to stop bringing dese bitches around here?" Gena shot back. "You ain't gon' be happy 'til I beat one of their asses," she said, attempting to break for the truck.

Fox grabbed her again, stopping her from getting embarrassed. He knew Falisha was going to end up beating the shit out of her, so he was trying to save her.

"Why don't you get out the car, you dumb bitch?" NeNe, one of Gena's girlfriends, said tapping on the passenger side window. "You dirty-ass hood rat."

Falisha sat there and looked at the young girl like she was an alien. NeNe had no idea what she was getting herself into, but she was about to find out. Falisha didn't care that this wasn't her neighborhood, nor did she care about the crowd of people standing outside of the projects looking on. There was just so much disrespect she was going to take.

"Tell ya fuckin' friend to get away from my car," Fox yelled at Gena as he held her back. The whole time NeNe stood outside of the car yelling and talking crazy about what she was gonna do. Falisha calmly prepared for the fight.

"These li'l girls is working my fuckin' nerves," Falisha mumbled as she began taking off her earrings. "Don't go nowhere," she yelled through the window while pulling her hair into a ponytail.

She looked down at her brand new cream Michael Kors wedges and shook her head, only mad that she was about to mess up a pair of good shoes. That made her a little angrier in itself.

As soon as Falisha stepped out of the car, the fight was on. NeNe rushed her, but Falisha grabbed her by the head and started kneeing her in the face. She was slinging NeNe around like a rag doll by her hair. Gena snapped seeing that. She wildly broke away from Fox, who was standing there fascinated by the work Falisha was putting in.

Falisha didn't see her coming but she damn sure felt Gena sneak her from the side. Gena was a little wilder when it came to fighting. She threw what seemed like a hundred punches in ten seconds. Falisha caught the brunt of most of the punches because she wouldn't let go of NeNe. She eventually let NeNe go, then turned around and went toe to toe with Gena.

It didn't take long for Falisha to get the upper hand on Gena, and when she did, she beat the hell out of her. All you could hear was a bunch of oohs and aahs coming from the crowd of people who had tuned into the fight. Falisha had beat NeNe up so bad she didn't want any more trouble. She just lay on the ground looking up at Falisha whooping Gena's ass.

"A'ight, a'ight, dat's enough," Fox yelled as he made his way through the crowd and stepped between the two girls. It took him a minute or two but Fox eventually pulled Falisha off of Gena then put her back in his truck. Fox was laughing the whole time, finding it amusing that young, beautiful women would still fight over him. He also knew how much Falisha could get down and found it entertaining when she did her thing. Her fight game was one of the many reasons why Falisha was his main chick; and, until somebody stepped up and knocked her off her throne, she was going to continue to be his main and number one chick.

A couple of nights ago Kim had called Lisa and warned her that Ralphy had come to her office and found out about Dre being home. Lisa stayed home and waited for the confrontation, but when Ralphy got home he didn't have much to say. Lisa tried to talk to him, but he insisted on not talking. Lisa, not really being in the mood either, just left it alone.

Today was a different day. Lisa had been walking around the house on eggshells long enough and the silent treatment Ralphy was giving out was killing her. As soon as Lisa came back from dropping Naomi off at day camp, she went right at Ralphy.

"Yo, we need to talk," Lisa said in a demanding way when she walked into the bedroom where he was at.

Ralphy stood in front of the mirror fixing his tie and ignored her request. Lisa wasn't taking no for an answer. Ralphy tried to walk out of the room but Lisa ran over and slammed the door, pressing her back up against it so he couldn't leave.

"Move from in front of the door, Lisa," Ralphy said in a calm voice, patting her on the arm.

"No! I'm not moving until we talk," she said.

"What do you wanna talk about?" he asked, stepping back and taking a seat on the edge of their bed. "Make it fast 'cause we both gotta go to work."

His calm and relaxed demeanor was throwing Lisa off. She expected Ralphy to have snapped out by now about what had happened, but he didn't. "Baby, I fucked up and I'm sorry," Lisa began to plead, walking over and kneeling in between his legs.

Ralphy gave her a confused look like he didn't know what she was talking about, but in that same look, it showed that he knew exactly what she was talking about. Lisa sat there stuck for a minute. She couldn't believe he was going to make her say what she had done. He wanted to hear it from her own mouth and for Lisa it was like being tortured. She looked up at him and could see the hurt in his eyes. She just put her head down, unable to fix her mouth to say the words.

"Why you ain't tell me dis nigga was home?" Ralphy asked, breaking the silence.

"I don't know, babe. I really didn't think it was something you wanted to know. He came—"

"Did you fuck dat nigga?" he asked in an angry tone, just thinking about it. "Don't fuckin' lie to me."

Hearing him ask the question in the manner that he did kinda scared Lisa. It wasn't the fear of him possibly putting his hands on her, but it was the fear of losing him that made her lie.

"No!" she answered quickly. "I did not have sex with that boy," she lied flat out with a straight face.

"So why da fuck is you callin' his name out? And you did it while I'm in the middle of—"

"I know, I know, babe. I'm sorry," Lisa cried out.

Lisa cried like a baby, but Ralphy wasn't impressed. He had a gut instinct it was deeper than what Lisa was telling him. "Look, I gotta get to work," he said, getting up from the bed. "I need some time to—"

"No, babe, wait!" Lisa whined, getting up from her knees and following him. "Ralphy. Please!"

Ralphy stopped at the door and turned around. He never heard Lisa cry like this and, naturally, he became sympathetic toward his wife. He grabbed her and pulled her into his arms, trying his best to suppress his anger so that he could comfort her.

"I don't wanna lose you. I love you so much," Lisa cried out as she held on to him tightly.

"Shhhh! It's cool, babe. You not gon' lose me. We'll get through this together," he said in a soft voice.

What he said was comforting, but how he felt in his heart was uneasy. He didn't want to show it but he was hurting inside, and until he got to the bottom of the situation he was going to continue to hurt.

"Yo, you good, shawty?" Fox asked before putting his truck in park.

Falisha flipped the sun visor down to see what her face looked like. She had a long scratch running down the side of her face, and a cut on her bottom lip that burned every time she licked it. Her hair was all over the place and her Michael Kors wedges were pretty much ruined. But her bruises were nothing compared to what Gena's and NeNe's faces looked like.

"You need to keep ya li'l hoes in check, Fox," she said as she put her hair back into a ponytail. "This is the last time I'm fighting over you."

Fox didn't say anything. He just looked at her and smiled. This wasn't the first time he heard this from her and he was sure this wasn't going to be the last. He wasn't worried about her going anywhere. There weren't too many niggas in the hood who could do for her financially what he could do. It was probably his only advantage and, for now, he was going to soak it up.

Chapter 12

Lisa, Falisha, Kim, and Tammy sat on Tammy's steps watching the kids play in the street. This was more like a daily ritual after everybody got off of work. This was the time when they all talked about what was going on in their lives and tried to give each other advice. Today, everybody had some type of drama.

"Hey, bitches!" Ernie said, walking up and taking a seat on the steps. "The vibe over here is dead," he joked.

Ernie was the gay brother who lived on the next street over, but became one of the girls after he finally came out of the closet two years ago. When he did come out of the closet, he came full steam ahead, wearing female clothes and letting his hair grow down to his shoulders. He had his ears pierced, nipples pierced, and he had a tongue ring. He was as gay as they come but he was cool as hell.

"Ernie, what da hell do you got on?" Kim asked, pointing to his orange and black striped pants.

"What, girl? Dese my tiger pants. Arggg," he growled, jumping up and striking a pose.

He was known for his fashion sense and some of the time the girls did bite his style, but today he missed. The pants were a mess, and he had the nerve to be wearing a gold blouse with it and some black Chuck Taylors.

"Boy, if you don't sit ya crazy ass down . . ." Kim laughed, throwing an empty potato chip bag at him. Everybody laughed at the same time.

"Ha-ha! Laugh now, but cry later when y'all asses don't get invited to my party," Ernie shot back with a few snaps of his neck. "Me and my tiger pants gon' be droppin' it like it's hot," he joked, jumping back up, but this time bending over and shaking his ass.

"Oh, shit. I forgot ya birthday was this weekend," Falisha said as she cracked open her sunflower seeds.

"Yup! And I'm having my party at the Mandingo's Den," Ernie bragged.

"What da hell is the Mandingo's Den?" Tammy asked.

Kim went into deep thought. She remembered hearing that name before, but couldn't place it to save her life. It wasn't until Ernie said something that it came back to her.

"The Mandingo's Den is a gay strip club," Ernie said.

"And who da hell is gonna be dancing in front of a bunch of gay men?" Falisha asked, shocked that there could be such a thing.

"Well, let me see," Ernie said, digging into his satchel. "You have Dustin the Dangerous, Anaconda Frank, Jake da Snake, and Mr. Billy D. himself," Ernie said, fanning himself with the flyer he just read from.

"Oh, I heard of Billy D.," Kim chimed in, grinning from ear to ear. "Dat boy don't just dance; he do porno, too." She chuckled.

"How da hell do you know he do pornos?" Falisha asked.

"Shit, a bitch get lonely sometimes and my rabbit and a nice porn will always take me there." Kim laughed. Everybody laughed at her.

"No, but seriously are y'all coming?" Ernie asked. "I got y'all a VIP table right up front. And, Tammy, I don't wanna hear you can't find nobody to watch the kids. I will pay Ms. D to watch the babies so you can go," he said.

Everybody got quiet for a minute thinking about whether they had plans for this weekend. One thing that they all could agree on was that they needed to go out. It'd been a long week for everybody.

"Hell, I'll go," Kim said, breaking the silence.

"Yeah, I'll go too," Tammy agreed. "But Ms. D want her money up front." She chuckled, giving Ernie the nod.

Everybody eventually agreed to go to Ernie's party. Liquor, music, and naked men dancing on the stage were exactly what the girls needed. It wasn't going to take away their problems but it sure was going to relieve a little stress, at least for that night.

Ralphy sat at his desk looking into the computer screen at the long list of shipments he had to make sure got to their destination. His newfound position at the postal office required him to supervise mail being distributed throughout Charlotte. Most of the time the job was easy but today it was busy as hell.

"Ay, John, you think you can handle this while I make a run?" Ralphy asked his assistant.

Today, Ralphy wanted to go down to the bank and transfer some of the money in his joint account with Lisa to a separate account that only he had access to. It was something he had thought about doing a long time ago but never got around to it. It was for a couple of reasons but the main one was so that he'd have some money put away in the event he and Lisa didn't work out. Part of the prenuptial agreement he and Lisa agreed to stated that in the event of a divorce both parties would agree to split the monies within the joint account they shared, and keep what was in their own personal, separate accounts. It wasn't until a few months ago Ralphy came to his senses and decided to open up another bank account. Now, he was glad he did because things were starting to look rocky in the marriage.

There was no telling how much longer it was going to last and he needed to make sure he had some money put aside.

Truth be told, the relationship was already over. There was no way in the world Ralphy could forgive Lisa for calling out her ex's name while they were having sex. He wasn't that type of guy. Something like that could lower a man's self-esteem and have him wondering whether he's sexually gifted. Every man feels like they got the best dick game in the world. They think that they are capable of sexually pleasing the whole female race. To make a man feel like he's not the one who's pleasing in bed, it can really ruin a relationship, and that's exactly what Lisa did. It would take an act of God to make their relationship work after this, and neither Ralphy nor Lisa had been to church lately, so the chances of that were slim.

Falisha sat on her step getting her hair braided by Annet when Lamar pulled up and parked a couple doors down. He got out of the car looking handsome as ever, and all he had on was a Polo tank top, some True Religion shorts, and a pair of Jordans. He made the basics look good, and not the other way around.

"Hold up for a second, girl," Falisha said, jumping up and walking down her steps. She hadn't seen Lamar in almost two days and was wondering where he had been. In fact, that was the first question she asked.

"Where you been at?" she snapped, walking up to Lamar while he went to get his things out of the trunk.

When he turned to look at her the first thing he noticed was the scratches and bruises on her face. They were starting to heal but they were still noticeable. "What happened to your face?" he asked, looking at the scratch running down the side of her face.

Falisha shook her head. "Fighting with these ratchet-ass bitches around Fox's way," she responded.

Lamar chuckled, then shook his head back at her. "That's what you get," he said, turning back around to grab his duffle bag out of the trunk.

"I didn't lose," she shot back. "I whooped their ass."

"Well, you should have lost," Lamar said, slamming his trunk. "You like dat shit, don't you?"

"Like what? What are you talking about, Lamar?" She could tell that Lamar had copped an attitude by the way he looked.

"You like being treated like shit, don't you?" he answered.

"He don't treat me like shit."

"Oh, yeah, so what da fuck is dis?" he said, pointing to the bruises on her face.

"He didn't do this to me. I told you—"

"Yo, you crazy as hell," he said, cutting her off. "But, you know what? It's not even none of my business. Do you," he said, then turned around and walked off.

"Oh, you gonna walk away now?" she yelled as he crossed the street.

"Grow da fuck up, Falisha," he turned around and yelled back before walking up his steps and disappearing into the house.

Tammy got to work about twenty minutes late today. Ms. D had a dialysis appointment and got back home late. Tammy thought that she was going to get an earful from her boss because she didn't call to let him know that she was going to be late, but when she passed by him on her way to customer service, he just smiled and kept it moving.

"I see you're back from your OBGYN appointment," Darious said, coming out from the back.

"What?" Tammy asked, confused.

"I told Tim you called in and said that you was going to be a little late 'cause you was at a doctor's appointment," he said, walking over and taking a seat next to her.

"Thanks for covering for me. I know he was going to be tripping as soon as I walked through the door," Tammy said.

"Well, you just better hope your next coworker is as nice as I am." Darious chuckled. "You know I'm outta here soon."

"What! I thought you didn't graduate until next month," Tammy said, shocked that he was leaving.

"Yeah, I do graduate next month but I already got a job. I'll be working at the hospital in the pharmacy department," he told Tammy.

"Wow, that's a good look for you. Congratulations."

"Thanks. You know I'm going to miss you, right?" Darious said in a sincere manner.

Tammy had to stop and look over at him to see if his facial expression matched the way he sounded and looked serious when he said it. "Boy, you better stop playin'. You ain't gon' miss nobody," Tammy said, waving him off before turning back to the computer screen.

"I'm dead serious, Tammy," he shot back. "Can I be honest with you about something without you taking offense?"

She didn't know whether to answer that, but she really didn't have time to because Darious just kept going.

"Yo, I think you're beautiful, Tammy. I been wanting to get with you from the moment you started working here. Truth is, I'd be kicking myself in the ass if I didn't tell you this before I left. I like you a lot, Tammy."

Tammy was blown back by his confession. She always thought that he used to flirt with her, but never did she know that he liked her to this magnitude. It was flattering in a sense, enough to have her blushing like a teenage girl with her first cousin.

"I don't know if I'll ever get this chance again so I was wondering if I could call you sometime?" Darious asked.

Tammy's defenses went straight up. It was the same block she put up on all the other men who tried to hit on her. It was something that came automatically because of her feelings for Chris. "I can't dooo that," she said with the sorry face.

"Tammy, I just wanna be ya friend. I wanna be the person you can call on when you need to talk," he said, turning his chair around to face her. Darious wasn't giving up that easy. He was trying his best to break down that wall Tammy had put up and, from what he had said, it looked like it was starting to work.

Tammy sat there in silence thinking about it. The thing was, she couldn't deny the fact that she could use a friend right now in her life. Times were hard and just to have someone to talk to about life's struggles was exactly what she needed. The fifteen-minute phone calls with Chris weren't enough, nor could he call all the time.

There's no harm in just talking, she thought, looking over at Darious. "I guess you can call me," Tammy said, writing her number down on a sticky pad and passing it to him.

Darious whipped out his phone immediately and put the number into his phone book. This wasn't just a big step for Tammy; it was also one for Darious. He waited patiently for months to get to this point. Now that he was here, there was only one more thing for him to do, and that was to keep pushing forward.

"Good afternoon, Mr. Windsor," the bank manager, Larry, greeted Ralphy when he entered the office.

Ralphy greeted him back then took a seat in the chair in front of his desk. He looked around the office at all the plaques hanging up and pictures of Larry standing next to a couple of celebrities, such as Usher, Bow Wow, and Kelly Rowland.

Damn, he sure know a lot of black artists. "I had opened up an account here a couple of months ago and I just wanted to transfer some money into it from a joint account I have with my wife, also at this bank," Ralphy explained.

"That shouldn't be a problem; just let me see your ID," Larry said, adjusting his computer screen.

Ralphy gave him his ID then watched as Larry began pulling up his file. Now that he was actually sitting in the bank, Ralphy starting to question whether he should go this far. Saying it and doing it were two totally different things. He wasn't even sure if Lisa had slept with Dre, nor did he even attempt to rectify the situation. He didn't even give Lisa a chance to fix what she had done. After all, she was his wife and most of the time when married couples have serious issues in their relationships, and they love each other deeply, they try to work things out, either with a marriage counselor or by themselves. Ralphy didn't attempt to do either one and it was starting to weigh on his conscience.

"Okay, Mr. Windsor, here's a look at what's in the joint account with your wife, and here's what you have in your separate account," Larry said, passing Ralphy the paper from the printing station.

Ralphy held up both papers in each hand, scanning over them carefully. The numbers on the paper with his and Lisa's joint account caught his attention immediately. He put his separate account paper down and focused in on the other.

"Is this what's left in this account?" Ralphy asked, pointing to the bottom of the page.

"Yup, you have $8,422 in this account," Larry confirmed. "Is something wrong?"

Damn right something was wrong. There should have been at least $13,000 in their account. Ralphy wasn't spending any money, so if it was missing it was because of Lisa. Ralphy normally kept tabs on the account transactions, mainly for budgeting purposes; but, as of late, he had been slacking in keeping up with it, but it was obvious Lisa wasn't.

"Is it possible I can see the last transactions within the last couple of months?" Ralphy asked with a suspicious look on his face.

"Yeah, sure. I can do that," Larry said, tapping away at the keys. "Here you go."

He passed Ralphy the two pieces of paper as soon as they came out of the printer. Larry was well experienced in the field of banking and knew that Ralphy may have had some marital problems. It was pretty much confirmed by the way Ralphy looked strongly at the two pieces of paper.

"Look, Mr. Windsor. I know this isn't any of my business but you seem like a nice guy," Larry said, sympathizing with Ralphy. "I know it's not professional for me to do this but we men gotta stick together," he said, looking back on the computer. "I don't know if you know this, but your wife also has an open separate account at this bank."

"Oh, is that right?" Ralphy said, raising one eyebrow.

He had no idea Lisa had another account open and, from what Larry was telling him, she had it open for about a year now. Larry even told him how much she had in the account, which was double what they had in their joint account.

Ralphy was hot as hell. The extra money she had in her separate account was one thing but the list of transactions made in the past two months was a whole other situation in itself. The credit card transactions showed purchases from Nordstrom, Neiman Marcus, Footlocker, and several other clothing stores, none of which Ralphy was at in the past six months. A million and one thoughts ran through his head at once, so much so he didn't even hear Larry talking to him.

"How much would you like to put into your account, Mr. Windsor?" Larry asked again, this time snapping his fingers to bring him out of his daze.

Words couldn't explain how Ralphy felt at that moment. All he wanted to do was leave; but, before he did, he answered Larry's question.

"All of it," he said, grabbed his ID, and walked out of the office.

Chapter 13

Tammy got off the bus and walked the rest of the way to Chris's mom's house. With Sinniyyah in the stroller and Anthony walking up front, Tammy pulled out her phone to check her text messages. Darious had sent her a text, basically checking up on her to make sure she was all right. She smiled at the text then hit him back to let him know that she was good.

"Anthony, slow down!" she yelled out to him.

"But Grandma house right there." He pointed, then began running toward the house once Tammy got closer.

By the time she got to Ms. Elaine's house, Anthony was on the porch knocking on the door. It was a pop-up visit so Ms. Elaine didn't even know they were coming. Hell, Tammy didn't even know if she was home, but Ms. Elaine was there standing behind the door with her head in her hands.

"Grandma!" Anthony yelled out again as he continued to bang on the door.

Ms. Elaine couldn't ignore Anthony any longer, even if she wanted to. She just wanted to avoid the drama that was about to unfold. She swung the door open with a big smile on her face, reached down, and gave Anthony a big hug along with a few grandmom kisses.

"Hi, Ms. Elaine," Tammy greeted her, carrying the stroller up the steps. "What, were you asleep?" she asked, pulling Sinniyyah out of the stroller and grabbing the diaper bag.

"No, I wasn't 'sleep. But I wish I was," she answered, mumbling the last part to herself.

When Tammy got into the house she headed back toward the kitchen to make up a few bottles. When she got there, a young white female was sitting at the kitchen table standing a baby up on her lap. Tammy slowly walked by the girl and her baby, speaking to her before opening up the refrigerator.

Tammy couldn't see it at first because of the angle the girl was sitting at when she entered the kitchen, but on the side of the white girl's neck, big as day, was the name CHRIS. Not that she had to, but Tammy looked a little closer at the fancy cursive writing.

"Excuse me, but what's ya name?" Tammy asked, closing the refrigerator door and walking over to the female.

"Oh, my name is Amy. I'm Chris's baby mother," she said, tilting her head to the side so that Tammy could see Chris's name on her neck, not that she had to.

Tammy looked down at the little girl and there was no denying the fact that Chris fathered that child. Her hair was long, thick, and curly just like Sinniyyah's, and she had his golden eye color along with his flat nose. The little girl and Sinniyyah looked almost like twins.

"Ms. Elaine!" Tammy yelled out.

She was so focused on Amy and the little girl, she didn't even notice Ms. Elaine standing at the entrance of the kitchen. "Now that you two finally met, I think it's best we sit down and talk," Ms. Elaine suggested.

"Talk about what, Ms. Elaine?" Tammy shot back with an attitude. "You knew about this and didn't tell me."

"It wasn't my place to tell you. It was Chris's and he promised me that he would, so I left it alone," Ms. Elaine explained. "I'm sorry you found out like this."

"Do she know?" Tammy asked, cutting her eyes over at Amy. "Do she know that me and Chris are . . . Let me rephrase that. Do she know me and Chris was together?" Tammy asked.

Ms. Elaine just put her head down. Amy knew as much about Tammy as Tammy knew about her. In both of their eyes, they both were Chris's girl. Tammy obviously had more time being with Chris than Amy did, and it was shown by the way Tammy took over the floor, and how Ms. Elaine was more sympathetic toward her. Amy, on the other hand, was so green to what was going on she didn't seem to care at all.

"You know what, you can keep his ass," Tammy told Amy, then stormed out of the kitchen.

Just as fast as she unpacked Sinniyyah's things, she packed them back up. Ms. Elaine was trying to talk to her but Tammy wasn't trying to hear shit right now. She left without saying another word, leaving Amy and Ms. Elaine sitting and looking stupidly at each other.

Ralphy sat at the kitchen table listening to Luther Vandross sing "A House Is Not a Home" on the radio. He had been drinking all evening, sitting there, waiting for Lisa to come walking through the door, but she never did, even hours after he knew she had gotten off of work. The only thing he could think was that she was with Dre, probably getting her back blown out. The more he thought about it, the more he drank and the more he drank.

Right while Ralphy was taking another swig from the bottle of Jack Daniels, Lisa came walking through the door. At this point, Ralphy was so drunk he couldn't even talk, nor could he find the strength to reach in his back pocket and pull out the paperwork he had gotten from the bank. He was torn up.

"Baby, what's going on?" Lisa asked, putting her bag down and walking into the kitchen. "What's the matter?" she asked with a concerned look on her face as she pulled out a chair and sat next to him.

Everything he wanted to say was in his brain, but the words just wouldn't come out. He sat there with a look on his face like he was taking a crap, looking her right in the eyes. He couldn't talk, but his tears were working just fine 'cause the more he thought about it, the more he would cry.

"Baby, please talk to me," Lisa pled, now wiping the tears falling from her eyes. She knew that she had hurt Ralphy and to see him sitting there drunk, and crying, was heartrending. She'd never seen him cry before, ever.

For a moment, it looked like Ralphy was going to say something, but he didn't. All he managed to do was crack a smile through the stream of tears falling down his face. He also found enough strength to get up from the table, knocking the bottle of whiskey over in the process. He stumbled toward the steps in an attempt to go upstairs and when Lisa tried to help him, he turned around and raised his fist. He only wished that he had enough power to punch her square in the jaw, but he didn't. He barely had enough strength to make it up the steps; but after two or three stumbles, a pause here, and a pause there, he finally make it to the bedroom. That journey took everything he had left in him, 'cause once he hit the bed it was lights out.

In the federal prison system, e-mailing is a feature everybody uses in order to communicate, aside from the phone calls and what many people now call snail mail, via the postal service. Any time Tammy needed Chris to call home she would e-mail him then get the phone call within an hour or so. She e-mailed Chris as soon as she left his mom's house so by the time she had gotten home Chris was calling. Tammy heard her phone ring the moment she stepped through the door. She hurried up and dug into her bag and pulled out the phone, leaving Sinniyyah still sitting in her stroller.

"You have a prepaid call. You will not be charged for this call," the automated system announced.

Tammy pushed 5 to accept the call, taking a seat on the couch with Sinniyyah in front of her.

"Wassup, babe," Chris spoke, unaware of what was going on at home.

"I just left ya mom house like an hour ago and guess who was there? Ya white baby mom and ya daughter," Tammy said as she unstrapped Sinniyyah.

It got real quiet on the phone. Chris was stuck. He didn't know what to say. It was pointless for him to even try to lie because he knew Tammy wasn't trying to hear any of it.

"So you don't have anything to say?" Tammy asked, breaking the dead silence on the phone.

"I mean, what you want me to say?" Chris answered, feeling the agony of defeat around the corner.

"I was faithful to you this whole time and this is what I get in return. I stood by you when you didn't have a damn dime in ya pocket. None of these bitches was around then. And you gon' sit here and have a fuckin' baby on me," Tammy yelled.

"Yo, we can't do this over the phone. We'll talk about it on the visit. I'll explain everything then," Chris said.

He didn't realize that it was a little too late to try to explain. Instead of being real and honest from the beginning, he lied and eventually got caught. That was the straw that broke the camel's back.

"Chris, I know I said this before and you might even think that I'm lying, but it's over. I don't wanna be with you anymore. Please don't call my phone. Please don't write me letters, and please don't expect any visits from me. I'll drop the kids off at ya mom house so she can bring them up there from now on. Take care of yourself. Bye," she said then hung up the phone.

She didn't even give him a chance to respond, not that he had a response anyway. Right then and there Chris knew for sure that he had lost his girl: the very thing he never wanted to happen.

Chapter 14

Lamar got out of the shower, wrapped a towel around his waist, and headed for his bedroom. It was a beautiful day today. The sun was shining bright and it wasn't hot and humid like it'd been all week, so Lamar was going to take full advantage of this time and do a little shopping downtown.

He walked over to his window and became irritated instantly once he saw Fox's truck sitting outside. Neither Fox nor Falisha was in the truck, which meant that he was inside of her house.

"I see you, playa," he mumbled to himself, backing away from the window then heading out of the room to go downstairs.

As he walked down the hallway he stopped at the top of the steps and stood still. He thought his ears were deceiving him 'cause it sounded like a female was moaning somewhere in the house. It was odd because he thought Kim had gone to work; but, then again, when he woke up this morning the only place he had been to in the house was the shower.

"Ooooh yesss!" the moans continued.

Lamar quietly walked over to Kim's bedroom door, placing his ear up against it to see if the noise was coming from there. It wasn't though, which caused him to look around. He walked back to the top of the steps where the moaning got louder, indicating that it was coming from downstairs. Every step he took after that revealed more of where the moaning was coming from.

He cleared one step, and could see the couch, then another, by which he could see a pair of legs moving around. By the time he got to the bottom of the steps he could see everything. Kim was laying on the couch asshole naked playing with herself. She was rubbing her toy in and around her pussy with one hand and squeezing and pinching her nipples with the other hand. Her eyes were closed the whole time from the pleasure she was feeling, so she didn't even notice Lamar standing in the room.

The vibrator was cool, but Kim wanted some penetration, for which she had a dildo sitting next to her on the table. She opened her eyes to grab it and saw Lamar standing there looking at her. Surprisingly, Kim didn't stop. It was feeling too good and she was chasing the ultimate orgasm; plus, she was just horny as hell.

She grabbed the dildo, looked up at Lamar, then slowly slid the long, thick plastic dick inside of her. Lamar stood there stunned. He never really looked at Kim sexually until today and by the way his dick was rock hard under his towel, he was feeling her.

"Damn, Kim! You need my help?" Lamar asked, unraveling his towel to show Kim his dick.

Kim didn't say anything. She was zoned out. It was like she was high off something. Lamar dropped the towel and slowly approached the couch. She watched him the whole time, biting down on her lower lip. He kneeled down right next to the couch, reached over, and grabbed the hand that was pushing the dildo in and out of her. He grabbed the dildo, pulled it out of her, then tossed it across the room. Before Kim could say anything, he lifted her leg up, put it over his shoulder, then stuffed his tongue inside of her wet box.

Kim inhaled deeply, holding on to the back of Lamar's head with one hand. His mouth felt so good in between her legs. It didn't take but a couple of minutes for Lamar to make her cum. Her whole body locked up as he continued to lick and suck on her clitoris.

"Put it in me," she whispered, pulling Lamar up to her.

He climbed on top of her, grabbed his dick, and guided it into Kim's soft, warm, wet vagina. He pushed it in inch by inch until Kim yelled out.

"Oooh. Yess!" she moaned grabbing on to his lower back.

His dick was two inches bigger than the dildo so after about seven inches of real meat Kim was barely able to take any more of it. Lamar couldn't see it going down no other way. He pushed the rest of his dick inside of her, all the way up to his balls. Kim stuffed her tongue in his mouth and kissed him passionately.

Feeling the lumps in the couch and the way it hindered his stroke, Lamar gripped Kim up off the couch, never taking his dick out of her, and walked her up the steps to his bedroom. When he got to his bed he fucked Kim each and every way for the next two hours. One leg up, two legs up, from the back, from the side, her on top, him on top, reverse cowgirl, up against the wall, on the floor slow, fast, medium pace. Lamar slayed Kim, then two nuts later for him and four explosive orgasms for her, they both fell asleep from exhaustion.

Ralphy woke up damn near twenty-four hours after he had passed out from all the alcohol he consumed. He never, in his life, drank that much alcohol at one time. He was vomiting in his sleep all night. Lisa stayed there with him all night and when the morning came around and Ralphy was still vomiting, Lisa had to call out from work. She didn't wanna leave him like that and for a moment she was about to call the poison control center thinking Ralphy may have had alcohol poisoning.

"What time is it?" Ralphy asked, sitting up on the edge of the bed and looking over at Lisa.

"It's two o'clock in the afternoon," she answered, walking across the room with a cup of water and a pack of Alka-Seltzer.

"I gotta get to work," he said in a groggy voice.

"Don't worry about that. I already called ya job and spoke to John. I told him you had a family emergency."

That was an understatement. Ralphy and Lisa had more than just a family emergency. They were on the brink of a family split. Last night while Ralphy was knocked out, Lisa found the papers he had gotten from the bank. She read them and saw all of the transactions from the cabin she rented out for Dre when she and Ralphy did the getaway trip. She was caught red-handed with her hand in the cookie jar and the only thing that was left for her to do was confess to her infidelities.

"We need to talk," she said, putting her head down to hide the shame of what she was about to say.

Ralphy looked over at his pants sitting on the chair, and then he looked back over at Lisa, who was now holding the papers from the bank in her hand.

"I guess you wanna talk now. If I never would have found out, you wouldn't have told me shit," he snapped. "So I guess this is the part where you feel guilty and wanna tell me everything."

"No, it's not like that, Ralphy. I just fucked up real bad. I don't know what I was thinking."

Ralphy already had an idea about the events that took place, but he still wanted to hear it from her mouth, or at least he thought he did. "How long have you been sleeping with him?" he asked.

"Ralphy, that's not gonna make anything better."

"How long?" he asked again in a more serious tone.

Lisa didn't want to answer him but she was tired of lying to him. He was her husband and for that Lisa felt like he deserved to know the whole truth. "I been sleeping with him since he came home about two months ago," she brutally admitted.

"Did you sleep with him while we were on our getaway?"

"Come on, babe, don't do this," Lisa pleaded.

Ralphy wasn't trying to hear it. He wanted to know everything. "Did you sleep with him at the cabins?" he asked again.

This interrogation was killing her. The tears began to fall down her face. The answer to this question was the worst of her affairs but, as a woman, she felt compelled to tell him.

"Yes, I slept with him while we were at the cabin," she answered, wiping the tears from her cheeks.

Hearing that, Ralphy buried his face in his hand. To hear her admit to it felt like a dagger was being driven through his heart. It was the toughest blow yet, and in a sense he wished that she would have lied to him about it. He was finished.

"Yo, what da hell did we just do?" Kim joked, smacking Lamar on his arm as she lay next to him, naked.

They both found it amusing that for the first time since they lived together, they had sex. They flirted with each other a couple of times, but never did it get this far. Not only did they have sex, it was backbreaking and the chemistry between the two just clicked.

"Wake up, nigga. I know you hear me," she said, punching him on the arm.

Lamar smiled, opening his eyes to see Kim staring at him. He too was still a little shocked that it went down the way it did. He wasn't mad, though. Kim had some bomb-ass pussy and looked sexy as hell without her clothes on. Hell, after having sex, Lamar looked at her totally differently.

"You better not say nothing to nobody, either," Kim said, punching him again.

Lamar chuckled then climbed on top of her. She spread her legs apart for him, too. He looked down at her and shook his head. "You better not tell none of ya friends what I just did to you," he joked.

"Boy, shut up," she shot back. "So now what?" she asked, trying to get some clarity on where they stood now.

Lamar leaned down and kissed her. "I don't know, Kim. That's' up to you. We can look at it like it was a mistake and never do it again, or we can look at this as a benefit of being friends," he said, leaning in to kiss her again.

Kim was surprised that Lamar was even giving her an option. She actually had to think about it for a moment and weigh the pros and cons. No relationship required, in-house dick just about whenever needed. Hell, those two things alone were good enough for Kim. The only thing she had to worry about was birth control, because Lamar had that good baby-making sex.

"So what you think we should do?" Kim asked, wanting to see what he thought before she committed to anything.

Lamar didn't say anything. He leaned over and kissed her again. The whole time Kim was in thought, weighing the pros and cons, Lamar's dick was getting hard all over again. When Kim opened her mouth to ask him again, Lamar pushed his member inside of her, then stuck his tongue into her already open mouth. Just like that, it was official. Kim and Lamar were now friends with benefits.

***

The room had been silent for over ten minutes now and Lisa hadn't the slightest idea what to say. She had hurt the man she loved and the only thing she could do was pray for his forgiveness. As crazy as it seemed, she still loved Ralphy and wanted to make things work out between them, but at the same time she knew the cut was deep.

"Ralphy!" she called out, ending the silence in the room. She was looking for something, anything to let her know what he was thinking.

Ralphy took in a deep breath then exhaled. He got up from the bed, walked over and grabbed his pants from the chair, and put them on along with a T-shirt he grabbed from his dresser. When he came walking over to Lisa, she thought that he was going to put his hands on her, but he didn't. He leaned over, put both hands on the arms of her chair, and looked her right in her eyes.

"I want a divorce," he said without remorse. "I swear I hope that shit was worth it," he said, leaning up then walking over to the closet to get his suitcase.

Lisa feared this was going to happen, but expected it when it came to Ralphy. He was a no-nonsense type of guy so anything short of a divorce wouldn't be like him. Lisa just sat there silent as he packed his things then left the house without saying bye.

***

Fox thought that Falisha invited him into the house so that they could fuck, but Falisha had some other shit on her mind. She had to get down to the bottom of something before she messed around and missed out on something good, that being Lamar. Fox was the only obstacle standing in the way and if he didn't answer this one question right she was done with him. Falisha made up her mind that she wasn't going to waste another minute being with Fox if he wasn't willing to be the man she truly needed in her life.

"Fox, I'ma ask you something and I want you to keep it a hundred with me. You know you talk all that shit out here in the streets about how real of a nigga you are, so I need you to be real with me just this one time," Falisha said, turning to face him as they sat on the couch.

"Yeah, wassup, shawty. Talk to me, I'll talk back," he said with his slick Southern accent.

"Do you love me, Fox?" she asked with a serious face.

"No," he answered, flat out without having to think about it.

It was so cold the way he said it, Falisha felt some type of way about it. He just didn't say no, but he also looked at her like he didn't give two shits about how she felt about it. The only girl Fox loved was his daughter and the only woman he loved was his mother. All the rest of the females in his life were expendable, even Falisha, whom he did take a liking to.

"Damn, Fox, that was the wrong answer," Falisha said, getting up from the couch and walking over to the door.

"What? You told me you wanted me to keep it real with you. I care about you and I think you're a nice chick, but that love word is crazy."

"You don't gotta explain, Fox. I'm cool," she said, opening the door. "I just need you to do me one favor and I promise I will never ask you to do anything else for me."

"Yeah, and what's that, shawty?" he said, getting up from the couch.

"I need you to lose my number and don't ever try to contact me again. I'm done with you, Fox," she said, stepping to the side so that he could walk out the door.

"You can't leave Big Fox. Bitch, I made you," he said, walking up to her. "Who else gonna treat you like me?'

One person popped up in her mind immediately. She knew that there was somebody out there waiting for her to treat her the way she wanted to be treated. That person was Lamar. Even though he didn't have nearly as much money as Fox did, Falisha knew that she could count on Lamar to do one thing and that was love her, something no man had yet to do.

"I'll take my chances. You have a nice life, Fox," she said with a smile on her face as she slammed the door behind him.

Chapter 15

A knock at the door caught Dre's attention while he stood in the living room of his apartment ironing his clothes. He walked over to the door and looked out the peephole to see Lisa standing there. When he opened the door he knew that something was wrong, because she was crying. Her husband must have found out about them. He reached out and grabbed her by the arm and pulled her into the apartment.

"Come on, sit down," he told her, pulling out a chair from under the kitchen table. "You hungry? You want something to drink?" he asked, opening the refrigerator.

Lisa shook her head, not really feeling like ingesting anything right now. She was sick right now and the only thing that kept going through her head was Ralphy telling her that he wanted a divorce.

Dre put a glass of water on the table in front of her then pulled out another chair for him to sit in. "So he found out?" he asked, scooting his chair up closer.

She just nodded her head. Dre was sympathetic, but only to a certain extent. He couldn't care less about how Ralphy felt. In his mind, she wasn't his to begin with.

"Ay, do you remember that time we broke up for like a week when we were in middle school back in the day?" he asked, grabbing her hand. "Do you remember what I told you the day that we got back together?" he asked.

Lisa managed to crack a smile. She remembered it like it was yesterday. Dre was always good with words. "You told me that we were going to spend the rest of our lives together," Lisa said, wiping the tears from her face.

"I swear to you, Lisa, my heart feels the same way it did back then. My love for you—"

"He's divorcing me," Lisa said, cutting him off. "My husband is divorcing me," she repeated.

Dre watched as a few tears fell from her eyes after she said that. Their relationship was deeper then what he thought it was. She really did love her husband and now Dre was starting to feel guilty because he was the one who broke up a happy home. It wasn't Ralphy he was concerned about; it was Lisa.

All he ever wanted to do was make her happy and he thought that if they were together he was going to be able to do that. Instead, he was doing the exact opposite of what he intended in the first place. Seeing how heartbroken she was behind being divorced, Dre saw that her intention to be with him was there, but her heart was in another place.

Annet stood behind Falisha in the middle of Ms. D's living room doing her hair. Falisha was only getting a touch-up to make her braids look brand new for Ernie's party tonight. The word in the neighborhood was that the party was supposed to be jumping. Ernie had about a hundred people coming, most of whom were gay.

"Daaaamn!" Falisha said, seeing Kim walk through the front door looking nice.

Kim had on a gray belted wrap dress that was well above her knees, and a pair of Valentino Garavani pointed-toe pumps. In her hand was a white Alexander McQueen clutch and on her face was a big-ass smile.

"You musta got some dick," Falisha joked, looking at the new glow Kim had.

"Girl, shut up. Ain't nobody got no time for humping," Kim lied, trying to hide it. "I'm just tryin' to make it rain tonight." She laughed, bouncing her shoulder up and down.

"Where da hell is everybody else?" Kim asked, looking around the house.

As soon as she said that, Tammy came walking in the door. She too looked different and she had a brand new attitude along with a nice outfit. It was rare that Tammy got dressed up but when she did, it was big. She had on an all-white Karen Millen mesh bandage dress that hugged her petite shape and a pair of black Salvatore Ferragamos. In her hand was a black-and-white tote, and on her face was a pair of Victoria Beckham shades. She definitely dug in the closet for this look.

"'Throw it up, throw it up. Watch it all fall out,'" Tammy sang, sounding just like Rihanna.

"Yo, I'm jealous," Falisha said, looking at Tammy and Kim. "What in da hell got into y'all bitches?" She laughed. They both were sitting there like two high school girls getting ready to go to a party.

"I don't know about Kim but I'm single and if I get drunk enough somebody's getting some pussy," Tammy joked but was kind of serious.

"Girl, Chris gon' kill you." Falisha smiled.

"Chris better worry about his other baby mother I just met the other day," Tammy responded.

Falisha's and Kim's jaws dropped and their eyes shot wide open.

"Yeah, and she's white. I saw the little girl and she look just like dat nigga," Tammy told them.

"Oh, my God, girl. Are you okay?" Kim asked, knowing that it must have hurt to find that out.

"Shit, girl, I'm fine. I'm not gonna let that ruin my night. We goin' out to drink, have fun, and make it rain on dem niggas at da club," Tammy said.

"Did anybody see Lisa? I haven't talked to her all day," Falisha said, getting up from the chair and walking over to the window to see if her car was out front.

"Girl, you know her and Ralphy goin' through something right now," Kim answered. "I doubt if she comes."

Falisha whipped out her phone anyway and tried to call her but she didn't get an answer. She then texted Lisa to see if she would answer, but she didn't. Falisha looked down at the clock on her phone and shook her head, seeing that it was already nine-thirty. Ernie's party started at ten o'clock and it was going to take at least forty-five minutes to get to the Mandingo's Den.

"Look, we running a little late as it is, so I'ma text Lisa with the address to the club and we'll meet up with her later. She got her own car so she should be all right," Falisha suggested.

Everybody agreed. Falisha, Kim, Tammy, and Annet all checked themselves one last time in the mirror before heading out the door.

Ralphy pulled up to his old block on Washington Avenue where at one point in his life he sold drugs.

It'd been so long since he'd actually been in the streets but, still, the hood knew who he was. Before he started dating Lisa, he was the man in his hood. A lot of people feared him but most loved him. Aside from the countless shootings, the many fist fights, and the unlimited amount of cocaine he sold, Ralphy showed the hood love.

"Seeing you is like seeing a ghost," Scoop, an old friend, said, walking up to Ralphy. He gave Ralphy a thug hug, mainly because he missed him. They were like best friends when Ralphy was on the block and ever since Ralphy got married and had his daughter, Scoop only saw Ralphy every once in a while.

"Aw, playboy. Don't do me like dat. You know ya boy still love ya." Ralphy laughed, throwing a jab at Scoop's arm.

Ralphy and Scoop walked down the street, catching up as much as they could with the current events going on in the neighborhood. Scoop even managed to grab a forty-ounce bottle of Olde English for old times' sake.

"So what's really going on, brah? I know you ain't stop by just to catch up on old times," Scoop said, knowing there was a reason behind this visit.

"Damn, a nigga can't just chill with his partna?" Ralphy laughed, seeing Scoop was still sharp as a knife.

"Come on, nigga. I knew you for how long? Ten years, my nigga." He smiled. "What, you tryin' to get back in da game?" Scoop asked with a little excitement.

"Nah, playboy. I'm done with da game. But what I do need is some heat," Ralphy said with a straight face.

Scoop looked at him and saw that he was dead serious. He knew something or somebody must have ticked Ralphy off for him to be wanting to deal with his problem by way of pistol. Scoop wasn't going to ask any questions, though. The less he knew the better. Scoop reached under his T-shirt and grabbed a black ten-shot .40-caliber off his waist. He cocked it back slightly to make sure a bullet was in the chamber.

"Yo, dis my bitch. You take good care of her, and I wouldn't care who you shoot with it. Bring my baby back to me. I'll give you a more permanent gun tomorrow," Scoop said, but not before kissing his gun, then passing it off to Ralphy. "Do you need a codefendant?" Scoop asked, willing and ready to ride with his boy.

Scoop was a wild boy. He reminded Ralphy of O-Dog from *Menace II Society*. He was young, black, and just didn't give a fuck. He would shoot anybody, and wouldn't care if it was broad daylight with a hundred people looking on. If it were any other type of drama, Ralphy would have taken him along for the ride. But this trip was a solo trip. Ralphy only had one person in mind he wanted to kill, so it was best that he did it on his own. Shit had gotten real now and the only thing that could save the person he wanted to kill was God.

"Happy Birthdaaaay!" the crowd yelled out all together. Bottles starting popping, the music started thumping through the speakers and everybody started dancing. Ernie had the club jumping with all of his gay friends. Surprisingly there were a lot of females there, most of whom were lesbians, but there was also a nice amount of straight women as well to support.

One thing about the gay community is they do it big. Gay men always seem to have the most beautiful female friends, so for the few straight men who were in the building, it was like heaven.

"Happy Birthday, baby girl," Falisha walked up and said to Ernie, leaning over and kissing him on the cheek. Tammy, Kim, and Annet all did the same thing as they passed him their gifts they brought for him.

"Thank y'all," Ernie spoke, sitting up in his birthday chair. "I hope y'all brought a lot of dollars." He laughed, swaying back and forth to the music.

On cue, the music shut off and the lights went dim. In Mandingo's Den, the strippers had three stages to dance on so once the music cranked back up, everybody who knew better rushed the stages.

Mongoose the Stripper crawled out onto the center stage, seductively freaking his body to Lil Wayne's "Lollipop" song. He had on a pair of 7 For All Mankind jeans and some construction Timberlands boots. His tank top was ripped off immediately, revealing his cut-up body. The gay men who knew better had taken up the front of the center stage. They were throwing dollars like it wasn't nothing.

Tyson, another stripper, came out on the other stage, but he danced his way to the floor level. He had on nothing but a pair of Speedos and a lifeguard T-shirt. He seductively ripped his shirt off as well, crunching his stomach to flash his six pack. A crowd of men, and a couple of women, gathered around him and made it rain all on top of him.

Elephant Trunk, Louisville Slugger, Bananas, and Foot Long all danced their way out from backstage onto the floor. The whole club went crazy.

"Oh, shit!" Falisha yelled out as Elephant Trunk danced over to their section.

A crowd gathered around him almost instantly, including Tammy, Kim, Falisha, and Annet. They were all yelling and screaming and throwing dollars on top of him as he humped the floor to the rhythm of the music.

"Make it rain, bitchessss!" Tammy shouted, flicking ones from her stack onto him.

Tammy was having a ball. Hell, everybody was having a ball. Ernie was really showing his ass, though. He jumped up on the table and started shaking his ass. His gay friends were throwing dollars at him like he was one of the dancers.

"Ernie ballin' out, yo," Annet yelled out, pointing across the room to where he was at.

After about thirty minutes of the dancers being out on the floor, all of them as if on cue danced their way back behind stage. Everybody clapped at their performance thinking that it was all over. Then, the lights went dim and the music shut off again. You could still hear clapping and whistling in the crowd.

When the lights came back on, Harold, Ernie's best friend, was standing on the center stage with a microphone in his hand. He motioned with his hands for the people to settle down and, when they did, he spoke.

"Thanks for coming out, everybody. I wanna call my good friend Ernie up to the stage," he said, waving for Ernie to join him.

Ernie and his chair were escorted to the stage where he sat like he was a diva.

"You know we had to save the best for last," Harold said, smiling and clapping. "Happy Birthday, Ernie," he said, and then backed down off the stage.

The lights got dim again, then they began flashing wildly all throughout the club. Ernie looked around trying to figure out what was going on, smiling from the excitement. Then a voice spoke through the speakers: "Now coming to the stage, the moment you've all been waiting for: Mandingo!"

Kelly Rowland's song "Motivation" came through the airwaves, then from behind the curtain and onto the stage came Mandingo, the best male dancer in the club. He was such a good dancer they named the club after him.

He glided out onto the stage with a cowboy hat down over his face, a pair of leather pants with fringe on them, and some cowboy boots. He danced around Ernie's chair seductively, making Ernie have to fan himself with the stack of dollar bills he had in his hand. First, the dancer danced out of his leather pants, and then he took off his hat to reveal his face. Ernie threw the whole stack of money in the air, and then fell back in the chair like he had passed out.

When the dancer turned around to dance for the crowd, he beat on his buff chest and snarled. Falisha and the girls were sitting at their tables pouring shots of Patrón. Annet just so happened to look up on the stage, and damn near choked on her own spit when she saw the dancer gyrating his body all over the place. She tapped Falisha, who looked up at the stage. Falisha tapped Kim, who looked up and actually did choke on her shot of Patrón.

They all sat there with their mouths wide open and in total shock that, before their eyes, standing on the stage wearing nothing but a G-string and a pair of cowboy boots, was none other than their very own Lamar.

Chapter 16

Tammy pulled up in front of Chris's mom's house in an all-white 2009 Chrysler 300 with tinted windows. It looked just like a dope boy's car, equipped with chrome twenty-inch rims and a touch-screen TV in the dashboard. The car was nice, and it looked pretty much brand new.

Ms. Elaine walked out onto the porch, shocked to see Tammy behind the wheel. "Whose car are you drivin'?" she asked as she came down to help Tammy unload the kids' things from the vehicle.

"It's a friend's car," Tammy responded. "I'll be back to pick them up tomorrow, and here's a few dollars, 'cause I know they're going to want something out of the vending machines when y'all get to the jail." Tammy had stuck by her word and made sure that Chris was still able to see his kids. She just wasn't going to be the one bringing them up there to see him. That job now belonged to Chris's family.

"Tammy, are you all right?" Ms. Elaine asked with a curious look on her face. "I hope you're not still mad—"

"You know what, Ms. Elaine? I'm actually good right now," Tammy said as she passed her the last of the overnight bags.

"Is there anything you want me to tell Chris while I'm up there?"

Tammy just shrugged her shoulders and shook her head. She didn't have anything else to say to him. She was at the stage where she was trying to move on with her life. She didn't want to continue to dwell on the past. She forgave Chris for having another baby on her, but she would never forget it. How could she forget? The little girl was going to be around for a very long time, and that was a reminder for Tammy in itself.

Lamar focused his eyes over at Kim, who was lying next to him with a big smile on her face. They had been having sex every day for the past week, sometimes two times a day.

Kim was really taking advantage of the "friends with benefits" deal. She hadn't had this much dick in her life, or at least since she was a teenager. It was starting to become addictive, just like her rabbit or the bullet she couldn't stop using. In fact, ever since Lamar had been handling his business in the bedroom, she hadn't even been using her toys, except for the one time she brought the bullet to a sex session.

"What're you lookin' at, Kim?" Lamar asked, turning onto his side to face her.

"I still can't believe that you're a male dancer. I mean, I never pictured you being a stripper." She laughed.

Lamar smiled. "Yeah, well, I never thought yo' ass would be a paralegal, either. I always thought you would be a doctor, or maybe even working for NASA or some shit. But here you are, wasting ya time looking up case law all day."

"Shut up, boy! I like my job," Kim shot back, along with a jab to his arm. "I was thinking about taking the bar exam, maybe becoming a lawyer at my firm."

"A lawyer? Yeah, I can see that, 'cause you sure know how to lie ya ass off!" he joked.

Kim reached behind her and grabbed one of the pillows, and then hit Lamar in the head with it. He playfully retaliated, jumping up and hitting her back with the pillow that he was lying on. They both laughed and giggled.

Kim tried to wrestle with him, but Lamar was too strong. He pinned her down to the bed, then climbed on top of her. She struggled for a minute, then stopped once he leaned down and softly kissed her lips. He pulled back, and looked down at her as she looked back up at him. He leaned in and kissed her again, this time adding a little tongue to it. Although she was enjoying it, she caught on to what was going on. She pulled back and turned her head to stop him.

Lamar immediately saw that something was wrong. "What's the matter?" he asked, releasing her hand that was still pressed to the bed.

"Nothing. I'm cool," Kim answered, rolling from under him then grabbing her shorts and tank top off the floor. "I gotta go."

Lamar didn't dig it at first, but after watching her get dressed and storm out of the room, it hit him and became clear what was going on. The boundaries that were put in place in the beginning of this sexcapade were starting to get crossed.

Kim didn't want her feelings getting involved, and the way Lamar was treating her was starting to trigger something. It was like they were already in a full-fledged relationship, something that she was trying to avoid. Before it had could go any further, she was going to put an end to it, or at least slow things down a bit.

"I hope you put some gas in my car," Darious joked when he saw Tammy enter the customer service area.

"Boy, shut up!" She smiled and passed him his keys.

Over the past couple of weeks, Darious and Tammy had gotten cool. They talked on the phone just about every night, mainly about life and the goals they wanted to accomplish in the near future. Darious had become somewhat of a friend, somebody Tammy could go to for advice and even, on one occasion, a loan.

"Oh, did you think about what I asked you the other day? You know the weekend is right around the corner and I kinda wanna get an idea if you wanna go with me," he said.

"I don't know. I'm not sure if that's a—"

"Look, no strings attached," Darious said, throwing both of his hands in the air. "It's only two friends going out to the casino to do a little gambling," he continued.

One thing Tammy didn't have to worry about was Darious having any ulterior motives behind taking her out. He wasn't like most guys who always looked for something in return after they had taken a girl somewhere or bought her something. He was a gentleman, which was something that was rare in Charlotte. If he said they were going out as friends, then that's what it would be. "I'm not spending the night out there," Tammy said with a big smile on her face.

"Don't worry. I'll have you home by one, maybe two. Now, if I get on a hot streak, that's another story!" He chuckled.

They both shared a few laughs before having to get back to work.

Tammy wasn't slow by a long shot, though. She knew that this was a date, and Darious was going at it under the friendship card to ease any pressure. It was cute and innocent, and she didn't mind entertaining it for just one night.

Ralphy walked into the house, went straight upstairs, and got into the shower without saying a single word to Lisa, who was sitting on the couch. This had been his routine for the past week, and the only reason why Lisa didn't question it was because she didn't feel like she was in a position to. In her mind, she thought that he was sleeping with another woman, but even if he was, who was she to say anything? It was her fault that things were the way they were.

"Are you coming back?" she hurried up and asked as Ralphy came running back down the stairs toward the door.

"Naw. I'll see you tomorrow. I got some shit to take care of," he said, throwing the black hood over his head. "Is ya mom still watching Naomi this weekend?" he asked, stopping at the door.

Lisa took a closer look at him and noticed the unusual attire he was wearing. He had on all black from head to toe, and the look he had in his eyes was different. It was a look that she had never seen before, and it made her concerned. "Ralphy, what's wrong with you?" she asked, getting up from the couch and walking over to the door.

He gave her an empty look and shook his head. "I'm good. I just gotta take care of something," he answered.

Lisa had known Ralphy long enough to know when something wasn't right with him. It was one thing to come into the house, take a shower, and go straight to bed, but it was another thing to be dressed in all black and leaving the house with a deranged look on his face. "Ralphy, is this about us? 'Cause if it is, I can fix it, babe. Just give me a chance; I promise!" she pleaded, not wanting him to do anything stupid.

"I gotta go," Ralphy said, reaching for the door-knob.

Lisa stood in front of the door, blocking it. She was still very much in love with him and didn't want anything to happen to him. If she could take back everything she did, she would in a heartbeat just to have things back to normal. "Please, babe, can we work this out?" she pleaded while wiping the tears that fell from her eyes.

The crying wasn't going to help. Ralphy didn't have a place in his heart for sympathy when it came to her anymore. This whole ordeal forced him to dig into his past and be somebody he used to be. There weren't too many people who knew how vicious he once was in the streets of the Queen

City. He used to go hard, and he was part of the reason why Charlotte's murder rate was so high back in 2002, 2003, and 2004. It was as if Lisa had woken a sleeping giant. "Look, man, I gotta go," he said before moving her to the side, opening the door, and walking out of the house.

Lisa just stood at the threshold and watched him get into his car and pull off. She was sick. She didn't know what he was going to do. But, whatever it was, she could only pray that it didn't get him killed or thrown in jail.

"Do you have to go straight home?" Darious asked Tammy as they approached his car.

Stopping at the passenger side door, she asked with a curious look on her face, "Why? Where are you tryin' to take me?"

"I know this little spot where we can grab something to eat. I know you're hungry as hell, working in there all day," he said with a smile.

The truth of the matter was that she was starving. The only problem was that she didn't have any money to be eating take-out food. Rent was right around the corner, along with the electric bill, gas bill, and her cell phone bill. Money was tight right now. Plus, she already had a refrigerator full of food and her cabinets were stocked to the max. It wasn't take-out, but it was free courtesy of welfare.

"Boy, I ain't got any money for take-out." She chuckled before opening the car door and getting inside.

Darious got into the car too. He looked over at Tammy and shook his head. "How about dinner on me tonight? You need to stop worrying about money all the time." He smiled. He grabbed the remote control off the center console and began changing the CDs in the changer.

Tammy couldn't help but to find him attractive. The more time they spent together, the more things she began to notice about him, small things, like the way he walked with a slight ditty bop, the way he always talked in a calm manner, and how confident he was in himself, not to mention the fact that he had his own car, his own apartment, and he was financially stable. Plus, he was single. He was a good catch, but she wasn't at that stage in her life right now.

"What you know about this?" Darious said, pushing play on the remote control.

Dru Hill's song "Beauty" flooded the car. This was something else that she noticed about him. He was somewhat of a hopeless romantic. Tammy was feeling that too, and if she didn't get some control over the situation immediately, it would be possible for her to fall into temptation.

***

Falisha sat on her steps, sipping on a bottle of Moscoto and enjoying the quiet night, as she did one or two nights out of the week. Things had been a little quieter since she broke up with Big Fox. She expected Lamar to stand by all the promises he made to her, but as of right now he wasn't showing up. Falisha barely saw him during the day because he was always ripping and running around, and by the time she did catch up to him in the evening, he was too tired to do anything. That's part of the reason why she was sitting out on the steps tonight. She was hoping that she could catch him before he went to work. And like clockwork, at about 9:45 p.m., he was stepping outside with his duffel bag slung over his shoulder.

She got up off the steps and walked over to his car while he was putting his bag in the trunk. "Damn, Lamar! You don't know me anymore?" she said while leaning against the vehicle.

Lamar looked at her then chuckled. "Shouldn't you be out somewhere with Big Fox?" he asked, digging into his bag to get his identification.

"What's that supposed to mean?" she shot back.

"Just what I said, Falisha. I know any minute now he's gonna be bending the corner in his truck, and you're gonna go running to him. To be honest with you, that shit is getting old," he said, and slammed the trunk.

"I broke up with him," Falisha told him.

"Yeah, right! You love that nigga," he said. He was so caught up with sexing Kim that he didn't even notice Fox not coming around for a couple of weeks now. He didn't know if he even cared at this point. His brain was somewhere else, but Falisha snapped him right back to reality. She walked up to him, wrapped her arms around him, and looked him right in the eyes.

"I swear, it's over between me and him. I realize who I wanna be with now, and that's you," she said with a sincere look in her eyes. She got up on her tiptoes and pressed her lips up against his. This was the first time that she had ever purposely shown him public affection.

It caught Lamar by surprise, but it didn't stop him from returning the kiss. "Oh, shit, you're serious!" he said after pulling away from her.

Falisha nodded her head with a big smile on her face. He pulled her back in to hug her. This was some of the best news he had in weeks.

But while he was standing in the middle of the street and holding on to the woman of his dreams, his happy moment was ruined in an instant when he looked up at his building and saw Kim looking out the window at them. He could see the sad look on her face before she closed the shades, leaving him wondering if he had done something wrong.

***

Ralphy and Scoop sat in Scoop's car with their seats leaned back and the car turned off. Ralphy had done his homework on Dre, and found out that he was back in his old neighborhood, doin' his thing again. It took him about a week, but he eventually narrowed it down to a two-block radius where Dre was hustling. It was all about the waiting game right now, because Ralphy was sitting there in the passenger seat, waiting for him to show his face.

"Damn, brah! Dis shit's just like old times!" Scoop said as he looked over at Ralphy in the passenger seat.

"Yeah, dis shit crazy. Dis bitch got me coming out of retirement on some bullshit," Ralphy shot back. His mind had been made up a long time ago that he was going to kill Dre. He didn't know any other way to ease the pain that he was feeling. Not only was his heart broken, but he was mentally drained dealing with the situation. Visions of Dre fucking Lisa from the back constantly made their way to his thoughts, breaking him down even more.

"Yo, is dat da nigga right there?" Scoop asked, lifting his head up to see over the dashboard. "I think it's him."

Ralphy looked over the dash to see a red Chevy Tahoe LS pull up and park on the corner of the block.

When Dre jumped out of the truck, he headed right for the deli where a bunch of young trap boys were standing around.

Ralphy wasn't sure if it was him, so he whipped out his phone and went straight to Instagram to see a photo of him.

Meanwhile, Dre stood outside in front of the store, kicking it with his boys.

"Yeah, dat's da nigga right there," Ralphy said, holding the phone up so that Scoop could see the picture.

"A'ight, brah! Let's go air those muthafuckas out!" Scoop said, pulling out twin Glocks.

Ralphy looked over at Scoop like he was crazy, then remembered that he actually was a little crazy. This was part of the reason why Ralphy didn't want to bring him along in the first place. He knew that Scoop was the type who would make a mess out of things, whereas Ralphy was more of a smooth criminal. The only reason why he brought him along was because the west side of Charlotte was the most dangerous. Niggas killed over there for less than nothing.

"Hold up for one second, li'l brah," Ralphy said, checking out his surroundings. "A'ight, let's go," he said, exiting the car with a compact .45 automatic.

Scoop and Ralphy were about a half block away from the store. They both pulled their hoods over their heads as they walked unnoticed down the street.

Dre was coming down the front steps of the store when he noticed the two hooded men dressed in all black. Everything went into slow motion, and right before the storm came, it got real quiet.

Bullets began firing into the crowd. Pop! Pop! Pop! Pop! Boom! Boom! Boom! Pop! Pop! Pop!

Ralphy was more focused on his target, whom he hit with the first few rounds he fired.

Dre took the first bullet to his side, causing him to stumble down the steps onto the sidewalk.

All the little trap boys scattered, most of whom took off running down the street in the opposite direction. One of the li'l homies whipped out his gun and started firing back, but Scoop ended that relatively quickly, giving the young shooter double action.

Dre ran to his car holding his side, but he didn't even get a chance to get the door open before Ralphy ran up on him with the gun pointed at him. He grabbed Dre by his shoulder and swung him around to face him.

Dre's face was twisted up on some gangsta shit, ruthless 'til the end. "Fuck you, nigga!" he yelled right before spitting at Ralphy, but only getting the side of his hoodie.

Dre still didn't know who was behind the hood; that was, until Ralphy pulled it off. He wanted Dre to see who it was who was about to take his life.

This shit was personal, and Ralphy wasn't going to waste another moment. Without saying a word, he lifted the gun up and pulled the trigger. Pow!

The bullet crashed through the center of Dre's skull and rested in his brain. He was dead before his body hit the ground.

Ralphy wasn't done yet. He stood over Dre and emptied the rest of his clip into his face, and when he ran out of bullets, he began kicking him and stomping what was left of his face into the ground. Scoop had to run over and stop him.

"Yo, he's dead!" Scoop said calmly as he grabbed hold of Ralphy's arm. "Let's get da fuck out of here," he screamed as he pulled him away from Dre's lifeless, bloody, bullet-riddled body.

Both men took off down the street, jumped back into Scoop's car, and pulled off into the night, leaving behind two dead bodies, three wounded, and the night sky full of gun smoke.

Chapter 17

Kim looked back at Lamar as he pounded away, stuffing his long, hard dick in and out of her from the back. She held on to the headboard with one hand, and then reached under her and began playing with her clit with the other hand.

Lamar raised his hand and smacked the top of Kim's ass as he continued to stroke deeply into her guts.

Morning sex was the best for Kim. She couldn't lie; Lamar had that golden dick, and he knew how to work it. It was starting to become addictive, but she wasn't willing just yet to allow him to dictate the rules.

"Damn, Kim!" Lamar said, looking down at his shiny, wet dick going in and out of her.

Kim knew that he was about to cum. She looked back at him and began throwing her ass back at him. She too was about to cum, and preferred that they did it at the same time.

"Take dis dick!" Lamar said, speeding up his strokes. He raised his hand and smacked the top of her ass again.

Kim's walls tightened up, and a river of her juices lubricated his dick. He couldn't hold off any longer. Her pussy was too wet. He started banging away until he splashed his thick white cum inside of her.

Kim could feel the warmth of his fluids filling her insides, which almost made her want to keep going. "Damn, boy!" she said, pulling away from him and releasing his dick from her suction.

Lamar flopped down on the bed, expecting her to do the same, but she didn't. Not this time. She wanted to make it very clear that she was running the show, and not him.

She got off the bed, dressed, and was headed out the door within thirty seconds of Lamar cumming inside of her. This was her way of establishing the tempo and not allowing her feelings to get involved.

What this did for Lamar was the total opposite, though.

Tammy woke up to Sinniyyah trying to eat her face. All she could feel were her wet gums and the spit running down the side of her face. It actually kind of tickled a little. "NaNa, what're you doin'!" Tammy giggled while her baby sucked on her face.

Sinniyyah was so cute. Right now she was probably the best thing Chris had ever done for her, and it was times like this when she appreciated him for that. A lot of the love she had for him came from their kids, and there wasn't a second that went by that Tammy didn't look at them and then start to think about Chris.

She looked over at her cell phone vibrating on the nightstand next to the bed. She grabbed it, looked at the screen, and saw that the number was unavailable. There wasn't a doubt in her mind that it was Chris calling. It was crazy how she was just thinking about him, and now he was calling.

She stared at the phone, not knowing whether to answer it. She hadn't spoken to him in a few weeks, so she didn't know how the conversation was going to turn out. But after a few more rings, she decided to answer it.

"You have a prepaid call. You will not be charged for this call," the prerecorded voice announced.

Tammy pushed 5 to stop the automated system. "Hey!" she answered as she shifted Sinniyyah to the other side of the bed.

"So I see you're doin' ya thing out there, pulling up in new cars and shit like that," Chris said.

Tammy knew that was going to get around to him eventually. His mom told him everything that was going on with Tammy and the kids. The only thing about his mother was that she blew things out of proportion sometimes. "It's not like that, Chris," Tammy responded.

"Yeah? Well, I hope things work out between y'all two," Chris said in a slick tone.

Tammy saw that he was trying to be smart, so she copped an attitude real fast. "Is this what you called here for, Chris?" she snapped. "How about ya kids? You haven't said one word about them!" she went on.

Chris knew that his kids were good. He had just seen them last week. He was more concerned about who Tammy was messing around with while he was locked up. At the same time, he didn't feel like arguing with her either. There was no way he could win, nor would it help the situation. "Man, I'm not tryin' to fight with you, Tam. All I'm saying is that I hope dude is making you happy."

"Who are you talkin' about, Chris? I'm not messing with anybody. My friend let me use his car to drop the kids off to your mom. I know she said something to you. She needs to mind her own damn—"

"Watch ya fuckin' mouth, Tammy! Don't get beside yaself! That's my mom you're talkin' about!" Chris blasted, checking her before she got any further out of pocket.

"Well, she should have thought about that when she was harboring ya little secret," Tammy responded, but not in a nasty way. She definitely still felt some type of way about the whole situation. There wasn't a day that went by that she didn't. She had always thought that Chris was different from the rest of the men out there, but as it turned out, he was just like most of them: unfaithful, untrue, and very disrespectful.

"Look, Tam. I see you got ya life in order right now, and I really don't wanna be a burden to you. I guess you can say that I'm officially letting you go. I'm not gonna call you and bother you anymore. You don't even gotta worry about dropping the kids off to my mom so she can bring them up here."

"Hold up! Wait, Chris. You don't have to do all that," Tammy said, hearing the sincerity in his voice. She could hear the change in the way he was speaking and in his attitude when he said that. He sounded sad and tired. She'd never heard him sound so down.

"Take care of yourself, Tammy. Good-bye," he said, then hung up the phone before she could say anything else.

All that hardcore shit that Tammy was talking was now out the door. The shit had gotten real, and she was already feeling the effects of what just happened. Not only was Chris done with her, he was also done with the kids, and that's what hurt the most.

Ralphy thought that killing Dre would make him feel better, and it did a little, but it still didn't take away the fact that Lisa had cheated on him. The pain from that remained in his heart.

"Ralphy, what's good, homie?" Lamar yelled before Ralphy got up the steps.

"What it do, Mar?" he shot back after turning around.

"Yo, I need to holla at you about something," Lamar said, walking across the street. "Ay yo, I'm in a li'l dilemma right now," he said, looking from left to right to make sure that it was just them out there.

Ralphy looked around too with one eyebrow up.

"Yo, I need you to keep this between me and you, brah," Lamar said. "You know I'm fuckin' Kim right now," he said with a big-ass smile on his face.

"Oh, yeah? I thought y'all was just roommates," Ralphy inquired.

"Yeah, we were. But guess what?" he said, looking around again. "Yo, I'm fuckin' Falisha, too, homie!" Lamar told him, sticking his hand out for some dap.

"Damn! You fucked Falisha *and* Kim? What in da hell can ya dilemma possibly be?" Ralphy asked.

Kim was a nice-looking chick with a sexy body. She had a good job, and there weren't too many niggas who could say that they hit it. She was more of a conservative chick, and was very careful of who she dealt with. A lot of niggas tried, but most of them failed.

Falisha, on the other hand, was bad in every sense of the word. Her body was crazy thick, and she was cute in the face. She didn't have a job, nor could she cook that well, but she was young enough to mold, and she had the potential to be loyal.

"Homie, I think I'm in love with both of those bitches, ya feel me?" Lamar said, rubbing his hands together.

Ralphy scratched his head. He was having trouble staying in love with one girl, and here Lamar was, trying to love two women.

"I know eventually I'ma have to pick one of 'em. I just don't know who," Lamar said with a confused look on his face.

Ralphy shook his head and chuckled. He really didn't know what to tell Lamar. Females and love were the last things on his mind right now. But he had to tell Lamar something. He came to him for some advice, and that's what he was going to get.

Ralphy dug deep down and put as much of his own situation to the side, and then found some good words to say. "Whoever you feel can complete you, that's who you should be with," he said, sticking his hand out for a dap, which Lamar gave him in agreement.

On that note, Ralphy went into his house, and Lamar walked back across the street thinking about what Ralphy had just said. "The one who can complete me," Lamar mumbled to himself as he took a seat on the steps.

Just as he sat down, Kim came out of the house, on her way to work. She had on a black Balenciaga leather pencil skirt, a white blouse, and a pair of Yves Saint Laurent peep-toe pumps.

She looked a little overdressed for work, which made Lamar raise an eyebrow. "You goin' to work like that?" he asked, standing up to get a better look at her, and also to help her down the steps in her heels.

"Boy, you ain't my man. Don't worry about how I'm dressed," she playfully snapped back at him as she walked toward her car. "And don't wait up, 'cause I got a date tonight." She smiled right before she got into her car.

Lamar just sat there. He didn't know how to respond to that. All he knew was that he didn't like the sound of her going out on a date.

Chapter 18

Lisa sat at work thinking about Ralphy, as she did every day. Today she even thought about Dre, wondering why he hadn't called in a couple of days. When she tried to call his phone it went straight to voicemail every time.

"Lisa, I need you to certify Ms. Thompson's insurance for an extraction," Dr. Crosby said, coming out of the operatory.

"Sure, Dr. Crosby," she said. As soon as she got up from her desk, her cell phone started to ring. Her instincts made her reach for it. When she looked on the screen, it was Kim calling. She answered it only to tell her to call back. "Hey, girl. Can you call me back in like twenty—"

"Did you hear what happened?" Kim said, cutting her off.

It sounded too juicy, and Lisa couldn't resist. "What happened?" she asked, looking over at Ms. Thompson sitting in the waiting chair.

"Oh, shit, girl! You really don't know! Dre was murdered two nights ago in his neighborhood. My boss just told me five minutes ago," Kim told her.

The news was such a shock that Lisa had to sit back down in her chair. She was sick.

"They said that two men in black hoodies walked up and started shooting. I know you don't wanna hear this, but whoever did it had some personal shit on his mind. Dre was shot seven times: once in the side and six times in his face, all at close range," Kim continued.

Lisa covered her mouth and shook her head slowly. Her eyes began to water at how horrible Dre's death was. Her thoughts then shifted from Dre to Ralphy, and she began to immediately ask herself whether Ralphy was capable of doing something like this. Ralphy did have a past life, but Lisa wasn't sure if it was as violent as the way Dre was murdered.

"Lisa! Ms. Thompson!" the doctor said, snapping Lisa out of her daze.

"Oh . . . oh, yes, Dr. Crosby. I'm coming right now," she responded. "Girl, I'll call you back after I get off," she told Kim, and then hung up the phone.

A lunch date was the situation for Lamar and Falisha this afternoon. It was Falisha's idea, but Lamar didn't mind, especially since Kim was at work around this time. It wasn't that he was trying to be sneaky or anything, he just didn't want Kim to know the extent of his and Falisha's relationship.

"Look at you, looking all cute!" Falisha said, coming down her steps.

Lamar was wearing something basic: a pair of cargo shorts, a white V-neck Polo shirt, and white Gucci sneakers. It was simple, but he made it look good. A fresh haircut, a nice rose gold chain around his neck, and the sweet scent of Creed emanated from his body. He was well put together.

Falisha kept it simple too. She had on a pair of blue Citizens jeans, a white top, and a pair of SW1 pipette pumps. Her hair was pulled back in a ponytail, which always brought out her natural beauty.

Falisha really wasn't in the mood to go anywhere extravagant today. She just wanted to spend some time with Lamar, so when she chose to eat at Jack in the Box, it kind of shocked Lamar, but he went with it anyway. The chicken there was banging, so there weren't any complaints on either side.

"Can I ask you a question?" Falisha asked while digging into her box of chicken as they sat outside at a table in front of the restaurant.

"One day I was broke as hell. My homie Dutch pulled up on me and asked me if I wanted to make some money," Lamar began, figuring that Falisha wanted to know how he started dancing. "He ran the whole dancing thing down to me like it was the new thing. I didn't know how to dance until he showed me a couple of moves." Lamar chuckled.

Falisha sat there and listened to him talk while she continued to eat her food.

They shared a few laughs and talked about other things, like goals for the future, kids, and marriage. They even talked about stuff they remembered happening when they were in high school.

After lunch, they decided to catch a movie, and from there they went to the park, and from the park they did a little shopping downtown. They had dinner at the Outback Steakhouse, and headed toward home.

By the time they pulled back up to the block it was around seven-thirty in the evening. What was only supposed to be lunch turned into a full day of them being together, and they both enjoyed every minute of it.

Lisa drove straight to Dre's mom's house after work to pay her respects. His mom was cool as hell, and she knew Lisa and treated her like she was her own daughter. She was the only girl Dre had ever brought home, and because he loved Lisa so much, so did his mom.

"Ohhh! Hey, baby!" Ms. Alberta greeted her when she opened the door. "Get ya li'l tail in here!" she said, grabbing Lisa by the hand and pulling her inside.

Lisa expected Ms. Alberta to be strong the way she was. She was built Ford tough, but at the same time she had a heart of gold.

"You know my son was crazy about you." Ms. Alberta smiled, sitting Lisa down on the couch. "I just wish y'all two would have stayed together. What y'all had was real love. I remember when y'all were teenagers, I couldn't separate y'all with a stick!" She laughed.

"I'm so sorry about Dre, Ms. Alberta," Lisa said, wiping the tear that fell down her cheek.

"Oh, baby, don't worry about my son. He's up there with the rest of the thugs the good Lord forgave." Ms. Alberta chuckled.

It was amazing to Lisa how high Dre's mom's spirits were, and how she kept it together. She had just lost her only son to the streets, and here she was making jokes.

Lisa felt the total opposite, though. She was hurt and a bit confused. Something inside of her felt like she was out of place being there mourning over the death of a man she cheated on her husband with. It felt disrespectful, especially considering the fact that she and Ralphy were still married.

But another part of her felt obligated to be there because of the history she had with Dre and his family. For her not to show up seemed disrespectful, and to fake like she didn't have love for Dre would be wrong.

"Ms. Alberta, I wish I could stay, but I have to pick up my daughter," Lisa lied just to have a reason to leave. "I'll come back tomorrow if that's okay with you."

"You can come back here anytime, baby. And I know I'm gonna see you at his funeral. It's on Monday."

Lisa didn't even think her answer through. She just said the first thing that came to mind. "Of course I'm gonna be there. Front and center," she said as Ms. Alberta walked her to the door.

Lisa didn't know what she was thinking, agreeing to that. She knew that if Ralphy found out she attended Dre's funeral, it would only add more fuel to the fire, a fire that Lisa was hoping she could put out before she lost her husband forever. She really hated putting herself in these situations. It was getting to be all too stressful.

Falisha leaned in and wrapped her arms around Lamar as they stood in front of her house. They had been sitting out there talking and laughing since they got back. Kim's car was nowhere in sight, so Lamar didn't mind showing Falisha public affection tonight.

"So, now what, Lamar? Where do we go from here?" Falisha asked, looking up at him.

Before he could answer the question, a white truck turned onto the block, grabbing their attention. It was Big Fox, and he was in his zone blasting some music.

As Big Fox got closer to the house, Falisha turned around, and her first instinct was to walk over to the truck. But before she did, she caught herself.

Lamar leaned his back up against the wall and thought, *here we go again with da bullshit!*

Fox stopped right in front of Falisha and Lamar. The light from his stereo system shined enough light in the truck for Lamar to see him clearly. Fox looked over at Falisha and was expecting her to come over to the truck, but instead she backed up to Lamar, who was still leaning against the wall. She rested her back up against his chest, and then reached back and grabbed Lamar's hand and wrapped his arm around her stomach. The entire time, she looked Fox in his eyes with a look that said she belonged to somebody else now.

Fox could do nothing but respect it. He simply gave Lamar a nod to let him know that he was top dog now. After that, he just pulled off.

"Come on. Let's go in the house," Falisha said, pulling Lamar up the steps by his hand. They disappeared into the house, more than likely for the rest of the night.

Lisa walked into the house to find Ralphy sitting at the kitchen table, reading. She could hear Naomi upstairs playing with her toys, as usual. When she walked into the kitchen, Ralphy lifted his head up and briefly looked at her before focusing his attention back to what he was reading.

"Have a seat. I need to talk to you about something," Ralphy said as he shifted the papers around.

Lisa hesitated for a second, thinking about Naomi.

"She'll be fine," he assured Lisa, then nodded to the chair.

Lisa took the carry bag off of her shoulder, placed it on the table, then pulled out a chair. She was curious to know what he wanted to talk about, seeing as how he hadn't had much to say to her as of late. "What do you wanna talk about, Ralphy?" she asked in a submissive manner.

Ralphy gathered all of the papers from the table and set them to the side. "You know, Lisa, I still love you. I care about you more than you'll ever know, and I hate the fact that things happened the way they did between us," he began.

"Baby, I still love you too—"

"Just listen to me, Lisa," he cut her off. "For the past couple of weeks I've been thinking long and hard about everything, and I ultimately came to the conclusion that things will never go back to the way they were. A lot has happened, and I really don't want us to waste any more time out of our lives trying to fix what's broken. It's just too much work."

"I know it's gonna be hard work, but I love you enough to do what needs to be—"

"Here," Ralphy said, pushing the papers he was reading over to her.

"What's this?" Lisa asked, picking the papers up off of the table and reading the header. Her heart dropped, along with her bottom jaw at the sight of the divorce papers. She knew that he was angry, but to see that he actually went through with obtaining divorce papers was a tough blow.

Tears immediately formed in her eyes, and when she looked up at Ralphy, he too had tears in his eyes. This process wasn't any easier for him. He loved Lisa with just about everything he had. To end it now, and to end it this way, was devastating to him.

"Ralphy, why can't we try?" she pleaded, and got up off the chair and onto her knees in front of him.

"Come on, Lisa," he said, shaking his head. "Don't make this harder than it needs to be. It's over."

Lisa jumped up, grabbed the papers off the table, and began ripping them up. Ralphy tried to stop her, but she had ripped a nice amount of the papers before he got to her. "No, no, no!" she said as they wrestled for the rest of the documents.

After a while, Ralphy just gave up and let her finish what she had started. He watched as she stuffed the papers into the garbage disposal, turned the water on, and hit the switch. He just looked at her and shook his head before walking out of the kitchen.

Instead of chasing after him, Lisa fell to the floor in tears. She still couldn't believe it was all happening this way. She cried out like a baby at the thought of losing Ralphy, and she knew by the divorce papers that it was pretty much official. All she had done was prolong the process a little, because the fact still remained that Ralphy was done with her.

Chapter 19

The morning sunlight almost blinded Lamar when he left Falisha's house. He put his hand up to block the sun as he crossed the street to get to his residence.

Seeing Kim's car parked down the street let him know that she was home. Still having some energy left over from last night, he figured he'd take a quick shower, and then wake Kim up with some early morning head, followed by some slow, passionate sex.

When he walked through the door, the scent of bacon and eggs smacked him in the face. He walked into the kitchen, but Kim wasn't there, nor was the food.

"I know she didn't just cook for herself!" he mumbled to himself while leaving the kitchen.

He shot upstairs and stood at the top of the steps, debating whether to jump into the shower first or go mess with Kim about not making him anything to eat when she cooked. He looked down the hallway toward the bathroom, and then he looked the other way toward Kim's room. It might have been the music coming from her room that made him choose to have his talk with her.

As he walked down the hallway he thought his ears were deceiving him when he thought he heard a moan coming from beyond the music. As he got closer to the door, the moans got a little louder, and it became clear that it was Kim.

Lamar's dick got hard quick as hell at the thought of Kim lying in her bed and pleasing herself. *Fuck a shower!* It was time to play. When he reached for the knob and saw that the door was open, he walked in.

"Oh, shit! Lamar, get out!" Kim shouted after opening her eyes to see him standing there.

Marell lifted his face out of Kim's pussy to turn around to see who was standing behind him.

Lamar was still in shock, looking at another nigga eating Kim's pussy. Kim had to yell again for him to back out of the room.

Marell watched the door close, looked back up at Kim for a split second, and then drove his face right back into her wet box. She was going to stop him, but his mouth felt too good. She laid her head back on the pillow and grabbed a hold of his head.

"Dis bitch done lost her fuckin' mind!" Lamar mumbled as he walked into his bedroom, which was right next door. He was mad as hell. He started swinging punches in the air, working himself up for a fight he wanted to have. "She's bringing niggas home now!" he snapped to himself while pacing back and forth across the room.

It took Lamar a few minutes of pacing and letting off some steam before he came to his senses. It had hit him like a ton of bricks, and when it did, he walked over and took a seat on the edge of his bed. "What are you doin', Lamar?" he asked himself while rubbing his temples. "She ain't even ya girl!" he mumbled.

The more he thought about it, the calmer he became. He had to laugh at himself and the way he was acting over some pussy that didn't belong to him. Kim was free to fuck whoever she wanted to, and there was nothing he could do about it.

He flopped back onto his bed and stared at the ceiling. Everything was cool, and from the sudden silence coming from Kim's room, he felt like the worst of it was over; that was, until it started back up, but this time even louder. He could hear Kim yelling through the walls.

"Ohhhh! Yesss! Ohhhhh, harder! Fuck me harder! Mmmmmmmm! Give it to me!" she screamed.

The sounds of her bed squeaking, the loud moans, and her screaming out were a little too much for him to handle, so he got up, grabbed his car keys off the dresser, and rolled out.

It might have seemed petty, but he kicked Kim's door on his way past her room. He did it just to let her know that he was upset, not that it mattered at the time, because Kim was too busy getting her back blown out. The kick was barely even heard by either her or Marell.

Tammy was awakened by a loud knock at her front door. She looked over at Sinniyyah to see if it had woken her up too, but it didn't. She was still sound asleep.

Anthony, on the other hand, heard the knocks and was a little scared, so he darted into Tammy's room and jumped in the bed with her.

"Anthony, don't move," she told him, and then slipped on a pair of jeans and a T-shirt.

The heavy knocking continued the entire time she made her way downstairs and to the door. Before opening it, she leaned over and peeked through the small window on her inside porch. She was actually kind of relieved to see that it was Mr. Louis. "Hey, Mr. Louis! What's goin' on?" she asked when she opened up the door.

He looked at her sideways with one eyebrow up. Tammy really didn't have a clue about why he was there, but he didn't have a problem reminding her, either. "It's the first of the month, Tammy. This is the day I go around to all of my properties and pick up my rent money," he said in a sarcastic way. "Please tell me you got my money," he continued, while stepping past Tammy and entering the house.

"Mr. Louis, you know I don't get my check until around the third. As soon as the check clears I'll give you the rent money," she said, following him into the house.

"Let me ask you this: why do you stay here when you clearly can't afford it? I've got other properties that are a lot cheaper to maintain," Mr. Louis said, looking around the living room at the pictures on the wall.

The answer to that was simple. Tammy didn't want to live anywhere else. This block was all she knew. She grew up here, much like everybody else who lived on Parker Street, and she wasn't ready to move quite yet. "Mr. Louis, I'll have your money, and the hundred dollar late fee in a couple of days. Now, if you don't mind, I gotta get back upstairs to my kids," she said, walking toward the front door.

Mr. Louis knew when he had worn out his welcome, but he was also still stern about collecting his money. "I don't wanna have to come looking for you, Tammy. I love those kids, but I love my money more," he said before leaving the house.

Tammy knew that those words meant that he didn't have a problem putting her and her kids out on the streets if he wasn't paid.

What made things even worse was that her money was funny yet again this month. The electric, the gas, and the phone bills were sitting on the living room table, and she didn't have a clue how she was going to pay them, the rent, and get Anthony's school clothes. It wasn't going to happen on the $650-a-month welfare check, and a $380-a-week check from her part-time job.

Tammy really needed help, and as she walked back upstairs to get back into bed, she began considering what Mr. Louis said about moving into one of his cheaper properties.

By the time Lamar took his car to the car wash, got it detailed, and went to the store to get something to eat, Marell had finished his business and left the house.

Lamar came through the door to see Kim standing in the kitchen, doing the dishes in her nightgown. She had a towel wrapped around her head, so he knew that she either had just taken a shower, or she was about to take one. "Damn! I see you've been busy early this morning," he said, entering the kitchen and putting his bag on the table.

"Yeah, well, you better learn how to knock." Kim chuckled as she dried off a cup and set it to the side.

"Oh, so that's where we're at now? You found some new dick so you toss me to the side?"

Kim turned around from the sink to face him. She could see a bit of jealousy in his eyes, and maybe even a hint of hurt. "I know you ain't getting soft on me, Lamar. I told you from the beginning that it was just sex between us. Now, if you can't handle that, then maybe we should stop," she said, crossing her arms and leaning up against the refrigerator.

Kim had all the sense. Lamar didn't know it, but Kim had purposely left her door open so that he would walk in on her. She wanted to let him know a few things of importance, one being that she was the only person who would dictate who would be tasting her goodies, and when. The second thing she wanted to establish was that his ass could easily be replaced by the next man. Thirdly, she just wanted to reestablish the boundaries that friends with benefits had.

The only thing she didn't expect when she did what she did was to hurt Lamar. And from the way he looked at her when he came through the door and saw her getting her pussy eaten, she knew that it hit a nerve.

"Of course I can handle it," Lamar responded, trying to play it off and be cool about it.

Kim smiled, and then turned back around to finish doing the dishes.

Lamar bit down on his bottom lip in total frustration. The truth was, he couldn't handle letting another man fuck Kim, let alone do it under the same roof where he rested his head. At this point, he had to be honest. "But what if I wanted more?"

he said, walking over and leaning up against the sink next to her.

"Boy, what are you talkin' about?" She chuckled, not taking her eyes off the dishes.

"What if I wanted more than just sex? What if I wanted to be ya man?" Lamar asked with a serious look on his face.

Kim put the plate she was cleaning back into the soapy water and turned to face him. At first she thought he was joking, but then she saw the look he had in his eyes. "You're serious, aren't you?" she asked with a curious look on her face. "You catchin' feelings, Lamar?"

Lamar didn't even know he felt this deeply about her until today. His jealousy of Marell made him realize that there was more to him and Kim than just sex. Not only did he hate the fact that somebody else was pleasing her sexually, Lamar felt like he was losing a very good friend. "I'm sayin' . . . I really don't know what I'm sayin' right now. What I do know is that I care about you a lot. I know more about you than I do of any woman."

"Boy, what do you know about me?" Kim smiled, curious to know what was going on in his brain right now.

Lamar moved in a little closer to her. "I know that despite what you portray on the outside, on the inside you got a heart of gold. You care about others, and you find joy in helping people. That's why you work so hard at the law firm. I know ya favorite food is shrimp, and ya favorite color is yellow. I know that you're allergic to peanuts."

Kim stood there amazed at how much he really knew about her.

"I know you got this scar right here from falling on a glass table," he said, reaching down and touching the scar on her lower back. "I know ya period comes anywhere between the third and the fifth of every month. I also know ya favorite spot to be touched is ya waist," he said, grabbing a hold of hers.

Kim was intoxicated and captivated by his words and his touch. She felt herself about to melt in his arms, but she quickly got hold of herself. "Boy, you don't know me!" she said, and playfully smacked his hands off of her waist.

"Com 'ere, yo," he said, grabbing her waist again and pulling her close to him. "I know you wanna be in love, but you're scared to get hurt, and you think all men have the potential to break ya heart. I know that when you love, you love hard, and you hate the same way."

"You swear you know somebody!" She smiled and lowered her head in a submissive manner.

"I know that guy you just had up in ya room didn't mean a damn thing to you, and I'm willing to bet anything you didn't even kiss him. You fucked him to make me jealous, and to let me know that you were in control. Shit, that's the only reason why the nigga left here with all his teeth!" Lamar chuckled.

Everything he said was accurate to a T. Kim was more than impressed with how much he paid attention to her, and how well he knew her so intimately. "What do you want, Lamar?" she looked up and asked him in a humble and soft tone.

Lamar reached up and unraveled the towel around her head. Her hair dropped down to her shoulders, still a little wet from the shower she just took. She was beautiful and sexy: a nice combination. He leaned down and softly pressed his lips up against hers.

This time Kim did melt in his arms. She was looking at him in a whole new light now, and found herself wondering how it would be if she gave him a chance to be the man she desperately needed in her life.

"Let's just see what happens," Lamar said, lifting her chin up so she could look him in his eyes.

Kim nodded her head, and then rested her head against his chest. She didn't know where this train was headed, but she definitely was going along for the ride to see where it ended up.

Chapter 20

"Why's ya face all frowned up?" Darious asked, walking into the back where Tammy was sorting merchandise.

"Everyday stress, that's all," she answered in a sad tone. "I'll be all right, though."

"A'ight. If there's anything I can do, just let me know," he told her before heading back out to the front.

Truth was, Tammy was thinking about how she was going to pay her bills this month. Not only were the bills an issue, but the kids needed things that she couldn't afford, like clothes and toys. Chris's family wasn't helping out with anything. It was as if he told them to cut Tammy off also.

The weight of being the head of the family was hard. It had gotten so bad that she even thought about trickin' just to get the money she needed. Her only problem with that was she only knew one person who would pay for her goods, and she wasn't up for the degrading feeling she knew she would have afterward if she fucked with Mr. Louis.

While thinking about her situation, she took a seat on one of the crates. She couldn't control the tears that fell down her face. It was hard and stressful being a single mother with two kids. Tammy needed help, much like the rest of the young, black, struggling single mothers out here.

"Tammy, what da hell is wrong with you?" Darious asked, coming back into the room where she was. Tammy tried to wipe the tears from her face before he could see them, but it was too late. Darius put the box he had in his hands on the floor and sat on top of it right in front of her. "Come on, Tammy. Talk to me," he said in a concerned voice. "Let me help you."

"You can't help me, Darious. I'm not who you think I am," she responded, now unable to hold back her tears.

"Just try me," he said, reaching over and grabbing a hold of her hand.

She looked up at Darious with her eyes full of tears. For some reason she felt comfortable telling him what was going on in her life. So, she did just that, breaking down and telling him about her financial problems and the situation with Chris and his other baby's mom.

They sat in the back for almost an hour, not caring too much about the customers who kept trying to get their attention.

"I know you look at me in a whole new light," Tammy said, wiping her face with her shirt sleeve.

"Nah, Tammy. I still see you as the same person. In fact, I got a lot of respect for you," Darious said, and stood up, reached into his pocket, and pulled out his small leather wallet. "Here. Use the rest of this. It's got a little more than a thousand dollars on it. Take care of ya bills and whatever else you need to do," he said, passing her a prepaid credit card.

"I can't take this from you!" she said, refusing the card.

Darious knelt down in front of her. "Tammy, before my mom died she used to give me little words of advice. She told me that sometimes we miss the blessings God sends to us because we look for the blessings in the wrong places. She said that most of the time the blessings are sitting right in front of our faces, and we still don't see them. From one friend to another, don't be one of the people who misses her blessings," he said, sticking the card out for her to take.

Tammy looked at the card then back up at Darious. His concern showed in his eyes. She hesitated for a moment, but reached out and took the card from him. The money was no doubt a blessing, and Tammy didn't want to miss out on it. "Thank you, Darious!" she said, and stood up to give him a hug. "I really appreciate it!"

Lamar drove down the highway on his way to work with more than enough to think about.

He looked out to the road as the highway lights beamed off the hood of his car. "Differences" by Ginuwine was pouring through the speakers, putting him in a relaxed state.

Lamar was trying his best to figure out how he got to the point where he was in love with two women. Each of them had certain qualities that were attractive, and while Kim was the one who was independent and more educated, Falisha possessed beauty and street smarts. Kim was more mature, but Falisha was young and willing to learn. Kim's pussy was good, but Falisha's head game was great. Kim knew how to cook, but Falisha knew all the good restaurants.

Lamar didn't know what he was going to do. But what he did know was that he had to choose one of them. It was impossible for him to go on with this love triangle without the possibility of losing both of them. He knew that he didn't have long, either, seeing as how they lived right across the street from one another and were the best of friends.

Something was going to have to give, and not leaning more toward one woman over the other was making it hard.

Tammy pulled into Darious's apartment complex to return his car. He had let her use it all day so she could run some errands and pay her bills. It was cool, because neither she nor Darious had to work that day, and she had dropped the kids off at Chris's mom's house so that she could take care of her business.

This was the first time that she had ever been to Darious's place, and as she walked up the steps to the third floor she felt kind of nervous. She didn't know why; she just did. As she walked down the hallway she looked up at the numbers over the doors, and saw 302, the apartment Darious told her he lived in. She knocked on the door and waited.

A couple seconds later he opened the door. "Damn! I thought you were going to be out longer than that!" he said as he was putting on his tank top. "Did you take care of everything?"

Tammy hesitated for a second. She was still thinking about the glimpse of Darious's abs she got before he put his tank top on. "Oh, yeah. I didn't have to do much. I can pay all my bills in one place," she said before reaching into her bag and pulling out his car keys.

"Come on in. Let me finish eating, and then I'll take you home," he said, stepping to the side.

Tammy became even more nervous, and she still couldn't figure out why.

"Or, you can stand there and wait!" He chuckled, seeing that she had a stuck look on her face.

Tammy laughed too, thinking of how silly she looked standing in the hallway. She stepped into the apartment and stood there looking around at how nice it was. Darious led her to the kitchen.

"Can I ask you something?" she said, taking a seat at the kitchen table with him.

"Yeah, you can ask me anything," he responded before taking a bite of his chicken sandwich.

"What's your angle? I mean, why are you helping me out like this?"

Darious put his sandwich down on the plate and finished chewing his food. "I'm helping you because that's what friends do. If I was fucked up and you were in a better position than me, I would hope that I could depend on you to be there for me," he answered.

Tammy wasn't convinced at all about that friendship talk. He was up to something, and she could see it in his eyes. "I hope you don't think you're getting any pussy!" she shot back.

Darious almost choked on his food when he heard her say that. He didn't know that she could be so blunt. But he did like her straightforwardness. It inspired him to want to come clean with his motives. "A'ight, Tammy. You wanna know the truth?" He rubbed his hands together to get the crumbs off, and scooted his chair over to sit directly in front of her. He then cleared the rest of the food from his mouth.

"Yeah, Darious, I want the truth."

"Look, Tammy. I helped you because I like you. And to be honest, I think the world of you.

Sometimes I think that I'm the only one who sees how good of a woman you are," he explained to her.

Tammy didn't see this coming.

"I'm not gonna lie, Tammy. I'm hoping that one day I can make you my girl. I don't know the status between you and ya baby daddy, but if y'all are not together, I'm tryin' to be the man in ya life," he continued.

Tammy definitely didn't see that coming. She was at a loss for words, but at the same time she was flattered. For a nice guy like Darious to want to be with her made her feel somewhat special. She felt wanted, a feeling she hadn't felt in a long time. "I don't know what to say. I mean, I like you too; but I'm not ready to be in a relationship right now. I just broke up with my kids' father, and I just need some time to get my shit together. I don't wanna bring anybody into this mess of a life I have," she said, damn near ready to shed a few tears at the thought of it.

Darious smiled. "Ya life ain't that bad, Tammy. You just hit a few rough patches. I know with a little polish, you'll be good as new. I also know that I'ma be here for you until you're ready to let somebody in. Just when you do decide that you're ready, make sure you call me first." He chuckled before leaning over and giving her a kiss on the forehead.

Tammy smiled and confirmed with a simple nod that she would call him first. If she ever thought about being with anybody, it would have to be with somebody like Darious. He was kind, sweet, smart, and handsome, not to mention the fact that he had a bright future ahead of him . . . and he was single. He was a good catch, but truth be told, she was still holding on to her past.

She didn't want to say anything to him, but the real reason why she wasn't ready to be with anybody else was because she was still in love with her childhood sweetheart, Chris.

Lisa sat in the front row with Dre's mom and his other family members she was familiar with. So many people turned up at the funeral. Lisa expected it, though, because he was well liked in his hood. Despite the fact that he terrorized the streets before he got locked up for murder, he helped a lot of people out. That's why there wasn't a dry eye in the building. Everybody was crying, even Lisa. She couldn't hold back if she wanted to, looking over at Dre lying in a coffin a mere fifteen feet away from her.

The priest gave a beautiful sermon about life and death, and how people should be living their lives here on Earth while they were still alive. It had Lisa thinking about her situation and how she

needed to make some changes in her own life. All
she could think about was having a chance to fix
what she had broken in her marriage, and get back
to being the loving wife she knew she could be.

After the viewing, it was time to take Dre to his
final resting place. Four large men stood around
his casket, lifted it up, and walked it down the aisle
toward the hearse that was parked outside. Lisa
followed them, along with Dre's mother and a few
other family members.

As the casket passed by the last pews, Lisa just
so happened to look over, and saw Ralphy sitting
there. She couldn't believe that he had come, and
for a moment she wanted to jump into the casket
and die right along with Dre. It was humiliating
getting caught at the funeral by Ralphy with tears
still rolling down her cheeks.

At first, Lisa didn't know if she should have
stopped to acknowledge him, but from the way he
was looking at her, she really didn't have any other
choice. He got up out of the pew just as the casket
passed by him. He was dressed for the occasion
with a suit and a tie, and in his hands was a white
envelope. He didn't have to say anything to get
Lisa to stop. Dre's mom kept it moving without
inquiring who Ralphy was.

"I'm sorry!" Lisa said, looking up into Ralphy's
watery eyes.

"Yeah, me too," he said back. He tapped the
envelope against his thigh while looking into the

eyes of the woman who claimed to have been his wife. Seeing her there at the funeral and crying as if Dre was her husband was the final straw. Any hope of trying to save their marriage was out the window, and this time Lisa couldn't argue with him or justify her actions. She was out of pocket all the way around the board.

"I guess I can only wonder whether you could have loved me as much as you loved him," Ralphy said, and passed her the white envelope and then a pen he retrieved from his pocket. "Do the right thing this time," he said, nodding at the envelope.

Lisa knew the divorce papers were the contents of the envelope. She didn't even have enough strength to put up a fight if she wanted to. This whole ordeal had taken its toll on her as well, and she felt like she had hurt Ralphy long enough.

She took the papers out of the envelope and began signing and initialing them in their correct places. It took Lisa and Ralphy every bit of five hours at their wedding to get married, but it took less than two minutes for them to get divorced. Their marriage had begun in a church, and by God's will, a church was where their marriage was going to end. Ugly, but fair!

Chapter 21

John Legend's voice filled the large bedroom as it flowed from the Bose speakers on the small table by the window. Kim lay naked on her stomach on the queen-sized bed. Lamar caressed the back of her thighs, and slowly caressed her soft, full hips with his large, rugged hands. Her body was toned, and as he massaged her soft spots, he memorized every curve of it.

"Damn, boy, you better stop before this turn into some—"

Kim's last word was cut off by a gasp as Lamar's warm tongue slid down the crack of her ass. Kim rocked with his tongue as it explored her. He slowly left her aching box, and formed a trail of hot kisses up her spine. He stopped at the center of her back and bathed it with his tongue.

"Nigga, why you gotta play so much?" Kim chuckled, while rolling over onto her back. "You better finish what you started," she teased, spreading her legs and seductively rubbing on her inner thighs.

Lamar stood up on the bed, looking down at her as he began to peel his shirt off. A pair of sweatpants and some boxers were the only things standing between his rock-hard dick and Kim's soft, gushy candied yam. Kim smiled mischievously as she began to caress her engorged clit. Lamar licked his lips and kicked off his sweatpants.

Boom! Boom! Boom! Boom! Boom! Ding Dong! Ding Dong! Ding Dong!

"Fuck!" Kim yelled, throwing her head back on to the pillow, pissed that someone was interrupting her morning lovemaking session.

Lamar jumped down off the bed, grabbed his pants, slid them up, and stormed out of the room and down the staircase. Kim was right behind him, grabbing the first piece of clothing she could get her hands on. Placing the red bathrobe over her body, she ran down the steps. Lamar did not look out the window to see who was at the door. He flung the door open and was met by a set of eyes that were full of shock, and then hurt. Falisha stood in front of him, looking like a lost child. All the anger he felt disappeared and was replaced by guilt and shame.

"Who da fuck is banging on my door?" Kim shouted as she walked up behind Lamar and peeked her head around him to see who it was.

Falisha looked at Kim and then back at Lamar. Neither of them was wearing much, and they were agitated at the interruption. She had obviously interrupted something, but what? Lamar was her man, and this shit was about to be answered.

Sitting in the passenger side, Tammy flipped the sun visor down to check her makeup and hair in the mirror. She had been looking forward to tonight all week. It was date night with Darious, and being with him was like floating on a cloud. She was free from kids, and no work tomorrow! It was the Lord's day, and her day of rest.

"Can you stop at the Rite Aid?" Tammy asked, looking over at Darious, who was humming to himself.

"Yeah, sure, it's one coming up in a couple of minutes," he said, taking her hand and kissing it. "You know you don't have to try so hard. You got a natural beauty," he said, cutting his eyes over at her.

Tammy smirked. She loved being complimented by him. It made her feel beautiful and desired. He was smooth enough not to make it sound corny or insincere. They had been spending more time together, getting to know each other, and Darious had been nothing less than a gentleman. Darius had catered to Tammy's every need, and he had displayed great restraint in the sex department. There had been no pressure from him, and he seemed genuinely interested in getting to know her as a person. That made Tammy's lower region tingle more for him, and she had made the decision that tonight she was going to put her rabbit away, and slide down on something bigger than two inches. She rested her hand on his thigh, leaned over, and kissed his cheek, sending a jolt from his thigh to his dick.

Darious turned into the parking lot of the Rite Aid. He put the car in park and turned off the engine. "A'ight, missy, hurry up." Darious said jokingly.

Tammy laughed and got out of the car, headed toward the store. As she disappeared through the doors, her cell began to ring in the passenger seat. Darious looked down at it. The phone trilled like it was trying to make him pick it up and answer it. He bit his lip and looked out the window.

"Damn, is her voicemail going to pick up?" Darious said, picking up the phone to swipe ignore. Instead, he hit answer. "Shit." He looked toward the doors of the store and put the phone on speaker. "Yo."

The automated message stated, "You have a prepaid call. You will not be charged for this call. This call is from Chris."

Darious hung up the phone. He sighed and laid the phone back on the seat. He had planned this night for a minute, and he didn't want anything to interrupt it. He picked the phone up again and pressed the power button. He wanted tonight to be perfect and flawless.

Tammy chewed her bottom lip as the cashier rang up the condoms, four bottles of 5-hour Energy, chips, and the Fiji water she knew that Darious liked.

"Umm, girl, you look like you 'bout to have a good night. That will be $22.50," the cashier said, placing her items in the white plastic bag.

Tammy laughed and swiped her ATM card. She keyed in her code, and the cashier handed her the receipt. "Thank you," Tammy said and walked toward the doors.

"You went in there to get some snacks?" Darious asked when Tammy got back into the car with a small bag. He was hoping that she didn't notice that her phone was off, but Tammy picked right up on it. She looked at the blank screen then over at Darious. He had to think of something quick, and said the first thing that came to his mind.

"Just me and you tonight." He smiled as he grabbed his phone from the center console and turned it off right in front of her face.

Tammy studied him for a moment. She caressed his face, and leaned over and kissed him slowly. She was glad they were on the same vibe. Darious slid his hand down her back. Her kiss almost made him forget about the jailhouse phone call. For now, he wasn't going to think about it too much.

However, at some point, they would have to talk about it.

Lamar applied pressure with the dishtowel to the right side of Ms. D's head. There was a pool of blood on the floor, some on the sink, and blood on her face.

"Come on, Ms. D, the ambulance is here. Stay wit' me," Lamar yelled as he cradled her head.

Ms. D had been watching Tammy's kids. Falisha had stopped by to check on them and found Ms. D face down in a pool of blood. Ms. D's wound was bleeding so much that she had to grab a second dishtowel for Lamar.

"Shit, she bleeding a lot!" Falisha said.

The EMTs came into the kitchen. Lamar stood slowly as one EMT placed oxygen over Ms. D's mouth. "We got it, sir," the EMT said, placing an inflatable pillow under her head and a neck brace on her neck.

Lamar walked out onto the porch to join Kim, and Falisha followed. Falisha looked down at the trail of blood that led from the kitchen; it looked like Ms. D was trying to crawl out of the kitchen and had collapsed. When Falisha saw her, she wasn't sure if someone was still in the house, and she ran over to Lamar's for help.

"Shit, the kids! I need to go check on them,"
Lamar said, stopping by the steps. The EMT had
Ms. D on the gurney, and they were rolling her
through the doors.

"No," Falisha said, grabbing Lamar's arm. "You
go with Ms. D; me and Kim gon' stay here with the
kids," Falisha said, cutting her eyes at Kim. Even
with the shit that was going down, she wanted to
get at what the hell was going on with the two of
them. Falisha was going to get answers as to what
the fuck was going on with him answering the door
half naked, and Kim wearing his robe, obviously
with nothing on under it. She had to be cool about
it, so Lamar wouldn't pick up on how pissed she
was, and she knew asking him what was going on
would only result in a lie. She was going to get the
truth out of Kim, and she needed his ass out of the
way while she got her answers.

Lamar looked at Ms. D on the stretcher and
then back at Falisha. He walked slowly to the
ambulance. Before stepping in, he turned to look
back at the two women, and his stomach tightened.
Leaving the two of them alone could not result in
anything good, but Ms. D needed him. He stepped
into the back of the ambulance. He had a feeling
his cake was about to be destroyed; he had each
woman thinking she was wifey. One thinking they
had somewhat of a relationship, and the other
thinking they were on their way to becoming an

official couple. Shit was crazy with Ms. D, but he had a feeling that his head could end up bleeding like hers once the two woman talked to each other

"Let me try to call Tammy," Kim said, walking over to the house phone.

"You fuckin' Lamar?" Falisha asked bluntly.

Kim placed the phone down and turned to Falisha. She was aware of the fact that they messed around from time to time, but that was it, or at least that was what she thought. "Why you asking me about Lamar?" Kim shot back.

"Because Lamar is my man," Falisha said, placing her hands on her hips.

Kim laughed and waved her hand at Falisha, but the look in Falisha's eyes made her stop laughing. "Are you serious?" Kim asked jokingly, thinking Falisha was playing.

Falisha sat down. "Yeah, man."

"Oh, you serious?" Kim said, walking over to the couch. The look on Falisha's face wasn't that of a woman who was joking around. Looking in her eyes, Kim could see that Falisha was serious. She was shocked at this crazy turn of events. The room became silent, and all Kim could do was shake her head.

Judging from the expression on Kim's face, Falisha could tell that Kim, like her, had fallen for the lies Lamar spewed. Whatever the case may have been, all of Lamar's dirty little laundry was about to come out.

Chris went back to his cell, sick as a dog with worms. After hearing another man answering Tammy's phone, all kinds of thoughts ran through his head. He knew that Tammy had been seeing someone, but being hit in the face with the reality of it made his emotions run out of control. Hurt, anger, and betrayal all coursed through his body with each step he took. He felt his head spin, and his vision had a red haze.

"Damn, my nigga. The police is about to call lockdown," Chris's celly, Deacon, said, coming into the room. "You gon' heat ya food up?"

"Nah, homie, I'll eat dat shit in the morning," Chris replied and leaned back on his bed. Food was the last thing on his mind. At the moment, the vision of Tammy riding another nigga's dick played in his head like a 3D movie. The thought of her fucking another nigga, and the dude being around his kids, made his stomach tighten and burn. He stared at the ceiling.

"Man, you okay?" Deacon asked.

"I'm good, man," Chris said, turning over to face the wall. There wasn't anything he could do about the situation at the moment. He closed his eyes and prayed for sleep.

***

Falisha crossed her legs and listened to Kim break down everything about her relationship with Lamar. Kim expressed her love for Lamar, and how they were on their way to planning a life together. They had been seeing each other for a while, but had kept their relationship between the two of them. They wanted to ensure that it was solid before announcing it to the world. Kim sat back on the couch; the women were quiet. Kim thought she was playing it smart with Lamar. She knew that Lamar had some situations to handle, like his fling with Falisha. Kim had decided to sit back, be patient, and keep things private until he worked his issues out. In her heart, she knew that Lamar needed to get things in check, and she didn't want any of his issues to become hers. At the end of the day, Kim had felt that she wore the crown, and would get the jewels because she did live with him, and he came home most nights to her bed.

Kim made things crystal clear for Falisha, and it explained Lamar's behavior lately. He had toggled between being friends, and being together. Lamar was the best at keeping her off keel.

The best trick of the devil is to convince you he doesn't exist, and Lamar's trick was his honesty. He had told Falisha that he was still seeing other females because he wasn't sure about how sincere Falisha's feelings were for him. She had hurt him a couple times before, and he couldn't bring himself to commit to her until he was sure she was really ready for there to be a "them." She knew he had been playing around, but she thought the chicks were random. Now she was finding out they weren't random, but one steady: Kim.

"So now what?" Kim asked, having laid all her cards out on the table.

Falisha looked over at Kim with one eyebrow up. She then reached for her tote bag over on the coffee table. She shook her head as she rummaged through the bag until she found what she was looking for. For a second, Kim thought that Falisha was going to pull out a gun and shoot her. If anybody was crazy enough to do something like that, it would have been her. But instead of a gun, Falisha pulled out a sandwich bag of some Ol' Gran' Daddy Kush, along with some swisher sweets to roll up with.

"I'm not letting him go," Falisha said as she crumbled up some weed on the table.

Kim looked at her like she was crazy; she felt the same way. After all that was said, neither woman was ready to let Lamar go so fast, and the only reason the two women weren't rolling around on the ground fighting like cats and dogs right now was because of their friendship and the love they had for each other. There was no way possible they were going to let a man ruin their friendship; but, at the same time, love was very unpredictable.

"Well, I'm not letting him go either," Kim said, which Falisha expected. "So may the best bitch win," Kim said as she dug in the bag of weed and pulled out some Kush to roll up for herself.

They both just sat there blowing on the weed, trying to figure out how in the world they were going to deal with this situation. It seemed crazy, but Lamar was the type of man most women hoped to have in their life. Kim and Falisha both knew his potential, and they knew that whoever he chose to give his heart to would be happy.

Ms. D lay back in the bed. She had eight stitches on the side of her skull, and an IV to replace the fluids and blood she'd lost. Lamar had spoken to the doctor; he told the doctor he was Ms. D's son so that he could get the information he needed about her condition. She had gotten dizzy and fallen. She hit her head on the sink, and the last thing she remembered doing was washing the dishes and drying out NaNa's bottles. Everything after that was a blur. Although she was getting on up in age, she told herself that she was healthy. She had been having dizzy spells, but none when she had been babysitting. She wasn't on any medication and felt great most of the time. Lamar shook the doctor's hand and took a seat beside Ms. D's bed.

"Did he say when I could get out of here?" Ms. D asked, looking at Lamar.

"No. They need to run some more tests on you. So just sit back and relax. That is a nasty gash," Lamar said as he poured a cup of water for her. The door opened and a petite brown-skinned nurse entered.

"Excuse me, Nurse. When can I leave?" Ms. D asked, ignoring Lamar.

"Dr. Patrick wants to check you out before he discharges you. I'm going to take some more blood from you in a few minutes," the nurse answered.

Ms. D smacked her lips, and began mumbling curse words to herself under her breath. Lamar tried to hide his smile as he watched her pout like a toddler.

Ms. D looked out the window. Hospitals, doctors, needles, medicine, and fucking bills. The cherry on top is usually some kind of bad news about your life. That was why she had stayed away from doctors and anything medical for the last two years. Her head began to throb, reminding her that she had no choice now but to sit, wait, and pray about the damn tests they would be running on her. Patience wasn't one of her strong suits, and waiting was going to be more painful than the stitches in her head.

Chapter 22

Lisa sat on the porch waiting for Naomi's father, Ralphy, to drop her off from her weekend visit with him. This was the first weekend in two weeks that he had been able to spend time with Naomi, due to his schedule. Lisa wasn't sure what his schedule was, but it was no longer her concern. They had filed for divorce, but it wasn't official. Yet, Ralphy was living his life like the papers were signed by the judge and filed. He had a new look, new house, new cell phone number, and a new group of friends. His world was exclusive, and it excluded her. She had no way to contact him directly, so she communicated with him through his relatives, or on days like today when he would personally drop their daughter off. Despite everything, Ralphy loved Naomi with all his heart, and she was a daddy's girl through and through.

Her cell phone began to ring. She looked at the table beside her chair on the porch and then realized she had left it in the house on the chair by the door. She grabbed it in time to hear the click on the line. She checked the caller ID, but the call showed as private. She cursed, thinking she could have missed a call from Ralphy. She heard a horn beep twice, and she opened the screen door and stepped outside. The white 2012 Range Rover seemed to glisten in the sunlight. It had tinted windows and a set of twenty-four-inch rims complementing the already stunning SUV.

As the SUV parked, the back door opened and Naomi jumped out beaming. "Mommy!" Naomi yelled, trying to grab the bags from the back seat.

Lisa walked down the steps, and held her arms out for Naomi, who giggled and placed bags in her open arms. The driver's door opened and Ralphy walked around the car to help Naomi get her bags from the back seat of the Range. Ralphy, like his truck, seemed to glisten. The dude had more than stepped up; he had flown up an entire level. The last car he had was a 2007 Buick LeSabre.

"She gonna need some help with these," Ralphy said, pulling the bags from the back seat.

"Mommy, we went shopping." Naomi said, taking a bag from her father.

"Wow, I see," Lisa said, looking at Ralphy. He wore a white fitted V-neck T-shirt under a black leather Polo jacket. The shirt hugged his slim waist, tight stomach, and broad shoulders. His dark True Religion jeans sat just on top of the Louis Vuitton sneakers. The aviator frames complemented his rich brown skin, low-cut wavy hair, and neatly trimmed beard. She inhaled the scent of Creed that emanated from him as he handed her the bags. She swallowed. The scent, the clothes, and his swag actually made it hard for her to focus.

"You look good," Lisa said, reaching over and grabbing the iced-out letter R Ralphy had dangling from his chain. "I see the single life treating you good," she said, letting the piece go and looking over at the Range.

"Who said that I was single?" Ralphy said, laughing as he walked back to his SUV. Ralphy got in and rolled the passenger window down. Lisa then noticed the dark-haired, young, beautiful Latin chick sitting in the passenger seat texting or something on her phone. She never looked up to even acknowledge Lisa.

"Drop her off at my mom's house next week at the same time," Ralphy said to Lisa before rolling up the window.

He pulled off before Lisa could respond. She was trying to process what had just happened. Her brain was playing catch-up as she stood on the sidewalk with her mouth open, watching the SUV head toward the stop sign.

"Mommy, let's go inside so I can show you my clothes. Mommy!" Naomi said, pulling on Lisa's shirt.

"Yeah, baby, sorry, come on." Lisa slid the bags up her arm and walked up the sidewalk to her house. She put on a smile for her baby. Naomi skipped ahead of Lisa, as she tried to mask the hurt and shock she was feeling. He had left her, and had moved up and moved on.

Tammy felt her legs being opened and something warm caressing her clit. She opened her eyes and blinked a few times to focus them. She looked down to see Darious's long, strong tongue caressing the walls of her wet box. His tongue slid in and out of her, and she moved her hips to meet his strokes.

Darious looked up at Tammy and smirked. "Good morning," he said before covering her clit with his mouth.

"Goo . . . ugg shit!" Tammy said as Darious sucked her clit and thumped it with his tongue. Instinctively, she tried to pull away from his mouth, but his strong arms held her still as he devoured her clit.

"Oh, baby. Oh, D . . ."

Darious slowly slid his hand up her stomach to her right breast. He held his tongue still for a moment, and gently pulled her long nipple with his index finger and thumb. He pulled her clit into his mouth and attacked it with his tongue. Tammy screamed and wrapped the sheets around her hands. Her eyes rolled to the back of her head as her juices dripped down Darious's chin.

Her screams vibrated through his body down to his dick, which twitched against the bed. He flipped her over and pulled her back to his lap. She was panting and still riding her orgasm when he slid his hard rod between her fat pussy lips. The sound of her breathing sent fire through him. This morning was not going to be gentle like last night; this morning, she was going to feel the power of his body.

"I'm about to tattoo my name inside that pussy. You're mine, you understand?" Darious grabbed her arms and held them behind her back with his left hand. She looked back at him curiously, and he began to pound her pussy. Yeah, he was going to thug fuck that pussy so damn good that her pussy couldn't even respond to another nigga's dick.

Lamar walked into Ms. D's hospital room and sat down in the green chair beside her bed. "Hey, Ms. D, I gotta go do some thangs. Falisha is on her way down here."

"Y'all can go on. I don't need nobody here with me." Ms. D said, wiping the tears from her eyes.

Dr. Patrick had her take a few more tests, and a mammogram earlier. The mammogram told her what the doctor wasn't saying. They had found a lump in one of her breasts, and she didn't need any damn test to tell her that the monster that had plagued the women in her family had now caught up to her. Most of the women in her family were usually diagnosed before the age of fifty. She was five years beyond that point, and she knew that her number was now up.

"No, you don't need to be alone. We are here for you," Lamar said, taking her hand. There was a light knock at the door, and Dr. Patrick entered with a large folder and small laptop in his arms.

"Ms. Hudson, how is your head feeling?" Dr. Patrick asked as he sat down on the small black rolling stool.

"My head will be fine, Doctor. Please, just tell me what you got to say. I don't like beating around the bush. Just say it."

Dr. Patrick turned the television on and turned to channel four. He placed the laptop on the cart, and typed something on its screen. Images appeared on the television screen. Ms. D sighed as she stared at the dark mass on the X-ray.

"The tissue we took tested—"

"I don't give a shit; and, no, I don't want no damn chemo. Just give me my oxycodone for my head and my damn marijuana card, so I can smoke my weed in peace," Ms. D said jokingly.

Dr. Patrick turned the television off, and turned to Ms. D. "Ms. Hudson, we have made so many advances in medicine. I would like to discuss your options."

"What did I just say, Dr. Patrick? I ain't doing shit!"

Lamar looked at Dr. Patrick. "Hey, can you give us a few minutes, Dr. Patrick?" Lamar said.

Dr. Patrick nodded, and grabbed his laptop. He looked at Ms. D one last time before walking out the door. Ms. D began mumbling and staring out the window.

"Ms. D, he is just trying to help. You acting like you giving up without a fight."

"Boy, I'm fine. I don't want to hear any of that bullshit he got to say. I've seen what this thing does to women, and I don't want to go out like that. Just let nature take its course."

Although Ms. D was trying to mask her fear, Lamar could see it in her eyes. She was the closest thing he had to a mother and, at the moment, it seemed the roles had reversed. He would have to be the one to tell her what was best for her, even if it meant he would have to knock some sense in her on the other side of her head.

Tammy turned on her phone, and it immediately began to vibrate and beep. The text messages buzzing across the screen were all from Falisha, saying something had happened. She dialed Falisha's number, hoping that it was just some Falisha drama and nothing had happened to her kids.

"Damn, bitch, dat dick must be good," Falisha said, answering the phone.

"You need to mind ya business," Tammy joked. "What you want anyway?"

"You need to go pick ya kids up from Kim's. Ms. D fell and split her head open last night, and she's in the hospital," Falisha said as she walked to her car.

"What?" Tammy said as she jumped up from the bed looking for her clothes. "Shit, she okay? Are the kids all right?" Tammy didn't bother looking for her underwear. She slid the shirt and jeans on as Falisha explained to her what happened.

Darious awoke to Tammy searching for her shoes, and talking on the phone. "What's wrong, baby?" Darious asked, getting up and grabbing his pants.

"I gotta go pick my kids up. The sitter in the hospital. She got hurt last night," Tammy said, strapping on her shoes. Darious put on his white Duke T-shirt and grabbed his white Nike tennis shoes.

Tammy grabbed her purse and walked down the stairs to the door. Darious followed without asking any questions. He locked his door, and clicked the alarm on the car. Tammy opened the passenger side door and sat down. She nervously chewed on her nail as she waited for him to get in the car.

***

Falisha walked down the brightly lit hallway with trepidation; hospitals always made her anxious. As she made her way around the corner, she thought back to the last time she had been down the halls of a hospital. Memories of visiting Fox when he was shot flooded her mind for a minute. She found room 807 and knocked on the door.

"Hey, Ms. D, the party can start now. Or maybe you don't wanna party anymore; you drinking some of that shine and hit ya head!" Falisha said, laughing.

Falisha walked over to Lamar and plopped down on his lap. She kissed his cheek and caressed his face. "Hey, baby," she said, making sure her ass was on his crotch.

"Now, girl, why you down here? They 'bout to let me go. Just got a little cut on my head is all." She cut her eyes at Lamar, warning him with her eyes to keep his mouth shut about the cancer situation. She didn't want to hear the sympathy shit; all she wanted was for them to release her, so she could go home to her own bed.

"So what did the doctor say?" Falisha asked, concerned about Ms. D's well-being.

"Oh, nothing. I fainted, then hit my head on the sink on my way to the ground. I'll be outta here in a minute," Ms. D answered.

"That's good," Falisha said, kissing Lamar on his cheek again.

"Look, I don't want to see y'all making no babies in front of me. You better go to one of dem broom closets," Ms. D said, laughing.

"That sounds like a good idea, Ms. D. Listen at you talking about getting freaky in the hospital!" Falisha said, rubbing Lamar's chest. There was a knock at the door, and Dr. Patrick entered with a petite Asian nurse.

"Ms. Hudson, we got the rest of your tests back, and I need to keep you overnight. We want to watch that head wound," Dr. Patrick said, looking at Ms. D and then Falisha. "Those types of injuries can be tricky, and require monitoring. Nurse Hong will give you something to help you sleep. You need to get some rest," Dr. Patrick said with a smile.

Ms. D forced a smile, but she wanted to jump off the bed and slap the hell out of him. Staying overnight was not what she wanted to do. Lamar looked at her with pleading eyes for her to listen to the doctor. She inhaled and nodded. She knew that her situation was serious, and that she needed to at least try to listen to what the doctor had to say. She also needed to know what stage the cancer was in, so she could prepare herself for what was ahead of her.

"Are the kids okay?" Darious asked, looking over at Tammy as she put the phone down. She had just spoken to Kim, who assured her that her babies were good.

"Yeah, they're fine. Kim got them right now," she answered, looking out of the window with a sad look on her face.

Darious could see the stress in her eyes. "Come on, shawty. Don't beat yaself up about that," he said, trying to make her feel better.

Darious wasn't a parent, so he really didn't know how it felt not to be there for your children when they needed you. She knew that turning off her phone was irresponsible; that was something she couldn't do as a mother with small children. She knew there wasn't any way for her to predict Ms. D getting hurt, but she knew better than to cut off the only line of communication to her. Anything could go wrong without a moment's notice, and it did last night.

She turned to Darious. "I was thinking, maybe you should—"

Tammy's cell phone began to ring before she could finish her sentence. She looked down at her phone and saw that the number was blocked. Thinking that it was probably Falisha calling from the hospital, Tammy answered it.

"Hello," she answered.

"You have a prepaid call. You will not be charged for this call. This call is from Chris."

Tammy's stomach gurgled and then tightened. She looked over at Darious; she knew that answering the phone would be an issue. She quickly hung up the phone. A few moments later, it rang again. She turned the ringer down, placed it in her purse, and stared out the window. Talking to Chris with Darious in the car would not be the ideal situation. Chris would grill her, and ask her about a million questions, and then after he had interrogated her, he would tell her he loved her. He would expect to hear her say it back, and that was not something she wanted to say in front of Darious. She knew not saying it to Chris would send him into a rage. Her brain fired, and she remembered she was supposed to take the kids to see him today.

"Shit," Tammy said to herself, not noticing how loudly she had spoken.

"What? Is something else wrong?" Darious asked as he stopped at the intersection.

"Nothing, nothing, I just remembered something I needed to do today."

Lisa and Naomi sat in her room folding up the new clothes Ralphy had bought her. As she listened to Naomi's chatter, her mind kept going back to how good Ralphy looked and smelled. He had transformed himself back into the dope boy Lisa fell in love with years ago. The new truck, clothes, and swag made Lisa want him but, even more than that, she had one question she needed answered.

"Was that Daddy's new girlfriend?" Lisa asked Naomi while they put the clothes away.

"Yup. Her name is Johanne," Naomi answered.

"Does she live with Daddy, too?"

"Umm, sometimes. Sometimes she sleep in Daddy's room," Naomi answered, playfully holding up a dress to her body to show Lisa how she looked.

"Does she have any kids?" Lisa asked as she placed one of the shirts on a hanger.

Naomi shook her head. "No," she said, then ran off to her dresser to put away some clothes. Naomi's mind was on her beautiful clothes and new books her daddy had bought her. Lisa felt some shame in interrogating her child, but she had no other way to get the information she desired. If she had his cell phone number, she would ask him right out herself. Ralphy was looking damn good, and she wanted to know about the chick in the passenger seat. The only way she could get what she needed was to question her little one. Besides, she needed to know about who Ralphy had her child around, right?

Chapter 23

"Look, I gotta get ready to go to work," Lamar said, standing up and stretching. He had returned to the hospital the night before after running some errands. Falisha was asleep in the recliner when he had come back, and he slept in the other chair. He was tired, but his pockets were hungry. Tonight was Sunday, and he knew there would be women packing the place. He would easily walk out with two and a half to three stacks. He was not about to miss that for nobody.

"Can we go somewhere tonight? I was thinking we can go to a hotel," Falisha said, wrapping her arms around his waist.

"I don't know. I'm tired as hell. After I get off, I'm trying to get some sleep," he responded.

Falisha looked over at Ms. D then back over at Lamar. She was horny as hell, and had thought about fucking him all day. She pulled his head down to her, kissed him with her juicy mouth, and swiped her tongue across his bottom lip.

"You better stop playing," Lamar warned as his hands gripped her ass.

Falisha giggled. "Come 'ere," she said, pulling him into the bathroom.

Lamar followed her into the bathroom. Falisha wasted no time dropping to her knees and unbuckling Lamar's pants, taking his dick out, and putting it into her mouth. Lamar moaned from the wetness, and as Falisha held on to his waist for support, she shoved as much of his meat into her mouth as she could. It was three quarters in and it had already hit the back of her throat. He held on to the back of her head to guide her. It felt so wet and so soft, that at this point, Lamar wanted some pussy.

He grabbed a handful of her hair, pulling her up to him, and before Falisha knew it, Lamar had spun her around, bent her over the sink, and slammed his stiff dick inside her. Falisha grabbed a towel from the rack and bit down on it. She looked at Lamar in the mirror, watching him caress her pussy with his thick dick. She could see the lust in his eyes as he looked back at her.

"Give it to me, daddy," Falisha whined, poking her ass out and arching her back a little, so that Lamar had a clear shot at it.

Lamar grabbed her ass, spread her ass cheeks apart, and pushed the rest of his long, hard, thick black dick within her soft, wet box. Falisha bit down again on the towel.

Sinniyyah sat in her high chair playing with the cereal Tammy gave her to snack on while she finished cleaning the kitchen. Tammy felt a little better being home with the kids and knowing that they were safe. It was always a blessing to have friends like Kim and Falisha to be there when she needed them.

"Mommy!" Anthony yelled, running into the kitchen with her cell phone in his hand. "My daddy want you," he said with a big smile on his face as he passed her the phone.

Tammy almost regretted showing Anthony how to accept his call. Tammy took a deep breath as she put the phone to her ear. Ever since Darious had dropped her off, he had occupied her mind. There was a time she looked forward to Chris's call, but now she wanted the battery in the phone to die.

"Wassup," Tammy said with a bit of attitude.

"What happened to my visit today?" Chris asked. He only had a couple of minutes left on the call. The phones would be turned off at nine-thirty, and it was nine twenty-seven. He knew that there was no time to start an argument with Tammy. He wouldn't get any answers from her in that short period of time.

"Look, you know I work, and I slept in today. I will bring them next weekend or whenever I get the chance."

"Whenever you get a chance?" Chris asked with an attitude. He bit down on his lower lip before he said something else. She was talking reckless, and if he had his way, he would have reached through the phone and punched her in the mouth. He felt his blood pressure rise, he breathing became labored, and he slammed the phone down. He stared at the wall, and swore it was turning red.

As Kim walked into Ms. D's room, Falisha and Lamar exited the bathroom. Lamar was zipping his pants, and Falisha was smoothing her hair. Falisha smirked at Kim, who placed the flowers in the empty vase beside Ms. D's bed. Seeing the two of them adjusting their clothes and hair, Kim knew that they had just had sex. Kim disguised her hurt and played it cool.

"Wassup, girl. How long have you been here?" Falisha asked, walking over to Ms. D's bedside.

Falisha knew exactly what she was doing when she took Lamar into the bathroom. Kim had texted her that she was downstairs just before she pulled Lamar in the bathroom. She wanted Kim to walk in and catch them in the act, but for some damn reason it took her longer to get to the room. Falisha's plan still worked, because Kim caught enough of it.

"I just walked through the door. How long has she been asleep?" Kim asked, sitting on the other side of Ms. D's bed.

"Not long!" Ms. D said, cracking her eyes open and cutting them over at Lamar and Falisha. "Y'all two are a mess," she said, shaking her head, letting them know that she heard them in the bathroom.

Kim glared at Falisha, who smiled deviously at her, while Lamar looked down and then at Ms. D before walking toward the door. He did not want to make eye contact with Kim, but before he could reach the door, Falisha jumped in front of him. She smiled and kissed him. Lamar didn't pull away, and returned her kiss before exiting the room. Falisha smiled to herself as she watched the door close.

She turned around and smirked at Kim. "What?" Falisha said, shrugging as she walked back over to her seat.

"Sit yo' crazy ass down, girl," Ms. D said. "And you better have cleaned up in there."

"Yes, ma'am, I did. I made sure nothing went to waste," Falisha responded.

Kim shook her head. "That is all you got to offer? It gets old after a while," Kim said, putting away her compact.

"Maybe in the world you live in," Falisha shot back. "Instead of hating on me, you should be trying to get ya weight up. You'll never keep a man at the rate you're going," she said, rolling her eyes at Kim.

Ms. D looked back and forth between the two women. "What da hell is going on between you two?"

Neither woman spoke.

Ms. D shook her head. "I know y'all not even trying to get at each other about no nigga. You been friends for as long as I can remember. Friendship, unlike dick, should always come first. These dudes out here run through y'all girls for a minute, and then they on to the next. Then what you left with?"

Normally, Falisha and Kim would listen to Ms. D's advice, but this time it was different. They didn't want to admit it to each other, but their feelings were heavily involved. Kim had love for Lamar, but Falisha was in love with Lamar, and that was a big difference. And the crazy part about it was Lamar had love for both of them, almost equally for that matter.

One thing Ms. D knew for sure was that if Falisha and Kim continued to go down the road they were on, things would get ugly real fast.

Chapter 24

Ever since Darious stopped working at the store, it had been super boring for Tammy at work. Her new coworker was a female who could barely speak English. The limited conversations they had were primarily about work, and nothing else. Tammy sighed as she thought of Darious. She missed his humor, which made her workday enjoyable, and passed the time. However, she knew that him moving on to his new job at Charlotte Medical Center was a good look.

"Yo, I'm bringing all this shit back," a voice yelled from the other side of the counter, startling Tammy, whose back was turned.

When she turned around, she was relieved that it was Darious standing there with his fist over his mouth, laughing at her. "You was scared as shit." He laughed.

"Shut up," Tammy said, reaching over the counter and punching him in his arm. "What are you doing here anyway?" she asked.

"I got off early today, and I figured I'd take you to lunch. I already talked to ya boss, so you good," he said and smiled.

Tammy cleaned up her workstation and let her coworker know that she was going on her lunch break. She wasted no time taking off with Darious. She only had a half hour, so they walked across the street to McDonald's.

"Yo, I need to talk to you about something," Darious said, taking a seat in the booth with Tammy.

"Uh-oh. That don't sound good," she said and took a bite of her burger.

Darious smiled, assuring her that it wasn't bad at all. He just had something that he needed to get off his chest before it killed him.

"I'm in love with you, Tammy," he said, looking into her eyes.

The burger that Tammy was chewing on seemed to expand in her mouth. She grabbed her Sprite to help wash it down.

"I don't . . . Well, wow." Tammy had a hard putting her words together.

Darious smiled and took her hand. "Every night that I get home from work and walk through the front door, I be hoping that you're there sitting on the couch waiting for me. It takes me every bit of an hour to get to sleep once I'm in the bed, because I can't stop thinking of you, and wondering if you're thinking about me. I think about all the ways I wanna make you happy and try not to do anything that would make you unhappy," Darious said.

Hearing the sincerity in his voice, Tammy felt warm all over. She was feeling something for him too, but she wasn't sure it was love just yet. He made her feel incredible. It had been so long since she'd felt adored, and protected. He had given her the resources to provide for her kids, made sure everything was straight, and had the bedroom game beyond incredible. Everything he had just expressed mirrored what she felt about him as well. She checked her watch; thirty minutes seemed like only five at the moment.

"Can we talk about this later?" Tammy said, touching Darious's face. "I gotta get back to work, but I definitely want to talk about this."

"Yeah, yeah. I will call you later," Darious said, taking a sip of his soda.

"We can talk at my house. Come by tonight around nine o'clock," Tammy told him. Inviting Darious to her home was a huge step. She had never allowed any man to walk across the threshold other than Chris.

She took a few more bites of her burger, and placed the rest on the tray. "I guess I need to get back over there."

Darious took the tray to the trashcan and extended his arm to Tammy. "Yeah, I guess so. You sure about me coming over?"

Tammy shook her head and kissed his cheek. "I'm sure," Tammy said, and then kissed his lips.

***

Ralphy pulled up to the block, jumped out of the Range Rover, and dapped all his homies who were standing out there. Being back in the hood had never felt better, and now that he was back on dope boy status, the hood was loving him once again.

Killing Dre had made the decision to get back in the game easy. Catching that body brought back memories of the power he had held back in the day in the streets. Scoop had looked out for him by giving him a couple of ounces of heroin on the strength of his game. Like a chick seeing her man after his bid, the streets had welcomed him back. Once he got the taste of what it felt like to pull down them stacks, Ralphy had not looked back.

"Damn, big homie, what it do?" Scoop said as he walked out of the store to meet Ralphy.

"Ain't shit, li'l nigga. Business as usual," Ralphy responded, letting Scoop know that he was there to pick up his money.

"Damn, playboy, I hate when you talk to me like that. I'm starting to feel like you treatin' me like the rest of these niggas out here. Don't forget who got you back in the game, homeboy," Scoop said, walking over to his car and grabbing the small backpack from his back seat.

Scoop might have said it in a joking way, but he was serious about what he said. When Ralphy got back in the game, he stepped on the gas and rose over his peers in a very short period of time.

Ralphy's street hustle was that of a Princeton scholar, which pushed him above the rest.

Ringo Street used to be Scoop's, but now it was Ralphy who was supplying the block. He had also picked up Thomas Road, Belmont Avenue, and the Academy Projects. Scoop knew firsthand how Ralphy could kill and destroy people who stood in his way. So for now he could only stand down, and submit to his takeover. Ralphy grabbed the back pack and headed back to his SUV.

"Yo, what up wit' homeboy?" one of Scoop's homies asked as he watched Ralphy pull out of the parking lot. He stared at the truck; he had heard the way the dude had spoken to Scoop, and found his tone to be arrogant. "That nigga think his shit don't stank," the young'un said, taking a pull off his Black.

"Yeah, well, the rise of some folks can make them think they can't ever fall," Scoop said before walking back inside his store.

Chris waited in line in front of his counselor's office to get inside, so that he could make a social phone call unmonitored. What he had to say couldn't be said over the regular inmate phones, because someone was always listening. Here in the counselor's office, anybody could say whatever they want freely without worrying about it coming back and biting them in the ass. Talking reckless on a fed phone can get a nigga a whole new indictment.

When Chris finally got into the office and was approved for the call, the only person he wanted to call was his little brother, Outlaw. When it came down to Chris, Outlaw would do just about anything for his big brother. Outlaw wasn't sweet by a long shot; at the young age of nineteen, he had half the neighborhood scared of him, and the other half respected his G.

"Wassup, li'l bro," Chris said into the phone when Outlaw picked up. "My counselor gave me a phone call," he told him, letting Outlaw know that the line was secure. "Yo, I need you to take care of something for me," Chris said, lowering his voice some so the counselor wouldn't hear him.

"Yeah, whatever you need, big bro. Just let me know."

"Yo, I think my baby mom got a nigga around my kids. I need you to swing through the block and see what it do," Chris instructed.

"Say no more. I'm on top of it like yesterday. You good, bro? I'ma put some money on ya books when I get off the phone wit' ya," Outlaw said.

"Nah, bro, I'm good. I just need you to take care of that situation for me," Chris said, looking back at the counselor.

He hung up and nodded to his counselor. Just like that, he had taken care of whoever was trying to be in Tammy's bed and around his kids. Outlaw would take care of it quickly, and without questions.

Chapter 25

Lisa walked down the hallway toward Naomi's room. It was quiet, so Lisa knew that Naomi was either playing in Lisa's makeup or she was asleep. She slowly opened the door to see Naomi fast asleep, dressed in one of her new outfits with her backpack on. Lisa laughed at how adorable she looked, and ran to her room, grabbed the phone, and snapped a couple of pictures.

"This will come in handy in a few years," Lisa said to herself. She placed the phone in her pocket and began pulling off Naomi's shoes and removing the backpack. As she placed it on the bed, she noticed a cell phone on the side of the backpack. She pulled it out, and swiped the screen. The wallpaper on the phone was a picture of Naomi and Ralphy. Lisa turned the phone over.

"Galaxy 4?" she whispered to herself. She looked at the photo again; it appeared that they were at an amusement park, but it wasn't the local one. Ralphy was standing behind Naomi smiling and pointing to the camera. Seeing the two of them together brought up memories of the three of them. She sighed and undressed Naomi down to a

T-shirt and panties. She pulled the covers up over her and kissed her cheek.

Before turning out the light, she noticed a laptop at the foot of Naomi's bed. He had really taken Naomi on a shopping spree. "What did you do, Lisa?" she asked herself as she watched Naomi sleep.

Every day, Lisa kicked herself for tearing her family apart. She hated sleeping alone, her heart ached for her husband, and at times the pain was so intense she had actually thought about suicide. Naomi's face would enter her mind, and save her from committing something so stupid.

She looked at Naomi's phone. She wanted to put it down, but curiosity took over. She swiped through the pictures on the phone. Ralphy and Naomi smiled at her from each one. She went to contacts and saw Ralphy's phone number under My Daddy in Naomi's contact list. She stared at the number with her finger hovering over the call icon. She thought better of it. After all, what would she say to him? He would probably hang up as soon as he heard her voice anyway.

She lay back on the bed with Naomi and took a photo of the two of them. She attached it to a text message and typed, I miss my family. She hit send and then cuddled up with her daughter for the night.

**

Darious parked his Charger on the street, a few houses down from Tammy's due to the orange cones and blue flags in front of her house. The city was working on the water line, and the asphalt had been torn up. He began walking toward her house, not paying much attention to the two hooded men standing at the stop sign smoking. He pulled his cell phone out and called Tammy to let her know he was outside. Tammy told him she would be heading downstairs to open the door for him. When he got to her building, he called again, to let her know that he was outside.

Darious was oblivious to the two hooded men. Outlaw and his boy, Ratchet, had been waiting all day to see if anybody showed up at Chris's house. Outlaw recognized the white Charger from when Tammy had dropped the kids off at his mama's house a few times.

"You ready, li'l nigga?" Outlaw asked, pulling out a black Glock 9 mm.

Ratchet reached in his waist and pulled out his black automatic .45 and cocked a bullet in the chamber. Neither one of the men said another word as they both proceeded to walk toward Tammy's house with their guns out.

As Darious approached Tammy's house, he noticed the men walking quickly toward him with guns drawn. His heart began to pound; he couldn't see the men's faces, but he could clearly see their guns. He froze at the front door, bracing himself for what was to come. He held his breath as they got closer. He felt the wind on his back as Tammy opened the door, but he didn't look away from the approaching guns.

Lamar rolled the cock ring to the base of his dick, and then stuffed it in his G-string. He looked at himself from the side and was satisfied with his member's appearance. The harder and bigger the bulge, the bigger the tips.

"Yo, you're up," Chip, the manager of the club, walked in and told Lamar.

Lamar put the rest of his outfit on and headed for the stage. It was ladies' night, so he didn't have to drink alcohol the way he had to in order to perform in front of the gay community. He was on a natural high and his game face was on.

Lamar stood behind the curtain, waiting for the MC to introduce him. He popped his neck and stretched. After a few moments, he realized that it was quiet on the other side of the curtain. He peeked out and noticed the silhouette of a woman sitting in the chair on the stage, but he couldn't make out the face from where he was standing. He looked out in the club, and no one was there: no servers, security, or DJ. He walked closer to the woman in the chair, and realized it was Kim. Lamar laughed and exhaled.

Kim knew the owner of the club, and she had decided to call in a favor. Her law firm had represented the owner, Moose, in a tax evasion case. She had put together the motions needed to get his case dismissed. When she called him, he didn't hesitate to oblige her request to give her the club for the first thirty minutes.

"What you doing, Kim?" Lamar asked, looking out into the empty club.

"I came to see you dance," she said seductively, tossing twenty dollar bills at him.

"How am I going to dance without any music?"

Kim raised her hand, and Lil Wayne's "Lollipop" song rushed through the speakers. Lamar looked at Kim as she uncrossed and crossed her legs.

"Dance; entertain me," Kim said as she let the twenties flow from her hands. She had a few stacks, and showering Lamar with them was nothing. Lamar moved around her like a panther on a prowl. He had to admit dancing for her like this was making his dick even harder. He leaned down to kiss her, and Kim raised her hand. She moved away from his lips and stuffed a few more twenties in his G-string, then pushed him back. She stood up, pressed her breasts against his chest, and looked into his eyes.

"Eventually, Lamar, you will have to make a choice, and you will need to do it sooner rather than later," Kim said, tracing his lips. "You see,

I'm a woman who can do this," Kim said, pointing to the empty club. "I'm about my business, but if you like fucking little girls in a hospital room bathroom, to each his own. Get your shit together and do it quickly. So by the time you get off tonight, you need to have made a decision, or I will make it for you."

Kim walked off the stage, leaving a trail of twenties behind her.

Lamar watched her disappear into the darkness. The doors of the club opened, and women began to fill the club. Lamar stood center stage with a hard dick, and a lot to think about.

Chapter 26

Darious looked down the barrel of the gun, closed his eyes, and braced for impact. Right before Outlaw began to fire, Tammy opened the front door, causing Darious to fall inside the home. She had the baby in her arms, so Outlaw decided not to start shooting wildly at the house. Instead, he walked up on the steps to get a better shot at Darious.

"No, Outlaw!" Tammy yelled, standing over Darious to shield him from the danger. "Please!" she pled, holding out her hand.

If Tammy didn't have his niece in her arms, Outlaw would have shot Darious right there. Looking into Sinniyyah's eyes, Outlaw backed off, but not before letting Tammy know what was on his mind.

"Next time I catch ya boyfriend 'round here, I'ma blow his fuckin' head off. You gon' show my brotha some fuckin' respect, whether you like it or not. Make this the last time we have this conversation," he told Tammy, before tucking his gun back into his waist.

He gave Darious a stern look before he and Ratchet turned around and walked off into the night. Tammy kneeled down to help Darious up, but he snatched his arm away from her, got up off the ground, and headed for his car. Tammy ran behind him, looking over her shoulder in the direction were Outlaw and Ratchet went.

"Darious, please don't leave," Tammy begged, knowing that it wasn't quite safe for him to leave yet.

"He was about to shoot me," Darious said, stopping at the driver's side of his car. "Ya people is crazy. I ain't got time for this."

"I know, I know, and I'm sorry, but please don't leave right now," she said, looking over her shoulder again.

She knew Outlaw, and was well aware of what he was capable of. Chris had told her enough stories of his and his brother's murderous ways. She knew that as soon as Darious pulled off from the block, Outlaw was the type of nigga who would be waiting for him, to finish what he had started. The best thing for Darious to do now was go inside her house, where he was protected by the presence of Chris's kids. After Tammy had a chance to explain all of that to him, Darious did just that.

Visiting hours were almost over for Ms. D. She had been given the good news that she was being discharged the following morning. Falisha decided to head home for the night and wait for Lamar to get off work. She had something special planned for him, and it involved some new lingerie she had purchased earlier in the day. She had it all planned out how she anticipated the rest of the night would go, and what she was going to do to Lamar.

"Damn, wassup, stranger?" a familiar voice said from behind, while Falisha was waiting for her cab.

She turned around, and there was Fox, standing there with his phone up to his ear. It had been awhile since Falisha had seen him, and she couldn't quite put her hands on it, but he definitely looked different for some reason. It wasn't his clothes, or the new haircut he was rocking, nor was it the fact that he had lost some weight. It was something else.

"How have you been, Fox?" Falisha greeted him, leaning in for a friendly hug. "Is everything all right?" she asked him, looking up at the hospital.

"I've been doing all right. My dad had a heart attack a couple of days ago. He's good, though," Fox answered. "So what about you? How have you been?"

Falisha explained that there was the same old stuff going on, and how she was trying to get back into school. They sat there and talked for a minute, forgetting about their prior engagements. Conversation was something that came naturally for them, and if it weren't for Falisha's cab pulling up, they would have been there talking awhile longer.

"It was nice seeing you, Fox," Falisha said, walking over to the cab.

He reached out and grabbed her hand, stopping her before she got into the car. He honestly missed Falisha, and didn't want to let her go right away. "Let me take you home," Fox offered.

Falisha thought about it for a second, but declined the offer after thinking about what Lamar would do if he saw her in the car with him. She knew there would have been drama, the kind of drama Falisha didn't feel like going through, especially now when she was trying to win over Lamar's heart.

"Well, since I can't take you home, can I at least call you . . . as a friend?" Fox choked up. "I really need to talk to you about something important."

Falisha didn't hate Fox, nor did they break up on bad terms. She didn't see any reason why he couldn't call and talk as a friend, of course as long as Lamar wasn't around. She also knew that Fox followed instructions to a T.

"Call my phone in the morning, around ten o'clock," Falisha told him before walking over and getting into the cab.

Fox nodded his head with a smile as he backed away from the curb. He'd rather take that than nothing. He also knew that when he did call her, he was going to make what he had to say count. He definitely had something on his mind that he'd wanted to get off his chest for a while now, and if Falisha wasn't careful, she could easily get caught up again.

"You should be good to leave," Tammy told Darious as she looked out the window.

Darious sat on the couch, still zoned out about having a gun pointed in his face. He was from the hood, but he was more of the square type, not really getting into too much trouble. That was actually the first time he'd had a pistol pointed at him, ever.

"If ya brother-in-law would have shot me, what would you have done?" Darious asked out of curiosity.

"I would have called the cops on his dumb ass," Tammy answered. "Look, I'm sorry, Darious. My baby father probably sent him around here."

"So you didn't tell him about us yet?" he asked, referring to Chris.

Tammy took a seat on the couch next to him. "I wanna tell him, but I'm scared," Tammy began.

"You shouldn't be with a man you got to be scared of. That's no way to live," Darious spoke.

Tammy had not been all the way upfront with the uncertainty she was feeling inside. "I'm not scared of Chris, Darious. I'm just afraid that once I leave him to be with you, you may leave me, and then I'll be alone. I really wanted to make sure I was good enough for you, before I said anything to him," Tammy confessed.

"Damn, Tam. You really think I tell you the things I do because I wanna hear myself talk?" Darious said, turning to face her. "Look, I told you that I love you and I meant that. You just gotta believe me, and trust me. If you can't do that, then what's the point of us being together? Let me ask you something, Tammy: do you love me?" he asked, reaching over and turning her chin so she could face him.

"Damn, I almost took a bullet for you tonight. Doesn't that count for anything?" Tammy said and laughed.

Darious had to chuckle at her comment as well, and in some crazy way, that was a way to show her love, but Darious wanted to hear the words come out of her mouth. "Nah, seriously," he said, getting back to the question.

Love was a big word to be throwing around and, for days, Tammy had contemplated whether her feelings for him were at the stage of love. At times, it got a bit confusing because she also had love for the father of her kids. It was like Tammy's heart was being torn down the middle, but at the end of the day, she knew she was in love with Darious, and she didn't want to hide it anymore.

"Yes, I love you, Darious," she said, then leaned in and kissed him softly.

Ralphy looked down at Johanne's head bobbing up and down on his dick. Her long, black, curly hair was pulled back in a ponytail, so nothing was getting in the way of her stuffing his whole dick down her throat. She was pretty as all get-out, and in Ralphy's eyes, there was nothing like having a bad bitch suck on his dick.

"Keep going wit' ya nasty self!" Ralphy said, grabbing the top of her head and pushing his dick deeper within her mouth. "You better not stop!" he told her.

Johanne was a freak. She liked when Ralphy talked to her like that. It made her pussy so wet to the point where it began to feel orgasmic. Not too many females could have an orgasm just by sucking their man's dick, but Johanne was one of them, and that was one of the many things Ralphy liked about her.

After Ralphy's phone chirped on the nightstand a couple of times, he finally reached over and grabbed it to see who it was. That too was a turn-on for Johanne. She took it as a challenge, which made her want to suck his dick even harder.

"I miss my family," Ralphy mumbled to himself, repeating what was written in the caption under the picture that was sent to him.

He looked at Lisa and Naomi lying in the bed asleep, and for a moment, he too felt like he missed his family. There wasn't a day that went by when he didn't think about being back at home, but the reality of the matter was that Ralphy wasn't going back. He was reliving an era in his life where he was having his way on the street. That, along with the fact that he would never be able to trust Lisa again, was more than enough for him to want to stay exactly where he was.

It was almost seven o'clock in the morning when Lamar pulled up to the block. After he got off work, he drove around all night thinking about what he was going to do. He always knew that it was going to come down to choosing either Kim or Falisha, but what he didn't expect was for Kim to go hard with the ultimatum she gave him. Even at that very moment, while parked at the top of the block, Lamar still didn't know what he was going to do.

It was a sure thing that both of them were waiting up for him, and no matter which house he finally went into, the other person was going to be hurt. He didn't want to, but today he was about to lose one of the two. Which one? He still didn't know.

"Come on, Lamar. What are you gonna do?" he mumbled to himself as he grabbed his gym bag out of the trunk. "Think, dummy, think!"

Lamar walked down the street with his workout bag over his shoulder. The street seemed shorter today for some odd reason, because after only a couple of steps in, he was already pushing up on both houses. Living directly across the street from each other didn't make things any easier for Lamar, who was only a few feet away from making one of the most important decisions of his life.

Standing in the middle of the street, Lamar stopped right in front of their homes. He could feel both sets of eyes looking at him, and as he looked up at Falisha's house, then back over at Kim's, Lamar made his choice. He lowered his head and walked up Kim's steps, praying and hoping he hadn't made the wrong selection.

Tammy got up bright and early in order to catch the van service that took the families up to the jail. This wasn't a family visit for Chris, as Tammy had dropped the kids off at Chris's mom's house. She wanted to talk to him alone this time, and didn't want the kids interrupting the conversation.

When Tammy got into the visiting room, she became even more nervous, not knowing how this was going to turn out. She felt in her heart that

Chris had the right to know about Darious, and it was best, and more respectable, that he heard it from her mouth instead of someone else's. She knew it was just a matter of time before Outlaw or one of his friends said something.

Chris walked out onto the visiting room floor with the standard federal-issued khaki set, his freshly groomed haircut, and tan Timberland boots. He looked so good, Tammy almost forgot what she came there to do. Chris, however, quickly reminded her of her mission when he walked over and took his seat without even attempting to give her a hug.

"Wow, no hug, no kiss?" Tammy asked.

"Nah, I'm good. Wassup wit' you, Tammy?" Chris asked in a nonchalant way, sitting back in his chair.

"You want something to drink or something to eat?"

"Tammy, why are you here?" he asked, cutting her off.

This was going to be harder than she'd thought. It was obvious that Outlaw had beat her to it. She didn't see a way to break the ice and have this conversation, but he was already five steps ahead of her.

"Are y'all together? I mean, are you in a relationship with this nigga?" Chris asked, getting straight to it.

Tammy paused before answering. "Something like that," she said, putting her head down in shame. She could see the disappointment and hurt in Chris's eyes. "I was tired of being alone," she spoke softly, trying to hold back her tears.

She knew that what she was revealing to Chris was killing him, and the last thing she wanted to do was hurt the person she'd been in love with for years. The pain increased almost immediately in Chris's eyes and, for a second, Tammy thought about getting up and leaving the visiting room. She could barely stand to look at him. In all their time together, she had never seen Chris cry. He was always a rock with his emotions.

"Do you love him?" Chris asked, wanting to know the whole truth of the matter.

That's when it hit Tammy. She couldn't hold back the tears, and as they fell from her eyes, Chris knew that his worst fears had come true. Tammy couldn't even speak. All she did was nod her head up and down, as she wiped the tears from her cheek. Chris felt like all the air had been removed from his chest. Even when the judge had given him his sentence, he took it on the chin. But the reality of losing the one woman he really loved and the mother of his children was overwhelming, and his eyes began to fill up with water.

"I'm sorry," Tammy managed to get out, looking over at Chris, who wiped his eyes.

All kinds of thoughts ran through his mind. After the hurt, he felt anger. He wanted to jump up and beat Tammy's ass until the cops pulled him off of her, but he didn't. He knew he couldn't. He even thought about spitting in her face, but he didn't. Instead, Chris just kept his cool. He wiped his face and cleared his eyes then looked over at Tammy. He searched his mind for the words that he wanted to leave with her, if he never had the chance to say anything else.

"I wish you the best, Tammy," Chris said, then bit down on his bottom lip in frustration. "Take care of yourself," he continued, while getting up from his seat and walking off to the officer's station.

He terminated the visit, leaving Tammy sitting there in her sorrow. As he disappeared into the back, the reality of the situation hit Tammy like ton of bricks. It was no longer "Tammy and Chris." It had been that way as far back as she could remember. Even when they were in their roughest times, never in a million years did she think they would not be together. But, somehow, she had messed around and fallen in love with somebody else. She wasn't sure if it was fear or regret that was now setting in.

Lamar walked into the house singing "You" by Jesse Powell. He went upstairs and walked straight

to Kim's room, but she wasn't there. He checked
the bathroom and then the guest room in the back,
and still there was no sign of her. "Kim!" he yelled
out, then paused in the hallway, listening for a
response. Still nothing!

"Come on wit' da dumb shit," he said, walking
toward his room. "I know I ain't made this decision
and she done spent the night somewhere else," he
continued.

When he opened the door, Kim was lying in his
bed asleep with nothing but one of his T-shirts on.
He walked over and sat on the edge of the bed,
waking Kim out of her sleep. She opened her eyes
to see Lamar looking down at her with a smirk on
his face. Seeing her lying there so peaceful brought
happiness to his heart, and it was at that point he
understood that his heart had made the choice for
him and not his dick.

"Is this what you want?" Kim asked in a soft
tone.

Lamar reached over and removed some hair
that was covering part of her face. The more he
looked at her, the more his heart was content and
at ease. He had never felt this way before, and it
felt good.

"Please don't hurt me, Kim," Lamar said with
pleading eyes.

Kim sat up in the bed and placed her chin on
Lamar's shoulder. She could feel his concerns

without him even having to say them. In a sense, she felt the same way, and didn't want to be hurt, but everything was telling her that Lamar was the one for her.

"I love you, Lamar, and I promise you that I will do everything in my power to protect your heart. I just need your all in return," she said, wrapping her arms around his waist.

Lamar turned to face her, kissing her softly and laying her back on the bed. He climbed on top of her, positioning himself between her legs. Looking down at her felt so right. This was surely where he belonged.

"I love you, Kimberly Levin," he said before kissing her yet again, this time with more passion.

To consummate their newfound bond, Lamar made love to Kim for the rest of morning, only stopping for water and bathroom breaks. It was probably the most intense sexual moment either one of them had ever experienced, and for the record, they enjoyed every last second of it.

The ride back from the jail seemed like forever in Tammy's eyes. She had more than enough on her mind, and really didn't feel like doing anything but going home and getting in the bed. Breaking up with Chris was by far the hardest thing she'd ever had to do. It seemed like she missed him now more than ever. The one thing Tammy was certain of was that it was over. She knew Chris well enough to know that he was so prideful he would never want to be with her again. That hurt Tammy more than anything, and the more she thought about it, the more she started to question if she had done the right thing.

Hearing her phone ring, Tammy almost broke her neck trying to get it out of her bag. A part of her was hoping it was Chris calling, so she could talk to him, but it wasn't. It was Darious, someone she really didn't feel like talking to right now, but she answered it anyway.

"Yeah," Tammy answered, looking out the window at cars passing by the van.

"Are you okay?" Darious asked, hearing the sadness in her voice.

"I'm a little stressed out right now, but I'll be all right," Tammy responded. "Wassup wit' you?"

Darious was aware of her intent to tell Chris about them. They had spoken about it the night before, and even though Darious told her it wasn't necessary, Tammy had insisted on doing it anyway. Darious kind of figured today wasn't going to be a good day for her.

"Look, I got a lot of stuff to take care of today, so if you wanna talk, then just call me after eight o'clock tonight. Also, I know you gotta go to work tomorrow, but I need you to call in sick," Darious said.

"Why, what's going on?"

"Try not to ask too many questions. I'll be there in the morning to pick you up. I'll tell you everything when I get there," Darious explained. "So let me get out of here. I'll talk to you later. I love you."

"I love you too," Tammy responded instinctively. She didn't know what it was, but Darious had her wide open. He always seemed to brighten up the worst days Tammy had. Plus, he was so understanding when it came down to her relationship with Chris. That's probably the reason it was so easy for Tammy to have fallen in love with him. It was wrong in a sense, but it felt so good to love and be loved back. This was life.

For the rest of the ride home, Tammy took her mind off Chris and thought about Darious and what in the world he had planned. Whatever it was, Tammy knew that it was something special. Darious never fell short when it came to surprises and trying to please her. That was one of the many things she liked about him. Never in her life did anyone ever cater to her the way that Darious did, not even Chris. It was as if he made Tammy the center of his world, and he didn't just run off at the mouth saying it. Darious really showed how he felt through his actions.

Falisha sat in her bedroom windowsill looking over at Kim and Lamar's house. She started to call him and curse him out for not coming straight to her apartment when he got home, but she thought against it, even though she felt some type of way. The Victoria's Secret lingerie set and pair of Christian Louboutin heels she had on all night looked amazing on her. He didn't know it, but Lamar had really missed out on something epic last night.

"Don't call now, nigga," Falisha said, looking across the room at her cell phone vibrating on the nightstand.

She walked over to grab it, ready to give Lamar a piece of her mind. The only thing was, it wasn't Lamar calling. It was Fox. Falisha answered it, interested only to see what he had to talk to her about.

"Oh, now you wanna follow instructions," Falisha playfully answered, as she sat on the bed.

"Well, you know Obama said that change is good," Fox replied with a laugh. "You know, I was thinking about you the other day."

"And what was ya little nasty mind thinking?" Falisha asked, rolling off her fishnets.

"It didn't have anything to do with sex. I thought about how much I miss having you around. You wasn't just my girl. I seen you as good friend, believe it or not."

She knew that Fox had game for days and it came in many forms, but this was new. It actually sounded sincere, and it had Falisha thinking. She kind of missed chillin' with Fox also. Despite all the drama she had to go through with his many, many side pieces, Fox really did know how to make a girl feel wanted.

"Look, I got a party coming up next weekend, and I was wondering if you could come out and support me, you know, as a friend?" Fox asked.

Falisha thought about it. She didn't want to make Lamar mad but, at the same time, she did want to show Fox some support. *He's not asking to sleep with me, and who says Lamar has to find out anyway?* Besides, Falisha was a party animal, and she knew that if Fox rented out a club, it was going to be bananas.

"Let me see what I got going on that weekend. If I'm free, then I'll come through," Falisha told him. "I'll let you know in a couple of days. Is that cool?"

"Yeah, that's cool, baby girl. Make sure you do that so I can have ya VIP passes ready for you. And if you wanna bring ya boyfriend wit' you, that's cool, too. I don't got no ill feelings toward him," Fox assured her.

This definitely wasn't the Fox Falisha knew. The change that he was talking about became more apparent in his words and, oddly, it was somewhat attractive to her. It wasn't to the point where she thought about getting back with him or anything;

she just admired the maturity in an older man. It was definitely a good look on Fox.

"A'ight, Fox, I'll give you a call," Falisha said.

"A'ight, baby girl; and don't hesitate to call me if you need anything," Fox ended before hanging up the phone.

Chapter 27

Lisa and Naomi headed out the door, ready to start their day. Lisa had adjusted her work schedule in order to be able to take Nomi to school in the morning. It used to be Ralphy's job, but just like everything else in her life, she now had to learn how to adapt.

"Mommy, look," Naomi yelled, pointing to the street.

Ralphy had pulled up, getting all the attention from the little kids on their way to school. His Range Rover was a head turner, like most luxury vehicles rolling through the hood.

"Daddy!" Naomi yelled, running up and jumping into his arms when he got out of the SUV.

"Hi, princess," he said giving her two fat-faced kisses.

Lisa wanted to run up and kiss him too, but opted to just say hello with a smile. This was the hard part for her, standing there in front of him while he stood there looking sexy as hell to her. "You gon' take ya princess to school this morning?" Lisa asked, smiling at how much Naomi looked just like him.

"Yeah, I think I can do that. I really don't have much to do today. If it's okay, I'll probably pick her up, too. What do you think about us going out for dinner?" Ralphy asked as he put Naomi in the back seat.

"I think that would be nice," Lisa answered.

"I might as well take you to work too, then pick you up after I get Naomi. After dinner, I can bring both of you home," Ralphy suggested.

Lisa wasn't about to protest that in the least. This was a big step in their relationship, and she was more than willing for them to spend time together as a family. Naomi needed that, so did Lisa, and, in all honesty, Ralphy needed it too.

"Wake up sleepyhead," Lamar said, tapping Kim on the shoulder. "You gon' be late for work." He laughed.

Kim cracked her eyes open and Lamar cupped his hand over his nose and made a stinky face. She punched him in the stomach for teasing her about her morning breath.

"Boy, my breath don't stink," she defended, puckering up her lips for a kiss. "Stop playing," she said after Lamar backed away from her.

He leaned back in and kissed her anyway, and to his surprise, her breath really didn't stink nor did her tongue taste salty. That was something new he didn't know about her, and it was pleasing to find out that he could wake up every morning to her kiss. "So what time are you going on ya lunch break today?" Lamar asked, climbing out of bed.

"Why, you gon' bring me something to eat?" Kim asked.

"I was thinking about it. Just call me and let me know what you want me to get you," he said, heading for the shower.

Kim stretched and yawned, then got out of the bed to join Lamar in the shower. When she got to the bathroom, Lamar was sitting on the toilet taking a shit. He looked up in shock when she walked in. Kim laughed at his facial expression.

"We are a couple now. You don't got no privacy anymore." Kim laughed, climbing into the already steaming shower. "And since I'm on the topic of us officially being a couple, when are you going to tell her?" Kim yelled through the running shower water.

Lamar hurried up and wiped his ass then joined Kim in the shower. This was the first time he'd been in the shower with Kim, and the way the water beaded off her body made his dick hard. She was looking so sexy.

"I'ma get around to it. You know I'm not the kind of guy who intentionally hurts others. I just wanna do it at the right time," Lamar said, wrapping his arms around Kim under the water.

The only reason Kim didn't object to his way of doing things was because she kind of felt the same way. Falisha was a very close friend of hers, if not her best friend, and when she found out that Kim and Lamar were together, it was going to hurt, despite how much Falisha would try to deny it. Kim knew she didn't want to be the one to tell her, so she would respect Lamar's timeline in revealing their relationship.

"I love you, boy," Kim said, turning around to face him.

She looked down at his rock-hard dick and couldn't help herself. She moved from the front to the back of the shower, out from under the water. Lamar's eyes followed her as she bent straight over and held on to the edge of the tub. Her soft, wet, pink pussy spread apart, giving him a clear shot of it. A good, stiff dick was exactly what she needed to get her day started, and Lamar was more than happy to provide it for her.

Darious pulled up to Tammy's house with another car following him. Darious wasn't in the streets like that, but he did have a couple of his close friends who were, and they didn't mind putting in work for him. When Darious got out of the car, so did they, and there wasn't a question as to whether they had guns on them, because they were clearly visible, poking out of their waistline.

They stood in front of Tammy's house like they were guarding the president.

"Why you ain't dressed yet?" Darious asked when Tammy came to the door looking like she had just woken up.

"I'm sorry. I fell back to sleep when I took Anthony to school and dropped the baby off at the daycare center," Tammy said, stepping to the side so he could come in. Tammy looked outside and saw the two thugs standing in front of her door, then she walked back into the house with Darious. "What's going on?" she asked, walking up to him.

"It's nothing. Just hurry up and get dressed. We got somewhere to be in less than an hour," he said, leaning in and giving Tammy a kiss.

Having already taken a shower that morning, Tammy went upstairs and got dressed. About ten minutes later, she was back downstairs and they were heading out the door. It didn't take long for Tammy to look up and see that they were on the highway.

"So where are you taking me today?" Tammy smiled, reaching over and softly scratching the side of Darious's head.

"You said you love me, right?" he asked, looking in his rearview mirror before getting off on the exit.

"Of course I do, babe," she answered.

"Well, I love you too, and I wanna be able to chill wit' you without having to look over my shoulders, wondering if ya baby father's brother gon' shoot me. I wanna be able to spend the night wit' you and not rush to get up and leave in the morning because it's checkout time at the hotel," Darious said.

"I understand how ya feel, but how do you plan on fixin' that?" she asked with a curious look on her face.

"Look around, Tammy," Darious told her, pointing out the window "We're twenty-five minutes away from the hood, and look at your surroundings."

She looked out of the window and noticed the quiet suburban area Darious was driving through. It wasn't too upscale for the average white family to live in, but it was definitely better than the rough, drug-infested neighborhood Tammy had lived in all her life. It was hard for her to deny wanting to live in a better community. Her only problem was deciding if she was ready to move into a house with Darious this early in their relationship. Before Tammy could even bring up that issue, Darious pulled into the garage of the first house he had on his three-house viewing agenda for the day.

"Wow," Tammy said, getting out of the car and looking at the beautiful townhouse.

Tammy looked at Darious then back at the house. She could already picture herself coming home from work and sticking her key in the front door. So far, Darious didn't fall short in any aspect of being a real man, and Tammy could see that he wasn't going to make it easy for her to deny packing up her things and moving in with him.

After Kim went to work, Lamar tried to get some sleep, since he had been up all night and most of the morning. The doorbell ringing really put a monkey wrench in his plan, especially since he was almost 100 percent sure who it was. He started not to answer, but that wouldn't have done him any good, because Falisha wasn't going to let him sleep anyway.

He shot downstairs and answered the door, and there she was, standing there with a miniskirt and tank top on, and some Chuck Taylors on her feet. Lamar couldn't lie. She was making basic hood clothes look oh so good. He thought about how good her body always felt, and just her standing there made his dick start to get hard.

"Nigga, where you been all night?" Falisha asked, brushing right by him and walking into the house. "Did Kim go to work yet?" she asked, already knowing the answer.

"You know she's gone already. Ay, listen. While you're here, I need to talk to you about something," Lamar said, taking a seat on the arm of the couch.

Falisha didn't pay him any mind. She walked over to Lamar and straddled him on the couch. She began kissing him with small pecks against his lips, which he was finding difficult to deny. She went from his lips to his neck, and for a moment, he almost forgot what he needed to talk to her about.

"Hold up, Falisha. Chill for a second," Lamar said, pulling his neck away from her lips.

It was as if Falisha wasn't hearing anything Lamar was saying. When she got into her sex zone, there wasn't too much that could stop her. She pulled her tank top over her head, allowing her bare chest to flop out. Feeling them against his chest had Lamar at his breaking point. His dick was so hard, and Falisha could feel it through his sweat pants, right at the entry point of her pussy. She looked at him and bit down on her bottom lip in a seductive manner.

"Stop playing, boy. You know you want this pussy," she said, standing up and dropping her skirt to the ground. "I'm wet as hell." She smirked.

Lamar couldn't take it anymore. It was like his brain shut down and his dick started running the show. In a lustful rage, he jumped up from the couch, grabbed Falisha by her throat and her waist and lifted her in the air. She wrapped her legs around his waist and held on to the back of his neck as he walked her across the room to the nearest wall. He slammed her up against it, dropped his sweatpants and pushed his dick deep inside of her. Mad at himself and at Falisha for seducing him like this, he viciously fucked her to the point where she could barely take the dick. He pounded away, making sure every inch of his meat dug inside of her. Falisha yelled out in both pain and pleasure, and within a few minutes of Lamar giving her the business, they both exploded at the same time: Falisha all over him, and Lamar all inside of her; but unlike every sex session that seemed so amazing between them, this one had a very heavy price tag on it. A price that Lamar knew he probably couldn't afford.

Chapter 28

"Scoop, what it do, my nigga?" Manny greeted him, hopping out of his black Yukon Denali.

Manny was from the west side, but had grown up all over Charlotte, and pretty much knew everybody. Scoop used to score dope from him awhile back when things dried up. He had some good prices, too. Ralphy had put a halt to all that once he got back in the game, so it had been a minute since Manny had been around this way.

"Tell me something good," Scoop said, giving him dap.

"I know ya boy Ralphy got da block back, but I thought you should know that I got dat work for da low, low," Manny said, lighting up a cigarette. "Whenever you ready to do ya own thing, just let me know. I got a steady connect who's blessing me right now. I can get you right. All you gotta do is give me the word."

Scoop looked at all the dopefiend traffic walking up and down the block and thought how much he wanted his block back. Ralphy had his claws dug in deep, and he wasn't trying to let go. Scoop was making good money too, just not as much as Ralphy was.

"Ay, yo. You remember da boy Dre who got killed on the other side?" Scoop asked.

"Yeah, yeah. Good dude, just gave back a life sentence before coming home," Manny said, nodding his head.

"Yeah, well, homicide detectives came around here asking a bunch of questions. They think Ralphy had something to with that. Between me and you, I don't think my boy gon' be out here much longer," Scoop added.

"Damn, you sure about that?" Manny asked, picking up on where Scoop was going with his comment.

"Yeah, they said he stood over Dre and hit him up close range. Punk-ass police asked me if I gave him the gun to do it. I said, 'Hell no.'" Scoop chuckled.

Scoop didn't have to talk direct in order for Manny to understand that Ralphy was the one who killed Dre, and Scoop was the one who supplied the gun and was possibly there. Scoop wasn't trying to get Ralphy locked up directly, but he knew that if Manny spread the rumors to the right people, niggas was going to be gunning for Ralphy. With Ralphy all the way out of the way, Scoop could get his block back and probably be the number one man on the east side. Now that he had Manny ready to supply him with whatever he needed, there was no need for him to keep pinching pennies and riding Ralphy's coattails. It was time for a change. This was the part of the game Ralphy had forgotten about; but he was going to be reminded of in the worst way, real soon.

Falisha sat in the waiting area at the OB/GYN clinic waiting for her name to be called. A lot of unprotected sex had been going on between her and Lamar, and since Falisha knew that Lamar and Kim were also having unprotected sex, it was time for her to get checked out for any STD she could have contracted from them.

"Hey, Linda," Falisha greeted her, walking into the room. She and her doctor were on first-name basis since Falisha didn't hesitate when it came down to her health. After changing into her gown, lying back on the table, and getting an STD swab, Falisha sat there and waited for her results. After about twenty minutes, Linda came back into the room.

"You got a clean bill of health, Falisha," Linda said, looking at her clipboard. "Now, here's your vitamins. Take one a day. Studies show that babies mature better when the mother takes her—"

"Wait, did you just say 'baby'?" Falisha interrupted.

"Oh, my God! You didn't know that you were pregnant?" Linda asked. "You're about six weeks along."

"I can't be. I just had my period about two weeks ago." Falisha laughed, thinking it had to be a mistake.

After Linda explained to Falisha that it was possible for her to get pregnant and still have some bleeding, the laughing stopped. Falisha sat there on the patient table and let her head drop into her hands. She didn't know what she was about to do, and for the next fifteen to twenty minutes she continued sitting there, allowing the shocking news to settle in.

Tammy sat on her bed, looking at the set of keys Darious had just passed her, and still couldn't believe that he had rented out a three-bedroom home in the country for them to live in. He put Tammy's name on the lease along with his, just to let it be known that they were in this together.

"What about my kids? Chris is going to always be in their lives and so will his family. I don't wanna bring that kind of drama out there," Tammy said, looking over at Darious standing by the window.

"Look, we can keep this as a front. His family can still come over here to check up on the kids but, at nighttime, I need you home with me," Darious explained.

"And how long is that supposed to go on?" Tammy asked.

"Until ya baby father and the rest of his family get it through their head that I'm not going anywhere." Darious meant every word of it, too. The lengths he was willing to go in order to be with Tammy had no boundaries, and Tammy was loving the fact that she had somebody like him willing to stand up and fight to be with her.

"Come here," he said, walking over and grabbing her hand and pulling her off the bed.

When they got downstairs, Darious reached in his pocket and pulled out his car keys. Tammy looked at him with one eyebrow up. She wondered what he was up to now. They both walked out onto the front steps. Darious's two homies were still standing in front of the house and, in the middle of the street, Darious's white Dodge Charger was double parked.

"Dis ya car now," he said, separating his house keys from his car keys and passing them to her. "This is so you can get back and forth from here to home whenever you need to. I'll transfer the title over to your name when I get off of work tomorrow," Darious said, leaning in and giving her a kiss. "It's team us. Is you wit' me?" Darious asked, sticking his fist out for a dap.

Tammy dapped him, looked into his eyes, and smiled. She threw her arms around his neck and pulled him down to give him another kiss. "Yeah, it's team us," she confirmed, kissing him yet again.

Just when Tammy was in a state of bliss, she looked down the block and saw an all-black Chevy Impala creeping up. Knowing whose car it was, Tammy tapped Darious for him to pay attention to what was about to go down. Outlaw was back on his bullshit again but, this time, Darious was on point.

"Now don't be over here cryin' an' shit," Ms. D said, walking into the room where Falisha sought refuge. "Women get pregnant every day. All the fun and games are over. It's time to put on ya big girl panties now," she said, taking a seat in her love chair.

"I don't even know if I'ma keep it," Falisha said, wiping the tears from her face.

Ms. D shook her head, reached over, and grabbed her stash of weed from the corner of her chair. Ms. D always was and always would be against abortion, except for in certain situations like rape or incest. Other than those two things, she felt like a baby being terminated was an act of cowardice.

"You listen to me, Falisha, and you listen good," Ms. D said in a serious manner while she poured some weed into her rolling papers. "That is a blessing from God, and He don't give you more than you can bear. That baby you got forming in ya stomach didn't do nothing to you. You was woman enough to lie down and spread those legs, so be woman enough to become a mother as a result of those fifteen minutes of glory you enjoyed so much. What if your mother didn't wanna have you?" Ms. D asked, rolling the joint up and licking the tip.

"Lamar ain't ready for no baby," Falisha spoke.

"Well, that's Lamar's problem. He'll get his mind right; and if he don't, oh well. Plenty of women have done it by themselves. That baby is going to have you in its life, and that's all he or she really need," Ms. D said, lighting up her joint and taking a puff.

Falisha looked at Ms. D in confusion. Despite the good jewels she had dropped on her, Falisha was trying to figure out why Ms. D was smoking weed. Her whole time of knowing Ms. D, she had never seen her smoking weed, and here she was blowing it out of her nose like a steam dragon.

Ms. D had forgotten that she didn't tell the girls about her cancer. She wanted to, but she still wasn't up for the pity party she knew was coming after she revealed it. She sat there thinking about it while Falisha waited for an explanation. She realized that she wasn't going to be able to hide it forever. So, as an afterthought, she made it known.

"I have cancer, Falisha."

***

Outlaw and Ratchet got out of the car, but only Outlaw walked over to where Darious and Tammy were standing. Ratchet stood between the passenger side door with a Mack-90, as he was instructed by Outlaw. Darious gave his boys a look, letting them know that drama was approaching. They both put their hands on the butts of their guns sitting on their waists. Outlaw noticed it, but didn't care, nor did he show any signs of fear. He walked right past them and right up to Darious and Tammy. If looks could kill, Tammy and Darious would have been dead by now, 'cause all they were getting from Outlaw was the mean mug.

"So, my brotha tells me to leave you alone and you free to be wit' whoever you wanna be wit'," Outlaw told Tammy, but looked over at Darious. "He's not gon' call you, write you, or bother you about seeing the kids while he's locked up. I also give you my word that I'm not gon' mess with you or your sucka-ass boyfriend. But you can rest assured that I'll be over here to check on my niece and nephew often. I shouldn't have to tell you what I'll do if you ever put ya hands on one of them," he said, looking at Darious.

Darious was silent. Tammy was so shocked at everything he said, she didn't even know how to respond. What she did know was that everything that came out of Outlaw's mouth came from Chris, and if this was what he said, then this was what it would be. Outlaw was about to walk off, but stopped and turned back around. He had something else he wanted to get off his chest.

"You know, I'm kinda glad my brotha finally finished with you. The nigga really loved you too much. Y'all been together all these years, and from day one he took care of ya ungrateful ass. He sacrificed his life out here on these streets to make sure you and his kids didn't struggle. Yeah, he could have been a bitch-ass square sucka," he emphasized, looking at Darious. "But that wasn't him, and you damn sure didn't complain when all that money was rollin' in. But now since he's at the worst place in his life and you got the upper hand, you got the nerve to turn ya back on him. Of all people. Shit, to me that shows a lot about your character and the kind of woman you are. You couldn't even be there for him. That's foul, and I don't respect that. Some wife you are. Buddy, I hope you know what you getting." Outlaw smirked. "Good luck with dis chick," he told Darious before walking off.

Darious was going to set him straight, but figured he would leave well enough alone. He knew what he had in Tammy, and there was no need to try to tell a nigga like Outlaw what he or his brother couldn't see.

Chapter 29

"Ralphy, what are you doing here?" Lisa asked, surprised, when she walked out into the waiting room and saw him sitting there reading a magazine.

"Did you forget I had an appointment to get my teeth cleaned today? This is still my dentist's office right?" Ralphy smiled, putting the magazine down.

Lisa smiled, too, and walked over to the receptionist desk to check the log. He wasn't lying. It was for today at two o'clock. "I'm sorry. Come on to the back," she directed, leading the way to the second room near the rear of the office.

Small procedures like cleanings were minor enough for Lisa to handle by herself. Ralphy knew this too; that's why he didn't mind when Lisa put on her mask and latex gloves and began adjusting the chair.

"Hold up. Before you get started, I know I really haven't been around that much, and I know you been handling the bills all by yourself. So, here, I got a li'l something for you," Ralphy said, coming from under his cape with a brown envelope. "I'ma start dropping you off something every week for you and Naomi," he continued.

"Thank you. I really do appreciate it," Lisa responded with a huge smile.

They stood there and had a moment, staring into each other's eyes. No matter what had transpired, both knew that they would forever have love for one another. Lisa had always been Ralphy's one true love, and now with Dre dead, Ralphy was the only man alive Lisa had ever wanted. The intense mood was interrupted by a loud commotion coming from the waiting room. Lisa walked to the door and peeked down the hallway to see if she could hear what was going on. Out of nowhere, two men with hoods over their heads and automatic pistols clutched in their hands came walking down the short hallway. They kicked in doors as they passed them by, as if they were looking for somebody.

"Oh, shit," Lisa whispered, backing up into the room.

Ralphy saw the fear of God in her eyes, causing him to jump up from his chair.

"They got guns," Lisa told him in a low tone, hoping they didn't hear her.

Ralphy pulled his gun from his waist, and by the time he spun around to head for the door, there was a loud sound and he felt a bullet strike him in his left shoulder. Ralphy stumbled backward, but not before firing his weapon and hitting one of the gunmen in the chest. The other shooter dipped behind the partition, but stuck his arm inside the room and let off at least another eight rounds, hoping one of the eight hit Ralphy. The gunman got himself together and darted down the hallway toward the exit.

"Ralphy," Lisa called out, sitting on the floor in the corner with both of her hands over her stomach.

Ralphy was in pain, but he needed to make sure that the threat was neutralized. He walked over to the gunman who he had shot in the chest, stood over him, and fired another round into his head.

"Ralphy!" Lisa called out again, now lying on her side.

Ralphy ran over to her, laid his gun down, and sat her up. When he moved her hands, he could see the blood on her coat. He wasn't sure where exactly she had been hit, because by now both of them were covered in blood. From the look she had on her face, Ralphy knew that the bullet was starting to burn, just like the bullet that hit him in his shoulder was.

"Look, baby, just hold on. Help is on the way." Ralphy was concerned, but he also knew that a situation like this could turn ugly from a legal standpoint quickly. "Listen to me, Lisa. You gotta say that I wrestled the gun out of this guy's hand," Ralphy said, pointing to the guy lying dead in the hallway. "Remember, babe, he had two guns and I took one," he said again.

Ralphy was thinking on his toes, getting his story right before the cops got there. Trying to explain a dead body could be hard, and even though he was protecting himself and his wife, self-defense didn't work too well when you were a black man.

"I need a doctor! I need a doctor!" Ralphy yelled out. "Somebody help me!" he continued yelling.

The only person who had courage to come down that hallway was Dr. Mathew, one of the dentists. He was only a dentist, but he knew his way around the medical block. If Lisa had any chance of making it, Ralphy was going to have to get out of the way and let the Doc do what he could.

Tammy and Falisha had decided to go to the mall to relieve some stress. So much had been going on in their lives, and the only thing that could make them feel better was to shop. It wasn't just a few items here and a few items there; they really were getting it in like money wasn't an issue.

"Wow, girl, you really about to be a mom?" Tammy said as they sat at the food court, eating.

"Yeah. I'm scared as shit, too. I don't know the first thing about being a mom," Falisha responded.

"I didn't neither, but as soon as I pushed that big head—ass boy out of my little vagina, my motherly instincts kicked in, and everything came to me like second nature. You gon' be a'ight, I promise you. Now the million dollar question is who in the hell is the daddy?" Tammy grinned, pointing her cheesy breadstick at Falisha.

The only person who knew that Lamar was the father was Ms. D. Falisha wasn't sure how she was going to tell Lamar, and feared that he would either deny it or tell Falisha he wasn't ready to be a father. She wanted to wait for the right time to do it, and since Ms. D was having a dinner for everybody tomorrow, she figured that would be a good time. So, for now, Tammy was going to have to wait to find out.

"You'll find out along with everybody else, at Ms. D's dinner," Falisha said, stuffing her face with funnel cake and ice cream. "Until then I need you to keep this between me and you."

"A'ight, girl, no problem. But you better make me the godmother, or I swear as soon as you have that baby, we gon' fight," Tammy joked.

They shared a laugh then went back to eating.

Kim and Lamar ran through the hospital, straight for the emergency room in search of Lisa and Ralphy. Before the ambulance and police got to the dentist's office, Lisa made Ralphy call Kim so she could pick Naomi up from school. After dropping Naomi off at Ms. D's house, Kim grabbed Lamar and headed for the hospital.

Unfortunately, Lisa and Ralphy were still in surgery by the time they arrived.

"Who in the hell could have done something like this?" Kim asked, wiping the tears from her eyes.

Lamar pulled her in and held her. "Everything is going to be all right," he told her in an attempt to comfort her fears.

They waited there for hours before the nurse came out to the waiting room and informed them that Lisa was out of surgery. Although he was only shot in his shoulder, Ralphy had lost a lot of blood. The bullet went in and out, but Ralphy had been so focused on making sure Lisa was okay, he hadn't thought to apply pressure to his wound to stop his bleeding. He was now in the process of receiving a blood transfusion, on top of patching up his wound.

Kim walked into Lisa's room with her hand over her mouth in shock at the many tubes that were sticking out of her girl. Lisa was out of surgery for now, but not yet out of trouble. The bullet had penetrated her spleen, causing massive internal damage. It was going to take several more surgeries in order to remedy the problem. For now, the doctors wanted her to get some rest and allow her body to heal from the first surgery before they went back in.

"It can't be that bad," Lisa said in a groggy voice when she cracked open her eyes.

Kim dropped her hand from her mouth and smiled. "You know I wanna rock that outfit," Kim joked, tugging at Lisa's hospital gown.

"Where is everybody?" Lisa asked, looking around the room. "Naomi?"

"She's wit' Ms. D. When I leave here, I'ma take her to my house. Lamar just went to check up on Ralphy."

"How is he?" Lisa asked in a weak voice.

"He's doing a lot better, but—"

Before Kim could finish her sentence, Falisha and Tammy busted into the room. "Oh, hell no. We came as soon as we heard what happened," Falisha said, putting her shopping bags down and walking over to the bed. "How is she?" Falisha turned and asked Kim, while hovering over Lisa.

"I see y'all bitches went shopping wit'out me?" Lisa asked jokingly. "Y'all better have something—"

"Shhhhh! Don't be worrying about that. You try to get some rest, girl," Tammy said, walking over and grabbing Lisa's hand.

Lisa smiled. It felt good having her girls all around her, even though she was in hospital. She could feel the medicine kicking in, and although she could hear the conversation, she began to drift back off to sleep.

The girls just sat around the bed talking quietly among themselves. Nobody could figure out why somebody would have done this to them. Not to mention at Lisa's job for that matter.

"Yo, I just came from Ralphy's room," Lamar said, coming into the room. "He's awake but the homicide detectives are down there questioning him. They're on their way down here, too."

Falisha jumped up from her chair and tried to kiss Lamar, but only came away with a hug. He turned his head when she tried to kiss him and he informed her that now wasn't the time. She looked at him with an obvious attitude written all over her face. Kim turned her head, trying not to smile from the way Lamar had dismissed her. She knew that Lamar hadn't told Falisha about them, and she was tempted to do it herself, but Lamar stepped up before she could.

"Let me talk to you out here for a second," Lamar told Falisha, pulling her by the arm.

Now was probably a bad time, but he knew he had to handle this immediately. He was tired of hiding and playing games about what was going on. He had love for Falisha, but now it was time for him to draw the line. Once they had gotten far enough from Lisa's door, Lamar took a deep breath and began.

"I really don't know how to explain this, so I'm going to get right to the point. This right here between me and you has to stop. You know I got love for you as a friend, and I hope we can continue to be that. But as far as anything more is concerned, that can't happen. Also, before you hear this from somebody else, I want to let you know first: me and Kim are together."

"Nigga, are you fucking serious?" Falisha asked, cocking her head back.

"Look, I didn't mean for it to happen like this," Lamar tried to explain. He knew that Falisha was about to snap. He expected her to make a scene right then and there, but to his surprise, she didn't say another word. Instead, Falisha turned, walked back into the room, and grabbed her bags. Lamar kept his eyes on her the whole time, just in case she started swinging on Kim.

"Please call me if anything changes with Lisa or Ralphy. And congratulations," she told Kim before walking out of the room.

The whole room was quiet. Tammy didn't know what was going on, and it showed by the confused look she had on her face. "What's up with that?" Tammy asked, still confused. Neither Kim nor Lamar said anything. "Well, she came with me, so let me make sure she gets home okay," Tammy said, grabbing her bags and heading out of the room.

The homicide detectives asked Ralphy question after question about what happened at the dental office. They even threatened to lock him up if he didn't tell them the truth, but Ralphy stuck to his guns and told them the same story he told the first responding officers when they got there. Two men came into the room and one of them began shooting. Ralphy wrestled the gun away from one of them and began firing back, dropping the man to the ground. The second gunman fired several more shots into the room blindly before taking off down the hallway. Ralphy said that when he went into the hallway to make sure the other gunman was gone, the shooter who was on the ground pulled out another gun, and that's when Ralphy shot him in the head. That was his story and he was sticking to it. Lisa gave the same story to another officer who rode with her to the hospital. The detectives didn't believe the whole story, but really they couldn't do anything, since both had the same version. After a few more questions, they left him and Lisa alone, calling it a justifiable homicide.

"Falisha! Falisha!" Tammy yelled, coming out of the hospital. "Wait up!"

When Tammy caught up to Falisha, she was crying and arguing with herself about something.

"What's going on wit' you?" she asked, getting Falisha to turn and face her.

Falisha looked at her, wiping the tears from her eyes. "Did you know?" Falisha asked.

"Know what?" Tammy responded in confusion. "What are you talking about?"

"Kim and Lamar being together," Falisha responded.

Tammy was shocked. She never thought they would be together, especially knowing how much in love Lamar was with Falisha back in the day. Kim always stood firm on the "no dating the room-mate rule" and always denied ever having sex with Lamar, or looking at him in that way. One thing Tammy was aware of was the fact that Falisha had been seeing Lamar off and on for the past couple of months.

"Girl, don't stress over dat nigga. It's plenty of fine men out here," Tammy said to counsel her. "I'ma go get the car and take you home."

"My ride is on the way here," Falisha said, cutting Tammy off and looking down at her phone.

Before Tammy could say anything, Falisha was waving her hand in the air. Tammy turned around, and there Fox was, pulling up in his Cadillac truck.

"Falisha, let me take you home," Tammy suggested one more time, knowing that being with Fox was not such a good idea right now.

Falisha cracked a smile through her sadness, then leaned in and gave Tammy a hug. Even though she was trying, Falisha couldn't hold back the tears, and her reasons were understandable. "I'm pregnant by Lamar." She wiped the tears from her face. "He's my baby daddy," she said before turning around and walking to the passenger side of Fox's truck.

Tammy stood there stuck as she let what Falisha said register in her brain. As Fox's truck pulled off, Lamar walked out of the hospital to try to check up on Falisha. He noticed Fox's truck, and knew nine times out of ten, Falisha was in it. He turned to confirm it with Tammy, but she rolled her eyes at him in disgust and walked off. She really didn't have anything to say to him right now.

He just stood there with a stupid look on his face.

Chapter 30

Tammy looked back at Darious as he fucked her from behind like a rabbit. She moaned loudly, holding on to the headboard as she tried to throw her ass back at him. Darious was too much for her, though. He pushed her back in and arched her ass up, slowing his strokes down, but digging deeper into her guts.

"Ahhhh!" she cried out from both the pain and the pleasure of his long pole tapping against her back wall. "Oh, yes. I'm cumming, baby," she yelled, reaching under and rubbing her clit.

"Yeah, cum all over daddy dick," Darious encouraged her. "Who pussy is dis?" he said as he continued to stroke. "Who pussy is it?" he yelled again, raising his head and smacking down on the top of her ass.

Tammy's pussy tightened up around his dick then a burst of her juices spilled out onto his member. She cried out as the orgasm sent chills through her entire body. "Dis ya pussy, daddy," she managed to get out through the waves of pleasure.

Darious sped up his strokes, this time trying to chase down the nut that was brewing in his balls.

Tammy had that wet pussy, and her ass cheeks were soft as cotton. This was actually his second time about to let off. "Where you want it at?" he asked, feeling himself about to explode.

The first time, Darious pulled out and came all over her stomach, but the sheets had wiped most of it off. This time, Tammy was in the zone. She was still feeling the effects of her orgasm and knew what would make it feel even better.

"Cum all in dis pussy," she moaned, looking at him through the mirror on the wall, pounding away at it.

Darious did as he was instructed, erupting and shooting his warm, thick, creamy lava inside of her. The feeling of it extended Tammy's orgasm even further, and as she felt herself about to cum again, she pushed her ass back against him. She bit down on the pillow and damn near tore the headboard off from the pleasure. Her insides were so soft and wet, it pushed Darious's now semi-hard dick right out. He couldn't go back in if he wanted to. Collapsing on her back was the only thing he could do, and just like that, they both flopped down onto the bed.

Kim stood outside the women's clinic, hesitant about going inside. She watched as a car pulled up in front of the building and its hazards began to flash. Seconds later, a woman got out of the passenger side, apparently about six or seven months pregnant. She didn't look happy at all, carrying around her load. And to make matters even worse, this wasn't her first time being a mother. The loud yells and screams from the two kids in the back seat pierced Kim's ears, and a quick verbal lashing from the young mother followed swiftly. Kim stepped to the side and allowed the little boy to storm into the building. The mother and another five-year-old boy went in right behind him.

"Nah, I can't do it," Kim mumbled to herself, shaking her head as she walked through the lobby area.

Kim's mind was made up that she was wasn't going to keep the baby she had conceived about a month ago. All that unprotected sex she had been having with Lamar had caught up with her, and although the thought of motherhood entered her mind and felt kind of good for a moment, Kim had to be real with herself. She wasn't ready for a baby and, in her mind, neither was Lamar.

"Hi, how can I help you today?" the receptionist asked when Kim walked up to the desk.

She really didn't know how to say it, since this was her first time. She wanted to be as discreet as possible, not wanting her business to get out. "Do y'all do abortions here?" Kim asked in a low tone.

"Yes, we do. You need to fill out these forms and doctor will see you in a little while," the receptionist said, passing Kim the clipboard.

When Kim turned around, she felt like all eyes were on her. There had to be at least ten females in the small waiting room, most of whom were there for the same reason she was. Kim sat right next to the female who was yelling at little Marcus on their way into the building. Surprisingly, Marcus was sitting over in the children's playroom, playing quietly with his little brother.

"The first time is always hard," the female looked over and said to Kim. "My name is Jazz," she greeted her, sticking her hand out for a shake.

"Kim," Kim replied, accepting her hand. "How did you know?" she asked, wondering if it was that obvious.

"Girl, I'm very familiar with those forms you got on that clipboard." Jazz chuckled. "I swear I probably got the most fertile eggs in this city."

Kim smiled. "So why do I feel so bad?" Kim asked while looking around at the other females.

"Oh, that's just your motherly instinct kicking in. As women, we're naturally inclined to protect our young, so when we go against that, it feels wrong," Jazz explained.

Kim didn't know how much truth it held, but it definitely made a lot of sense. They sat there and talked until Jazz was called for her check-up. A few moments later, Kim's name was called. It felt like she was being led to the slaughterhouse as the nurse led her down the hallway, into one of the small rooms.

Tammy dismounted Darious and fell into the bed, exhausted and thirsty as hell. They had been in the house all morning, fucking then making love, then fucking again, right before making love for the final time.

Tammy couldn't feel nothing from the waist down, and Darious's dick felt like it caught a cramp from all the work it had put in. Neither of them could honestly say that they'd had that much sex in a morning's time before. It was incredible and intoxicating.

"You can't be doing this to me," Tammy said, pulling up under Darious. "You gon' get us both in trouble," she said, thinking about the unprotected sex they continued to have.

"I'm already in trouble." He smiled as he leaned down and kissed her on her forehead.

"What you mean by that?" she asked, looking up at him.

Darious turned on his side and faced her. In his eyes, Tammy was beautiful in every way. He didn't mind showing and telling Tammy constantly how much he loved her. "Every day I spend with you,

I fall deeper in love with you. I can't lie, shawty. I'm in too deep. You got my heart, and I don't plan on going anywhere anytime soon," Darious said, removing some hair from in front of her face.

When he spoke, Tammy could see the sincerity in his eyes. She could just feel the love pouring off him and, being honest with herself, she was falling deeper in love with him too as the days went by. He treated her like she was the only thing that mattered in this world, and for any woman who had a man like that, the feeling was good.

"Darious, I'm yours. I only ask you to do one thing for me," Tammy said, looking into his eyes. "Please don't hurt me," she told him as her eyes began to tear up.

All she could think about was how happy she was right now, and how she didn't want to lose Darious. Her tears came at the thought of them not being together. Tammy knew that it was true love because the only time she ever felt this way about a man was when she was with Chris, and now that she thought about it, Darious probably treated her better in the spoiling department. But when it came to the sex, Tammy had to be real with herself. Darious was a good lover, and his dick was a little longer than Chris's, but the truth of the matter was that Chris did some things sexually that Darious would never be able to compete with. Hell, Chris did some things to Tammy that even she couldn't explain. Her heart wasn't with him anymore, but that was one thing she couldn't take away from Chris. He was the truth in bed.

Since Kim was a walk-in, she couldn't get the abortion done the same day. The doctor took her blood samples and got Kim's medical history, all for the procedure scheduled for the next day. Kim was about seven to eight weeks pregnant, so the extraction wouldn't be difficult at all. The cost of it was $375, and that was with the anesthesia. The last thing she wanted to do was be awake and watch as her baby got sucked out of her through a tube.

On her way to her car, Kim looked through her phone to see who would pick her up from the doctor after the abortion. After being instructed that she couldn't drive, Kim immediately began to think. She even thought about just telling Lamar what was going on, but opted not to, out of fear of how he would feel about his baby being on the chopping block.

"Ms. D," Kim said, leaning against the driver's side door of the car.

"You better be calling me to let me know that you're on ya way to come get me and take me to my doctor's appointment," Ms. D shot back.

Ms. D had been sitting by the window waiting for Kim's car to pull up on the block. With all that was going on, and her covert mission to the abortion clinic, taking Ms. D to the doctor's had slipped her mind.

"I'm so sorry, Ms. D. I am on my way," Kim said, getting into the car. "Can you call and tell them that you're going to be a few minutes late?"

"Don't worry about it. I already called," Ms. D told her, not upset at all. "So besides that, what was you calling me for?" Ms. D asked, taking a bite of the celery stick she was munching on.

"I'm on my way to you right now. We'll talk then," Kim told her, looking both ways before pulling out of her parking spot.

Kim really didn't want to explain her whole situation over the phone anyway. It was personal. Ms. D needed to know how important it was for her to keep the pregnancy between them, and in order for that to happen, Kim needed to talk face to face. Sometimes Ms. D could be a chatterbox, especially when she had that devil juice in her.

Chapter 31

Naomi leaned over on her tiptoes and kissed Lisa on the cheek. It woke her up, and when Lisa cracked open her eyes, she gave her daughter a huge smile. Today was supposed to be the day Lisa was released from the hospital. She was doing a lot better, and had improved over the past two weeks. Her wound was healing well and the doctors were even optimistic about Lisa being able to have more children one day.

"Good morning!" Ralphy greeted her, getting up from his chair and walking over to her bedside. "You ready to go home?" he asked as he leaned over and kissed her forehead.

Lisa smiled. The thought of going home sounded good, but feeling Ralphy's lips on her skin felt even better. She couldn't believe that through every-thing that was going on right now, his lips was all she could think about. "Are you coming too?" Lisa asked, wanting to make sure he wasn't just talking about her and Naomi.

Every day, Ralphy sat in the hospital looking over at Lisa. He had a lot of time to think about the more important things in life, and at the top of his list was his family. He couldn't deny how much he missed being home, nor could he continue to hide how much he still loved Lisa.

"Yeah, I'm coming home too," he said, placing his free hand over hers.

Lisa was damn near ready to jump up out of the bed and get dressed. Tears began to run down her face. Hearing those words come from his mouth let Lisa know that there was still a chance for them to be back together, and if all it took was a bullet to the gut for Ralphy to come back home, Lisa would have volunteered to get shot months ago. Hell, being shot was a lesser pain than the pain she felt the day Ralphy walked out of her life. Whatever the case may be, Lisa was going to make the best out of this bad situation.

Tammy pulled up to Chris's mom's house with the kids to drop them off as she did every other weekend. Ms. Elaine couldn't front, though; Tammy was looking like a totally different woman from what she did a couple of months ago. Darious had her looking right. New car, new clothes, hair done just about every week, and even her attitude changed. She was way more confident in herself, and the stress bags that used to sit under her eyes had cleared up.

"Hey, Ms. Elaine," Tammy greeted her, walking up the steps with Sinniyyah in her arms.

"Grandma!" Anthony yelled out, running with the diaper bag over his shoulder.

When Tammy walked into the house, she was a little startled to run into Outlaw, who came out of the kitchen. In the living room sat Brea, Chris's older sister, who used to like Tammy until she found out that Tammy had left her brother.

"You do know that it's Thursday, right?" Ms. Elaine said, walking into the living room.

"Yeah, I know. Here," Tammy said, passing Ms. Elaine some money. "I got something to do. I'll be back Sunday night to get them," Tammy said in a nonchalant fashion, sitting Sinniyyah on Brea's lap like she was in a rush to get out the door.

Ms. Elaine looked at Tammy like she was crazy. She wasn't feeling Tammy's attitude one bit, and neither was Brea for that matter. When Tammy turned around to leave, she noticed the way Ms. Elaine was looking at her.

"What?" Tammy said, looking around the room. "If you don't wanna watch them, I can take them somewhere else," Tammy said with an attitude.

"Tammy, sit down," Ms. Elaine said, nodding to the empty seat next to Brea.

Tammy was feeling herself, but not that much to flat out disregard Ms. Elaine's request. She knew that in a split second it could get real ugly in that house.

"Now I don't know if you lost ya mind or you just don't have any respect for my son and this family, but don't come up in my house with passion marks all over your neck and throwing around money like you dat girl now. Now don't forget that my son took care of you and this family took you in when you didn't have shit. Anything you needed, I gave you, and I treated you like no less than my own daughter from day one," Ms. Elaine snapped.

Tammy sat there in silence listening to Ms. Elaine give it to her, but Tammy too had a lot of hostility built up inside, and wanted to share her thoughts. "I don't mean any disrespect, Ms. Elaine, and I hope you don't take it that way, but I am a grown-ass woman, and I don't owe nobody shit, not even Chris. Don't get me wrong, I love ya son, and I know everything he did for me. But let me tell you this, ya son left me out here by myself with two kids, and he ain't coming home no time soon. Forgive me if I'm moving on with my life," Tammy said, getting up from the couch. Tammy grabbed Sinniyyah from Brea's lap then called out for Anthony, who was upstairs.

"My niece and nephew don't have to go anywhere," Brea said, getting up from the couch and standing in front of the door.

Tammy looked at Brea like she wasn't a threat at all. Brea could fight her ass off, but Chris had taught Tammy how to get down too, so if it was about to get physical between the two, it was going to be a bout to remember.

"Brea!" Ms. Elaine shouted. "Get away from that door. If she wanna leave then let her go."

Just then, Anthony came down the steps with Outlaw, unaware of what had just happened. Tammy simply grabbed him by the hand and walked out the front door. After strapping Sinni-yyah into her car seat and putting the seat belt on Anthony, Tammy got into the car and pulled off, not even worried about the baby bag she had left in the house.

Lamar looked up from drying his car off to see Falisha coming out of the house. His car was parked right in front of her apartment, so it was impossible for Falisha to ignore him, much like she'd been doing as of late. She still didn't tell him that she was with child either, and that's because she wasn't sure if she was going to keep it.

"Wasssup, Falisha," Lamar greeted her, standing in front of her steps. "You gon' keep ignoring me or can we talk like two civilized adults?" he asked.

Falisha finished locking her front door then walked down the steps. She tried to brush by Lamar without saying anything to him. He grabbed her arm and stopped her. Falisha snatched her arm away from him then gave him a stern look. "Don't touch me. I'm good," she said then bumped him as she walked past him.

Lamar thought about chasing after her, but decided against it, not wanting Kim to pull up and get the wrong impression. He just watched as she walked down the street with her cell phone up to her ear. What happened next took Lamar by surprise. The all-too-familiar Cadillac truck pulled up and stopped at the end of the block. It was Fox and, before Lamar knew it, she was hopping into the passenger side and he was pulling off.

"What da hell," Lamar mumbled to himself as the truck disappeared into traffic. He really didn't know what to think, and an unexpected wave of jealousy came over him and made him wonder what she was doing with him. He had made it clear that he wanted to be with Kim, but Lamar never thought about how he would feel if he saw Falisha back with Fox. He surely didn't like it, and became mad as hell. He loved Kim and didn't want to hurt her, but after seeing Falisha and Fox together, Lamar questioned himself on whether it was possible that he still loved Falisha as well. It was a question that he needed clarity on, and he was bound to get it at some point.

Kim sat in the lobby area waiting for Ms. D to pull up. She was still a little groggy and tired from the anesthesia, but was well aware of what had just happened. Getting an abortion was more difficult than what she thought it would be. Kim had heard many of her friends talking about their abortions, and on some occasions she even encouraged it, but talking about it was easier than actually getting it done. The emptiness in her gut began to tear away at her conscience almost immediately after she woke up. She began to wonder if she had done the right thing, and wished that she could reverse time and give it a little more thought before terminating her pregnancy.

As she sat there in her thoughts, Ms. D walked into the lobby and spotted Kim sitting there with her head down. She knew the feeling Kim was going through, having had a couple of abortions in her lifetime. It was a feeling that couldn't be explained. Ms. D sat in the chair next to Kim's. Kim was so zoned out she still didn't acknowledge her.

"You gon' be all right, baby girl," Ms. D said, putting her arm around Kim. "You can't dwell on it. What's done is what's done. You gotta keep it moving now," she said, rubbing Kim's back.

The more Kim thought about it, the worse she felt. The tears began to pour out of her eyes as the reality of the situation set in. "I . . . I killed my baby," Kim cried, lifting her head up to look at Ms. D. "Oh, God, I killed my baby," she continued, now bawling her eyes out.

"Shhhhhh. Everything is going to be okay," Ms. D said, laying Kim's head on her shoulder.

It was an emotional moment for Kim, and even the tough, hard as nails Ms. D couldn't hold back her tears. She felt for Kim, but she also knew that this was part of being a woman. This was something Kim had to stand by and live with for the rest of her life. No matter what happened in her life from this point on, she would never forget this day. This was going to be her life-changing moment.

"Are you sure you wanna do this?" Fox asked, looking over at Falisha sitting in the passenger seat.

Falisha stared aimlessly out of the window at the medical center and thought about the last time she was there, terminating a pregnancy at the age of fifteen. "Can I ask you something?" Falisha said as she continued looking out of the window.

"Naw, shawty. I can't help you make up ya mind on dis one. You gotta put ya big girl panties on and make ya own choice," Fox told her, eliminating himself from the equation.

Falisha looked over at him and wanted his advice bad, but the truth of the matter was that Fox was right. Falisha just had to make the choice on her own whether to get another abortion. One thing she could count on was Fox keeping it real with her at all times. That's the reason why she confided in him of all people with her secret. Fox wasn't going to judge her, no matter what decision she made, nor was he going to leave her stranded at a time like this.

"Look, Falisha, whatever you decide to do, I'ma roll out wit' you. I told you a long time ago that I got mad love for you, and I meant that."

Falisha looked at him and smiled. It was very comforting to know that she had somebody like Fox in her corner. She turned to look out of the window again, and right before she was about to open the door to walk across the parking lot, Ms. D pulled Kim's car up in front of the building. At first Falisha thought that she was trippin' but then Ms. D exited the car and walked up to the glass double doors where Kim was standing. Ms. D helped the still crying Kim to the car, got her into the passenger seat, then pulled off.

Falisha didn't have to wonder about what had just taken place. She was still too familiar with the process of getting an abortion, and knew that Kim coming out of the abortion clinic, crying her eyes out, and Ms. D being the designated driver, could only equal up to one thing: a termination. It blew Falisha's head back to have witnessed it with her own eyes. After seeing this, it made Falisha's decision a little easier.

"So whatcha gon' do, shawty?" Fox asked, unaware of what had just gone down.

She sat there quiet for a moment, allowing everything to register. She knew how bad she felt, even at the young age of fifteen. Every time she saw Lisa's and Tammy's children, she always wondered, what if she had kept hers? Would it have been a boy or girl? Would it have looked just like her or the father? "Nah, yo. I think I'm good," Falisha said, reaching for her seat belt. "Let's get out of here before I do something I might regret."

Chapter 32

Lisa sat up in the bed, inching her way to the edge of it. She sat there, looking down at the patch on her stomach covering the bullet wound. Right when she was about to get up, Ralphy walked into the room, stopping her before she could get to her feet.

"Come on, Lisa. Chill out, yo. Whatever you need, just let me know," Ralphy said, pulling his arm out of the sling. "The doctor said that you still need to rest."

Lisa smiled at how good it felt to be catered to by Ralphy again. She missed him so much, and so did Naomi. Having him home just felt right. "Can I ask you something?" Lisa said, looking up at him.

"Yeah, what's going on?" he asked, taking a seat next to her on the bed.

"Who was that? I mean, who were those men who shot us, and what was it about?" Lisa had been curious about that the whole time she was laid up in the hospital, and the way the detectives questioned her about Ralphy's involvement made her a little concerned.

"I don't know who those niggas were," Ralphy answered and, right there, Lisa knew that he wasn't telling the truth.

"You know you can't lie to me," Lisa said, raising her hand up to the back of his head and smacking it playfully. "Just tell me that we're safe."

Ralphy looked over at her with a serious face. "Yeah, you're safe, and I don't want you to worry about that situation. I'ma take care of it," he assured her.

That was a problem in itself, because Lisa was well aware of how ugly the streets could get. The hood didn't have any picks when it came down to killing, and since Ralphy was back on the block, he was now fair game, and subject to be held for court on the streets.

Lamar looked into the glass case, staring at a nice ring that caught his eye. He'd been in Tiffany's for over forty-five minutes looking for the perfect ring. The bank employees thought that he was going to rob them the way he browsed around without saying a word.

"Can I see that ring?" he asked the older white lady standing behind the glass.

She hesitated for a moment then called over to a male employee, Tim, to assist her. Lamar could see that she was a little nervous, so he reached into his back pocket and pulled out a wad of money and placed it on the glass counter.

"Don't be so quick to judge black people," he looked over and told the lady, then turned back to Tim. "I'm looking for an engagement ring for my girl, and I like that one," Lamar said, pointing to the ring.

Tim pulled the ring from the display case and set it on the glass. He felt a little bad for how his fellow employee had treated Lamar, so he tried to be as kind and pleasant as he could to make up for it. "This is a beautiful ring. It's a two-karat princess cut, surrounded by a half karat of canary diamonds," he said, passing Lamar the ring.

Lamar looked at the ring and then at its price tag. It cost a little more than five grand. Money truly wasn't the issue at hand. His real concerns came as he fought with himself over whether he was ready to make this kind of commitment this early on in the relationship. Things had been going well for him and Kim, but was proposing the right move at this point? There was no question whether Lamar loved her, because there wasn't a day that went by when he didn't think about starting a family with her. He just wasn't sure if Kim was on the same page; and he didn't want to make a fool of himself asking her to marry him if she were to say no. Rejection never sat well with him, and he didn't know how he would take it if it happened.

The crazy part about it was that Lamar loved Kim so much he was willing to take a chance, even if it cost him $5,300.

Ralphy turned his head from the stove as he sat in the kitchen cooking Lisa something to eat. He grabbed his gun off the kitchen counter and took the safety off then tucked it into his back pocket. He wasn't taking any chances, and wasn't about to get caught slipping again. He walked over to the front window and peeked out the curtains. It was Falisha and Tammy, standing on the porch.

"Hey, ladies. If you're looking for Lisa, she's—"

"Boy, if you don't move out the way . . ." Falisha said, pushing right by Ralphy.

"We just got off the phone with her." Tammy smiled, smacking Ralphy in his gut with the back of her hand, as she too brushed by him.

Ralphy's shoulder hurt too much to even play around with the girls. Besides, Falisha was already at the top of the steps before Ralphy got the front door shut.

"Hey, bitch!" Falisha yelled out playfully when she walked into Lisa's bedroom.

"Hey, crazy," Lisa responded, giving Falisha a kiss on her cheek. "I thought you and Tammy was going shopping."

"We were," Tammy cut in as she entered the room. "We just came to chill out wit' you for a minute," she said, leaning in to give Lisa a soft hug and a kiss.

Lisa reached over and grabbed the joint that was sitting in the ashtray. She wasn't too big on taking pain killers, or any kind of pill for that matter, so she turned to Ms. D's remedy, which was the cannabis.

"Oh, you gangsta. You got shot and you smokin' weed now," Tammy said, sitting on the bed next to Lisa.

Lisa took two pulls then tried to pass it to Falisha. "Nah, I'm good," Falisha said, waving the smoke from in front of her face.

Lisa put an eyebrow up at her, then looked over at Tammy, who looked off, trying her best not to blurt out Falisha's business. It only made Lisa even more curious. "What's wrong with you?" Lisa asked, taking another puff of the weed before putting it back in the ashtray.

Falisha took a seat on the bed on the other side of Lisa. She wasn't sure if she was ready to let the whole world know that she was with child, but after considering the fact that she was going to keep it, it wasn't going to do any harm letting her girls know. She only wanted to keep the news away from Lamar.

"Girl, I'm pregnant," Falisha announced to her, shocking the hell out of Lisa.

"Pregnant? Who in da hell is crazy enough to knock you up?" Lisa chuckled through the pain in her stomach.

"It's by Lamar, but please don't say anything."

Falisha got quiet when she heard Ralphy coming down the hallway. He had Lisa's baked tilapia fish and sautéed vegetables on a tray, along with some apple juice and Patrón. He also brought fresh bandages for Lisa's wound. He had Lisa covered.

"A'ight, we ain't gonna interrupt y'all little family time," Falisha said, jumping up from the bed, not wanting Ralphy to hear anything about her pregnancy. "You want something from the mall while we're out?" she asked.

Lisa shook her head, still smiling from the news. She got her hugs and kisses and watched as Falisha and Tammy made their speedy exit. If it weren't for Ralphy standing there looking handsome as he wanted to, Lisa would have gotten some more of the juicy gossip she'd missed out on while she was laid up in the hospital.

Johanne walked out of the supermarket with two bags of groceries in her arms. When she got to the car and put the bags in the back seat, she pulled out her phone to call Ralphy and see if he'd be coming home for dinner tonight. He hadn't been there for a few days, but Johanne was optimistic about tonight, because he gave her his word that he would come.

"Yo, shawty," a deep voice said from behind while Johanne was leaning up against the driver side door. She looked back and saw a young black guy leaning against the passenger side door, looking right at her. He was rough looking, too. He was black as motor oil with two missing teeth in the front and a scruffy beard to match the nappy hair he had on his head. Before she could say anything, another rough-looking man walked up to her from the side. He was a little more clean cut, but the scar running down the center of his eye made it look like he'd been through some things in the streets. Johanne looked around to see if anybody else was coming out of the woodwork.

"Where's ya li'l boyfriend at?" the man who walked up from the side asked. "Think about it," he warned, lifting his shirt up slightly so Johanne could see the butt of his gun.

"Hello! Hello!" Ralphy yelled into the phone. Johanne forgot that she had dialed Ralphy's number and still had the phone to her ear the whole time. She thought about dropping the phone and running across the parking lot, but decided against it, not wanting to risk being shot in the back. So Ralphy could hear what was going on, Johanne let the call run; but she took the phone away from her ear.

"I don't know where Ralphy's at. I haven't seen him in a few days. Please don't hurt me," Johanne pled.

"You think it's a fuckin' game. Bitch, I'll blow ya fuckin head off," the man said, pulling his gun from his waist and resting it on the side of his thigh.

"I swear, I don't know where he's at," she cried, looking around to see if somebody would notice she was in danger and come to her aid.

Where she was parked, nobody could see what was going on. Ralphy sat there listening to the whole confrontation, wishing he could jump through the phone and start blasting. All he could do was sit and listen, and hope that they would let her go.

"Next time you see ya boyfriend, give him this message for me."

"Please, I'm pregnant," Johanne yelled.

The gunman let off a single shot, hitting Johanne in her shin. She fell to the ground, dropping the phone and her car keys in the process. She held on to her leg, yelling out in pain as the gunmen walked over and stood over her. She knew for sure that this was it, and in what she knew were her last moments on earth, she called out the only name she could think of: "Ralphy!"

The phone went dead before Ralphy could yell back into the phone.

Lisa looked over at him standing by the bedroom window with a distraught look on his face. She knew that something was wrong and wanted to ask him what it was, but by the time Lisa finished swallowing her food to clear her mouth out, Ralphy was headed out of the room, only saying that he'd be back in a couple of hours.

Lamar pulled up to the block, only to see Ralphy's Range Rover driving down the street. He beeped his horn at him a couple of times, but Ralphy kept moving. Lamar wanted to get the opinion of a once-married man, to see if the whole husband and wife thing was as good as some people said.

When he got in the house, Kim was lying down in the bed, balled up under the sheets. She wasn't exactly asleep, but was more daydreaming about how her life would have changed if she had kept the baby.

"What? You got off work early today?" Lamar said, diving into the bed next to her.

"Yeah, I took off a half day. I'm not feeling good," Kim said, closing her eyes so she wouldn't have to look at Lamar.

"Awwwweeee! My baby sick right now," Lamar said in a playful manner, leaning over and kissing her. "You know, I been thinking about a lot of stuff as of late and I wanted to run a few things by you to get your take," he said, reaching into his back pocket and grabbing the small suede box containing the ring he'd just bought.

"Not right now, babe. My period is on, and I don't feel like doing anything but lying here and going to sleep," Kim said, turning over and giving Lamar her back.

Lamar could see that now probably wasn't the best time for him to pop the question. It was frustrating, because he'd waited all day and rehearsed his words a thousand times, hoping that they would come out the way he'd planned. Now that he was lying beside her, the mood was the only thing that wasn't right; and instead of trying to force the issue, Lamar placed the little suede box back into his pocket, scooted up behind her, and wrapped his arms around her waist. They both eventually fell asleep without saying another word.

Chapter 33

"Mommy, Mommy, whose house is this?" little Anthony asked as he got out of the car.

"Why do you have to ask so many questions, Anthony?" Tammy said as she unstrapped Sinniyyah from her car seat.

"I wanna know who's house it is, Mommy," Anthony continued, looking around at the unfamiliar area. It was a far cry from where he was used to living. There had to be about twenty kids out on the street, riding their bikes and running up and down the sidewalk. Anthony had never seen this many white kids in one place before, although there were a few black children among the crowd. This definitely was something new for him.

Darious, who was in the garage with the door up, walked out to the driveway, surprised that Tammy had the kids with her. She walked up to him with Sinniyyah in her arms, waiting to see what he was going to say.

"Are you sure?" Darious asked, wondering if she was ready to bring her kids into his life.

"Mmmm hmmmm." She nodded, leaning in to kiss him.

This was a big step for their relationship, but Tammy felt comfortable enough to have Darious around her kids on a more permanent note; plus, she was tired of always having to find a babysitter in order to spend some quality time with her man. Tammy felt that if they were going to be together, then Darious might as well get to know the kids. He'd only seen them a couple of times, and that was due to Tammy trying to give Chris some respect by not having his kids around another man. That way of thinking had run its course, and it came by way of the fact that Darious wasn't just another man, he was Tammy's man and the person she planned to spend the rest of her life with. Darious being a part of her kids' lives was inevitable, and that was something Chris was going to have to learn how to respect.

When Ralphy pulled up to the block, Scoop was in the cut, sitting on some steps a nice distance away from the heavy dopefiend traffic heading for the workers. The moment Scoop saw Ralphy pull up, he removed the gun from his waist and set it on his lap. He wasn't sure what type of shit Ralphy was on, or if he'd put it together that he had something to do with the shooting at the dentist office, but just to be on the safe side Scoop had his gun at the ready.

"What it do, big homie," Scoop greeted him, extending his fist for some dap, which Ralphy returned.

"Yo, I think we might have to go to war with these niggas on the west side," Ralphy said, easing his arm out of the sling.

"War? Niggas don't go to war like that anymore." Scoop chuckled. "Especially when the beef is personal. And what makes you think it was the niggas from the west side?" Scoop asked, trying to see where Ralphy had come up with that idea.

"Man, it had to be. Them niggas came for blood not money. I don't know how, but I got a feeling Dre's people know I had something to do with his death."

Ralphy didn't sound all that sure, which made Scoop feel like he was in the clear. "Yo, my nigga, you ain't been out here in a while, and I tried to warn you."

"Warn me about what?" Ralphy shot back with a little attitude behind it.

"This street life ain't you anymore. You're a family man now, and that's where you belong. Shit gets ugly out here if you're not careful," Scoop told him.

Ralphy was a little shocked by what Scoop had said. It was as if he didn't have any respect for Ralphy's G card anymore. The more Ralphy sat there and thought about it, it also sounded like

Scoop didn't want him out there on the streets at all. It wasn't what he said, it was how Scoop said it that caught Ralphy's attention.

"So you're gon' put dis work in wit' me or what?" Ralphy asked, but only to check Scoop's temperature on the matter.

"Homie, I really don't got the time for war. I'm trying to make some money right now," Scoop said, turning his head away to look down the street. "Just let that shit die down before you get yaself killed," Scoop said, before getting up from the steps and walking off down the street toward his workers.

Ralphy knew right then and there that Scoop was no longer on his side. He didn't know if or to what extent Scoop had something to with the shooting, but if it came out that he did, Ralphy wasn't going to hesitate in putting a bullet through his head, so-called friend or not.

Just about every Sunday, Ms. D had a dinner, and it was a guarantee that everybody would show up. She fried chicken breast, fish, and a few other seafood creatures like shrimp and crab cakes. Mashed potatoes with gravy, macaroni and cheese, greens, corn, and white rice were also on the menu. Her house smelled like a soul food restaurant, and in the midst of the great smell, the aroma of her specially made apple pie blended in the air. Ms. D could cook her ass off.

"All right, somebody clear this table off," Ms. D yelled out from the kitchen.

Lamar wasn't getting up from in front of the TV and neither was Ralphy. The football game had them locked in, so it was up to the females to get the job done. Lisa couldn't do much of anything with her wound, and Falisha was upstairs in Ms. D's bedroom talking on the phone. Tammy and Kim were left to take care of the dinner table.

"Are you okay?" Tammy asked, seeing the blank look on Kim's face as she sat at the table.

Like many women, Kim still had the abortion on her mind, and she wanted so bad to tell Lamar what happened. She just didn't know how he was going to react to it. She loved him, and didn't want to risk losing him. At the same time, she didn't like hiding things and keeping secrets from him. It just felt wrong all the way around the board.

Ms. D finally got everybody to the dinner table. Little Anthony, Sinniyyah, and Naomi all sat at the kitchen table, with Ms. D going back and forth to check up on them. As soon as everyone was seated, Falisha said grace.

"Heavenly Father, thank you for this food you have provided for us, and thank you for allowing friends to come together and enjoy this meal. God, I ask that you protect us from the evil plot of the devil, and to make us all strong enough to move on.

God knows that strength is what we're gonna need. And please protect us from these wolves in sheep's clothing. In the name of Jesus. Amen!"

Lamar looked up at Falisha knowing that after that sarcastic prayer there was more to follow, and nine times out of ten, it wasn't going to be good at all.

Ms. D even gave her a look as if to say, "Don't start ya shit."

Falisha kept her cool and began to eat along with everybody else. For the first few minutes, it was pretty much silent except for the sounds of spoons and forks hitting the plates and a couple of moans from the delicious taste of the food.

"I got an announcement I wanna make," Tammy said, wiping her mouth with the napkin. I'm moving next week," she said, taking a sip of her juice.

"What? I know it's not with that boy," Kim spoke, surprised to hear that coming from her.

"His name is Darious and he's far from a boy," Tammy quickly corrected her. "Besides, he makes me happy."

"That's right, girl. That's all that matters," Falisha cut in.

"You know Chris gon' kill you and him when he gets home." Ralphy chuckled.

"Chicks ain't got no loyalty nowadays. A nigga go to jail, and a female is so quick to forget about everything a nigga did for them before he got there," Lamar said with a slight attitude. "I don't respect it," he concluded, taking a bite of his chicken breast.

"Lamar!" Kim yelled, smacking his arm, "Don't be rude."

"Nah, nah, that's cool, Kim. I'm not mad at Lamar. He's only saying how he feels. But let me say this to all the niggas who's locked down in the pen: I didn't put a gun to nobody's head and make you be a trap boy. Chris did that on his own. I would have stood by his side if he worked at McDonald's in order to provide for his family. He knew what he was doing, and the possibility of being taken away from his kids. But, guess what, he kept doing it. Meaning he didn't give a damn about me or our kids. He left this pussy out here so he could be around a bunch of men and dicks. If you think I'm about to put my life on hold for the next ten years, you and every other nigga got another think coming," Tammy said, pointing her fork at him.

Lamar sat there and continued to eat his food. He really didn't have anything else to say. Chris had always been a cool dude to him and, from the outside looking in, it looked like Tammy was leaving him when he most needed her.

Ralphy, on the other hand, had something he wanted to get off his chest. He cleared his throat, reached into his back pocket, and pulled out an envelope. Inside were the divorce papers signed by him and Lisa, and ready to be processed. He held on to them for good reasons and the most important of them was that he wanted to make sure a divorce was what he really wanted.

"Me and Lisa been together for a long time now, and I know everybody is aware of what happened between us. I just wanna say that when you love somebody as much as me and Lisa love each other, you can make it through anything," Ralphy said, taking the papers and ripping the up into little pieces, "Me and Lisa are back together."

"You just sayin' that 'cause she got shot. Nigga, the streets is talking," Falisha said, biting down on her fish.

"You out of pocket, Falisha," Kim said.

"Look who's talkin'," Falisha shot back. "Don't you got something you wanna say, since everybody got announcements?"

"I got an announcement," Lamar said, reaching into his pocket for the ring.

"And who you screwing now?" Falisha shot at him. She wasn't taking any prisoners today. Her hormones were running wild and she was just saying whatever came to mind. Lamar was so shaken he put his ring back inside his pocket and continued eating without attempting to respond to Falisha's comment.

"Damn, you cold," Ms. D said, shaking her head at Falisha.

"Yeah, and don't think that I don't know you got cancer. You like a fuckin' mother to me, and you hide some shit like this from me . . . from us."

Ms. D leaned over and backhanded Falisha right in her mouth, splitting her bottom lip on the side. Falisha knew she was wrong, and that's why she did nothing but cover her mouth with her hands and remain quiet while Ms. D said what she had to say.

"Yeah, I got cancer, but that's my business. I was going to tell the rest of y'all, who didn't know, on my own terms, not yours," Ms. D said, cutting her eyes over at Falisha. "Now, if y'all don't mind, I wanna enjoy the rest of this meal without the negativity. So if you don't have anything positive to say, then don't say nothing at all," Ms. D concluded before digging into her plate.

Everybody was in agreement with trying to salvage what good was left in the Sunday dinner. Silence took over the table, and just when everybody thought that the day was over, Falisha rocked the table with her own shocking public announcement.

"Well, how about one more quick announcement. I'm pregnant!" Falisha said before turning around and walking out of the kitchen on her way to the bathroom.

***

Johanne sat in her hospital bed looking at the positive pregnancy test the nurse had given her. She was so astonished by the good news she could barely feel the metal rods keeping her shattered shin bone in place. This whole time, she had no idea she was absolutely with child and the more she looked at the test, the more excited she became.

"Excuse me, Nurse. Is it possible for you to find out how far along I am?" Johanne asked, reaching over and grabbing her cell phone off the stand.

"Sure, just give me a minute," the nurse responded.

Although Ralphy said that he'd be back around eight o'clock, Johanne couldn't help but to try to call him. She wanted to give him the news right away, hoping he would be just as happy as she was. Unfortunately, her few attempts at calling him ended up going straight to his voice mail. She thought about texting him, but that was a little too cheesy. Johanne would have to wait; but, in the meantime, in between time, she was going to bask in the beautiful gift of motherhood.

Chapter 34

"Babe!" Darious yelled out from the upstairs bedroom. "Come 'ere real quick," he shouted.

Tammy was in the kitchen feeding Sinniyyah in her high chair. She picked her up and headed upstairs to see what Darious wanted. When she got to the bedroom, he'd just wrapped up a phone call.

"Yes, babe," Tammy said, putting Sinniyyah on the bed, then walking over and standing in front of him while he sat on the edge of the bed.

"On ya way to go pick up Anthony, I need you to drop this medication off to one of my patients," Darious said, grabbing her by the waist. "I got a lot of running around to do before I go to work."

"Yeah, sure, babe. That's no problem," she said, rubbing the top of his head. "Are you okay? 'Cause you look a little stressed out," she said, pushing him back onto the bed. She then climbed on top of him.

She leaned in and kissed him then looked into his eyes. She still couldn't believe how far in love she was with Darious, and he felt the same.

"You know I love you, right?" he asked, reaching up and placing his hand on her cheek. "Promise me that you're not going to leave me," he said.

"I know you love me, Darious, and I'm not going anywhere. You got my heart," she responded, leaning back over to kiss him again.

This time, Sinniyyah interrupted the moment, crawling across the bed and grabbing a handful of Darious's face. Her finger was lodged in his nose and the saliva from her mouth dripped down into his eye. Sinniyyah was laughing and bouncing back and forth like she was having the time of her life. This was the first time Sinniyyah was this intimate with Darious and, to be honest, Tammy was feeling the bond.

Kim pulled up right in time to catch Falisha coming out of her house. She beeped the horn twice but Falisha only looked at Kim's car before going back into the house. Falisha really didn't feel like talking to anybody at this point.

"Here we go wit' dis bullshit," Kim mumbled to herself, getting out of the car with her briefcase in hand. Kim didn't want to, but she walked up to Falisha's front door and rang the bell. There was a lot of tension between them, and Kim wasn't the type to walk around with a chip on her shoulder. If she had a problem, she confronted it head-on.

"Come on wit' da childish shit and open the door," Kim yelled through the mail slot.

Kim was about to yell in the mail slot again but, before she could, the door swung open and Falisha was standing there with an obvious attitude. "What do you want, Kim?" Falisha asked, stepping out onto the porch.

"So it's like that? You sayin' that we're not cool at all anymore?" Kim asked, putting her briefcase on the ledge.

Falisha never said anything, but she felt some type of way about Kim wanting Lamar since day one. The only reason she entertained the whole race to capture Lamar's heart was because she truly thought that she had it in the bag. She never thought in a million years that he would choose Kim over her, given the history they had, along with amazingly great sex. When he did choose Kim, it was mind-blowing and it caught Falisha off guard.

"Come on, Kim. You know what it do. You took my man, and that was that. We cool and everything, but we're not friends," Falisha said.

"So we're not friends because of a man?" Kim asked.

Falisha didn't say anything right away. She looked down the street, trying to avoid any eye contact with Kim, but Kim walked over and stood in front of her, forcing Falisha to look at her. Kim could see the anger and the hurt in her eyes and knew that what Falisha felt was real.

"You know that I was in love with Lamar, and you still pursued him. You didn't give a fuck about me or how I felt. To you, this was all a fucking game, and Lamar was your prize. A friend? You can't be serious. A real friend would have backed off, instead of doing the shit you did. But guess what, I'm good. You and Lamar ain't gon' last another month once he finds out you got an abortion," Falisha said, looking down at Kim's stomach before walking into her house and slamming the door behind her.

Kim sat there on the porch with a dumb look on her face after being chewed out by Falisha. Not only did she feel bad, she also felt like a home wrecker, because if it weren't for her, Falisha and Lamar would be together. It was something Kim had never really thought about until now, and the more she thought about it, the more she could understand how Falisha felt.

What she couldn't grasp was the last comment Falisha made pertaining to how long she and Lamar had left to be together. She wanted to bang on the door and ask Falisha what she meant by it, but Lamar pulling up on the block made Kim leave it alone for right now. This definitely wasn't going to be the end of that conversation but, for now, Kim had another pressing issue to deal with, one that might make or break her and Lamar's relationship.

***

Darious had warned Tammy that the neighborhood was a little ghetto, but that was an understatement. When she pulled up to Milton Road, it looked like a zombie land. There were dopefiends everywhere and, for a minute, Tammy was scared to pull over. In fact, she drove right by the house she was supposed to deliver the medication to.

"Shit," Tammy mumbled, pulling over toward the end of the block after seeing that she had passed the house. Two luxury cars parked on the pavement caught Tammy's attention and, for some reason, she felt comfortable parking behind them. Plus, there weren't that many dopefiends at this end of the block.

"You lookin' for somebody?" a female voice asked when Tammy got out of the car.

Tammy looked over and saw a young girl coming down off the porch with one of her hands behind her back. Despite her intimidating approach, Tammy thought the young lady was cute, rocking a pair of 7 For All Mankind jeans, a white shirt, and some Yves Saint Laurent sandals. Her hair was straightened and draped over her left shoulder, allowing her diamond-studded earrings to bling in the sunlight. Tammy didn't know her, but she looked like somebody of importance.

"I'm going up the street to deliver this medication to a patient," Tammy said, looking down at the address she had written on a piece of paper. "Is it safe to even go up there?" Tammy asked, picking her head up as the young lady walked up to her.

The girl looked at the address then smiled. "Who sent you, Darious?" she asked, waving for Tammy to follow her up the street.

"Yeah, that's my man," Tammy said, establishing off the top who she was to him. "You know him?"

"I know Darious. He's a nice guy. He's been looking out for my uncle James for a while now. By the way, my name is Tiffany," she said, walking up the steps to James's house.

"I'm Tammy," Tammy responded, walking up the steps behind her.

Now that Tiffany was in front of Tammy, Tammy could see why she had her hand behind her back. The butt of a gun poked out of her back pocket, clearly visible to the eye. It kind of took Tammy by surprise, and even though she didn't have the guts to ask her the reason why she had the gun, Tammy made a mental note of it.

"Wassup, Uncle James," Tiffany asked when he opened the door. "Ya medication is here."

The drop-off was pretty simple, except for when the drop-off became an exchange at a dining room table with stacks of money sitting on it. Tammy didn't know the contents within the prescription bag, and didn't get a chance to see them either, because as quick as Tammy handed it over to James, he gave her a two-inch thick wad of money. Before she knew it, Tammy was being led out the back of the house by Tiffany, and escorted back to her car.

As Tammy pulled off, the chain of events that had just taken place bum-rushed her brain. She really didn't know what to think, or what Darious just had her do. All sorts of theories went through her head, and not one of them sat well with her. Before the day was over, she was going to get a clear understanding about what had gone down.

A nice, hot bath was exactly the thing Kim needed in her life right now, and from the looks of things, and how her body felt, it seemed as though her period was about to go off. Dealing with the abortion was starting to get a little easier and, because of that, Kim was ready to let Lamar know what she'd done.

Kim sat in the bathtub trying to figure out what words she was going to use to break the news to him. There really wasn't a delicate way to say to a man that she'd murdered his unborn child. The more Kim looked at it that way, the fewer words she came up with.

Lamar opening the bathroom door snapped Kim out of her train of thought.

"I was thinking, maybe we should go out for dinner tonight," Lamar said, taking a seat on the edge of the tub.

"I really don't feel like going out tonight, babe. Plus, I need to talk to you about something," Kim said.

"That's crazy, 'cause I wanna talk to you about something too," Lamar shot back, dipping his hand into the bathwater and twirling it around.

Kim looked as Lamar stared aimlessly at the bubbles floating in the tub. She wondered if he'd already found out about the abortion from somebody else, such as Falisha, or whoever else Ms. D probably told. Before she went into her defense mode, she had to see what Lamar knew, if he knew anything at all. "But what do you want to talk about?" Kim asked, wiping the suds off her arm.

Lamar sat there thinking about it. He wanted the moment to be right, but at the same time, he didn't want to waste another minute before asking for Kim's hand in marriage. It was now or never, and there was nobody or nothing that could interrupt him.

"Kim, I really need you to know that I love you, and there's nobody else in the world I would want to spend the rest of my life with," Lamar said, reaching into his back pocket for the little box.

Kim's heart started beating erratically when she saw the suede box and, from its size, she knew that it had to be a ring. Lamar got off the tub and got down on one knee. Kim sat up in the tub, cupping her hands over her mouth in shock.

"I just don't wanna spend the rest of my life without you. I wanna stand by your side and truly be the man who makes you smile from the time you wake up until the time you go to bed at night. I wanna be the person you can depend upon to be there for you through it all and be more than just your boyfriend. I wanna be your husband, Kim. Will you by my wife?" Lamar asked, opening the little case.

Kim was in tears and, for the first time ever, they were tears of joy. She had a few boyfriends in her time, some good and some bad; never did any of them propose to her. She was speechless, all except for the one word Lamar hoped to hear.

"Yes!" Kim said, then leaned out of the tub to kiss him.

Tammy didn't go and pick the kids up right away like she planned to do after she'd dropped the medication off to James. She called Darious, who told her to meet him at his job, because he was about to get off anyway. As soon as she pulled up in front of the hospital, Darious walked out and got right into the car. He could tell something was wrong by the look she had on her face.

"What did I do now?" Darious asked in a playful way.

Tammy wasn't up for too many games right now. "Are you selling drugs?" she asked flat out.

"Tam, you know I work in a hospital," Darious spoke.

"No, Darious, that's not what I asked you. I just came from Milton Road and James's house looked like a trap spot. He got money all over the table, bitches walking around with guns in their back pockets like it's legal," Tammy snapped. "I swear, if you got me delivering drugs and ain't telling me—"

"Tammy, I'm not selling drugs. James just had a disc put into his back, and the medication I gave him came from a doctor," Darious said, cutting her off. "I wouldn't do that to you, babe," he said, placing his hand over hers. "Do you really think I am a drug dealer?"

Tammy didn't question him on what he said. If James had a disc in his back, then that's what it was. With Darious, Tammy felt like she could trust him, and there hadn't been a time yet that he'd lied to her. For those reasons alone, Tammy left it dead, but one thing she knew for sure was that under no circumstances would she be making any more deliveries to Milton Road. Ever!

Ralphy pulled up to the hospital to pick Johanna up and take her to the house that he shared with her. She was waiting out front in a wheelchair, with her cousin, DeeDee, standing by her side. Ralphy felt somewhat bad that the niggas who were looking for him came after her as well. It showed Ralphy that whoever it was really meant business.

"Damn, mommy," Ralphy said, walking over and scooping her out of the wheelchair. "I'm sorry this happened to you but, rest easy, I'm going to find out who did it, and I'm going to bury them," he assured her.

Johanne didn't want that, not now or ever, for that matter. She was carrying a child, and couldn't afford to lose Ralphy to the streets. Johanne wanted her child to grow up with a father just like she did, and at the rate Ralphy was going that wasn't going to happen. She spoke the only words she figured could change his mind about getting revenge.

"Babe, I'm pregnant!" Johanne exclaimed.

Ralphy almost dropped her after hearing those words. To be sure, he made her repeat what she'd just said, which was the same as he thought. He stood curbside, holding Johanne in his arms, at a loss for words.

"Damn, you're not gonna say anything?" Johanne asked with a slight attitude, seeing that he wasn't excited as she was.

Ralphy wasn't excited because he didn't want to have a baby by her. Johanne was cool, and she looked good as hell, but Ralphy wasn't even sure if he loved her, let alone wanted to have a baby with her. His heart was always with his family, and that's something that would never change, no matter what. It wouldn't even be fair to give Johanne the impression that he wanted this baby.

"Don't worry. We'll talk about it when we get home," Ralphy said, putting her into the back seat of the Range Rover.

On the strength that DeeDee was with her, Ralphy opted to not embarrass Johanne with his disapproval. He had enough respect for her to do it in private, which he was sure to do just as soon as they got home.

Chapter 35

"Damn, homie, you ain't going out to the rec yard?" Willow, Chris's celly, asked while walking into the cell.

Chris wasn't too pressed about going outside right now. He had just received a letter from his lawyer, stating that the court of appeals wanted to have oral arguments on the several issues he had raised on his appeal. It was a bit of good news for him, as his issues were strong enough to either get a new trial or possibly even walk out of the front doors with time served.

"Yo, how often do people actually win their appeals?" Chris asked Willow as he stared at the letter.

"It depends, homie. If you got good issues, then you got a chance. Wit' these dudes around here, everybody has that crazy notion that appeals are easy, but they aren't. You really gotta box the government into a corner to the point where they can't legally respond to what it is that you're arguing," Willow said, as he changed into his basketball clothes. "Just stay focused, homie, and try not to be the defendant. Play devil's advocate and look at it through the eyes of the prosecution," Willow said before leaving the cell for the recreation move.

Chris sat there after Willow left, pondering what he had said. Looking at his case through the eyes of the prosecution was crazy, but it made sense. If Chris could figure out from what angle the government was attacking his appeal, he could prepare a better defense for the oral argument hearing coming up.

"Damn, let me make this rec move," Chris mumbled to himself, hoping to get a seat in the law library.

Darious sat in the driver seat, waiting for Tammy to come out of the pharmacy with a hundred oxycodone pills, all to be delivered to another one of his clients on the other side of town. Moments later, Tammy came out with the white and blue pharmacy bag in her hand. She got into the car holding it out, and then snatched it back before Darious could grab it.

"Now explain to me, why in the hell can't Mr. Mason pick up his own medication?" Tammy asked, waving the bag in front of Darious's face as he pulled off.

Tammy wasn't dumb by a long shot, and she knew that Darious was doing something he had no business doing with the medicine. To what extent,

Tammy didn't know, but by how limited her role in helping him was, she didn't think that it was anything that serious. She felt that, in the worst-case scenario, Darious would lose his job if he got caught. That was something he was going to have to deal with in the event that happened. Until then, Tammy was going to continue to help, just as long as the money kept rolling in.

"You know what? You too much for your own good." Darious smiled as he snatched the bag from her. "Now, listen, you got a full day tomorrow," Darious said, opening up the console and grabbing a wad of money from it. "You gotta pay the rent, the bills, and you gotta take ya car to the shop for a tune-up," he said, peeling off some money.

Tammy loved the fact that Darious depended upon her to take care of important things pertaining to their home. She felt more responsible than she'd ever felt in her life, and not only did she feel good about it, she embraced it. Until the day she started dealing with Darious and since Chris had been locked up, Tammy struggled to pay bills, let alone had a few thousand dollars in her own bank account. Not only did Darious treat Tammy like his partner, he had transformed the young-minded girl into a woman.

"You know I love you, boy," Tammy said, looking over at Darious.

"Yeah, how much?" He smiled, concentrating on the road ahead of him. Tammy leaned over, kissed him on his cheek, and then kissed the side of his neck. She sat in the passenger side on her knees, reached down, and unzipped his pants.

Darious kept his eyes on the road while Tammy pulled his dick out and began kissing it. It didn't take long for his member to become erect, and once it did, she took all of it into her mouth.

"Ohhh, shiiiitttt," Darious moaned, steering the car with his left hand and placing his right hand on the top of her head. "Damn, girl."

Tammy's head bobbed up and down on his dick, and the only thing that could be heard in the car was the slurping sound her mouth made from all the spit she was using. Nothing but the soft tissue of her mouth wrapped around his dick and, like a pro, Tammy made sure his mushroom head hit the back of her throat when she went down on it.

After about five minutes in, Darious had to pull over, feeling himself about to explode. Tammy could feel it too, so she sped up, sucking it deeper down her throat and moving faster. Seeing her full thick lips wrapped snug around his dick, Darious splashed off without warning.

"Don't make a mess," Darious said, feeling his cum fill her mouth.

Tammy didn't waste a drop, swallowing every last bit of it. She continued sucking, even after it was all gone, forcing Darious to grab a handful of her hair and pull her head up off him. Tammy came up chuckling, knowing Darious couldn't take any more of her dick sucking if he wanted to. She tried to lean in and kiss Darious, but he playfully palmed her face before she could, as he thought about all the cum he'd just shot in her mouth. They laughed and play fought for a minute, before Tammy eventually sat back in her seat, and Darious pulled back onto the road.

Lisa sat at the kitchen table, sipping on a glass of Gallo Moscato while she listened to Shirley Murdock and looked at a bunch of old pictures of her and Ralphy. There were a few things she knew that Ralphy had to take care of in the streets but, for the most part, he was home, and that's all that truly mattered. It had been rough for the past few months, being deprived of the love she and Ralphy once shared. It was pure torture, but then came the relief Lisa had only longed for.

"What are you in here doin'?" Ralphy asked, walking into the kitchen with Naomi on his back and a smile on his face. He leaned over and kissed Lisa on the top of her head, then allowed Naomi to do the same, while she was still on his back.

"I'm not doin' anything. Just sitting here looking at some pictures." Lisa smiled, pouring more wine into her glass. "Remember Jamaica?" she asked, pointing to the pictures.

Ralphy did remember; it was one of the best vacations he had ever taken. He wanted to sit down and reminisce about the good times with her, but knowing Lisa the way he did, she was trying to have some alone time, which he was more than happy to provide her.

"I was thinking about taking Little Miss Thing here to the mall with me. We should be back in a couple of hours," Ralphy said, hiking Naomi up higher on his back.

"Daddy said he was going to buy me some new shoes. Do you want some new shoes, Mommy?" the excited Naomi asked.

As Lisa was answering Naomi, Ralphy's phone began to ring in his back pocket. He usually didn't answer blocked numbers, but just out of curiosity, he hit the accept button. "Yeah," he answered, kneeling down to let Naomi off his back.

"*Hola, papi.* Did you forget you were supposed to be taking me to my doctor's appointment to see how far along I am?" Johanne asked while brushing her teeth in the mirror.

"Damn, I forgot that it was today. What time do you got to be there?" he asked, opening up the refrigerator door.

Lisa knew that he was talking to Johanne, but she wasn't the least bit upset. She knew that

Johanne was some of the baggage he had accumulated during their time apart, and she accepted it, only because Ralphy promised to end their relationship in the coming days. Giving him the time that he needed was a sacrifice Lisa was willing to endure to secure her family being back together. Plus, she didn't want to dig up any old bones by being demanding and nagging Ralphy to expedite the process.

"Just give me like twenty minutes, and be ready 'cause I got something else to do," Ralphy said, looking down at Naomi.

Johanne got an attitude quick, thinking of the way he'd been treating her ever since she told him about the pregnancy. It had been a week since she came home from the hospital, and during that week, it had been nothing but arguing. He only stayed at the house with her for about two nights, the other five were spent with Lisa and Naomi. If it had not been for DeeDee, Johanne didn't know how she would have survived being out of commission.

"Kim, I need to see you in my office," Mr. Wilson said, walking past her cubicle and straight into his office.

Kim logged out of her computer immediately, because it sounded urgent. When she got to his office, he was standing up by his window undoing his tie.

"Have a seat," Mr. Wilson offered, pointing to the chair sitting in front of his desk.

For a minute, Kim thought that she was about to be fired. She had a speech already formulated in her head that she would give in the event this day would ever come. Fortunately for her, today was the total opposite.

"Look, Kim, what I'm about to offer you is a once-in-a-lifetime opportunity," Mr. Wilson said, taking a seat behind his desk. "I got a friend out of Philadelphia who's looking for a paralegal to join his firm. His name is Denis Cogen, the highest paid lawyer in that city—"

"But I like it here," Kim said, cutting him off.

"And I'm not firing you, Kim. What he is offering, I can't give you. Guaranteed seventy grand a year, medical benefits, one year free housing; and, here's the kicker, he wants to pay for you to go to law school. Free ride all the way through," Mr. Wilson explained.

"Damn!" Kim wanted to go back to school and her dream was to pass the bar and become a lawyer. Mr. Wilson was right, this was a chance of a lifetime, and it had Kim thinking about it hard.

"I'm not complaining, and God knows I'm not declining the offer. I'm curious to know why me? I mean, you got Patty, Mitch; and Ray is an animal in the civil department," Kim spoke.

"He's a good friend of mine, and he asked me for the best. I don't know a soul in Charlotte who could research and put a motion together as good as you, and that's the God's honest truth," Mr. Wilson replied.

Kim was flattered, and almost started to tear up. "So how much time I do I have?" Kim asked, knowing there had to be a deadline before this offer was off the table. "And please don't say I have to decide—"

"You got until the end of next week when he comes back from his vacation," Mr. Wilson interrupted. "That's about ten days from now."

Kim really wanted to say yes on the spot, and almost did until she thought but Lamar, who was now her fiancé. She didn't know how he would feel about moving to Philadelphia while she pursued her career in the legal field, but this definitely was going to be the topic for the little getaway they had planned for the weekend. After leaving Mr. Wilson's office, Kim had more than enough on her plate to cipher through.

DeeDee and Johanne were standing in the doorway waiting when Ralphy pulled up with Naomi. He wasn't going to let Johanne ruin his plans to take his daughter shopping today, and despite the fact that Lisa didn't have a problem with Naomi staying home with her, Ralphy brought her along for the doctor's appointment.

"You gon' be one of those kind of fathers, huh?" DeeDee said in a smart manner when Ralphy got out of the car.

"And what kind of father is that?" Ralphy shot back.

"The kind who don't wanna be a father."

Before they got into an arguing match, Johanne stopped both of them. She really didn't feel like hearing the two of them go at it. The only thing on her mind was her doctor's appointment.

"Is that the prettiest little girl in the world?" Johanne chuckled, rolling up to the back door of the Range Rover and seeing Naomi sitting there with her seat belt on.

"Hi, Ms. Johanne," Naomi responded in a low tone, not really wanting to speak on account of Lisa making it clear to her that they weren't to become friends.

"Come on, NayNay, you can sit up front with Daddy," Ralphy said, helping her out of the back seat.

The sound of tires screeching to a halt grabbed everyone's attention, and when Ralphy looked over, one old-school Chevy Impala and a black minivan had stopped at the end of the driveway. The two occupants in the black minivan hopped out first, clutching large, fully automatic assault rifles, aiming them at everyone as they ran up the driveway. Ralphy noticed one of the men off the bat, remembering him from the shooting at the dentist's office. He was the one who got away. Ralphy knew that his time was up. The only thing he could think about was Naomi, who he still had hoisted in his arms.

The gunmen got within a few feet, and the only reason the man from the dentist shooting didn't open up fire was because of Naomi. "Put her down!" the shooter demanded, not wanting to hit an innocent child by accident.

"Come on, dog. Don't do this in front of my daughter," Ralphy pleaded, as he lowered Naomi to the ground.

"Oh, my God, please don't shoot him," Johanne said, holding her hands out while sitting in the wheelchair.

"Daddy," Naomi cried out, wrapping her arms around his leg. "Daddy, Daddy," she continued.

"Please, dog," Ralphy begged with tears in his eyes.

"Fuck you, nigga! You think dis shit is a fuckin' game?" the shooter yelled out, pointing the rifle a mere two feet away from Ralphy's face. The shooter's face was twisted up and you could tell that he was biting down on his teeth in anger. His finger hugged the trigger, and he was just about to pull it when Naomi spoke.

"Please don't shoot my daddy," she said with tears pouring down her fat cheeks.

"Man, fuck dat. Shoot dat nigga!" the other gunman encouraged him as he kept his eyes on DeeDee.

The shooter looked in Ralphy's eyes then glanced down at Naomi. Naomi didn't realize it, but she had just saved her father's life, because the shooter started to back down the driveway.

"I'm on ya fuckin top, nigga, and I don't care who you got wit' you next time," the shooter yelled out before getting back into the minivan.

The two cars both peeled out, leaving nothing but tire smoke in the air. Ralphy let out a huge sigh of relief then immediately got everybody back into the house where it was relatively safe. He would have to stay there until his boys came to back him up.

Chapter 36

Falisha rolled Fox over then climbed on top of him, straddling his long, thick baseball bat of a dick in order to get it over with. Fox had been fucking her for the past forty-five minutes straight, and didn't plan to stop anytime soon. The only way Falisha knew how to knock him down was by riding him. He loved the way she bounced up and down on his dick.

"Right there. Go faster," he coached, feeling himself about to bust a nut.

Falisha braced her hands against his chest and rocked her hips back and forth, just how he liked it. Her breasts swayed with every stroke and, just like second nature, Fox grabbed a handful.

"You gon' cum for mommy?" Falisha said in a seductive way, biting down on her bottom lip.

Fox couldn't hold it any longer if he tried to. Falisha could feel his warm, thick nut fill her insides. She continued rocking back and forth, making sure she drained every drop from his sack. Fox reached up and grabbed a handful of her hair, pulling her face down to his and kissing her wet lips.

"I missed you," he admitted, looking Falisha in her eyes.

This was the first time they'd had sex in months, but it wasn't by Fox's choice that he got some today. It was all Falisha. She was horny as hell and needed to relieve her thirst for some dick. Lamar was out of the question, and somebody random was a no-no. Letting Fox tap it was the more reasonable thing to do. She didn't have to worry about catching anything, because Fox stayed cleaner than the board of health, and since she was already pregnant, a condom wasn't necessary at all. The most important thing for Falisha was that she knew beyond a shadow of a doubt that Fox was going to please her. If she couldn't count on anything else, she sure could count on that.

"Come 'ere, where are you going?" Fox asked after Falisha jumped out of the bed, grabbed her clothes, and headed for the bathroom.

If she lay in that bed any longer, Falisha knew that it was going to start getting personal, something she was trying to avoid Fox doing. For her, it was just about the sex, and she didn't want to confuse or mislead Fox into thinking it was going to be anything more than that.

"Falisha!" Fox called out, walking up to the bathroom.

By the time he opened the door, Falisha was fully dressed and standing in the mirror putting her hair in a ponytail. Fox stood at the door with his boxers on, showing the head of his dick.

"Hit and run, huh?" he said, walking into the bathroom. Falisha smiled as he slid up behind her and wrapped his arms around her waist. He looked at her reflection in the mirror, taking in her beauty. "I thought we was a little better than that," he said.

"Don't be like that. You already know my situation, and I'm not gonna bring that kind of drama into ya life right now," Falisha responded, trying not to hold eye contact.

Fox was insistent. "Look at me, Falisha," he said, nudging her. "You don't think I know ya situation? If it mattered to me, you wouldn't even be here. You know me better than that, shawty."

"Yeah, I know, Fox. I just don't wanna—"

"Look, man, I know awhile back I fucked up big time when I didn't fight for you. I shouldn't have let you walk out of my life that easy."

This was the exact thing Falisha was trying to avoid with him. She had to admit that Fox was a nice guy and, given different circumstances, Falisha probably would have tried to give it another shot. But the truth remained that her heart was somewhere else, and although a future with Lamar didn't look that promising, Falisha wanted to make sure of it. She longed to be with Lamar, and with his baby growing in her womb every single day, the only man who was on her mind was him.

***

"So what are you going to do?" Tammy asked Kim as she drove down the street.

"I really don't know yet," Kim responded, looking out of her bedroom window at Lamar washing his car. Kim had broken down the whole offer that was presented to her by her boss, hoping to get some good advice from a friend. Tammy was the only person Kim had told so far, and she wanted to keep it that way until she had a chance to talk to Lamar about it tonight.

"I'm not gonna lie, girl. If I were you, I'd take the job," Tammy said as she turned onto the block where Chris's mom lived. "Medical, college, and free housing. Girl, you'd be a damn fool. It ain't shit goin' on in this neighborhood anyway. I wish I was in ya shoes."

Pulling in front of the house, Tammy could smell the drama brewing. Brea had two of her girlfriends out there with her, looking as jealous as they wanted. Tammy really didn't feel like the bullshit today. "Girl, let me call you back," Tammy said, ending the call.

Tammy put her hazard lights on then got out of the car, only to be eyeballed by everybody standing out there. "Is the kids in there?" Tammy asked Brea as she headed for the steps.

"No. My mom took them out to eat. If you wasn't so busy, you would have picked up ya phone when she was trying to call you," Brea replied in a slick manner.

Tammy didn't pay Brea's smart tone any mind. "Well, just tell ya mom to call me whenever she gets back. I'll have my phone on me this time," Tammy said, walking back to her car.

"I don't know what ya brother saw in that bitch," Aisha said to Brea, while watching Tammy walk off.

Tammy heard the comment and wasn't going to respond, but the "bitch" word somehow got under her skin. "Everything he would never see in you," Tammy shot back as she opened the driver side door.

"Oh, no, dat bitch didn't," Brea instigated, hyping Aisha up. "She's so disrespectful," Brea nagged on.

Before Tammy could sit down in the car, Aisha was tugging away at a handful of her hair. She pulled Tammy out from between the door and the body of the car, and began swinging wildly at her face. Going toe to toe, Aisha didn't stand a chance. Once Tammy got her footing, it was over. She pummeled Aisha, dropping her to the ground with just a couple of punches.

"Get dis bitch off of me," Aisha yelled out from the ground. "Brea, Kisha," she continued yelling through the punches to her face.

Feeling bad for Aisha, Brea and Kisha ran over to help. It took one wild punch from Tammy that landed on Brea's chin to really get it poppin'. Brea and Tammy were instantly locked in a brawl, throwing punch for punch at each other. Neighbors started coming out of their houses and off their porches to see the fight.

While locked in battle, Kisha and Aisha seized the opportunity and started swinging on Tammy. In a three against one fight, they whooped Tammy's ass, despite the lock hold Tammy had on Brea's throat. Tammy really didn't care about losing, just as long as she got the main culprit out of the bunch.

"Look, I want you to take some money and go stay with ya folks for a few days," Ralphy told Lisa, who had just walked into the kitchen. Ralphy had been sitting at the kitchen table all afternoon replaying the events that happened at Johanne's. He tried to think of an alternate way to handle the problem, without the use of violence, but none of his ideas mapped out a positive solution. There was only one way to deal with the problem, and that was by holding court in the streets.

"Babe, you really don't have to do this. We can just move away. I'll follow you anywhere," Lisa pleaded, seeing the vicious road Ralphy was heading down. Lisa didn't understand how Ralphy felt having a gun pointed at him and his daughter, with the threat to terminate his life. Although Naomi was physically okay, she was still a little shaken up from the confrontation. That in itself fueled the fire inside of Ralphy.

"We can still move away, but I gotta take care of something first," Ralphy said.

"I don't wanna lose you," Lisa cried, taking a seat on his lap. "Dis shit just ain't worth it." It wasn't worth it, but it was the street life, and running away wasn't the solution. "So when will it end? When will this all be over?" Lisa asked, laying her head on his chest.

Ralphy lightly put his hand on Lisa's stomach, over the bullet wound. Images of the gunmen opening fire on him and Lisa rushed thought his mind. All the faces Ralphy saw were locked into his memory, and his heart raced at the thought of revenge.

"It's over after I kill everything movin'."

Kim was in her bedroom packing her and Lamar's weekend bags when her phone started ringing on the nightstand. She walked over, looked at the screen, and saw that it was Tammy calling.

"These bitches just jumped me!" Tammy yelled into the phone the moment Kim answered it.

"What bitches, and where are you?" Kim shot back, dropping the shirt she had in her hand.

The phone went silent, but Kim could hear a car speeding down the street outside of her front window. She looked though the blinds and it was Tammy coming to screeching stop in front of her house. Kim shot down the steps, meeting her at the front door.

"Girl, what happened?" Kim asked, coming out of the doorway while Tammy paced back and forth across the porch.

Tammy's hair was everywhere and she had scratches all up and down her face. Her top lip was busted and her clothes were still disheveled from the fight. She could barely get any words out, but once Brea's name was mentioned, Kim knew exactly who it was.

"Hold on, dis shit ain't over," Kim said, shooting back into the house to change her clothes.

Kim moved faster than Clark Kent the way she ran upstairs, threw a pair of jeans on with a T-shirt, and put on a pair of Jordans. She put her hair in a ponytail, wrapped the end in a bun, then put one of her wigs on over it. She came back down the stairs in less than two minutes with a jar of Vaseline, some for her face and some for Tammy's.

When she got back outside, she was shocked to see Falisha standing at the bottom of the stairs tying her shoelaces tight. She had rings on every

other finger, and on both hands, so it was obvious
Falisha was there to fight as well. Lisa must have
heard the commotion, because she made her way
outside, curious to know what was happening.

"What y'all bitches up to?" Lisa asked, walking
across the street with a glass of lemonade in her
hand. "Oh shit, girl, what happened to you?" she
asked once she got close enough to see Tammy's
face.

"Chris's sister and her friends jumped me,"
Tammy answered, applying the Vaseline to her
face in the rearview mirror. "They couldn't beat me
one on one, so they had to jump me."

Lisa only wished that she could go with the
girls for an old-fashioned throw down. The last
time they did something like this together was
in high school. The bullet wound to her stomach
prevented Lisa from actually participating in the
festivities, but being the getaway driver was the
perfect part for her to play.

"Hold up, Falisha. Where do you think you're
going?" Lisa asked as they were loading into the
car. "You need to sit ya pregnant ass down somewhere."

"Yeah, Falisha, don't risk it," Tammy agreed.

Falisha looked at both of them like they were
crazy. "I'ma either ride on top of this hood or in
the back seat. Either one is fine with me," Falisha
replied, climbing into the back seat before anybody
could say anything.

Falisha was no more than four months pregnant and wasn't showing in the least. Besides, nobody in the car was going to be able to physically stop her from coming along, so the only thing they could do was just let her go. It was all crew love, and Falisha wasn't going to miss out on this for anybody. When it came down to her girls, she was willing to go all out.

"Yo, you sure you wanna go through with this, homie? I mean this is practically ya club," Tank, one of Lamar's fellow dancers, said as he poured the two another shot of Hennessy.

Lamar looked around the empty club and thought about how much he was going to miss dancing at Club Mandingo. He thought long and hard about this decision, and concluded that he wanted a different life for him and Kim once they got married. Over the past few years, Lamar had saved up more than enough money, and was in a position to give up dancing and try something new.

"You know, sometimes in life, you gotta make sacrifices in order to grow as a person. I'm at a stage in my life where I'm trying to chill out and enjoy what the world has to offer."

"Man, what da hell is you talking about?" Tank laughed. "You sound like an old-ass man."

They shared a laugh at the comment. Tank was still young, and young-minded, for that matter. Lamar wasn't that old either, but his mentality exceeded his age, and it showed by him taking a big step in wanting to settle down and get married.

"Well, big homie, if that's the road you're taking, then we gon' have to turn this mothafuckin' club up before you leave. Hopefully, after you leave we can call this Tank's Room," Tank said, throwing back another shot.

"I'm wit' you on that, li'l homie. We gon' give 'em hell for the next month," Lamar nodded before throwing back his last and final shot.

"There those bitches go right there," Tammy said as soon as Lisa turned down the block. Brea, Aisha, and Kisha were still standing in front of Chris's mom's house, and from the way they were smacking each other's hands and laughing, Tammy knew that they were bragging about the beat down they gave her. That only added fuel to the fire.

"Park up there," Kim told Lisa, pointing to an empty parking space a little farther down the block.

When Tammy's car passed by Brea, she knew it was about to be on and poppin'. The crowd of people who once dispersed had returned to see round two. Tammy, Falisha, and Kim all got out of the car. Lisa did too, but she stood by the car with a pocketknife in her hand.

"I got Brea," Tammy said as all three women walked up the street.

The talking was over, and as all six women stood in the middle of the street, they clashed like two armies on foot. Kim took Aisha while Falisha punished Kisha. Kisha didn't even get a chance to throw a punch. Falisha was all over her, pulling Kisha's head down by her hair and kneeing her in the face multiple times.

Aisha grabbed Kim's hair, only to pull off the wig that Kim had purposely put on for that reason. Kim threw about ten right-hand punches at lightning speed, all of which landed on Aisha's face. Aisha swung back wildly, hitting Kim a couple of times, but not fazing her.

Brea and Tammy was the main event everybody wanted to see. It was like Mayweather and Pacquiao, with Tammy being Mayweather. They stood in the middle of the street and exchanged blow after blow. Tammy pushed Brea against a nearby parked car, using it like it was the ropes. They were fighting like cats and dogs.

Kim beat Aisha up so bad, the girl took off running down the street. Meanwhile, Falisha had Kisha pinned down on the steps, whaling at her face. The rings on her fingers were cutting Kisha's face so bad, one of the men who was out there watching the fight had to stop it. He walked over and hooked his arm around her stomach and pulled Falisha off the girl. Thinking about her baby, Falisha didn't put up any resistance as the man carried her across the street, away from Kisha. Her point had been made.

"Beat dat bitch's ass!" Kim yelled out, looking at Tammy and Brea, who were now rolling around on the ground. "You got her, Tammy!" she continued yelling.

"Fuck dat bitch up!" Falisha also yelled, coming over to the fight.

After several more punches were thrown by each of them, fatigue started to set in, and the fight became a holding match. The same guy who broke up Falisha's fight came over and pulled Tammy and Brea apart as well. Once Tammy stood there and got herself together, she, Kim, and Falisha headed back to the car, knowing that they had come, handled their business, and left with a victory.

Chapter 37

Ralphy really couldn't sleep well with so much on his mind. He couldn't seem to figure how those guys with the guns knew he and Johanne lived at that house. Johanne swore that she didn't tell them, and there was no way they followed her home the day she was shot, because she went straight to the hospital. Nothing really made sense, and it was eating away at Ralphy like a disease.

Ralphy sat in a chair in the corner of his bedroom looking over at Lisa and Naomi, who were still asleep in the bed. They looked peaceful, to the point where it gave Ralphy a bit of tranquility. His thoughts were interrupted by a text that came through his phone, which he read promptly. It was from Scoop.

Heard about what happened. Are you good? the message read.

Ralphy started to hit him back, but paused for a moment. His brain went into overdrive and he couldn't help himself for making Scoop a suspect. First and foremost, ever since the day the gunmen ran down on him, Naomi, Johanne, and DeeDee, Ralphy had stayed at his house he shared with

Lisa as a precautionary measure. Ralphy put off all his drug dealing in the hood until the situation with Dre's people was taken care of. He never called Scoop, or saw him to tell him about what happened. The only people who knew about it were the people who were there. There was no way Scoop should have known what happened.

"Not you, homie," Ralphy mumbled to himself.

Then it hit Ralphy. Scoop was probably the only person who knew where he and Johanne stayed, plus he had been acting a little funny lately, making subliminal comments Ralphy didn't catch on to at the time. Now Ralphy was almost sure that Scoop had something to do with it; and, if that was true, it was possible Ralphy, Lisa, and Naomi were in danger at that very moment, because Scoop also knew the location of the house Ralphy was in right now. Ralphy started to regret not taking Lisa and Naomi to her folks', but now was just as good as ever; and getting his family out of the house was now the number one priority, and exactly what he planned to do.

Tammy was sore as hell when she finally woke up in her bed. Every part of her body was aching, and it was like a mission in itself getting out of the bed to go to the bathroom. When she walked past the mirror, she barely recognized herself, due to the many marks she had on her face, and the patches of weave missing from her head.

"Well, well, well. If it ain't Bernard Hopkins." Darious smiled while standing at the bathroom sink brushing his teeth.

"Shut up and move," Tammy replied, brushing by him and taking a seat on the toilet. Usually Tammy would be a little more private with her bathroom usage around Darious, but today wasn't one of those days. She pissed and farted like he wasn't even there. Darious couldn't do anything but chuckle.

"You should get back in bed," Darious suggested.

"No, no. I gotta go pick up the kids. I told Ms. Elaine I'd be there to get them this morning."

When Ms. Elaine finally did come home with the kids, Tammy was in her bed licking her wounds, and didn't feel like coming back outside. She also didn't feel like being chewed out about the fight, which was inevitable.

"You want me to take you?" Darious asked, not sure if it was safe for Tammy to go over there by herself.

"No, I'm good, babe. I think I got my point across yesterday," Tammy answered, getting up from the toilet.

"Well, look, while you're out, I need you to drop off Ms. Pam's medication. I got a lot of running around to do today, and I really don't have the time," Darious said, following Tammy out of the bathroom.

"Yeah, I got you, babe. Just make sure you call her and tell her to be downstairs waiting. God knows I can't walk up four flights of stairs today."

Darious walked over and wrapped his arms around Tammy's waist as she stood in front of the dresser looking in the vanity mirror. She pulled out what weave she had left in her head and fought through the pain in her scalp while combing her real hair into a ponytail.

"You too pretty to be fighting," Darious said, kissing Tammy softly on the neck. "You be careful going over there. If you have any problems, call me so I can come get you."

Tammy nodded her head before going into her drawer to grab some jeans and a shirt to slip on. She had to move fast, because Ms. Elaine had called about three times already. She didn't know it yet, but this was going to be the last time Ms. Elaine saw the kids for a while. After yesterday, Tammy was pretty much fed up with the drama in that family.

Lamar woke up to the feeling of his dick being sucked on by Kim. When he cracked his eyes open, her head was bobbing up and down at a slow pace, and the sensation of her warm spit spilling onto his balls seemed to have made his dick even harder. She looked up and saw that he had awoken, and pulled him out of her mouth.

"Good morning," she greeted him, kissing the head of his dick.

Lamar reached up, grabbed the back of her head, and pushed it back down on his dick. "You talkin' too much," he said, pushing his dick deep into her soft, wet throat. Kim smacked the side of his leg playfully, but continued to go down on him. It made her horny to see the look of pleasure on his face. So, while she sucked, Kim reached under and began playing with her pussy. Her moaning at the same time she sucked turned Lamar on so much, he could feel himself about to cum.

"Come 'ere," he demanded, pulling Kim by her hair up to him. "Sit down on dis dick," he told her.

"Shhhh, you talkin' too much," she shot back, climbing on top of him. Her pussy was super wet, and Kim damn near came when she sat all the way down on it. She bit down on her lower lip, swaying her hips back and forth while pinching her nipples, trying her best to fight a massive orgasm that was just about at its peak.

"Come on, baby. Give it to me," Lamar said, knowing Kim was about to cum. "Dis ya dick, baby. Cum all over daddy's dick," he encouraged her.

It was impossible for Kim to hold it back any longer. It felt too good to even try. "Mmmmmm,

I'm cumming, daddy," she moaned, looking down into his eyes.

Her pussy tightened around his dick, followed by a stream of her fluids gushing out of her. Lamar could feel it pouring down his shaft, causing him to want to explode inside of her. Kim could see it in his eyes as well, but she had another plan for where she wanted his nut to go.

With one hand on Lamar's stomach for leverage, Kim rose up from his soaking wet member, grabbed it with her free hand, and guided it into her ass. His large mushroom head penetrated her rectum for the first time. It was too big for her to just sit right on it, so she inched it in, little by little, until it was all the way inside. Lamar didn't last a minute inside her ass. It was tighter, and seemed just as wet as her pussy, thanks to her cum being used as a lube. He held her waist and pushed his dick in and out of her at a fast pace. It took every bit of ten pumps before he shot his load into her.

Kim almost fainted from the pain, and as soon as she saw that he had cum, she jumped off of it and exhaled loudly. The pain was almost unbearable, but it was the price she was willing to pay in order for Lamar not to cum inside her pussy, and possibly get her pregnant before she could get on birth control. She was done, and she made it known by curling up under the blankets at the other end of the bed. Lamar couldn't even touch her, and when he looked down at his dick, he didn't want to either, because his number one priority became him heading to the bathroom to wash the blood and shit off of his dick.

Tammy pulled up to the red light and looked around before grabbing her cell phone to call Ms. Pam to let her know that she was a few blocks away from her apartment complex. Ms. Pam told her that she was sitting out front as they spoke. As soon as Tammy hung up the phone, the light turned green, but out of nowhere a cop car pulled in front of her before she could cross the intersection. She had to slam on the brakes in order for her not to hit the car. "What da hell?" she mumbled to herself, putting the car in park.

She looked around, and from behind her, an unmarked car pulled up to her rear, pretty much boxing her in. The plainclothes officer in front of her got out of his car, only to direct the heavy traffic around her. Tammy was still confused, but then a white male dressed in a suit tapped on her window. The guy didn't look older than eighteen years old, and fresh out of high school, but as soon as Tammy rolled her window down, he showed her that he wasn't a boy at all.

"DEA!" the man said, flashing his badge at her. "I'm gonna need you to step out of the vehicle, Tammy," he told her as he stepped back.

Tammy was blown back by the agent knowing her name before she told him. She was even more confused when she stepped out of the car and saw a K-9 unit coming down the street toward her. Another unmarked car joined in the stop, and two more white men got out of their cars and were staring at Tammy like she was a T-bone steak with A.1. Sauce on it.

"Can I ask you what's going on?" Tammy said, realizing that she was being detained.

"Where's the drugs?" the agent asked while waving for the K-9 unit. "If they're in there, then you need to give them to us. Otherwise, this dog is going to rip this car to shreds, and ten times out of ten, he's going to find it."

"What drugs?" Tammy asked with a confused look on her face. "I don't know what you're talking . . ."

Tammy stopped in the middle of her sentence and remembered Ms. Pam's medication sitting in the center console. Thinking that what she had was not that serious, she tried to go into the car and grab it. The agent reacted by yelling at her not to. He wasn't sure if she was going to reach for a gun, and he definitely wasn't going to take the chance.

"Just tell me where it's at," the agent said, pinning Tammy against the car with his hand.

"It's in the console," she told him.

For safety purposes, he put Tammy in hand-cuffs, which she didn't like one bit; but she had no other choice but to comply. The agent then went into the car and retrieved the pharmacy bag full of pills. "Is that it?" the agent asked, holding the bag up in front of her face.

"Yes, that's all. Now can you please tell me what's going on? I have to pick up my kids," Tammy complained, still not aware of the trouble she was in.

"Don't worry about ya kids right now. I'm gonna need you to come with me," the agent said, taking her to the back of his car.

Once she had gotten into the back seat of the unmarked car, it hit her. All this had to be about something Darious was doing, and from the looks of it, Tammy knew that she was on her way to jail. It didn't matter any that she wasn't aware of anything illegal going on, and the agents surely didn't seem to care about her ignorance, as the three white men gathered around laughing and holding the bag of pills. Tammy couldn't help but to sit there and cry.

By the time Lisa and Naomi woke up, Ralphy was gone. The whole time she made breakfast for her and Naomi, she had a gut feeling that something was wrong. She couldn't quite put her finger on it, but she knew that it had something to do with Ralphy.

"Baby, sit here and eat your food. Mommy gotta make a quick phone call," Lisa said, walking into the living room and grabbing her phone off the charger.

When she called Ralphy's phone, she could hear it ringing upstairs. She went upstairs and grabbed the phone, curious as to why he left it behind. Not only did he leave his phone behind, he also left the keys to the Range Rover; and, sure enough, when Lisa looked out the bedroom window, the car was parked a little bit down the street.

"What da hell are you up to, Ralphy?" Lisa mumbled, looking down at his cell phone.

Tammy sat in a room waiting for the federal agent to come in and tell her what was going on. He didn't say anything to her the whole ride downtown, despite Tammy asking several times where they were going. Sitting there was nerve-racking, and for some odd reason it was cold as the North Pole.

About thirty minutes went by before an agent entered the room. It wasn't the same one who arrested her, and that was due to the first one not being the lead agent on the case. The agent who was in front of Tammy now looked a lot older, and way more seasoned.

"My name is Special Agent Grant, and I work for the Drug Enforcement Agency," he said, taking a seat in a chair on the other side of the desk.

"I don't understand what's going on," Tammy said.

"Well, I don't believe that to be totally true. We've been watching ya boyfriend for quite some time now, and you alone have made over forty deliveries for him in the past couple of weeks, half of which went to one of my informants," Grant said, pulling a couple of pharmacy medication bags out of his legal folder.

"He told me that the medication belonged to his patients, and that it was legal for him to—"

"Tammy, knock it off. You're not stupid, and given your history with Chris, you're not a stranger to the drug world."

Tammy sat there quietly. It seemed as if Grant knew everything about her.

"Right now, you gotta make a choice, and that is whether you wanna walk out of here today, or go to jail, more than likely for a very long time."

One of the best tactics the feds used in building their cases was going after the weakest links in the organizations and turning them. Not only were they good at it, they were great, and most of the time, women with something to lose were their main targets. Tammy was perfect. She had two kids whom she loved more than anything in the world, and Grant was well aware of it.

"What do you want from me?" Tammy asked, rubbing her arms together, trying to get warm.

Grant had a pretty good case against Darious, but he wanted it to be stronger than it was. He needed more, like prescription receipts, names of his clients, the number of pills he sold, and how much he made from them. Percocet was the new thing, and it was highly addictive, like heroin. Profit from selling it was through the roof, but at the same time it left behind an alarming death rate. The feds wanted it off the streets immediately, and they were locking people up for a very long time if caught.

"I want you to be an informant for me. I want you to wear a wire and break down Darious's whole—"

"No, I'm not doing that," Tammy said, cutting him off. "I'm not getting involved with that."

"You're already involved and, to be honest with you, you're in over your head. Do you know how much time you're facing if I go out there and file these charges against you? You delivered forty prescriptions, around one hundred pills per bag. The mandatory minimum for that is twenty years in federal prison," Agent Grant lied.

There wasn't any mandatory minimum for that amount of pills, but Tammy didn't know that. It was a scare tactic that had Tammy deep in thought. Agent Grant wasn't done with his verbal assault.

"You need to think about your kids, Tammy. Don't lose them on account of a man you've only known for a few months. How do you think Anthony's going to feel coming to see you in prison, or Sinniyyah, whom you'll watch grow up from your jail cell? Their father is already in prison; what you think will happen to them with both parents locked up?" Agent Grant asked.

He used her kids as a weapon, as most agents do when it comes to women. It was their weak spot, and Tammy wasn't any different. When threatening to separate her from her two kids, the choice to cooperate was easy. She loved Darious, but she loved her kids and her freedom even more, and wasn't going to risk losing them for anybody.

"Just let me know what you need me to do," Tammy said, crossing her arms over her chest.

Chapter 38

Kim's asshole was still in pain when she walked out onto the pool deck with her towel wrapped around her waist. The only reason she came out was because she wanted to talk to Lamar. Too much was going on right now.

"It's hot as hell out here," Kim said, taking the towel from around her waist and laying it on the ground right next to Lamar. "You gettin' in?"

She looked sexy as hell in her lime green and yellow Lenny Niemeyer bikini, and on her feet were a pair of green Chuck Taylors, which she took off before jumping into the swimming pool. Lamar took his shades off and dove right in behind her, swimming up and lifting her out of the water.

"Ya ass still hurt?" Lamar chuckled, thinking about how funny her walk looked when she came outside.

"Shut up," she replied, pinching him in the chest. "Never again." She smiled, wrapping her arms around his neck.

Lamar walked around the pool, holding Kim up with her legs wrapped around his waist. It was peaceful, and this was exactly how he'd hoped this getaway would go.

"Babe, I need to talk to you about something," Kim said with a serious look on her face.

Still walking her around the pool, Lamar became attentive. "What's going on?" he asked, seeing that something was bothering her. "Talk to me."

"I got a job offer the other day, but it's not in the city. Shit, it's not even in the same state, but it's the chance of a lifetime," Kim began. She broke down the whole proposal that was given to her by her boss, leaving nothing out; but when she got to the part about moving to Philadelphia, Lamar lost interest.

"So what did you tell them?" Lamar asked, hoping that she didn't already say yes.

"I told them I had to think about it, and they gave me until next week to decide. I had to talk to you first, because how you feel matters to me."

"I'm not gon' lie, shawty. I'm not tryin' to move to Philly. I'm a country boy, and those niggas up North move too fast for me," he told her.

Not surprised at all, Kim figured Lamar would say something along those lines. "So you're telling me not to go?" Kim asked, wanting to be clear.

Lamar turned his head, trying not to keep eye contact. "I'm not telling you that you can't go. All I'm saying is that I'm not going with you to no Philadelphia."

"Wowwww!" Kim said, pushing off him. "I didn't expect that from you, but I'm good," Kim said, before climbing out of the swimming pool and storming off back into the hotel.

Lamar called out for her, but Kim kept trucking. He started to feel bad, and smacked the water in frustration before climbing out of the pool to head back into the hotel.

Tammy walked into the bedroom where Darious was counting money on the bed. There had to be at least $70,000 in all denominations, and now the money that Darious told her was for a rainy day was sure starting to look like drug money to Tammy.

"Can I ask you something, babe?" Tammy said, taking a seat on the edge of the bed.

"Yeah, wassup?" he responded, not picking his head up.

Tammy was nervous as hell, especially since she had a wire and a small camera hooked up to her Gucci bag sitting on the nightstand. All she had to do was reach over, grab the bag, and turn it on. She looked at Darious and thought about how much she really did love him, despite how long they had been together. Doing so made her not reach for the bag right away to turn on the device. She struggled with wanting to help him or throw him to the wolves.

"Are you trappin'?" Tammy asked flat out.

Darious picked his head up from counting the money to see her looking at him dead in his eyes. The question kind of caught him off guard, but he played it cool. "What makes you think I'm trappin'?" He chuckled, looking back down at the money.

"I know you might think that I'm green, Darious, but I'm not. I only turn a blind eye 'cause I love you," she said, reaching over to lift his head up.

"Why you asking when you already know?" he replied.

"I just want you to tell me the truth. I think I deserve to know, and I should hear it from your mouth. Shit, I have two kids living here."

"You know I'll never let nothing happen to you or the kids," Darious spoke in a serious tone. He got up off the bed and walked around to where Tammy was sitting. He got on his knees and sat between her legs. "Tammy, I love you, and there's nothing in this world I wouldn't do for you," he said, looking around the room. "I want us to live comfortably, and I wanna be able to buy you nice things and take you nice places. It's a sacrifice—"

"It's a sacrifice I don't need you to make," Tammy said, cutting him off. "I don't need all of these things to be happy. All I need is you."

Tammy found herself giving Darious the same speech she gave Chris when he was out in the streets trappin'. She had been down this road before, and taking into consideration all that had happened today, Tammy could see that the same outcome was going to repeat itself with Darious.

"Darious, I need to tell you something," Tammy said, putting her hands over his.

"What is it, babe?" he asked, kissing her hand.

Tammy looked over at her Gucci bag then back at him. She wanted to tell him so bad about the DEA and how they wanted her to get certain information for them concerning his drug transactions, but the conversation she had with Agent Grant kept running through her mind. She kept thinking about her kids and them being taken away from her right before they threw her in federal prison. "I'm pregnant," she lied, knowing that in a couple of months, Darious would be in jail.

The thing Tammy didn't expect from her little white lie was how happy Darious was to hear the news. He smiled from ear to ear then kissed Tammy's empty stomach. It was almost as if he was trying to get her knocked up, and had finally succeeded. He was so happy, he kind of made Tammy feel a little happy too, as if it were true.

The fact of the matter was, Tammy was telling a lie, and even though Tammy wasn't reaching into her Gucci bag to turn on the device tonight, tomorrow was another day. One thing she wasn't going to do was continue to play around with her freedom, because she knew from experience that the feds were nothing to play with.

***

Ralphy parked his rental car around the corner from Cedar Street then sat there contemplating what he was about to do. His instincts told him that Scoop had something to do with Dre's people attempting to kill him. He thought about it, and everything seemed to come back to Scoop. It was hard for Ralphy to swallow the fact that his close friend would set him up like this but, at the same time, that friendship shit went out the door the minute Scoop chose his side.

Ralphy reached under his seat, grabbed a chrome .38 snub nose, and tucked it in his hoodie pouch. It was his throwaway gun, and out from the center console he pulled his back-up gun: a seventeen-shot Glock 9 mm. He was bringing that along in case things got out of hand.

"Do what you do," Ralphy spoke to himself as he got out of the car.

The sun was just below the horizon, so the sky was only minutes away from being dark, just the way Ralphy needed it to be. Everything in all black, Ralphy threw his hood over his head and proceeded down the street. Cedar Street was the next block over, and instead of walking around the long way, Ralphy cut through an alleyway, which led to the top of the block.

Scoop was sitting in his car watching the dope-fiend traffic down the block. Ralphy couldn't tell through the tint whether he had somebody in the car with him, but at this point it really didn't matter. Ralphy emerged from the alley and walked right up to Scoop's car. Only seeing a shadow out of his peripheral view, Scoop reached for his weapon.

"It's me, nigga," Ralphy said, pulling his hood back slightly so Scoop could see who it was.

Even after seeing who it was, Scoop kept his gun in his hand as he got out of the car. Ralphy kept his hand in his hoodie pouch, wrapped around the .38 with his finger hugging the trigger.

"Damn, homie, what you creepin' for?" Scoop asked, still not sure of Ralphy's intent.

Ralphy never was the type to beat around the bush, and today wasn't going to be any different, even if Scoop had a gun in his hand. "Yo, homie, let me ask you this," Ralphy said, standing directly in front of Scoop. "How did you find out about them niggas who ran down on me at da spot? I damn sure didn't tell nobody what happened," Ralphy questioned him.

Scoop's heart started pounding out of his chest. He couldn't tell him that the reason he knew was because he was actually there when it happened. Scoop never got out of the Impala that day, but he saw everything go down. He knew that Ralphy would try to kill him if he knew that piece of information.

"Come on, brah. What are you talking about?" Scoop said, trying to play it off. "Everybody knows about that."

From the look in Ralphy's eyes, Scoop knew that the answer he gave didn't sit well with him. They shared a quick, awkward moment of silence before Scoop looked and saw Ralphy's hand move in his hoodie pouch.

"What's all that about?" Scoop asked, gripping his gun a little tighter. "What, you gon' shoot me, nigga?" he said, hyping himself up for the gun battle he knew was about to erupt.

Ralphy didn't say anything, and in Scoop's eyes, it was either kill or be killed at this point. Scoop's gun was already out in his hand, so he felt he had the advantage. They stood there staring at each other like two cowboys in the Old West days, waiting for the clock to strike twelve so they could start fighting.

Feeling froggy, Scoop went to raise his gun up, but Ralphy blazed through his hoodie pouch. Pop! Pop! Pop! Pop! Every bullet hit Scoop in his upper body area, knocking him backward onto his car. Scoop still tried to raise the gun to get a shot off, but Ralphy grabbed it with his left hand, pulled the .38 out with his right hand, and gave Scoop a head shot.

Scoop's body went limp instantly, dropping to the ground between the parked cars. Seeing that the commotion got the attention of a few workers at the end of the block, Ralphy knew that he didn't have long before they ran up the street, guns blazing. He took his sleeve and wiped down the .38 real nicely before tossing it next to Scoop's body, and then walking off into the night.

Kim and Lamar's little getaway didn't turn out to be all that great after Lamar ruined the mood with his rude comments about the whole moving to Philadelphia situation. It was quiet for the most part in the room, and the only real conversation they had was concerning what type of food they were going to order. If Kim didn't care about wasting her money for the room, she would have gone home, with or without Lamar.

"Babe, can we talk?" Lamar asked, breaking the silence in the room.

Kim cut her eyes over at him. Seeing her mean face only made Lamar smile.

"No, for real, babe. I wanna talk," he said, scooting over a little closer to her on the bed.

Sitting there in silence for most of the night had given Lamar plenty of time to think. He weighed the pros and the cons of moving so far away, and remained firm about not wanting to go. But then reality set in.

"Look, first I want to apologize to you for being selfish and not being understanding toward ya situation. You have a great opportunity to do something major, and I'm sitting here being an asshole not supporting you," Lamar said. "I'm not going to lie, I really don't wanna move that far away; but I love you, and if you really want to move to Philly, then I'll ride out with you," he told her, taking her hand into his.

Kim sat up in the bed, holding her ring finger out. "We are about to get married, Lamar."

"I know, I know. And there's gonna be a lot of sacrifices both of us will make. I get it, and I promise you that I will communicate with you better in the future," Lamar assured her.

Kim's frown turned upside down. She leaned in and kissed him on his neck then lay down across his lap. She was so in love with Lamar, and it was moments like these when she felt that Lamar loved her back. It made everything they went through worth it. At the end of the day, she had his back and he had hers, the way that it is supposed to be.

Tammy's phone vibrated on the nightstand next to the bed, waking her up out of her sleep. She wasn't going to answer it, but it just kept buzzing to the point where it was about to wake Darious up too. She grabbed it and looked at the screen. It was

Falisha, and it was also two o'clock in the morning,
Tammy noticed from the clock that sat next to the
phone.

"Yeah," Tammy answered with a scratchy voice.

Tammy could hear Falisha crying and yelling at
somebody else in the background, telling them to
mind their own business. It was later determined
that it was Falisha's mom she was talking to.

"Girl, I'm stressed da fuck out right now,"
Falisha said, finally saying something to Tammy.

"Talk to me, Falisha. What's going on?" Tammy
asked, getting out of her bed and walking to the
bathroom so she wouldn't disturb Darious.

Falisha began pouring her heart out, something
Tammy had never seen before. "I don't wanna
have my baby by myself. I see young girls every
day struggling to take care of their children all
by themselves. I don't wanna be like that, and
this asshole got the nerve to get engaged to Kim,"
Falisha spazzed.

"Whaaaat!" Tammy spoke, surprised this piece
of gossip was just now hitting her ears. "So you still
didn't tell him yet?"

"Not yet. And I don't even know if I want to now.
Kim gon' think that I'm desperate and who knows
what Lamar is going to think. I wanna tell him
but . . . I don't know. This pregnancy shit is fucking
with my head right now," Falisha said, wiping the
tears away.

Tammy called these the single mother blues. Everything Falisha was going through right now, Tammy had been there and done that. Raising a kid alone wasn't easy at all, and Tammy wasn't going to lie and make her think that it was going to be.

"Look, Falisha, if you plan on keeping this baby, you gotta do what's best for your child. Don't worry about what Kim thinks or anybody else for that matter," Tammy told her.

The advice was a little tough, since all of them were friends, but Tammy did nothing less than keep it one hundred. What Falisha did with the advice was totally up to her, but in Tammy's eyes Lamar needed to know that he was about to be a father, and telling him now would be better than telling him later.

Ralphy looked up and down the block carefully before entering the house he had with Johanne. Once inside, he pulled the Glock from his waist and held it down by his side as he walked through the house. The light in the kitchen made it possible for him to see enough not to walk into things. He hadn't been there in a couple of days, nor had he spoken to Johanne much.

Feeling like the house was secure, he shot upstairs to his bedroom to see if Johanne was there or if she was staying over at DeeDee's house like she said she would. When Ralphy got to the bedroom and opened the door, the sound of a heavy snorer filled the room. Knowing that it was physically impossible for that to have been Johanne, Ralphy reached for the light switch and turned it on.

Johanne and another man were in the bed asleep. Ralphy walked up to the bed, and they still didn't wake up. It wasn't until he put the barrel of the gun on Johanne's forehead that she cracked opened her eyes. It was like she had seen a ghost the way her eyes popped out.

"Donny," Johanne called out to the man she'd been sleeping with. "Donny," she called again, this time waking him up.

Ralphy had backed up to the foot of the bed, but he kept the gun pointed at both of them. His eyes were locked on Johanne until Donny said something.

"Hold up, homie, we can talk about this," Donny said, attempting to get up from the bed.

"Lay ya monkey ass down," Ralphy said, pointing the gun at him now.

"I don't have nothin' to do wit' it. Lick want you dead," Donny yelled.

Looking at him for the first time, Ralphy couldn't believe Johanne was lying in his bed with another man. Not just any man, either. It was the second

gunman who insisted on killing Ralphy in front of
his daughter in the driveway. Ralphy never forgot
a face.

Johanne was literally sleeping with the enemy,
and for that, she was going to die with him.

Ralphy squeezed the trigger, sending a hot lead
ball at Donny, hitting him in the center of his forehead. His body slumped over onto Johanne, who
began to cry out. She pled for Ralphy not to shoot
her, and in a final attempt to preserve her life,
Johanne yelled, "I'm pregnant with your baby!"

Her words were ignored as Ralphy aimed
the gun at her. He was already on the path to
Murderville, and at this moment he didn't have
any picks. She was just as guilty as everybody else
who participated in the assassination attempts on
his life. His heart was cold toward each and every
one of them and, without further ado, Ralphy
pulled the trigger on her too. The first bullet hit her
in the chest, knocking her back against the headboard. Ralphy walked up closer, aimed the gun at
her head, and fired again, killing her instantly. He
wiped down his gun thoroughly, tossing it in the
bed before throwing his hood over his head and
walking out of the room.

Chapter 39

Sunday dinner at Ms. D's house took place as usual. The sound of grunts and silverware hitting empty plates was all that could be heard in the dining room. The whole gang was there, and Ms. D was so kind to have invited Darious as well, only so that everyone could officially meet him. He did good for the most part, answering a million and one questions by Tammy's closest friends. Lamar and Ralphy were a little overprotective, but made it perfectly clear that as long as Darious didn't put his hands on Tammy, he would be good.

"Listen up," Ms. D said, getting everyone's attention at the table. "You all know my situation, and I just wanna give you an update on what's going on. Considering the news I got over the course of my last three visits to my doctor, I have decided not to go through with the chemo," she announced.

As she expected, the crowd wasn't happy with her decision. Everyone at the table except Darious put up a protest, yelling out their opinions on the matter, but Ms. D really didn't want to hear it. Her mind was already made up, and there was nothing or nobody who could change it.

"Is everybody done?" Ms. D said, as the commotion wore down. "Now, I didn't ask for any of your medical advice. I told y'all because this is the only family I have left, and if the good Lord takes my soul," Ms. D spoke, "I want y'all to be ready."

When Ms. D started talking about life insurance and her funeral, Falisha got up from the table in tears. Ms. D was like a second mom to her, and pretty much everybody else who was sitting at the table.

"I got her, y'all," Lamar said, getting up from the table and following Falisha out to the porch.

Truth be told, he really didn't feel like hearing Ms. D talk about her situation either. For him Ms. D was like his only mom and he loved her as much.

"I don't like it either," he said, walking up to Falisha. "Come 'ere," he said, extending his arms.

Falisha leaned in and was wrapped up into his body. He spoke softly and gently, bringing Falisha a sense of comfort, one she hadn't felt for quite some time. As she rested her head against his chest, she had a moment where she felt the love that they once shared.

"I have to tell you something," Falisha said while he continued to hold her. "It's ours," she told him as she wiped the tears from her face.

"Huh? What are you talking about?" Lamar asked, pulling away from her.

Falisha looked Lamar in his eyes. "This baby I'm carrying in my stomach is yours, Lamar."

"Yeah, right! Stop playin' wit' me, Falisha," Lamar shot back.

"Do it look like I'm playin? Just think about it, Lamar. I wasn't fuckin' nobody else but you for the past three months," Falisha explained.

"Now, though? You gon' do this now, Falisha? What, you trying to fuck up what me and Kim got going on?" Lamar snapped.

"It ain't my fault. You da one who played me. I was pregnant before you decided you didn't love me anymore. You know what? Fuck you, Lamar!" Falisha tried to smack the fire out of his mouth, but Lamar caught her hand before it connected to his face.

"We don't need you. Now I see why Kim had an abortion," Falisha said, snatching her wrist away from Lamar's grip.

"Now I know you tripping. What the fuck you mean, you know why Kim had an abortion?"

"Like you said, I don't want to fuck up what you and Kim got going on, so maybe you need to ask her."

Falisha rolled her eyes and walked off the porch, leaving Lamar standing there deep in thought. He threw his head back and let out a loud sigh in frustration thinking about Kim possibly killing his child and not telling him about it. He became angry at the thought of it; and if it turned out to be true, it was surely going to be a problem.

After leaving Ms. D's house, Darious, Tammy, and the kids headed home for the night. Anthony and Sinniyyah were in the back seat knocked out cold from their stomachs being full and the night air seeping through the windows, which were cracked open slightly. Wanting to spend some time with Tammy, Darious took the long way home, enjoying the soft music playing at a low volume throughout the car.

"You never answered my question," Tammy said, breaking the silence between them.

Darious looked over at her, not really hearing what she said. "What's that?" he asked.

"I said you never answered my question," Tammy repeated. "That night I asked if you were you trappin', you never answered me," she said, reaching into her Gucci bag and turning on the recording device. She adjusted her pocketbook so that the little camera on the outside of the bag was aimed at him. Agent Grant had called her earlier and told her that she need to come up with something before the deal came off the table. Up until now, she hadn't provided anything that was of use to their case, so the DEA was starting to become a little impatient.

"You're right. I did avoid the question, and that's only because I felt that the less you know the better. If the wrong person got a whiff of what I'm doing, the feds would be knocking at our door in no time," Darious said.

"I just want you to be able to trust me, and I don't want us to have any secrets between us," Tammy spoke.

Darious looked out to the highway, thinking about what Tammy was saying. In a sense, she was right, and there were times when Darious hated the fact that he couldn't share certain aspects of his life with her. Even though what he was doing wasn't considered to be a violent crime, Tammy did deserve to know the truth.

"I trap, but it's not the kind of trappin' that you think," Darious began. "I sell pills. Percocet, Xanax, oxycodone, and every now and again I get my hands on some Molly. I got a doctor in the hospital who forges prescriptions for me, and most of the time I go down to the hospital's pharmacy to get them. Other times, so I won't draw any attention to myself, I take the scripts to the—"

"The neighborhood pharmacies," Tammy said, finishing his sentence. "Damn, boo, is it really a lot of money in pills?" she asked with a curious look on her face.

"Put it this way: I make five dollars off of each pill, wholesale, and I'm moving close to one thousand pills a day. In some cases, depending upon the quality of the pill, that number doubles," Darious explained. He went into detail about his operation, but the information he gave was basic compared to what was going on behind the scenes.

Tammy recorded every word of it. This was sure to be enough for her to get back in good graces with the DEA, and if they needed more Darious was more than comfortable enough to share just about everything with Tammy.

"What's ya problem?" Kim asked, nudging Lamar, who was sitting on the couch with his face balled up. "So you not gon' talk now?" she said after he glanced over at her then turned his focus back on the television without saying anything to her.

The idea of Kim getting an abortion behind his back was the only thing that was on his mind all day. A part of him wanted to know, but then another part wished that it weren't true. So many nights Lamar lay in the bed with Kim talking about wanting to start a family with her, and telling her how good of a father he was going to be. Kim had also expressed her desire to have a child with Lamar, and didn't object when he came inside of her just about every time they had sex. Lamar was confused, and being confused was one of the things that made him so upset.

"Yo, I'ma ask you something, and if you love me as much as you say you do, you won't lie to me," Lamar said, grabbing the remote control and turning the TV off.

"Sure, babe, what is it?" Kim asked.

Lamar didn't know quite how to formulate the question to her without being ignorant. He simply said it the way he felt it: "Did you kill my baby?"

Kim almost choked on her spit when he asked her that. It wasn't what he said, it was how he said it that messed Kim's head up. It was bad enough she had to live with what she had done, but now in the eyes of her soon-to-be husband, she was considered a baby killer. It was a little too harsh, but Kim stood by her decision, and was willing to face the music.

"Yes, I was pregnant by you, and yes, I got an abortion," Kim confessed, putting her head down in shame.

Lamar's heart sank into his stomach after hearing those words. He looked over at Kim, who couldn't find it in herself to even look at Lamar. All the emotions she experienced after the procedure came back, this time tenfold.

"Damn, was I not good enough for you? Did I do something wrong that made you not want to carry my seed inside of you?" Lamar asked, looking over at her.

Kim just sat there for a few minutes saying nothing.

"Oh, now you don't have anything to say?"

"I'm sorry, Lamar. I fucked up, and I regret ever doing it," Kim cried, letting her tears flow freely. "I was scared, and I didn't know if we were going—"

"Kim, I haven't done nothing but love you up until now," Lamar said, cutting her off. "I told you that I wanted a child. Shit, I got down on my knees and asked you to marry me," Lamar snapped.

Kim tried to say something, but Lamar got up from the couch, grabbed his keys off the table, and left the house before she could think of anything. She sat there crying her eyes out, thinking how she might have ruined their relationship. Lamar was crushed, and Kim didn't even know where to begin to try to fix it. All she knew was that the most important man in her life had just walked out the door, and she wasn't sure if he was coming back.

"I don't know what Kim did, but Lamar sure looked mad as hell," Lisa said as she sat on the couch looking out the window.

"You so nosy." Ralphy chuckled, walking over and peeking out of the window too.

"Shut up. And where do you think you're going, dressed like that?" Lisa asked, seeing that Ralphy had on all black.

Ralphy leaned over and kissed Lisa on the forehead. "I gotta take care of something. I'll be back in a couple of hours, babe. You gon' wait up for me?" He smiled.

"You know I am, and I think I might be ready for you," she said, biting her lower lip and giving Ralphy a wink.

Lisa had been feeling extra horny as of late, and not even a bullet wound to the gut was going to stop her from trying to get some tonight. It had been a minute for Ralphy also, considering everything he had been going through lately. He really didn't have sex on his mind, because all he wanted to do was kill.

"You know I love you, right?" Ralphy asked, pressing his forehead against hers.

"I love you more, babe," Lisa responded, grabbing the sides of his face. "Now what are you about to do?" she asked, pulling her head back away from his so she could look him in the eyes.

"Nothing!" Ralphy answered, leaning in and stealing a kiss from her before turning away and walking out the door.

"Do you got ya phone wit' you?" she yelled out the window as he walked down the street.

He held it up in the air right before he got into a rental car. All that leaving the house with no way to contact him was out of the question.

Lamar didn't even bother getting in his car. Instead, he took a walk, hoping that the cool night breeze would calm him down. The night breeze was cool, but it wasn't working at all. He found himself walking into a local playground where several kids were still out playing basketball. Lamar took a seat on the bleacher by himself, checking out the game. Everything that Falisha had told him about Kim turned out to be true, and he couldn't help but to think that maybe the baby that was growing inside of her was his. Thinking back, he was a little out of pocket with his reaction toward the news, and Lamar couldn't blame her for being mad at him. He pulled out his phone and scrolled through it until he got to Falisha's number. Her phone rang several times before going to her voicemail. Lamar tried again but there wasn't an answer.

If anybody had an excuse to get an abortion, it would be Falisha, due to the way Lamar had been treating her. It was crazy, but in Lamar's mind, he hoped that she wouldn't do it. The more he thought about it, the more he needed to talk to Falisha to see what she was going to do.

***

The west side had a big party over at Club 935 and just about everybody was going to be there to see the rapper Young Jeezy. Ralphy knew beyond a shadow of a doubt that Lick was going to be there repping his crew. One thing about the west side boys, they showed out at parties, clubs, and whatever events that went on in the city.

"My man, you can't come in here dressed like that," the bouncer said, stopping Ralphy at the door.

"Dressed like what?" Ralphy responded, looking around at other partygoers who were admitted with no problem.

"No jeans, no boots, and you damn sure ain't coming up in here with no hood on," the bouncer informed him.

Ralphy sized the bouncer up. He had to be every bit of six feet four inches, 300 pounds, and all muscle. Forcing his way in was out of the question, so Ralphy spoke in a language just about everybody understood. He reached in his pocket and pulled out a wad of money about an inch thick, nothing but twenties. The bouncer thought that Ralphy was going to peel off a couple hundred, but he didn't. He extended his hand, offering the whole wad. The bouncer's eyebrow went up, then he looked around before grabbing the money from him.

"Don't start no shit up in here," the bouncer said, stepping to the side and letting Ralphy in.

Ralphy walked right by him, throwing his hood over his head. Inside was a whole lot better than the outside. The party was off the chain, and there had to be well over 1,000 people there, some of whom were females walking around with the least bit of clothing on. Ralphy was like the sore thumb by the way he was dressed, but there were so many people there, nobody seemed to notice him.

Ralphy was like a wolf walking through a herd of sheep. He looked around attentively as he made his way through the crowd of people on the dance floor. Lick wasn't anywhere in sight at first, but then several waitresses parted the crowd as they walked by with sparkle-lit champagne bottles, heading for the VIP section. Ralphy followed the last waitress, but veered off once he got close enough to see Lick, his boys, and a bunch of women holding down the biggest VIP section in the building.

Ralphy went straight to the bathroom, and when he got there he went into one of the stalls. He pulled down his pants to reveal a small, compact .45 automatic that he unstrapped from under his nuts. He cocked it back slightly to make sure he had a bullet in the chamber before tucking it into the front of his hoodie. He had ten shots, plus one in the head, and he needed to be sure that each and every one of them counted for something. Ralphy had to, because after he initiated the gun battle, somebody out of Lick's crew was sure to be blazing back.

"Show these niggas what you're made of," Ralphy mumbled to himself before exiting the stall.

"Dis shit jumpin' tonight. Who you goin' home wit' tonight?" Lick asked the female who was sitting on his lap. "You roll wit' me tonight, I'ma change ya life," he said, looking down at all her thickness.

She leaned in close to his ear and spoke. "If I go home with you tonight, I'ma fuck da shit out of you," she said, and licked his earlobe.

Lick's dick got hard instantly, and if it weren't for the second wave of champagne coming through the crowd, he would have called it a night and taken her straight home. "Yeah, I'ma hold you to that," he told her.

Waitress after waitress, all in a single-file line, walked up and dropped bottles of champagne off at the table. Lick was so focused on the female he had sitting on his lap he didn't notice that the last of the waitresses was actually Ralphy, holding a bottle in one hand and the gun in the other. When he got close enough, Ralphy dropped the sparkling bottle, clutched both hands around the gun and aimed at Lick.

Hearing the bottle crash to the ground, Lick looked up and saw nothing but a gun aimed at his face. He tried to hide behind the female, but Ralphy's aim was superb.

Everybody in VIP dropped to the ground. The first of the three bullets hit Lick in his chest, the second one struck the female he had on his lap in the ass, and the third knocked a chip of wood off the top of the booth they were sitting in. People scattered like roaches, screaming and running out of the VIP area for dear life. Lick sat in the booth holding his chest, trying to put some type of pressure on the wound. It hurt like hell, and he found it hard to breathe. Ralphy kicked the table that stood between him and Lick to the side. Blood from his chest started to fill his lungs, causing Lick to cough up blood. Ralphy walked up on him and pointed the gun at his head.

"Look at me," Ralphy said through clenched teeth. Lick didn't want to. He didn't want the last person he saw to be the person who killed him. Ralphy had to physically lift his chin up to look Lick in his eyes. Ralphy backed up and fired the fatal shot to Lick's head, sending brain matter all over the booth.

When Ralphy turned around to leave, the bouncer who had warned him not to start no shit was standing there with a 12-gauge pump aimed right at him. Ralphy went to drop his gun, but his movement startled the bouncer, forcing him to let off one shot from the shotgun. The impact from the blast lifted Ralphy off his feet, sending him crashing into the table he had previously kicked.

The bouncer walked over, unsure of what he had just done. Ralphy lay there struggling to take his last breaths.

Within a few minutes, while waiting for the medics to arrive, Ralphy died with his eyes open, and only two people were on his mind before his final breath, and that was Lisa and Naomi.

Chapter 40

Stressed out to the max, Kim and Tammy took the day off from work to go to the mall and do a little shopping. There was something about spending money that made life a little easier to live, and that was the common bond that they shared.

"So did y'all even plan the wedding date yet?" Tammy asked, picking up a sundress off the rack and holding it up.

"No. He told me that whenever I was ready, just let me know. Girl, I'm not gon' lie. I don't think it's going to be a wedding," Kim said, looking down at her ring.

"Dat boy just mad right now. He loves you, and I think that all he needs is a little bit of time—"

"He didn't come home last night," Kim said, cutting her off. "He didn't call, leave a text, or anything, and when I tried to call him, he didn't answer."

"Yeah, that's crazy, but it's typical. Men do dumb shit like that when their little feelings get hurt," Tammy said, shaking her head at the dress's color blend. "I'm telling you, girl, he's going to walk through that door today and he's going to be fine."

Kim hoped so. Since Lamar agreed to move to Philadelphia with her, Kim called her boss early that morning to let him know that she was accepting the offer. She thought that the move would give them a chance to start fresh, and if Lamar got her pregnant again anytime soon, she would be sure to keep it.

"So what about you and Darious? How are things going with y'all two?" Kim asked as she headed for the register with a couple of items in her hand.

Tammy couldn't even get into the details of their life. She was confused herself about wanting to tell Darious that the DEA was watching them. There was even a time during the course of their nightly pillow talk when Tammy almost slipped up and told him. Agent Grant's voice continuously repeating, *"twenty years in federal prison,"* always seemed to keep her in check.

"Everything's good. He bought Anthony an Xbox—" Tammy was interrupted by her phone buzzing in her bag. She reached in, grabbed it, and saw that the screen read number unavailable. At first she wasn't going to answer it but she decided to take the call just in case it was Agent Grant.

"You have a prepaid call. You will not be charged for this call. This call is from—"

The operator didn't have to go any further before Tammy pushed 5 to accept Chris's call. This was the first time he'd called since her visit.

"Damn, stranger!" Tammy answered, paying for her stuff then excusing herself away from Kim.

"Wassup wit' you?" Chris replied, leaning back against the wall. "How are you doing?"

Tammy was smiling from ear to ear. He sounded so good, all she wanted to do was stay quiet and let him talk. Being honest with herself, she missed Chris a lot, and thought about him daily, wondering if he would ever call her again. The current situation Darious had her in made her appreciate Chris even more. There was no way he would have ever involved her in his illegal activities.

"I'm good. The kids are good, and I'm still working my ass off. I got some pictures right here in my bag, and as soon as I see a mailbox, I'm going to send them out to you," Tammy said, taking a seat in the food court.

"Yeah, thanks. I haven't seen my kids in a while and, believe it or not, I do love them."

"I know you do, and I'm sorry for not bringing them up there. You know me and ya sister got into a fight a few days ago, so I haven't had a chance to see if ya mom wanted to ride out there with me. You know I don't like to drive by myself." Tammy smiled.

"Yeah, I heard about that, and I told my sister just because we not together no more, you still the mother of my children, and don't make me fuck somebody up for fucking with you. By the way, I miss you," Chris said, putting his head down.

Chris had always been so protective over her. Tammy's eyes started to water and the ball in her throat prevented her from being able to swallow. She missed him too, and wished that he were home to enjoy watching their children grow. She hated him being locked up in prison.

"I know you don't have long on this call, and I give you my word that I will bring the kids up there to see you this weekend, even if I gotta come by myself," Tammy spoke.

"That would be so nice," Chris responded.

"I want you to know that no matter what I do out here, and no matter what you hear from anybody else, Chris, I do and will always love you no matter what. And whenever you get home, I'll be right here to help you in any kinda way I can," Tammy said, wiping the single tear that fell down her cheek.

Chris stayed quiet on the phone. He didn't think that Tammy would ever love him again, nor did he expect for her to be there for him when he came home. As far as he knew, it was over between them; but listening to her, he couldn't help but feel that there was some hope for them to get back together.

They sat and talked for the rest of the time about the kids, school, and work. Kim sat across from her at the table, smiling while Tammy glowed. She hadn't seen her friend smiling and laughing that hard in a long time. Even though she was with Darious physically, and may have even loved him, a part of her heart would always belong to Chris.

Falisha yelled up to her mom to see if she wanted something from the store while she was going. Hunger had set in, and for some odd reason she wanted a large breakfast this morning, including eggs, sausage, bacon, pancakes, home fries, toast with jelly, and some orange juice. After the morning sickness phase of her pregnancy had passed, the cravings hit her full blast.

"Oh, shit! Boy, you scared the hell out of me," Falisha said when she stepped out on the porch and Lamar was standing off to the side. "What do you want and why da fuck is you out here on my porch?" Falisha snapped.

Lamar had been sitting out there just about all morning, hoping to catch Falisha either coming in or going out. He had more than enough time to think last night, and he really felt bad about how he handled the news of the baby. "Can we talk?" Lamar asked, lowering his head in humility. "I really need to talk to you."

"About what, Lamar? You said what you said and that's it."

"I know, I know, and I'm sorry. I really didn't mean for it to come out that way, and I should have let you punch me," he said.

Falisha unbuttoned her shorts and adjusted them so they wouldn't feel so tight. Lamar couldn't help but to notice that she was picking up a few pounds around her waist. Her thighs were also looking a little thicker. Lamar thought it was cute.

"Look, I'm hungry, so unless you plan on taking me to get some breakfast, I'll talk to you later," Falisha said, turning around to lock the front door.

Lamar smiled. "Yeah, I'm kinda hungry myself. I've been out all night," he said, leading the way down the steps. The closest spot was Grandma's Diner, which happened to be Falisha's favorite breakfast spot. It was only about five minutes away by car, so there really wasn't much conversation during the ride. Falisha used that time to check her missed call log and her text messages, most of which were from Lamar.

"Damn I can't believe Grandma's is still da shit," Lamar said when they walked into the diner and saw that it was a full house.

Falisha didn't need a menu. As soon as she got into the booth, she called the waitress over and began ordering. It was everything she had a taste for when she left the house. Lamar kept it simple and got some egg whites, toast, and some orange juice.

"So can I ask you something without you getting an attitude?" Lamar asked, not wanting this conversation to turn into an argument. "Are you really keeping it?"

"You think I'm buying all this food for nothing? Of course I'm keeping my baby, and if you don't want to be a part of our lives, then that's fine, Lamar. The only reason I told you is because I wanted to give you chance to step up and be a man. You and I both know that I can take care of her by myself."

"Her?" Lamar asked, excited about the gender.

Falisha chuckled. "I'm hoping it's a girl. I don't know what I'd do if I had another you running around here."

Lamar got up and sat in the booth next to Falisha. He reached over and placed his hand over her stomach. Falisha put her hand over his. His touch was gentle, and the little tummy ache she had earlier went away the moment he touched her.

"Damn, that's really my baby in there?" Lamar asked with a huge smile on his face.

"Yeah, you're gonna be a daddy ," she answered, also smiling at the thought of motherhood.

Hearing those words made Lamar happy. So happy he leaned over and kissed Falisha on the cheek. She turned and could see the joy in his eyes. They sat there staring at each other for a moment, and then inevitable happened. Lamar leaned back in, but this time he kissed Falisha's soft, full lips. In her mind, she wanted to resist, but her lips were calling the shots right now, and they were begging him not to stop.

A guilty shock raced through his body, causing him to pull back. "Damn, I'm out of pocket," he said, scratching the top of his head.

Falisha was about to respond, but stopped when the waitress brought the food to the table. His guilt was a reminder to Falisha that he still belonged to someone else. It was so embarrassing and humiliating that Falisha lost her appetite. It was ugly, but it was a reality check both of them needed at the time.

Tammy and Kim pulled up to the block to see several cop cars sitting in front of Lisa's house. At first, Tammy thought that they were there for her, and she was about to back up and take her chances running. Lisa's loud screams made Tammy and Kim abandon the car and race down the street toward her.

"Nooooo! Nooooo! Oh, God, nooooo!" Lisa cried out, falling to the ground in tears.

"What happened! What happened!" Kim and Tammy yelled, pushing their way through the crowd of police officers and homicide detectives.

"He's gone. Oh, my God, Ralphy's gone!" Lisa yelled, kicking and punching the air.

"What? What do you mean gone? What happened, Lisa?" Tammy questioned her.

Kim kneeled down next to her and wrapped Lisa in her arms where she cried like a baby. Tammy couldn't hold back the tears as she kneeled down and began rubbing Lisa's arm. They all sat there for a while until finally they had to help Lisa up. Her legs were totally gone and the girls had to drag her limp body toward the house.

"They killed my babe, my husband. My Ralphy is gone," Lisa kept repeating.

"We would like to ask you a few questions about your husband, ma'am," the detective said, as Kim and Tammy led Lisa up her steps.

"Can't you see that now is not a good time?" Kim responded. "Damn, have some fucking decency."

The women disappeared into the house and slammed the door behind them. None of them, especially Lisa, had anything to say anyway. Right now, Lisa really needed to be around some people who loved her and not be questioned about her husband's death.

Chapter 41

It had been a week since Ralphy's death, and Lisa still hadn't left the house. His funeral was tomorrow and Lisa wasn't even sure if she was strong enough to make it. Ralphy's mom had to go down to the morgue and identify his body, because Lisa didn't want to see him lying on a cold metal table. She didn't want that image to be stuck in her head.

"Mommy, Mommy!" Naomi said, coming into the bedroom where Lisa was. "Is Daddy coming home today?" she asked so innocently.

Lisa had already explained to Naomi that her daddy wasn't coming back, but Naomi still didn't fully understand it. She didn't know any better, and every time Lisa tried to explain she felt her heart break all over again

"Baby, come here for a minute," Lisa said, patting the bed. "I wanna talk to you about your daddy."

Naomi got up on the bed and sat between Lisa's legs with her teddy bear. Lisa began taking out Naomi's barrettes so that she could redo her hair.

"Remember, I told you that you weren't going to see him again for a while, because he went to heaven," Lisa told her.

"But I don't want my daddy to go to heaven. I want him to come home," she said in a sad voice.

Lisa fought back the urge to cry. She knew that she had to be strong for Naomi and help her understand. As her mother, Lisa was all she had left as a parent.

"I don't want Daddy to go to heaven either, baby, but guess what?" Lisa said, trying to sound excited. "He's gonna be watching over us from heaven every day." Lisa smiled, kissing Naomi's head.

The road ahead was going to be rough, but Lisa had no other choice but to prepare for it. First and foremost making it through Ralphy's funeral was the top priority, which was going to be a task in itself. Physically, her body was able to do it, but mentally Lisa was out of it. It was going to take a near act of God for her to bury her husband tomorrow or, at the bare minimum, some type of medication to help relax her.

Tammy walked up and got into the back seat of Agent Grant's car on Market Street. She had more than enough information for Grant to go to the grand jury with an order to get an indictment.

She had video and audio recordings of her and Darious talking in detail about his drug operation. She also brought names of clients and people she was to deliver the pills to every week, along with receipts from all the prescriptions she went to the pharmacy and did herself.

"You know you're doing the right thing," Agent Grant said as he looked over the evidence.

"But why does it feel so wrong?"

Grant put the Gucci bag down and turned to face Tammy, who was on the passenger side. He went through this on a regular basis with females cooperating against their boyfriends or fiancés and, in some cases, their husbands. He could see something in Tammy that he had seen in every woman he'd ever dealt with.

"It feels wrong because you love him. He treats you good, gives you money, and probably makes you feel like the only person who matters," Grant spoke.

"Yeah, he does." Tammy smiled, thinking about how much of her life Darious changed.

"But don't be fooled, Tammy. Darious doesn't love you. If he did love you, he wouldn't be out there selling drugs and putting you and your kids' lives in danger. Do you know how many home invasion cases I worked where nobody in the house survived? Too many. When the stick-up boys come, they don't care who's in the house. If somebody holds you and your kids for ransom, do you think he's coming for you, or when these indictments start getting tossed around, do you think for one second that he won't sacrifice you in order to get a lesser sentence?" Agent Grant spoke. "Trust me." He chuckled.

Tammy sat there listening to him, wondering if he was right about Darious. She began to question whether Darious did in fact love her.

"Next week, I'm going to need you to testify in front of a grand jury," Grant said, interrupting her thoughts. "After that, it's pretty much over."

"Just call me, and I'll be there," Tammy said, then got out of the agent's car.

"Now, I'm going to apply some gel," the nurse said, rubbing the green goo on Falisha's stomach.

Lamar opted to go with her to this doctor's appointment to show his support, since it was established that Falisha was keeping the baby. He stood on the other side of the bed looking into the monitor at pretty much nothing. The baby wasn't formed yet, but after adjusting the device against Falisha's stomach, the faint sound of a heartbeat could be heard.

"That's your baby," the nurse said, turning the volume up on the monitor.

She explained to Falisha and Lamar that over the course of the next few weeks, the baby would start to take its form, and by the fifth month she would be able to tell them what the sex was. This was the experience of a lifetime for the both of them, and something that they would be able to share for the rest of their lives.

Looking down at Falisha lying there with her shirt up over her stomach did something to him. It was a reality check that he needed, and a reminder that there was more to life than what he knew. He also had a newfound respect for Falisha, and standing there in that room, listening to his baby's heartbeat, he also had a newfound love for her.

Tammy pulled up in the driveway, put the car in park, and just sat there. The conversation she had with Agent Grant was weighing on her. Some of what he said did hold some truth to it, but she also was well aware that Agent Grant was trying to manipulate her into doing what he needed her to do.

Darious tapped on the window. He was right on time, because there were some questions that she needed to ask him, questions that might change the way she felt about him. She got out of the car, closed the door, then leaned against it with her Louis Vuitton bag in her hand. Darious could see that something was bothering her.

"What's wrong?" he asked, reaching out for her waist.

She pushed his hand away then gave him a stern look to let him know that she was serious right now. Darious didn't like the rejection at all, but he stood there to see what was really on Tammy's mind.

"Let me ask you something, Darious," Tammy spoke. "Do you love me?" she asked, but continued before he could answer her. "And don't say yes because you think that is the right thing to say. Be real with me," she said, looking into his eyes.

"You buggin' out right now. Let's go in the house to talk," he said, reaching out again to grab her arm.

Tammy didn't budge. She wasn't trying to go in the house or do anything else but stand there and wait for Darious to answer her questions. Seeing that she wasn't moving, Darious stood there too.

"I guess you don't listen to anything I say," he began. "I really don't know what else there is for me to say or do to prove to you that my heart belongs to you, Tammy."

"So why do you sell drugs, knowing the dangers it brings? I told you this before: I got kids who live here with us. Anything can happen," she snapped.

"It's funny you said that, because I just told the doc that I was about to fall back. I made more than enough money, and now that I have someone like you to spend the rest of my life with, I'm good," Darious told her.

"So you're saying that I'm the reason why you're getting out of the game?" Tammy asked.

"Look, Tammy, I don't know who you've been talking to, and I really don't care. Just don't let anybody else try to tell you what's in my heart. I give you my word that sometime in the near future, you're gon' come to know that my love for you is that of nothing you could ever imagine. When that time comes, I just hope that the love you say you have for me is half as strong as the love I have for you," Darious told her.

He really didn't feel like talking about it anymore, because to continue to question his love would only irritate him. Tammy couldn't see it right now, but he was making a crazy sacrifice as well.

Lamar followed Falisha into the house, reading the label on the prenatal pill bottle aloud. He was excited the entire ride home. "I hope you feel this way when I'm going through my mood swings," Falisha said, flopping down on the couch.

"I'm not worried about ya little mood swings," Lamar shot back, sitting on the arm of the couch. "I think I can handle you." He laughed.

"I'm hungry," Falisha said, jumping up from the couch. "You hungry?" she asked, walking off to the kitchen.

Being in the hospital all day did have him a little hungry. He followed Falisha, shaking the bottle of pills. "Come on, you might as well start taking these now," he said, walking up behind Falisha at the refrigerator. When she bent over to grab some leftover spaghetti from the bottom shelf, Lamar looked down and pictured himself inside of her. His hands must've been feeling the same way, because they wrapped around her waist and pulled her ass up against his dick. Falisha looking back at him didn't make things any better.

"You wish," Falisha said, standing upright.

She tried to step around him, but Lamar stood in front of her. She tried again, but Lamar cut her off.

"Come 'ere" he said, grabbing her by the waist and pulling her body close to his.

She resisted a little, but Lamar wasn't letting up. He pressed her body up against his some more then kissed her forehead. The kiss sent chills down her spine, and before she could drop the plate of spaghetti, she reached over and put it on the table.

"Look at me," Lamar said, reaching up and grabbing a handful of her hair from the back and yanking it down so that she looked up at him. "You still love me?" he asked, looking into her eyes.

Falisha closed her eyes and tried to put her head down, but Lamar yanked at her hair to stop her. The pulling of her hair actually turned Falisha on, but the question he asked did something else to her. At that very moment, she felt submissive and unable to deny him in any way, shape, or form. She didn't want to tell him, but she did love him and probably even more now than ever.

"Do you still love me?" he asked again, demanding to know how she felt about him.

Falisha still didn't say anything, so Lamar leaned in and kissed her. She pulled back, but he went in for another, and this time Falisha felt the need to indulge. She kissed him back passionately. It got hot and heavy within seconds, and before she knew it Lamar was unbuttoning her jeans.

"Yes. Yes, I do still love you," Falisha whined through his kisses. "Take me upstairs," she commanded, wrapping both of her arms around his neck.

Lamar lifted her up, wrapped her legs around his waist, and began walking toward the steps. He kissed Falisha the whole way up to her bedroom and, once inside the room, he closed the door behind him and slammed Falisha on the bed. She pulled his shirt over his head while he yanked her pants off, and never once did they take their eyes off each other.

"I missed dis pussy," Lamar said, pulling her to the edge of the bed as he stood over her. He dropped to his knees, grabbed her thighs, and pushed them back, spreading her soft pink pussy apart. He slowly French kissed her clit, licking and nibbling on it before taking it into his mouth and sucking on it. Falisha was going crazy, biting down on her bottom lip and rubbing on her breast.

"Oh, my God, Lamar. Don't stop, baby," she told him.

Lamar didn't have any plans to stop anyway. He licked the inside of her pussy lips, and then the outside, and then back to the inside before twirling his tongue around the whole of it. He could see her fluid seeping out every time her vaginal muscles tightened up.

"I'm about to cum," Falisha moaned, pushing her titty up and putting her nipple in her mouth.

Lamar stuffed his tongue inside of her and started flicking it up and down at a fast pace. He looked up at Falisha, who was moaning in pleasure as she sucked on her nipple. Her whole body began to jerk.

"Ahhhhhh!" she yelled, grabbing the sheets and tearing them off the bed. "Gimme dat dick," she begged.

Lamar stood up, and dropped his pants and his boxers at the same time. His dick was cinder block hard, and looking down at Falisha's sexy body, he knew he was about to beat da pussy up. She crawled backward onto the bed, still shaking from the massive orgasm she'd just had. Lamar climbed on top of her and looked Falisha in her eyes and cracked a smile.

"I love you too," he said before pushing his long, thick member inside of her honey pot.

A knock at the door took Lisa's attention away from the stove. When she walked to the front to answer it, she was shocked to see Ms. D standing there with two plates in her hand.

"You gon' stand there or are you gon' let me in?" Ms. D joked, squeezing her way into the house.

It was such a shock because Ms. D hardly ever went to anybody else's house. Everybody normally went to her home.

"I brought you and that baby something to eat. I know you in no condition to be trying to cook," Ms. D said, heading to the kitchen. She took the lid off the frying pan and shook her head, seeing the overcooked fish still cooking in the grease. "God knows y'all need it," Ms. D mumbled, turning the stove off.

"I came over here 'cause I wanted to talk to you," Ms. D continued, while taking the foil off the plates.

"Ms. D! Ms. D!" Naomi yelled, running into the kitchen.

Ms. D picked her up and gave Naomi a big hug and a couple of fart kisses to her cheek. "Come on, I want you to sit down and eat ya food," she said, unveiling a buttered roll. "Ms. D got some pie for you later on," she told Naomi before walking out the kitchen with Lisa.

Ms. D and Lisa went into the living room and took a seat on the couch. Lisa looked dead to the world, and the bags under her eyes told the tale of her not getting any sleep at night.

"You need to rest," Ms. D said, combing Lisa's hair with her fingers.

"I know. I will after the funeral. Ralphy's mom is gonna take Naomi for a few days, so I should be okay."

"I know it may seem hard right now, but things will get easier," Ms. D said, patting Lisa's hand. "One thing I know about you is that you're strong, and I'm not talking about any kind of strong. I'm saying you're strong up here," Ms. D said, pointing to Lisa's head. "And let me be the first to tell you that the worst thing you can do right now is drown yourself in sorrow. That little girl needs you, and you need her, you understand?" Ms. D said, reaching up and turning Lisa's face toward her.

Lisa nodded her head, wiping the tears that began to fall from her eyes. She agreed with everything Ms. D said to her, but there was something more serious weighing down on her, something that was hard to shake.

"You know this is all my fault," Lisa said, covering her mouth to muffle her cries.

"What? What are you talking about?" Ms. D said, pulling Lisa close to her. "Don't say that."

The detective who was on Ralphy's case had informants all over the streets, and once he put the whole story together, he called Lisa and asked her if she wanted to know. At first, she was unsure if she wanted to hear the gory details, but thought that one day, Naomi might inquire about her father's death when she got older. So for that reason alone, Lisa agreed to hear the detective's theory about what happened.

Lisa almost threw up when she learned that everything that happened was a result of her affair with Dre. After hearing that from the detective, it all made sense to Lisa. She didn't want to explain everything to Ms. D as they sat on the couch, but the tragic events that took place would forever be embedded in her thoughts. Had she not slept with Dre, Ralphy would still be alive today. Getting easier, as Ms. D put it, would never be the case with Lisa. This was something that would haunt her probably for the rest of her life.

Tammy lay in the bed naked, hugged up under Darious, who had fallen asleep after the crazy sex session they just had. Tammy didn't know when the DEA was going to be kicking down the door to come get Darious, so until then she was going to get as much dick as she possibly could. It was a little selfish, but this might be the last time she had sex for a while.

"Darious! Darious!" she said, nudging him out of his sleep. "Come on, get up," she said, dipping under the covers and going straight for his dick.

She popped it in her mouth and began sucking it until it got hard. By then, Darious was awake, getting himself ready for round two. Tammy wasted no time climbing on top of him and sitting down on his dick. She grunted, feeling all of him inside of her, and after a minute or two, she started grinding her hips back and forth while pressing her hands against his chest. Darious looked up to her, and could see the pleasure written all over her face. He grabbed her waist and began bouncing her ass up and down on his dick, sending her breasts flopping all over the place.

Tammy hissed, then yelled out his name as she felt another orgasm building up in the pit of her stomach. Within a few minutes, Tammy had reached her peak, cumming all over Darious's dick for the third time today. He too splashed off inside of her for the second time that day, and didn't consider one time pulling out.

He felt like Tammy was a lioness in heat and his only job was to please her. For the rest of the day, he did just that. Since she was now on Depo and couldn't get pregnant, all she wanted to do was give them both something to remember for the darker days ahead.

On Saturday morning, everyone gathered at Lisa's house preparing to go to see Ralphy laid to rest. Lisa needed her friends now more than ever before. She had requested for them to all ride in the family car with her and Ralphy's mother. Looking outside as the large funeral limo pulled up in front of the porch, Lisa noticed that there was a silent rain coming down. The flowers that she, Ralphy, and Naomi had planted last year had fully bloomed, but on this morning, they appeared to be frail. The morning dew had formed on top of the petals, dragging them down as if they were paying their final respect to the dead.

Lisa knew that she had to be strong, if not for her mother-in-law, for her daughter, who was still thinking that her daddy was coming home. The funeral director came into the house to let everyone know that it was time to leave. Lamar opened the passenger door for Kim, Falisha, and Tammy to climb inside. Ms. D, Lisa, Naomi, and Ralphy's mother got in on the driver's side. Although Kim, Lamar, and Falisha still had tension in their love triangle, all parties understood that today was not the day to deal with that stuff.

When they arrived at St. Luke Baptist Church, the sanctuary was filled to capacity. There was a mixture of former classmates, people from Ralphy's old job, and street dudes. Lamar straightened his tie as they all piled out the car. All of the women were already crying, and he knew it wouldn't take much for him to start. Ralphy was always like a big brother to him, and looking at Naomi and knowing that she would have to grow up without a father was pulling on his heartstrings. He silently made a promise to Ralphy that he would be there for his daughter, like she was his own. The old lady playing "I Have a Home" on the piano was singing so loud that it was as if she was trying to drown out the wails and whimpering that were going on throughout the church.

When they arrived at the front row, Lisa looked over to see Ralphy laid in the custom casket she had picked out for him. The blue Ralph Lauren suit she had purchased lay on him so perfectly that he looked as if he was going on a job interview. When Ralphy's mother cut her eyes over to the body, the realization of her son being gone was overwhelming. She dropped Lisa's and Naomi's hands and went up and stood over her dead child.

"Lord, why? Please tell me why. It wasn't supposed to be like this. I wasn't supposed to be burying my baby. Why, Lord, why? God, please, somebody tell me, why?" Ralphy's mother's plea to

God had everyone's tears flowing like a never-ending waterfall. Lamar went up to her, and with the help of one of the ushers they managed to get her to her seat.

Little Naomi wasn't sure why everyone was crying so much. She went into Lisa's pocketbook to get her grandmother some tissue. "Mommy, why are you and Grandma crying?" she asked.

"It's just hard for us to see your daddy like this, that's all, baby."

"My daddy? Where is he at?" Naomi asked, getting excited.

Lisa figured this would be her last time seeing her father, so she walked Naomi up to the casket to view the body. Once Naomi saw her father's face, she went running, Lisa tried to grab her but was too late.

"Daddy? Daddy. Wake up, Daddy. Mommy, help me wake my daddy up. He can't be 'sleep with all these people here." Naomi was shaking the casket so hard, it was about to fall off the stand.

Lisa broke down at the sight of her daughter trying to get Ralphy up. All the guilt that she had tried to put behind her was coming back. Tammy and Kim went running to get Lisa, and Lamar and Falisha went to grab Naomi. Both were putting up a fight, and now, even the funeral director and his staff were tearing up.

The pastor did the best thing he could do. He said a quick sermon and asked that the body be removed, and cancelled the graveside ceremony.

Chapter 42

One Week Later

Lamar walked into the room while Kim was packing their things in large blue storage bins. The lawyer in Philadelphia was eager to have Kim on his team, and needed her there immediately to start working on a big case he had. Kim was cool with the moving date being bumped up, mainly because she was ready for her and Lamar to move forward with their lives. She needed it bad.

"So the moving company should be here in about an hour. Tell me if I left anything out," Kim said, looking around the room at all she'd packed.

Lamar entered the room and leaned against the stack of storage bins with a sad look on his face. Kim had a feeling he was going to be like this.

"Awwww!" she whined playfully, walking over to him. "Once we get there, you'll see that it's not that—"

"I'm not going," Lamar said, cutting her off.

"Boy, you better cut it out." Kim smiled, reaching up to kiss him.

Lamar turned his face so that she kissed his cheek instead of his lips. "I'm serious, Kim. I'm not going anywhere," he said, looking down at her with conviction.

"Lamar, don't do this right now. If it's about the abortion, we can get through it. We can have a baby—"

"Falisha is pregnant by me," he interrupted.

Kim looked up at him and saw that he was serious. She took a step back and looked to the sky. "Wow," she said, taking a seat on the bed.

Lamar stood there silent, giving Kim some time to let what he said sink in. It was a tough blow, and it took a minute, but Kim got herself together.

"So, I guess this is it, right?" she asked, looking over at Lamar. "This is how we end, huh?"

Lamar walked over and took a seat next to her on the bed. This wasn't easy for him by far and, in the past week, he had considered every possible outcome.

The one thing that tipped the scale was the abortion, and no matter what Kim did to make up for that, Lamar didn't think that he could ever forgive her for it. She aborted his first child, without even discussing it with him. Some men in this world wouldn't have cared much, but Lamar was different. He didn't have a family and the moment when he was about to create one of his own, Kim took that away from him.

On the other hand, Falisha was giving him back what Kim stole from him, and for that, Lamar planned to be there for her and the baby, possibly salvaging any chance of giving their prior relationship another chance. Sometimes a baby could do one of two things: it could either tear people apart or bring them together, and both Falisha and Lamar were hoping it would do the latter.

"I'm sorry, shawty," Lamar said, then got up and walked out of the room.

Darious sat outside on the backyard deck drinking a Corona, watching Anthony and his friends play in the swimming pool. Tammy came out with Sinniyyah on her hip, yelling at Anthony to be careful before joining Darious under the canopy. After going to the grand jury on Wednesday, the DEA would be coming to arrest Darious any day now, and serve him with an indictment. Although she was backed into a corner and pretty much forced to do what she did, guilt still hit her like a ton of bricks. Not only did she feel guilty, she felt disloyal and untrustworthy, among other things. All the good that happened in her life over the past few months was on the account of Darious being her man. New car, new house, new clothes, and a higher level of maturity were all because of him. She couldn't deny it; he made her a better person, and despite what Agent Grant said about him not loving her, Tammy was convinced that he did.

"I need to talk to you," Tammy said to Darious as she put Sinniyyah in her swing.

"If it's about the DEA, you don't have to say anything," Darious responded, not taking his focus off the kids in the pool.

Tammy looked over at Darious in shock. "Wait, wait, how do you know about the DEA?" she asked.

Darious explained to her that one night while she was asleep, he went to get her phone out of her Gucci bag so that he could get one of his clients' numbers. He had found the recording device and the camera attached to the inside of her bag. He figured that the feds had gotten to her, probably during one of the drop-offs, and had her working since then.

"Then last week I followed you when you told me that you were going to get ya nails done. You just had gotten them done a few days earlier, so I knew that was a lie. When I saw you get into the back seat of the unmarked car, I almost ran for the hills," Darious said, taking a swig of his beer.

"So why didn't you run? Why are you waiting around to go to jail?" Tammy asked.

Darious finally took his eyes off the pool, taking off his sunglasses and putting them and his Corona on the table. "Come 'ere," he said, motioning with his head for Tammy to come and sit on his lap.

She got up from her seat and sat down between his legs on the beach chair. He wrapped his arms around her and laid her head on his chest, then kissed her forehead.

"I chose to stay because of you. Whether you believe me or not, I really do love you, Tammy, and I can't imagine me living life without you."

"So you'd rather go to jail?"

Darious laughed. "I'm not goin' to jail, or if I do it shouldn't be for long," he replied.

"I don't understand. What are you saying?" Tammy asked, sitting up and giving Darious a confused look.

"After I found out that you were working with the feds, I turned myself in and cut a deal. I'm not as high up on the totem pole as they thought I was. They want the doctor and the rest of the hospital staff he has working for him. I told the DEA that if they left you out of it, I'll help them. That means no charges will be brought against you, and you don't have to do anything for them anymore."

"Damn, babe, dis shit is deeper than what I thought," Tammy said, lying back down on his chest.

"Yeah, well, the doctor don't pay me enough, so I work for the feds now," Darious said, reaching over and grabbing his Corona off the table.

Through it all, Tammy still couldn't figure out for the love of God why Darious would want to be with her after everything she had done. As she sat there laid up on his chest, the only thing that she could think of, which made no sense at all, was the fact that Darious must love her as much as he said he did. From that day forth, Tammy would no longer question the love Darious had for her, and never would he ever have to prove it again.

**

Lisa sat down on the toilet looking at the First Response pregnancy test she had bought earlier. For the past few days, she had been feeling nauseous and weak, and at first she thought that it might have been from the funeral and all the stress that came along with it, but then Lisa looked at the calendar and saw that she was at least a week late.

"Mommy, I gotta pee," Naomi yelled, knocking on the door.

"Here I come, NayNay," Lisa shouted back as she ripped open the box.

Lisa urinated on the little white stick then stuck the cap back on. She got up off the toilet in the nick of time, because Naomi burst through the door. She did her little potty dance, dropping her pants to the floor and almost falling into the toilet when she sat down. Lisa stood by the sink trying to hold her laugh in, looking over at half of Naomi's body sunk into the toilet as she swung her legs back and forth.

"Mommy is sorry," Lisa apologized.

After waiting the two minutes for the results, Lisa looked down at the test in her hand. It came back negative and Lisa felt both relieved and sad. She kind of hoped that she would have been pregnant just one last time by Ralphy. He always wanted a boy, and Lisa always used to promise him that she would give him one, no matter how many times it took. Being able to keep that promise would have meant a lot to her, but looking over at Naomi, looking just like her dad, Lisa's heart was content with just one.

Kim stood curbside, watching as the movers took several storage bins out of the house and loaded them into the moving van. It really didn't take long, since Lamar wasn't going with her, so she had a few minutes to blow. Not knowing if she would ever be coming back, Kim took one good look around Parker Street, the block where she was practically born and raised.

Tires screeching caused her to turn her head. It was Tammy, turning onto the block as though she had sped the whole way there. At the same time, Lamar came out of the house and walked down the steps. He had a stressed look on his face, but walked up to Kim and gave her a hug.

"You take care of yourself out there, and don't hesitate to call me if you need anything," Lamar said.

"Here!" Kim said, attempting to take off the engagement ring.

"Nah, you hold on to it for now," Lamar shot back.

Kim smiled and put the ring back on her finger. "Yeah, well maybe you can come visit me sometime," Kim said with a smile, trying to hold back her tears.

"All you gotta do is say when," Lamar replied, removing the hair from in front of her face.

He leaned in and kissed her lips, and at first Kim wanted to pull away, but she couldn't. She didn't know if she'd ever kiss him again, and if it was going to be her last she wanted to make it her best. It was slow, soft, and wet, and during the whole time, Kim kept her eyes open.

"A'ight, y'all two!" Tammy yelled, walking up and separating them.

Lamar looked into Kim's eyes then cracked a smile before walking off. He didn't want to stick around and watch her leave, because in all actuality, he really didn't want her to go. He had a lot of love for Kim, and after having a heart-to-heart conversation with her an hour earlier, Lamar realized that underneath all the anger he had inside of him about the abortion, their love had made an impact on his life that he would never forget.

"So are you ready?" Tammy asked, reaching out for Kim's hand. "I mean, are you really ready to leave us?"

"Yeah. I'm a little nervous, but I'm ready," Kim answered with a smile. "I'ma miss y'all," she whined.

"Bitch, you better not leave without saying good-bye!" Lisa yelled out, coming off her porch with Naomi by her side.

She walked over and gave Kim a big hug. Naomi did the same. "What's his problem?" Lisa asked, pointing up the street at Lamar leaning against his car with his head down. "He looks sick."

"He's an asshole!" Tammy yelled so Lamar could hear her. They all laughed a little. "No, he'll be all right. He has more important things to worry about right now."

"Girl, don't get to Philly and forget about us," Lisa said.

"Shit, I'm flying y'all in as soon as I get right. We gon' tear the clubs up," Kim responded, doing a little dance.

One of the movers got out of the van, holding his watch up in the air. "Your flight leaves in two hours, and we gotta be hitting the road," he rushed her.

"She's coming!" a voice yelled from across the street. It was Falisha, making her way across the road. Kim, Tammy, and Lisa all got quiet, praying that Falisha didn't ruin the mood. When she got across the street, she walked up and stood right in front Kim, who looked her in the eyes. They both had a mean mug on their faces, and for everybody who was standing there it became awkward. Falisha stared at Kim as long as she could before she broke first, cracking a huge smile. Kim smiled, then they both hugged. Lisa and Tammy were relieved.

"You make sure ya ass is back here for ya goddaughter's baby shower," Falisha spoke into her ear as she continued to hug Kim.

"Promise I will," Kim said, wiping the tears from her face. "I love you guys," she whined, bringing everybody in for a group hug.

There wasn't a dry eye within the crowd. The friendship and the bond that these four women had was like no other. From toddlers to adults, they went through the challenges of life, leaning on each other for support. They were the true definition of friends, and as they watched Kim's van pull off down the street with her inside of it, a piece of their hearts was leaving right along with her. A piece that would never be replaced.

The End!